T0163223

LEIGH REDHEAD's first novel, *Peepshow*, burst on the crime scene introducing PI Simone Kirsch to readers. Simone made her next appearance in *Rubdown* followed by *Cherry Pie*, Leigh's third crime novel.

cherry pie

LEIGH REDHEAD

ALLEN&UNWIN

First published in 2007

Allen & Unwin
83 Alexander Street
Crows Nest NSW 2065
Australia
Phone: (61 2) 8425 0100
Fax: (61 2) 9906 2218
Email: info@allenandunwin.com
Web: www.allenandunwin.com

National Library of Australia
Cataloguing-in-Publication entry:

Redhead, Leigh, 1971– .
    Cherry pie.

    ISBN 978 1 74114 736 0.

    1. Women private investigators – Fiction. I. Title.

A823.4

Set in 11.5/14 pt Bembo by Asset Typesetting Pty Ltd
Printed in Australia by McPherson's Printing Group

10 9 8 7 6 5 4 3 2 1

To Anthony, who did the hard yards in the 'hostility' industry and was always there for me.

prologue

It was dark and cold when she opened her eyes and her right leg throbbed with pain. Stars streaked and swirled in the sky above, like a sci-fi flick when the spacecraft hits warp speed.

Where was she? How the hell did she get here?

The ground beneath her palms was hard packed earth, studded with gravel. Sharp air stung her sinuses, smelling like leaf mulch and cold. Dust coated her tongue. A night bird screeched.

Every time she thought she'd caught it her memory skipped away, just out of reach. Had she taken drugs? Her right nostril was blocked and there was a powdery, alkaline taste at the back of her throat. Bad coke? Some rapist spiked her drink?

Didn't feel like she'd been raped. Jeans zipped, coat still on, but her head throbbed and there was something seriously wrong with her right leg. The pain was in her shin, pulsing and expanding like red globs in a lava lamp, with a splintery sharpness at its core.

Light exploded through the darkness, punching her eyes. Alien abduction, she thought, going weak and waiting for the sylph-like silhouettes with crustacean fingers and bulbous heads.

Her eyes adjusted and she lifted her neck. It was a car, headlights on high beam. It was a car, and she was lying on a dirt road cut into a mountain. The hillside to her right was tangled with slender trees and vines. Ferns struggled out of the exposed earth. To her left the road dropped away. She couldn't tell how far. Pebbles cast long shadows like rocks on the surface of the moon. And her right leg was twisted at an unnatural angle.

She waved at the car. The light was too bright to see the make or colour, or who was driving.

She yelled, 'Hey.'

The car started. She smelled exhaust. She thought of that Stephen King book about the demonic vehicle, Christine. How come she could remember all that crap when she couldn't even remember her own name?

The engine revved. The gears shifted.

Shit.

She rolled on her side, pushed her palms flat to the ground and hoisted herself up, balancing on her good leg as the car jerked forward, a rock released from a slingshot. She threw herself to the side but not fast enough. The bonnet clipped her hip and instead of pain she felt only pressure and then she was flying through the air, over the slope, and nothingness gave way to slapping branches, then something solid and her head cracked, a burst of pain and she was gone.

2

chapter**one**

Two days earlier

I kicked off denim hotpants with flames appliquéd over the arse, shook my long dark hair and shimmied in a red spangled bikini. A Warrant song blasted from the pub speakers and a bunch of tradies and smattering of lunchtime suits bellowed along with the chorus.

The Royal was on Punt Road, opposite the Richmond Cricket Ground and not far from the MCG. With its multi-coloured carpet and topless barmaids the hotel was delightfully retro and I wondered why all the inner-city thirty-somethings hadn't discovered its ironic joys, the way they had lawn bowls.

I swung my hips exaggeratedly to the left, then right as the lyrics suggested, unclipped the back of the bikini top and held the fabric to my breasts, squishing them together to create a cleavage. Not that I had a hell of a lot to work with.

'Take it off!' yelled a guy in dark blue King-Gees.

It was a strip show. That was the general idea.

The crowd formed a rough circle, perching on stools, lounging in vinyl armchairs, leaning against the bar. I went to each guy in turn, flashed a nipple and they stared, mesmerised, pupils dilating. Amazing what the sight of a B-cup could do to a grown man. Still, I wasn't complaining. Those puppies were financing the Simone Kirsch detective agency. I twirled the bra around my head and flung it onto the stage. One of the suits waved a ten buck note so I sashayed over and danced close. Every little bit counted.

Although it was a cold September day the pub was heated and I felt a line of sweat snake from the nape of my neck to the small of my back. The suit, balding and pasty, sat in one of the low chairs with his legs apart and I rested my red platform stiletto on the arm and indicated he should put the money in my garter. Thick fingers fumbled in the sequinned elastic as I ground my pelvis in time to the beat. I had just turned my head to smile at the other punters so I didn't see the sneaky fucker reach for my pussy until it was too late. Still swaying to the music I whipped my leg down, grabbed his hand and moved in close, holding it to my chest and resting my knee lightly on his crotch.

The other blokes thought I was a top sheila, pressing myself against the guy and letting him cop a feel of my tits while I whispered sweet and dirty into his ear. What they didn't know was, I had his middle finger bent back at an unnatural angle and was increasing the pressure of my knee on his balls as I said, 'Sweetheart, you try that again and I'll snap this thing off and shove it up your arse, understand?'

His face flushed puce and he nodded, vigorously, so I let go and skipped off.

I hadn't always been such a tough chick. There was a time when I might have giggled sweetly and told him to stop being so naughty, but a year of various scumbags trying to waste me with assorted weaponry meant I wasn't going to take any shit from a smarmy suit with wandering digits.

A pissed guy with plaster dust in his hair was doing a little dancing of his own. I grabbed him and we fell into a sloppy waltz, got a laugh, then it was onto the stage to squirt Nivea on my boobs, unclip the g and pretend to take it off a couple of times before finally removing it with a flourish. In the last thirty seconds of the song I got down on my fluffy white rug for what some girls delicately referred to as floor work, but I liked to call the money shot.

Over the other side of the bar a punky looking girl with chopped-up short brown hair and a pixie face was ordering a beer. She wore a red sleeveless ski jacket over a black and white striped top and I was sure I knew her but couldn't figure out where from. She grinned when she saw me looking and gave me the thumbs up. My first instinct was to respond by crossing my eyes and sticking my tongue in the side of my cheek but I suppressed it, maintaining the illusion that humping a carpet offcut in front of a bunch of baying drunks seriously got me off. Professional.

Inside the change room a young blonde in a school uniform was tying her hair into bunches with plastic bobbles.

'Cool song,' she said, 'what was it?'

What was that song? Only the most famous stripping anthem of all time.

'"Cherry Pie". You know, Warrant?'

She stared at me blankly as I pulled on black lace knickers and a matching bra.

'Cock-rock pseudo metal band? Big hair, tight trousers? C'mon, they were huge in the eighties.'

She laughed. 'I wasn't even born till eighty-eight.'

'Holy shit, what does that make you—five?'

'Eighteen, silly. How old are you?'

'Twenty-eight.'

She slapped her dainty hands on her cheeks. 'That's almost...'

'Yeah, I know.'

'Wow.' She turned back to the mirror, knotted the white shirt under her boobs and adjusted the blue and red striped tie. 'No way I'll still be stripping when I'm that old. I've got a five year plan, gonna open my own day spa.'

She must have caught my look in the mirror. 'Not that you look old. You could pass for, like, twenty-six. Easy.'

'Thanks.'

I quickly dressed in jeans, boots and a black v-neck sweater, shrugged into my denim jacket and wound a scarf around my neck. Hefting my bulging backpack over one shoulder, I told the blonde to have a good show and pushed through the door into the bar.

The chick in the striped top was still sitting on a barstool. From that side I could see she wore ripped black jeans with a studded belt, and was tapping her red Converse High-Tops to some internal rhythm and drumming her fingers against her glass. Her skin was tan and her eyes were big and brown, fringed by long dark lashes. She had a snub nose, a wide mouth and when she smiled at me again I saw a gap between her small white teeth. Where the hell had I met her?

I asked the topless redhead behind the bar for my usual and sat on the stool next to the girl. 'Let me guess, the Shaft peepshows?'

She shook her head, gulped her beer and wiped a froth moustache from her upper lip.

'Buck's parties for Kelvin's Extreme Promotions?'

'Way off. No one would want to see my hairy bush.'

'You'd be surprised.'

The barmaid handed me a glass of cheap champagne and my pay from the jug strip. Seventy bucks. I wouldn't be retiring in a hurry.

'I give up. How do we know each other?'

She turned to face me. 'Andi Fowler. Joy's daughter? Our mums are mates. We all shared a house in Potts Point years ago.'

I slapped my forehead. Of course. After Dad shot through in the late seventies Mum had gotten involved in the women's movement, met Joy and we'd all moved in together. My brother Jasper wasn't born then, he had a different father, so it was just us girls, and a steady stream of militant feminists assembling in our decrepit terrace, making up slogans and preparing placards for the demonstration de jour. The last time I'd seen Andi was at a barbecue at my mother's eight years before. Just after Mum moved back to Sydney from northern New South Wales to teach women's studies at Sydney uni.

'Remember that barbie?' Andi asked. 'Bored shitless by all those old farts talking politics so we locked ourselves in the bathroom and did half a gram of speed, then stole that hundred dollar bottle of shiraz and skolled it in the park?'

'Uh-huh. Saw a band at Max's Petersham Inn, turfed out 'cause you decided to stage dive, ended up at a pool hall ...'

'Totally kicking arse until we got into a fight with that bikie over the two shot rule. He chased us down Parramatta Road and we had to duck into a brothel to escape!'

'Jesus,' I said, 'just as well we never hung out more. Maybe you should leave, before we get in trouble again.'

'Nah, I'm straight now,' Andi said, motioning for another beer. 'Mostly. You?'

'Except for this.' I picked up my glass and clinked it against hers. 'So what are you doing here?'

'I moved to Melbourne last year. Finally got into journalism at RMIT. I'm still waitressing but I'm so fucking over it. You know I called you when I first moved down but you never got back to me.'

I vaguely remembered the message, and meaning to ring, but …

'Sorry, I—'

'Yeah, I was really cut.' She frowned and stared into her beer but I knew she was just messing with me. The glint in her eye gave her away. 'Wanna make up for it?'

'How?'

'I need a detective. I want to hire you for a job.'

'You need a detective?'

'Uh-huh.'

'Why?'

'Until we've got a contract all I can tell you is it's to do with an article I'm working on. I need some surveillance. I'd do it myself but I'm flat out with uni and working and the people involved might recognise me. I hear you're good at that sort of shit. Been reading about you in the paper.'

'Ordinarily I'd jump at the chance, but I'm saving to open my own agency and what with surveillance equipment, a new car and an ad in the Yellow Pages I'm gonna need at least twenty grand. It's footy finals this month and I'm so damn busy the only thing I've got time to investigate is my bikini line, for ingrown hairs. I can recommend someone for you …' I thought of my old boss, ex cop Tony Torcasio.

'I've rung around but they're all so expensive. I make good tips but not that good. I thought maybe you could do me a deal, sort of like …'

'Mates' rates? Give me a break.'

'C'mon, Simone. We go way back. Remember when you were three and I was four and I used to pull you round the concrete yard in that little red wagon? Remember how you cried when your mum got you Tonka trucks for Christmas, and I gave you my Baby Alive?'

'You repossessed her on Boxing Day.'

'And wouldn't it be a good idea to get back on the horse before you open your business? I reckon you're sick of stripping. You seemed a little bored out there.'

And I'd thought I looked orgasmic. Stripping was funny. When I didn't do it I missed it. When I did it gave me the shits.

'Is this what they teach you at journalism school? To pester someone till they give in?'

'I call it persistence.'

'I can't accept the case if I don't have a clue what it's about.'

Andi glanced left and right, like we were dodgy Cold War spies, and whispered, 'I reckon I've got something big on someone in the hospitality industry. Pretty explosive stuff. Can only tell you on a need to know basis. Aren't you dying to find out?'

'Not really, but I'll help you 'cause I feel bad about not returning your call. Maybe I can slot in the surveillance between shows.'

'Fantastic.' Andi skolled her beer, burped loudly and checked her watch. 'Shit. I've got to get to work. Meet me tomorrow at four and all will be revealed.' She scribbled her mobile number and an address in Elsternwick on the back of a coaster and looked at me, head tilted like a bird. 'Your mum ever talk to you about the old days?'

'Not really, thank god. Don't think I could face another

lecture about how it's impossible to be a good feminist while flashing one's gash. Why?'

'No reason.' She slid off her seat and clapped me on the shoulder. 'Good seeing you, Simone.'

'Which bit?' I asked.

chaptertwo

'Jelly wrestling.'

'What?'

'Phoenix called in sick for jelly wrestling this arvo, could you …?'

Chloe clutched my arm and bounced up and down, boobs nearly spilling out of her white crocheted bikini top. We were on the aft deck of the River Princess, gliding underneath the Bolte Bridge, industrial wharves on our right, the shiny new high-rises of the Docklands complex on our left. This was Chloe's first annual Footy Fever Boob Cruise and she was freaking out.

'Babe, you know I don't do that shit,' I said.

'It's an emergency. Just this once.'

'Uh-uh. Rolling around in a wading pool of lime jelly. It's ridiculous. What if some future client saw me?'

'You don't mind people seeing you naked.'

'Yeah, but that's erotic. That's art.'

'And this is a sport. You can't be against sport. What are you, un-Australian?'

'Forget it. Besides, I've got to meet someone this afternoon for my real job.'

Chloe pulled her mobile out of her bikini bottoms, punched some numbers and talked rapidly into the phone while I stood there in my bikini and thigh high boots, shivering as the sweat cooled, finishing off my champagne and the cigarette I'd nicked. All the guys were in the cabin clustered around a big screen TV, watching the game.

'Okay,' she said. 'Brandy will come and do the wrestling but you'll have to take over her shows. There's a half time strip over in Richmond and another in Moorabbin at the end of the game.'

'Chloe, I—'

'Please. If I can't come through with the girls I get a rep for being unreliable and Chloe's goes down the tubes. Just change your appointment. I'm that desperate I'll even let you keep all the money. Five hundred bucks for an afternoon's work.'

I thought about it. That was a mini spy camera, half a vehicle tracking device, a tenth of an ad in the Yellow Pages. And I was the one doing Andi a favour. She could wait.

'Okay. I'm in.'

Below deck I got changed and called Andi. 'Something's come up, I can't make it. How about tomorrow?'

'I have to fly to Sydney tomorrow.'

'How about when you get back?'

'If you don't want to do it, just tell me.' She sounded pissed off.

'No, it's just …' We'd docked at Crown and Brandy's driver was waiting, ready to whisk me to Richmond. Chloe was busy setting up the wading pool on the rear deck and I got a waft of synthetic lime. The guys roared as someone scored a goal. It was hard to hear. 'Look, I'll call you or you call me, okay?' I couldn't tell if she hung up on me or the connection was lost.

I had Monday off and spent it sleeping in, exercising at my gym—a no frills place above a chicken shop on Glenhuntly Road—and poring through spy equipment catalogues, circling pinhole cameras and directional mikes. I got a little restless in the evening and could have gone out, but that would have meant spending my precious business savings. I'd become the world's biggest tightwad in the previous four months, but it hadn't been such a bad thing. I'd saved twelve grand and my hangovers were virtually nonexistent since I could only stomach a couple of glasses of cheap four litre cask wine. And without indulging in my usual hobby of seeing bands, getting fried and flirting with guitar players, I'd even managed to stay faithful to Sean.

Sean was my boyfriend, if that's how you referred to someone you'd spent two weeks shagging and dodging bullets with. He was also the most unlikely cop I'd ever met, a red haired, chain smoking, vodka swilling vegetarian from Scotland who loved jazz, made me laugh, danced like a dream and spoke eight languages, so was very very good with his tongue. The perfect man. Except for a Virgoan tendency to alphabetise his CD collection and go mad at me for leaving wet towels on the floor, which I was sure we could work out. He'd been on an exchange in rural Vietnam for four months, with two more to go, and I hadn't even kissed another man. Chloe was convinced pod people had taken over my brain.

I checked my email. Ads for Viagra and penis enlargements, but nothing from him. That was okay. Internet access was a little touch and go where he was. I sent him one anyway, grabbed a couple of cheese singles and lay down on the couch to watch a Russ Meyer DVD, *Beyond the Valley of the Ultra Vixens*. It was great seeing those babes go, and nice to live vicariously for once. I'd had enough excitement earlier in the year to last me a lifetime. Things were quiet now. I was glad.

Tuesday I went for a run by the canal, did a lunchtime jug show at Hosies Tavern in the city, then an afternoon strip at the Clifton in Kew. After going home and showering I met Chloe at the Elwood Lounge, a groovy little hole in the wall just around the corner from my one bedroom flat. She'd called earlier and said she had a business proposition for me. Coming from her that was a frightening thing.

The pool tables were occupied so I found her by the window overlooking the 7-Eleven and the Catholic church, sitting at a scratched laminex table with a bottle of champagne and a plate of dips. I kissed her cheek, smelling her usual aroma of Paris perfume and bong smoke, then pulled up a mismatched vinyl chair.

She'd gone for a bit of a winter wonderland look that day, billowing platinum hair, tight white jeans and a white PVC jacket with fake fur around the collar and cuffs. Her platform boots were silver and spike heeled. She hated being short and I had a sneaking suspicion she couldn't actually wear flat shoes anymore, kind of like Barbie.

'How were the shows?' She poured me a glass of champagne.

'You know. Same old shit, different day.'

Her mobile started buzzing across the table and she glanced at it but didn't answer. I peeked at the screen. Curtis. He and Chloe had hooked up a few months before. He'd been a journo for the girly magazine *Picture*, but had recently found success as a true crime writer, mainly by following me around and waiting for the trouble to start. I tolerated him, though it was hard to completely warm to someone whose articles got you shit-canned from your last job. He argued that if it hadn't been him it would have been someone else, but still.

I raised my eyebrows and she tossed her hair over one shoulder and shrugged.

'Why do they always get so clingy?'

I couldn't answer that, since all the guys I went for ended up pissing off before I had time to get sick of them. My mobile started vibrating in sympathy. The screen read 'Andi'. Feeling bad about letting her down I chose the coward's way out and didn't answer.

'So let me tell you about my proposition.' Chloe dipped a thick finger of Turkish bread in bright pink beetroot dip and waved it in my general direction. 'I'm expanding the agency— more boob cruises, male strippers on the books, tours to country Victoria and of course the jelly wrestling, which is huge right now. I can't run Chloe's from my flat in Parkdale anymore so I've found this shop in Balaclava with a two bedroom apartment on top. You take the shopfront for the detective agency, I'll take the apartment as a home office. It'll be perfect—we can share the rent and hang out more. What do you reckon?' She jammed the dip in her mouth just before it splattered all over her faux fur.

'Running an inquiry agency from the same address as Chloe's Elite Strippers isn't really the image I want to project to a corporate clientele.'

'There are separate entrances.'

'So?'

'And with your reputation I seriously doubt the corporate types'll be beating down your door. I mean, c'mon,' she laughed.

I was hurt for half a second until a sudden rage bubbled up, blood rushing to my face along with a desire to tip the dip plate into her lap. I scraped my chair back and stood up.

'Back in a tick.'

I headed for the loos at the back of the bar even though I didn't need to go, locked myself in a cubicle and sat on the toilet lid, waiting to calm down. It wasn't Chloe's fault. I was only angry because I knew she was right: my reputation as a private investigator in Melbourne was shit. Not because I couldn't do the job, but because things got out of control whenever I did. I'd be lucky to get any bloody work at all.

Tears welled up but I refused to cry and stared at the graffiti instead, waiting for my eyes to dry. My mobile beeped and I pulled it from my bag. The message icon was blinking so I dialled the number, put the handset to my ear and heard the recorded voice tell me I had one new voice message.

A clunk. Heavy breathing, and then, in between gulping breaths, 'Simone, it's Andi. I'm in big trouble. You've gotta come get me or I'm gonna die.'

chapter**three**

'**S**o who is this chick?'

Chloe was smoking a Winfield and had the champagne bottle between her legs. We were barrelling down the Nepean Highway in my '67 Ford Futura, heading for Andi's place. Elvis danced on the dash and the mirror balls and beads on the rear vision mirror shimmied and swayed.

I told her about Andi contacting me at the Royal, and how I knew her from my childhood. Memories of the time were coming back to me, hazy and fragmented, like a fading dream. I remembered overalls, underarm hair, sweat and patchouli, trying to draw the feminist symbol and getting frustrated when I couldn't get the fist right. I remembered my matchbox cars getting their wheels caught in the seagrass matting and the soft spikes of Mum's new crew cut under my tiny palm.

I remembered Andi pulling me around in the wagon, and I remembered her mother, Joy. She was tall and brown skinned with a booming voice and a wild frizz of hair. I couldn't conjure up any facial features, just huge braless tits undulating beneath a t-shirt that declared: A Woman Needs a Man Like a Fish Needs a Bicycle. She'd scared the shit out of me in those days, and I wasn't sure if it was the boobs, the loud voice, or the way she'd take my mum's side when I acted up. 'Cut out the tantrum crap, Simone, she's your mother, not your slave.'

'Let me listen again,' Chloe said. I chucked her the phone and she replayed the message. 'It cuts straight off after she says she's gonna die. Can't hear any background noise but it sounds like she's in pain. Should we take it to the cops?'

'I dunno, Sherlock. I want to check her place first. Make sure it's not a wind-up. She's got a pretty warped sense of humour.'

'I'm gonna die. Who would joke about that?'

'You tell me. You're the one who reported a fake stalker to the cops so they'd send around a couple of hot guys in uniform.'

Chloe shook her head and ashed her ciggie out the window. 'I was bored in those days, young, irresponsible.'

'It was last year!'

'Should I try ringing her again?'

'Go for your life. But it keeps saying the phone's switched off.'

Andi's place was more Ormond than Elsternwick, a dilapidated weatherboard on a street that ran off North Road. In typical student house style the gate was rusted, the garden showcased a comprehensive selection of weeds, and the porch was home to a sagging brown couch and milk crates full of long necked beer bottles. A tatty awning hung from the veranda roof, striped in faded red, yellow and green.

We got out and slammed the car doors shut. High above us fluorescent pink clouds streaked the steel blue sky. A light wind froze the tips of my ears, flapped the awning and made the long grass hush. The house was dark and quiet and I realised my heartbeat had elevated and my pulse was pumping hard and fast at the base of my throat.

Chloe crushed her Winfield under her pointy boot and swigged from the bottle.

'Spooky,' she whispered. 'Don't you reckon the windows look like eyes?'

I ignored her, pushed through the rusting wire gate and walked up the concrete path. When I rapped hard on the front door peeling paint fell to the spiky welcome mat.

'Hello? Andi? Anyone home?' I put my ear to the door but couldn't hear any movement inside.

I turned to talk to Chloe but she was already picking her way through the overgrown grass, heels sinking into the dirt, heading for the concrete driveway that led to the back of the house. I hurried after her. The back was similarly overgrown and home to a wonky Hills hoist and a laundry shed with an old washing machine and concrete tub. The fence was corrugated tin and an open gate led to a cobbled back lane where the wheelie bins congregated. A train sighed as it pulled into a nearby station and I could smell charcoal chicken from the shop we'd passed on North Road. Chloe tried to slide the back windows up, to no avail, then pressed her face against the glass.

'Can't see much. A kitchen, I think. It's pretty dark. What if she's, like, dead in there?'

I flashed back to the time I'd found a body: the staring eyes and tangy metallic smell of blood. I went dizzy and leaned against the Hills hoist for a second.

Chloe squinted at me. 'You right?'

I straightened up. 'Fine. I'm gonna see if the front windows are unlocked.'

I walked back around the side to the front porch, trying each one. No go. When I returned Chloe had her face up against the back door, fiddling in the old fashioned keyhole with a rusted piece of wire.

'That shit only works in the movies,' I said, 'maybe I should find a brick …'

She stood back and turned the knob. 'Ha!' The door swung in.

I obviously wasn't utilising Chloe's talents enough. 'Where'd you learn that?'

'Wagging school in Frankston, hanging out with Colin and Worm.'

'Worm?'

'He was in and out of holes a lot.' She stepped back. 'After you.'

The gloom inside made the door look like a gaping mouth. I felt faint again but forced myself forward. It was ridiculous. I didn't usually scare easily and I'd been in a lot tougher scrapes than walking into an empty house. Christ, it was kindergarten stuff, Private Investigation 101.

I climbed the concrete steps, crouched and went in low, swinging left and right to check no one was lurking on either side of the door. Chloe snorted behind me, amused.

'You could have gone first,' I told her.

'And got decapitated by the psycho killer? No thanks.'

I felt around the walls and hit a switch. Fluorescent tubes flickered and hummed and my pupils constricted in the brightness. It was an old kitchen. Brown laminex cupboards, an ancient gas stove, orange and brown lino in a fussy, hexagonal pattern, lots of dirty dishes in the sink. A bathroom ran off one side and I checked it before I lost my nerve. Brown and orange like the kitchen. A toilet, sink, shower cubicle with frosted glass. I wrenched the shower door open. A couple of bottles of Herbal Essences shampoo, a thin sliver of soap, pale blue shower puff hanging off the tap, mould climbing the tiles.

Chloe stuck close behind me, still clutching the champagne bottle and standing on tippytoes to look over my shoulder. The kitchen and lounge room were separated by a curtain of hanging beads. I clicked through, turned on the light and found myself in a living room furnished with an old cane lounge set, the faded cushions printed with yellow palm fronds and brown bamboo. The carpet was floral and the wallpaper patterned with roses. A small TV sat atop a batik draped pillar, coathanger aerial poking out. I'd done my share house time and would have bet a hundred bucks three milk crates were lashed together under the cloth.

Doors on either side of the lounge had to be bedrooms. I turned the handle on the left one, and when it clicked open I nudged it with my foot so that it bounced off the adjacent wall and I knew no one was lurking behind it. Chloe giggled again. At least she was having fun. The room was neat and looked like it had been filled with a Fantastic Furniture package deal. A navy blue doona covered the wrought iron bed, IT texts and Dungeons & Dragons figurines crowded the bookshelf and five computer monitors were lined up on a huge desk along the far wall. I dropped to my knees and checked under the bed.

'Andi's room?' Chloe asked.

I slid out a stack of *Penthouse* and *Picture* magazines. 'I think not.'

We crossed the lounge and stood outside the door to the second bedroom.

'Can I do this one?' Chloe asked.

'Sure.'

She turned the handle and kicked so hard her spike heel dented the wood and the door slammed into the wall. I looked at her and she shrugged, took a slug from the champagne bottle and turned on the light. I scanned the room. No bodies. No blood. No staring eyes, thank Christ. My pulse finally returned to normal.

But Chloe was aghast. 'Someone's turned this place over!'

'I don't think so.' I gingerly picked my way into the room. The futon bed was a jumble of scrunched-up sheets and blankets. An empty beer bottle lay next to it, and a chipped cup with the remains of milky coffee, both balancing on a plate sprinkled with toast crumbs. Books, journals and news-papers covered every available surface and clothes escaped the rim of a wicker washing basket, migrating across the floor in a desperate bid for freedom. 'I'd say she's just messy.'

'And I thought you were a slob. At least she has good taste in music.' Chloe had wandered over to a shelf jammed with books and CDs. 'Iggy and the Stooges, Radio Birdman, the Ramones. I used to love the Ramones. Back in Frankston.'

'With Colin and Worm?'

'They were more into the Radiators.'

The only neat things about the room were the empty square on her old wooden desk where I guessed her computer had sat, and her two work uniforms. A length of pipe hung on chains secured to the ceiling, and at the end of a row of jackets the black pants and shirts were pressed and the aprons neatly folded and draped through the hanger. I told Chloe not to move or touch anything with her bare fingers, and stretched the sleeve of my jumper to cover my own as I riffled through Andi's desk.

The top drawer contained the usual detritus: paperclips, rulers, blank CDs. Her completed assignments crammed the next one down and I was quietly impressed that the worst mark she'd got was a distinction. The bottom drawer was stuffed with notes but nothing that appeared to relate to any big hospitality scandal. Her expanding file was overflowing with ancient electricity bills, transcripts, old superannuation statements, receipts, cards, but nothing remotely sinister and nothing that might provide a clue to her whereabouts. Not a single threatening letter composed of cut-out newsprint, no matchbook from a sleazy bar to follow up.

The bin underneath the desk was empty and the corkboard above blank in the middle, just a few current bills hanging around the edges, a card for a mechanic and hairdresser and a printout of library books she'd borrowed. I checked them off against the list and found one missing. *All That Glitters: King's Cross in the Seventies and Eighties* by someone named Chris Ferguson.

Chloe was crouched down flipping through a photo album with a tissue over her hand, humming 'I Wanna Be Sedated'. 'This Andi?' She held up the album.

'Uh-huh.'

'She's cute. Find any clues?'

I looked around the room, shaking my head. 'It's not what's here, but what's not. Computer gone, notes on whatever she was working on, a library book …'

'She could have taken them with her.'

'… bins emptied. Doesn't square with the rest of the mess. She could have done it herself, or maybe someone cleaned the place out.'

'Look at this.' Chloe carried the photo album over. 'A couple of pages from the end, some photos are gone. You can see the outline of where they were.'

'No shit. You're turning into a hell of a sidekick, babe.'

Chloe smiled and did a little wiggle. 'Thanks.'

I stared at the noticeboard again. There was a drawing pin

in the middle with a minute scrap of photographic paper hanging off it, like a picture had been ripped off.

'You find an address book?' I asked her.

'No.'

'Okay. Since we can't call anyone who might know where she is, we go to the cops. Report her missing, play them the phone message.'

We turned off the lights and left the way we'd come in. Back in the car I had an idea. 'The wheelie bin. I should check it.' I opened the glove compartment and pulled out latex gloves and a torch. Even though I hadn't worked a case for a while, it paid to stay prepared.

'Want me to come?' Chloe lit up a Winfield, drank more champagne.

'Nah, finish your smoke. I won't be long.'

Twilight was long gone and the night was black. My torch must have needed new batteries because the weak yellow light hardly penetrated the darkness, just seemed to bounce off it. I wasn't scared though. The jitters had disappeared once I'd searched the house and found no nasty surprises. I wondered about my dizzy spell before. Post traumatic stress? I didn't believe in that shit … well, maybe for other people, but not for me. If I'd suffered from it I'd have been a basket case long before now. I didn't much believe in counselling either. After the last violent incident I'd been involved in, both Sean and my mum had been at me to see someone, but I hadn't gone. What was wrong with pulling your own self together, stiff upper lip and all that?

The back lane was narrow and cobbled, built for the shit-cart to travel down a hundred years ago. I imagined being a shit-cart driver and decided it wouldn't be quite as bad as waitressing or retail. At least people would leave you alone.

I passed through the gate and found the wheelie and recycling bins on the left. Going through rubbish was a huge part of being an inquiry agent, and usually yielded all kinds of interesting bounty. Luckily I had a strong stomach. I opened the lid and peered in. Just a lone plastic shopping bag tied up down the bottom. I'd have to tip the thing over to reach it so I put the torch on the ground.

Just as I started to push I noticed a flash of movement behind the bin, and then a shadowy figure reared up and rushed me. My breath caught in my throat as I was body-slammed back onto the cobblestones, where I lay, gasping and winded, skin prickling with fear. I reached for the torch and had just closed my fingers round the handle when it was kicked out of my grasp and flew down the lane, plastic cracking. The light was extinguished and all I could make out was a shape looming above me, amorphous and shifting like something not quite human, and then the shadow lengthened and there was a rush of air and an incredible cracking pain on my forehead, and after a brief flash of light it was darker than ever.

chapter**four**

'**S**imone.'

I came to on the cane couch, Chloe softly slapping my face. I batted her hand away. My head was throbbing and I felt like throwing up.

'Codeine,' I croaked.

Chloe fumbled in my bag, popped a couple out, checked the champagne bottle and, finding it empty, swished through the curtain to the kitchen and came back with a glass of water.

'What happened?' I asked.

'You got mugged. Your wallet was lying beside you, open. The cards are still there but the money's gone. How much they get?'

'Ten bucks.'

'You only took a tenner to go out with me? Jeez, we were gonna have a ball.'

'I'm on a budget. How'd I get in here?'

'You walked. You said you were fine, picked up that rubbish bag, marched in here and passed out again on the couch.'

'My brain hurts.'

'No shit. You've got this red mark on your forehead. It's weird, kind of curved.'

I tried to lift myself up on my elbows but the room spun and little dots danced in front of my eyes.

'I'm driving you to casualty,' Chloe said.

'Forget it. You've drunk a bottle of champagne and I'm not sitting there for five hours just so a doctor can give me a couple of aspirin and send me home. Soon as these pills kick in we're going to the cops. First, open the rubbish bag for me. I don't think it was a mugger. I think whoever attacked me wanted what was in there.'

'Why didn't they take it?'

'I don't know, maybe you scared him off. Maybe he freaked.'

Chloe ducked into the kitchen and grabbed some old newspaper and a pair of washing-up gloves and upended the bag. I lay back, praying the tablets would act fast. I hadn't had a headache this bad since the night I'd mixed vodka, gin, whiskey, champagne and beer.

'Safeway receipt, tissues, hair. God, other people's hair is gross. A business card.'

'Whose?'

'The Doyle Food Group. There's a Sydney number and a picture of a fish and some cheese.'

'Put it aside.'

She glared at me.

'Please.'

'That's it except for an old toothbrush, double gross, and a bit of newspaper. It's that food section from the *Age*. "Epicure".'

'What's it say?'

She scanned the first page. 'Oh my god.'

'What?'

'I think I just creamed my jeans. Check this out. "Mad, Bad and Dangerous to Know. Meet Trip Sibley, Young Chef of the Year".' She held the paper in front of my face so I could clock the picture.

Trip Sibley reclined on a red chaise longue in what looked like a Parisian bordello but could have been any bar in the Melbourne metropolitan area. He wore dirty jeans, motorcycle boots and a black chef's jacket open to the waist, displaying a sinewy, muscular torso. His long wavy hair was tied back in a ponytail, a jagged scar traced his right cheekbone and his brows arched in a devilish, Jack Nicholson fashion. Plump cherries were scattered across the thick gold carpet and one, resting between his teeth, looked about to pop. I started to read and the letters danced around in front of my eyes. Gradually they settled down and I got through the whole thing.

Trip Sibley ran the Jouissance Restaurant and Bar on Fitzroy Street, St Kilda, and the place had won just about every food award in the year since it opened. It was the brainchild of Sibley and his Sydney based business partner, Sam Doyle. The article took the reader on a tour of Trip's St Kilda penthouse apartment, complete with view of Luna Park, pinball machines, home theatre set-up, gourmet kitchen and rooftop spa. There was even a mention of his bedroom. Black bed linen, mirrored walls and a selection of whips and chains that would put the House of Fetish to shame.

'"What are those for?"' the reporter asks. 'Trip chuckles and, with a wicked glint in his eye, replies, "Keeping the apprentices in line." Although his temper is legendary, once resulting in an assault case that was settled out of court, I don't believe him for a second.'

The article explained that Trip had served an apprenticeship under the great Rudolpho in country Victoria, and finished his training in London and France. The reporter went on to gush about his food, his rock hard abs, his appearance in *People* magazine's '50 Sexiest Issue' and his upcoming TV cooking show, *Chef of Steel*. Trip enjoyed such exciting hobbies as skydiving and rock climbing and had even taken the interviewer for a spin on his new motorbike, a crimson Ducati 996, breaking just about every road rule in the process.

Chloe looked over my shoulder and pointed at a picture of the bike. 'I'd kill for one of those.'

'You can't ride.'

'Yes I can. I used to hoon around on a two fifty, in Frankston.'

'With Colin and Worm?'

'Uh-huh. So is the article a clue?'

'Possibly. Can you check Andi's work uniforms, see if there's anything embroidered on them?'

She was back in two seconds. 'Jouissance Restaurant.'

'Interesting.'

'We'll have to investigate.' Chloe looked thoughtful. 'I'm prepared to fuck him for information, if I have to.'

'You want to fuck him you'll have to do it on your own time. We're not investigating shit. We're going to the police. Now.'

I struggled to sit up and that's when I heard it. Chloe did too. The front gate creaked open and footsteps scraped down the path.

'Shit!' She jumped up and stared at me like a rabbit in the headlights. 'What do we do?!'

'Sit tight,' I whispered. 'It's probably just the flatmate. We'll tell him what we're doing here. I think you're actually in a couple of his magazines so he'll probably be delighted to see us.'

The footsteps stopped at the door and I listened for a key turning in the lock but it never happened. Chloe and I held our breath. The steps started up again. I heard them scuffing around the side of the house.

'I don't think it's the flatmate,' Chloe breathed.

'Back door locked?'

'No.'

I attempted to get up but the room started spinning . I sat back down. Chloe grabbed the empty champagne bottle and stood just to the side of the curtained kitchen door, back flat against the wall. I tried to wave her over but she shook her head and held the bottle up to her chest. The back door opened. Footsteps crept across the kitchen lino. Stopped. The beaded curtain made the tiniest of clicks.

Chloe leapt out from the wall with the bottle held high, faced the figure through the curtain and bellowed like Mel Gibson in *Braveheart*: 'Aaaaarghgh!'

The figure yelled back. A short, sharp shriek. A hand jabbed through the curtain, karate chopped her wrist and the bottle soared. A foot shot out and kicked her ankle and Chloe flew up in the air, landing flat on her back. The whole person jumped through, screamed and stood above her in a karate stance, ready to drop a knee on her neck.

The woman was in her mid fifties, tall, dark skinned, hair a waterfall of black curls peppered with grey. She wore brown cords and a black skivvy with a burgundy shirt unbuttoned over the top. Wire framed glasses rested low on her nose, silver studs curved up each ear and a turquoise pendant dangled from her neck. It was Joy Fowler, Andi's mum. She could still scare the shit out of me.

chapter**five**

Joy was sitting on the couch, Chloe and I the armchairs. It hadn't taken long to sort out who was who and what we were all doing there. Joy had just come back from the police station where she'd been hassling the cops for an update. She'd reported Andi missing the day before. Luckily for Chloe, the floral carpet was thick and she hadn't been badly hurt.

'How've you been?' I asked Joy.

She took out a pouch of Port Royal tobacco and started rolling a cigarette. 'Karen left me after fifteen years. My mum's terminally ill in hospital, and now Andi's disappeared. Always comes in three's, huh? But I'm glad you're here. I've read about you girls in the paper. I'll hire you. Between the three of us we'll find her.' She licked the paper, stuck it down, struck a match and the tobacco flared.

Hire me? I thought back to when I worked for Tony Torcasio. He wouldn't touch missing persons, said they were bullshit. The individual either didn't want to be found, or was dead, in which case it was Homicide's problem.

'I wouldn't go that far. We'll help you look around, but it's best left to the cops. I mean, they've got all the resources.'

'The cops?' Joy snorted and smoke roiled out her nostrils. 'This smarmy little dickwad, Nolan, thinks Andi's pissed off, or met some guy and shacked up with him. Kept asking if she had a drug problem, or was depressed.'

'Was she?'

'No! The problem is I gave them her bank details and they found out she withdrew five thousand dollars, her whole savings, last week. So of course they think—'

'Five grand?'

'Yeah, anyway, I've hated jacks since I got bashed after a demo in seventy-nine and I went off, called him a pig and kicked over a fucking pot plant.'

Chloe giggled and clutched her ribs. 'Ow. Hurts to laugh.'

'Sorry, mate.' Joy reached out and patted her knee. 'Couldn't believe it. Thought I was being attacked by Buffy the fucking vampire slayer.'

'A smoke would make it better,' Chloe said.

Joy proffered the Port Royal pack.

Chloe shook her head. 'A smoke smoke. There any around here?'

Joy grinned, stuck her hand up her skivvy and dug around in her bra, finally producing a bent-up joint. It never ceased to amaze me, the way potheads immediately recognised their own kind.

Chloe perked up immediately. 'Don't suppose you've got a bottle of bourbon stashed in your knickers?'

'You're a cheeky one. Should be some home brew in the fridge.'

Chloe made a face.

'No, it's really good. Andi makes it.'

Joy sparked up the number and the room instantly filled with the thick, wet smell of marijuana. Chloe had a toke then tripped off to the kitchen, her spike heels catching on the carpet. I heard her open the fridge then rustle through cabinets. She returned with a long necked Coopers bottle and three glasses that looked like they'd been nicked from the pub.

'Couldn't find an opener,' she explained, levering off the bottle top with the base of her disposable lighter.

Joy smiled. 'Andi does that. She can knock the cap off with a metal spatula too.' She made a sweeping action.

'I'd like to meet her.' Chloe tipped cloudy brew into an inclined glass and handed it to Joy. 'Sounds like a cool chick.' She offered me a glass but I shook my head. Not if I was driving to the cop shop.

'She is.' Joy offered me the joint but I refused that too. Dope made me want to eat everything in sight, then hide in a closet, trembling.

'I remember your mum and I, years ago,' she said, 'wondering how you and Andi would end up, whether you'd follow in our footsteps or go the other way. My worst fear was Andi becoming one of those simpering girly girls who'd need a man to change a tyre or turf out a spider. But she didn't. Maybe kids don't rebel like we did. Maybe you all turn into your mothers these days.'

Chloe grabbed a handful of butt and jiggled it around. 'My arse is turning into my mother's.'

I shook my head. 'No way. Me and Peta are total opposites. I've seriously rebelled.'

Joy raised her eyebrows then skolled half her glass in one go.

'So tell me what you told the cops,' I said. 'How long has Andi been missing?'

'Two days. I was supposed to pick her up at Sydney airport yesterday morning. Don't know how much longer Mum's going to be around and I wanted Andi to be able to say goodbye to her grandma. Plane landed at nine but she never got off. Or the next one. No message on my phone so I called hers. Home and mobile. No answer. Tried her work but they were closed. Bloody dolly birds at the airport wouldn't tell me if she'd got on the plane or changed flights or anything, and I started imagining she'd had an accident on the way to Tullamarine. I called the hospitals. The morgue. Nothing. So I jumped on the next plane to Melbourne, with only my shoulder bag.' She pointed to a battered leather satchel.

'I know where Andi hides her key so I let myself in but there was no sign of her. Car's gone, laptop's gone, no note. It's like she vanished without a trace. I found her flatmate's mobile number. He's in Canberra for the week, and he thought she was in Sydney. I rang her best friend in Sydney, Daisy, and she hadn't heard from her, tried her ex boyfriend, studies with Andi at RMIT, but he was clueless, useless as tits on a bull. I called everyone in her address book, knocked on all the neighbours' doors, left notes for the ones who weren't home and then Monday arvo I went to the police.'

'What about Andi's father or other relatives? Have you contacted any—'

'Sperm donor.'

'What?'

'I guess you were too young to know back then.'

'I wish my dad had been a sperm donor,' Chloe piped up. 'He's an arsehole. In and out of jail for years. Only contacted me after he'd seen me on TV. Thought I was loaded and he could get some money out of me. What a prick.'

'All Andi's rellos are in New Zealand,' Joy said, 'and yes, I called them. No one's heard from her. Except you, this evening. What did she say exactly?'

I didn't want to do it but felt I had no choice. I fished in my bag for my phone, pressed the message bank number and handed it to Joy. She listened to it about five times before setting it down on the coffee table.

'I knew it. My baby. Somebody's got her.'

'Who?'

'You said she was writing an article about some scandalous stuff? Obviously, whoever she was writing about.' Joy set her jaw and stared at the wall opposite.

'We don't know that. She did take the money from her account.'

I was confused. Maybe my attacker was just a junkie. Maybe Andi was holed up somewhere down the Great Ocean Road with a hot guy, bottle of Wild Turkey and a couple of grams of coke. I would be, given half the chance. Maybe she was doing this to punish me for blowing her off the other day, and to punish her mother for god knows what. I hadn't seen her for years. For all I knew she was a total fucking fruit loop.

And then Joy's eyes teared up, her bottom lip started to tremble and she flung herself sideways on the couch and let out a keening wail, the kind you hear on news footage from the Gaza Strip. I didn't know what to do, so I stared at the carpet for a bit. When I looked up Chloe was glaring at me. She knitted her eyebrows and inclined her head toward the couch, where Joy was still sobbing, face pressed into a cushion, broad shoulders heaving.

I shrugged and mouthed, 'What?'

Chloe rolled her eyes and tiptoed over to Joy, sat next to

her and cradled her in her arms. She stroked her hair and made soft cooing noises and looked very much like a trampy Virgin Mary. I sat opposite and attempted an expression of thoughtful concern, but probably just looked constipated. Joy's sobs turned to hiccups, then rattly breaths.

Chloe reached for her silver handbag and gave Joy a travel pack of tissues. 'It's okay, hon. Me and Simone are on the case now. She's as good as found.'

Now it was my turn to glare at her. 'I'll go to the police, tell them what I know, let them listen to the phone message, but I'm not on any case.'

Chloe gave me a look like I'd just fired an automatic weapon into a petting zoo. 'She called and asked for your help!'

'I can't help her. The police can.'

'I'll stay here with Joy,' she said.

'Fine. What was the cop's name again?'

'Nolan,' Joy sniffed.

chaptersix

Constable Nolan listened to the phone message and frowned. He was in his mid twenties and looked like a poster boy for a police recruiting campaign, except the straight brown hair at his temples was rapidly starting to thin. We were sitting in an interview room at the Elsternwick cop shop while Joy and Chloe were at Andi's, drinking beer and designing a 'Missing' poster.

Nolan sat back in his chair, flicking a pen between his fingers, and frowned. 'You know her. Her distress seem genuine?'

'It's either real or she's a hell of an actress. Can you trace it?'

'We can try. You say Andi wanted to hire you to do surveillance on someone in the hospitality industry, someone she was writing about?'

'Yeah, but I didn't take her up on the offer.'

'Any idea who she was investigating?'

'No, but I found these in the bin out the back.' I handed him the card and the section of newspaper.

'Are you working for the family now?' he asked.

I shook my head. 'Joy wants me to but I think it's the sort of thing that's best left to you guys. She's afraid you think Andi went off on purpose, because of the five grand.'

'She needn't worry. We treat every missing persons case with the utmost seriousness. We've searched the car parks at the airport and there's no sign of Andi's vehicle, nor any indication she travelled along the Citylink freeway to Tullamarine. I've talked to her lecturers at RMIT but as far as they're concerned everything was fine. Her fellow employees at Jouissance last saw her leaving a staff party at approximately two am Monday morning and assumed she was going to be in Sydney for the rest of the week. And we've had a look around her house and found no sign of a struggle or foul play.

'We're still in the process of canvassing businesses on Fitzroy Street, where she works, and neighbours, to see if anyone saw or heard anything suspicious that morning. And of course Andi's photograph and car details have been circulated around the country and posted on the national missing persons website. Now we'll see if we can trace the mobile call and if she hasn't shown up by the seventy-two hour mark I'll be talking to the missing persons unit attached to the Homicide Squad. You can tell Ms Fowler we're doing everything we can and that the majority of people turn up within a week. Especially if they've done it before.'

'She's done it before?'

'Didn't Ms Fowler tell you? Andi went missing when she was eighteen. Apparently it was in the middle of her HSC, she was stressed, had personal problems. Took off but was back within the week. Hid out in the shed at a friend's place. It's possible the same thing could be happening here. She's been taking antidepressants.'

'There is another thing. See this mark on my forehead?' I told him about the attack on me and he asked if I wanted to put in a report. I declined. What would be the point? He also asked if I thought it was connected with Andi's disappearance and I told him I couldn't say either way. My first instinct had been that it was, but as time passed and my headache turned into a dull throb, I wasn't so sure. Shit happened when you lurked round skanky alleys in the dark of night.

I said, 'Joy also wanted to apologise for her, uh, little scene before. She was really stressed and she feels terrible …' That was not in the least bit true but I thought it wouldn't hurt to smooth things over.

'I've dealt with worse outbursts than that.' Nolan smiled. 'If being called a pig offended me I wouldn't have lasted more than five minutes in this job. Let Ms Fowler know she can call me any time. We're all on the same side here and I didn't much like that rubber plant anyway.'

Well what do you know, he wasn't such a dickwad after all. If only all my dealings with the constabulary were so civilised. It wasn't until I was outside that I realised I'd forgotten to tell him about the missing photographs. I hurried back in and the guy at the front desk told me Nolan had just knocked off but I could probably catch him in the parking lot out the back.

I walked around the front of the station to a driveway that led to the rear. The building was red brick and looked like it had once been an electricity substation or a toilet block. Low shrubs circled the perimeter, spiky with waxy green leaves. The building was lit by sodium orange lights that picked up a slight mist in the air. I shivered and buttoned up my denim jacket, reached the end of the driveway and was just about to turn the corner to the car park when I heard my name. Nolan's voice had gone all harsh and blokey. I stopped short.

'No, serious, it was her. Gave me a card.'

'Fuck me.' A gruff, older voice. 'The stripping detective. Nice cans?'

'Nothing to write home about. Good legs though.'

'Couldn't investigate her way out of a paper bag. She's a fuckin' joke.'

'Didn't she solve the Tamara Wade thing?' Nolan asked.

'Lucked out. You know she gets all her information from rooting people? Bit of a goer. Likes cops too. Heard she was fucking some bloke from the Asian squad. You might be in with a chance, son, play your cards right. But watch out—word on the street is she's an alcoholic nympho. Why was she here?'

'You know the crazy lesbian who tried to smash the place up? Mother of the missing waitress? Friend of the family, apparently.'

'That's all we need. Fucking amateur running around messing shit up. And she's a fucking jinx, mate. Troublemaker. People start getting killed whenever she turns up. I don't know how she's kept her licence, let alone stayed out of jail. You know Dick Farquar? Never charged, but she knocked him, mate. You can say what you like about Farquar but he was a good man. I came up with him in Southern suburbs.'

'Well she's not on the case so we should be right.'

My guts lurched, my scalp prickled and my face burned despite the cold. I hadn't felt this particular emotion for quite some time and it took me a while to recognise the nauseated feeling as shame. There was also a fair whack of anger, which is the only explanation for what I did next. I pulled my phone from my pocket, dialled Chloe's number, whispered for her to put Joy on, then walked around the corner to find Nolan and a bald, beer bellied cop leaning on a divvy van, smoking cigarettes. At least Nolan had the good grace to blush. The other one crossed his arms over his shirt–straining gut and lazily looked me up and down.

'Joy? It's Simone. Listen, I've decided I will help you look for Andi after all. It's the least I can do since she called me for help. Soon as I'm back we'll draw up a contract, yeah?'

I smiled sweetly at the cops. 'Hi, guys,' I said, in a girly, singsong voice. 'Looks like I am on the case after all, so we'll be seeing a lot more of each other. Isn't that super?' I checked my watch. 'Oh shoot. Love to stay and chat but I gotta go get drunk and shag somebody for information. You know how it is.' I blew them both a kiss and skipped off down the drive.

chapter**seven**

Back at Andi's Chloe and Joy were sharing a vegetarian pizza. Carbs and removing your clothes for a living don't exactly mix so I slid the cheesy topping off, folded it in half and popped it in my mouth. Chloe was used to it, but Joy gave me a funny look.

I'd swung by my flat on the way back from the police station and typed up a makeshift contract. Joy raised her eyebrows and I explained that due to a recent run-in with the licensing division I had to do everything by the book. She wasn't exactly flush but wrote me a cheque for five hundred. I'd have asked for more but Chloe might have given me another dirty look.

'So what's the plan?' Chloe asked.

I licked my fingers and scribbled in my notebook. My

headache had receded and what with getting badmouthed by the cops, I was raring to go.

'Last place she was seen was Jouissance, right? I'm going to talk to them, then go through Andi's address book, speak with the ex, the flatmate, people from uni.'

'Hasn't that already been done?' Joy said.

'Not the way Simone does it!' Chloe slapped her on the thigh.

'It's always good to look at things with a fresh pair of eyes, and talk to people face to face if possible. Hopefully the cops can trace the phone call in the meantime.'

'I'll get the posters printed tomorrow and we can stick them up round here and in St Kilda,' Chloe said.

I picked up my phone, called directory and got them to put me straight through to Jouissance. It was nine o'clock and I hoped they weren't too busy.

'Jouissance Restaurant, Yasmin speaking.' The voice was haughty and she pronounced her name Yasmeen.

'My name's Simone Kirsch and I'm a private detective looking into Andi Fowler's disappearance. She worked with you?'

'Yes, I'm her manager. I spoke with the police yesterday and told them we last saw her two am Monday when she left the staff party. As far as we knew she was off to Sydney. Has there been any word?'

'Afraid not. And since you guys seem like the last ones to have seen her, I'd like to come in and talk to you and your staff. Maybe later tonight or—'

'I'm sorry, but that won't be possible.'

'What?'

'I've asked around. No one saw her after she left. Look, she hasn't been gone long and she'll probably show up soon. We're just too busy here. It's madness since Trip won the award. I don't want my staff disrupted. Sorry.'

My first thought was, man, what a bitch. My second was to grovel.

'Please, I'm working for the mother and she's very worried. It won't take long and—'

'What part of no don't you understand?' Her voice, which had been cold, turned arctic. 'I've talked to the police and am attempting to run a very busy restaurant. I'm well aware of my legal obligations and I believe I've fulfilled them. Don't call here again.'

Joy and Chloe looked at me as I cut the connection.

'The manager won't talk to me,' I explained.

'That's weird,' Joy said.

'More than weird,' Chloe said through a mouthful of pizza. 'It's suss.'

Joy's phone buzzed and we all jumped. She snatched it off the coffee table and when her face sagged I could tell it wasn't Andi.

'Yeah,' she said. 'Oh no. Right. I understand. I'll be there as soon as I can.'

She hung up and looked from Chloe to me. 'It's my mother. She's taken a turn for the worse. I have to get back to Sydney.'

Joy gave us her contact numbers, Andi's address book and showed us where Andi hid her key. I told her I'd let her know as soon as I came up with anything, and shook her hand. Chloe hugged her, promised we'd find her daughter and waved at the cab until it disappeared down the end of the street.

We stood on the footpath. I didn't mind the cold, it was waking me up, making me feel alert despite the head injury and all the codeine.

'What do we do now?' Chloe asked.

'Head to Jouissance.'

'But they won't talk to us.'

'You've worked hospitality, right?' I said.

'Fuck yeah. Worst fucking job in my life. Getting paid shit to be nice to people. Now I get paid good money to be a bitch. Why?'

'What's the number one after-work activity of hospitality workers?'

'Besides screwing the crew?'

'Yeah.'

'Gossip?'

'Bingo.'

After stopping briefly at my place, we drove to St Kilda, left the Futura on Park Street and crossed Fitzroy at the lights opposite Leo's spaghetti bar, admiring all the red neon. The air was icy enough to mist our breath, and it smelled like the bay. The tables outside the Prince of Wales hotel were empty. We shoved our hands deep into our coat pockets and I wouldn't have been surprised if it had been snowing somewhere up in the Dandenong Ranges. Officially it was spring but you could have fooled me.

We stood outside the restaurant and looked in. Jouissance took up two shopfronts at the end of Fitzroy, just before it veered around and turned into the Esplanade. The smaller, on the left, housed a bar furnished with brown suede banquettes and red velvet wallpaper. Giant orange orbs hung from the ceiling, washing the room in muted golden light. An archway led to the restaurant on the right, which continued the interior design theme, except it had polished floors and dark wood tables set with white napery and candles in small glass bowls. All the tables were full. The kitchen was in the far right corner, separated from the restaurant only by a waist high stainless steel bench. I guessed there was no point in having a celebrity chef if no one could get a look at him.

'What's my mission, should I choose to accept it?' Chloe giggled. I realised that she was swaying slightly and had to be pretty stoned. Still, wouldn't affect my plan. I checked my watch. It was just after ten.

'We hang at the bar and it's your job to ingratiate yourself with the menfolk so we can stick around for staffies. They should be finishing up around eleven thirty. Think you can accomplish that in an hour and a half?'

'Puhlease. I could do it in thirty seconds.'

'Cool. Then be your usual charming self and I'll sort of slink into the background and listen in and hopefully someone will spill something interesting. And we shouldn't use our real names. I'm Vivien.' It was my stripping name and I used it more often than my own.

'Can I be Marilyn?'

'Can't you think of something a little less …'

'Madonna?'

'How about Michelle?'

'I'll think of something,' she said.

We pushed through the glass door and into the bar where the suede banquettes were all occupied by expensively dressed women and portly older men. A waitress approached and her eyes flicked over Chloe. Was it just me or did blondes always size each other up like territorial felines? She looked like a catwalk model, tall, flaxen hair pulled back in a tight chignon, collarbones jutting out of her open necked black shirt. A tag over her right breast said 'Yasmin'. So this was the Nazi I'd spoken to on the phone.

'I'm afraid we're all booked out tonight.'

'That's okay, mate, we're just here for a drink.'

Chloe pushed past, causing the woman's top lip to twitch, and we took a couple of empty stools at the bar. When Chloe's mobile rang I swung around to check the place out.

A glass panel had been inserted along the length of the wall so you could see into the restaurant and vice versa. Opposite us an archway joined the two spaces. When I swung back Chloe was hanging up the phone.

'That was Curtis. He's meeting us here in a sec.'

'What?'

'He was in the area and wouldn't take no for an answer. Don't worry, I'll get rid of him.'

An impossibly cute bartender whose nametag identified him as Dillon flung a napkin over his shoulder and smiled at us. 'Hey, ladies, what'll it be?'

'Lime and soda,' I said, and Chloe almost fell off her stool. I shrugged. Those cops were wrong. I so wasn't an alcoholic.

'Double bourbon and Coke and a cocksucking cowboy,' Chloe smiled.

'Now that's more like it.' He winked.

I felt a draft of icy air and turned towards the door. Curtis was coming towards us.

Chloe offered her cheek and he kissed it, leaned against the bar and nodded at me. 'How many librarians died to make your outfit?'

At home I'd changed into a knee length skirt with a sober, polo neck jumper and flat shoes. My hair was slicked down, clipped rather severely at the back of my neck, and I'd accessorised with a pair of wire framed glasses I kept for when I did the 'stitched up secretary who lets down her hair and becomes a total hornbag' show. I'd wanted to fade into the background.

'And which Carlton gangster's wardrobe did you raid for that ensemble?'

When I'd first met him Curtis had been a mullet and flannie man. A combination of moving to Melbourne and hanging with Chloe had styled him up but he'd started taking it a little too far.

'What's wrong with it?' He stroked his shiny black shirt and silver tie.

Dillon returned with our drinks and grinned winningly from beneath his floppy brown hair. Chloe paid and told him to keep the change. Curtis ordered a Stella. Chloe slammed back the shot then slowly spun on her stool like I had, not so much to have a look at the place but to ensure everyone got a look at her.

She stopped short, growled like a cat on heat and Curtis and I turned to look through the arch.

Trip Sibley stood at the grill, cleverly positioned so he was in the middle of the kitchen, facing out towards the restaurant. While the rest of the staff wore white outfits with hats and neckerchiefs, his black jacket was open at the neck and his long hair was tied back with a red bandana. He towered over the other chefs, who were all kind of chunky, and the leaping flames and swirling plumes of smoke and steam created the illusion that he was standing in the middle of a raging inferno. When he raised his arched brows and smiled in our direction, I fancied that below the stainless steel bench his legs were hairy and goat-like, with hooves of the cloven variety.

'So … hot …' Chloe murmured and slowly unzipped her jacket. Trip said something over his shoulder and four chefs looked up from what they were doing and stared into the bar. I couldn't help staring either. Underneath the jacket a tiny silver singlet with spaghetti straps made her breasts look even bigger than normal. Trip's grin expanded. Chloe winked, swung back to face the bar, picked up a coaster and fanned herself.

Curtis frowned. 'Do you have to keep doing that?'

'What?'

'Flashing your boobs.'

'I'm a stripper, hon, I flash a whole lot more than my boobs. I thought you liked it.'

'When we're home alone, but in public ... it's cheap.'

Chloe rolled her eyes, Dillon returned with Curtis's beer, and we all drank in a silence about as comfortable as a rectal exam. Chloe removed the straw and gulped her bourbon, slapping the empty glass onto the bar. Dillon was down the other end garnishing a daiquiri, so she asked, loudly, 'Who's a girl have to blow to get a drink around here?'

I cringed and Curtis's jaw tightened.

Dillon was there in a flash. 'That'd be me.'

She ordered Australian sparkling and a clitlicking cowgirl, whatever that was, and after she'd tipped him she pointed at the rim of her champagne glass and pouted. 'Where's my strawberry, hon?'

'Coming right up.' He raced to the other end of the bar and bent over into the fridge.

Chloe nudged me. 'Check it out—arse you could bounce coins off. And those lips. Kinda like little pillows. I know where he could put those babies.'

Curtis flushed red. I saw it crawl out his collar, up his neck and spread across his cheeks. His eyes narrowed and the vertical line between them deepened. He got in Chloe's face.

'Right, that's it. I've fucking had it. Find someone else to be your lap-dog. I'm out of here.'

Dillon came back with the strawberry and Curtis leaned over the bar: 'Buddy, she's not fucking worth it,' then stormed out.

Dillon looked at Chloe, eyebrows raised.

'Boyfriends,' she laughed. 'Can't fuck with 'em, can't fuck without 'em.'

chapter**eight**

My plan for the evening had been generally sound, only I hadn't figured on Chloe being in one of her moods. Normally she was gorgeous, a tough cookie, sure, but melted chocolate in the centre. Every now and then though, usually after a smoke and one too many drinks, she got a crazy glint in her eye and seemed determined to raise some hell. In half an hour she'd ordered every obscene shooter on the menu and flirted outrageously with Dillon. She'd also slapped the arse of a buff Italian waiter named Patrizio when he came to the bar to collect a tray of drinks, even after I told her he was definitely gay.

'Chloe,' I said, 'you're doing really great but you might want to tone it down just a tad.'

She wasn't listening. She'd swung around again to give the kitchen another flash. 'Check it out.' She nodded.

Yasmin was facing the stainless steel bench holding a docket out to Trip and it looked like they were arguing. Trip ripped the paper out of her hand and studied it, his big, scarred hands shaking. Yasmin backed away. Trip grabbed the largest chef's knife I'd ever seen, a wicked, gleaming sweep of steel, wedged it between his teeth and leapt over the stainless steel counter into the restaurant. The din of conversation and cutlery ceased immediately. Everyone froze, watching, some with forks half raised to their mouths.

Trip's boots clomped on the polished wood as he strode toward a table of four: two couples, fat men in gaudy shirts with their pinched, skeletal wives. He grabbed an unoccupied chair and in one fluid movement slid it toward them and stepped up and onto the tabletop. The couples grabbed their wine glasses as the candle tipped over, its flame extinguished in a puddle of liquid wax.

Trip transferred the knife from his mouth to his right hand, held the docket in his left and read from it, voice booming so we could hear him all the way out in the bar.

'Goat cheese salad, hold the goat cheese, add cucumber and carrot, dressing on the side.

'Porcini mushroom risotto with no truffle oil, butter or salt.' He pointed the knife at each patron as he recounted their sins.

'Whole fish of the day, no bones. And finally—' the blade was dangerously close to the fattest guy's nose—'Export quality Wagyu beef, grain fed, marble score of seven, hold the Bordelaise, replace the celeriac mash with fries, cover with ketchup and cook … well done.'

Trip raised the knife. My heart was beating fast. He let out the sort of guttural yell you'd expect to hear from a marauding Viking and hurled the knife into the centre of the table where it stood up, quivering. And then, no kidding, he

51

crouched down like some kind of gargoyle and actually hissed in their faces.

The foursome didn't stick around to see what he'd do next. They scraped their chairs back, the women grabbing their bags, and ran. Trip pulled the knife out and straightened up, breathing heavily, sweat rolling down his temples. I wasn't breathing at all. Would someone try to restrain him? Call the police? Would the diners panic and stampede for the exit?

But it was Melbourne and the place was packed with foodies. A man started clapping. Someone else followed. Then another and another and people actually stood up, cheering, tapping wine glasses with knives and stamping their feet. Despite her affection for blackened steak smothered in tomato sauce, Chloe got into the spirit of things, stuck two fingers in her mouth and whistled. Trip grinned, bowed like a musketeer, and yelled for Dillon to bring everyone champagne.

Mad, bad and dangerous to know indeed.

At midnight we were still sitting at the bar. The restaurant patrons had left, the tables had been reset and a crusty dishpig was swabbing out the kitchen. I was on my third lime and soda and Chloe possibly her thirtieth sex related shooter. Although she was pissing me off, the boys seemed taken with her. Dillon was flirting, leaning on the bar, and Patrizio, who'd instructed us to call him Patsy, was captivated, especially after she told him he ought to be a male stripper. The sous chef, a fat guy with a red face and orange hair, sat in a banquette surrounded by spotty apprentices, all drinking beer and sneaking looks at Chloe's cleavage. Great that she was entertaining the troops, but none of them were gossiping about Andi's disappearance.

Yasmin stalked over. If she'd sucked her cheeks in any further her face would have collapsed in on itself. 'I'm afraid we're closing up, ladies, you'll have to leave.' Her smile didn't reach her eyes. Hell, it barely reached her lips.

I was relieved. Time to cut our losses and skedaddle.

Chloe was about to protest when suddenly I felt a shift in barometric pressure. I glanced up at the mirror at the back of the bar and saw that Trip was behind us.

'You're not going anywhere. I'm the boss and I say you can stay.'

He'd removed his chef's jacket and wore a black Slayer t-shirt with the sleeves cut off. He had arms like an AFL player. Chloe shifted stools so he could sit in between us and Trip told Dillon to pour him a shot of tequila.

'Girls?'

'No thanks,' I said.

'Shit yeah.' Chloe bounced on her stool, then leaned forward and pointed at him. 'You're fucking crazy.'

Trip shrugged. 'Americans. What you gonna do?' His voice had a vaguely English accent. 'You know, I'm pissed off with you girls.'

'Why?' Chloe shrieked in the manner of women who have consumed their entire body weight in cocktails.

'You didn't try my food.'

Chloe scrunched up her face. 'Yeah, why didn't we try the food, Si—uh, Vivien?'

'Couldn't get a booking. And we ate before we came.'

'You want dessert? I have some clafouti left. It's my signature dish.'

'I'm stuffed.' I patted my tummy. 'Couldn't fit another thing in.' Man, I just wanted to get out of there.

'I can fit a lot more in,' Chloe smiled lasciviously. 'A lot.'

'Then I'll make you some. Cream?'

She licked her lips.

He slammed back his shot, slid off his stool, then turned at the archway and pointed at her. 'You remind me of someone. Have we met before?'

'Yeah,' said Patsy. 'It's been driving me crazy all night. I've seen you somewhere.'

Chloe smiled and squirmed in her seat. Oh god, don't blow it, babe, I thought.

'Guess,' she said.

My plan had been a disaster. No one had said a word about Andi and it was only a matter of time before they figured out who Chloe was. She'd become a kind of Z grade celebrity after being kidnapped the year before and had even been on television: appearances on *A Current Affair*, hosting a program about Melbourne's seamy side, and a bit part playing a lap dancer on a cop show. Once they knew who she was they'd see behind the conservative clothes and realise I was none other than Simone Kirsch, stripping detective.

Trip strode off to the kitchen and I was just about to grab Chloe and drag her out when I heard bottles clattering behind me. I turned and saw the dishpig dragging two big green garbage bags toward the corridor where the toilets were. I'd worked as a kitchen monkey and knew dishies saw and heard everything, while remaining completely invisible to the naked eye. I'd have to act quick.

'Just going to the loo,' I muttered, sliding off my seat.

The back of the restaurant was crowded with garbage bins and stacked milk crates and an ancient cobbled laneway separated the small concrete yard from the rear of a unit block. The backstreet Bangkok stench of rotting food invaded my nostrils and the air hummed with the sound of the cool room and extractor fans.

I found the dishie sitting on an upturned milk crate behind a rubbish skip, scoffing food from a takeaway container. He was small and haggard, of indeterminate age, with a ten day growth spiking from his fissured face. Despite the cold he wore a laddered t-shirt with the sleeves rolled up, tucked into black nylon tracksuit pants, and his head was covered with some sort of hanky.

He flinched when he saw me. 'You're not supposed to be out here.'

'It's cool.' I held out my hands. 'Got sick of all those wankers in there, thought I'd come out the back for a smoke. You got a light?' I'd filched one of Chloe's Winfield Blues on the way out.

'Yeah.' He looked around slyly like it might be a trick, pulled out a pack of matches decorated with the Jouissance logo and held them out. I lit my ciggie. It tasted like shit without a drink to wash away the flavour, but I soldiered on bravely and scraped over a milk crate to sit on.

'I used to be a dishie.'

He looked dubious.

'A while back. When I was going through uni.'

'Don't want a job, do ya? They're looking for someone. Coupla days a week.'

'No thanks. I know what you go through, man. Talk about overworked and underpaid. Jeez, the chef used to piss me off.'

'Trip's not such a bad bloke,' he said, and I was surprised. 'Gordon's a prick though.'

'Gordon?'

'The second chef. Fat ginger bloke.'

'Oh. You get on with the waiters? That Yasmin seems like a bitch.'

'Shit yeah. Pole up her arse. Thinks she's it and a bit, too high and mighty to clean food off plates. Patsy's not bad but he's a poo jabber so I watch out for him.'

leighredhead

It crossed my mind that his rancid little arse was probably quite safe around even the most desperate homosexual, but I held my tongue.

'Andi was the best. But she's gone missing.'

Hello. 'Yeah, everyone was just talking about it in there. Weird, hey? What do you reckon happened to her?'

'Dunno.'

Damn. 'This restaurant was the last place she was seen. Imagine that. Walks down Fitzroy Street and just vanishes.'

'Wasn't Fitzroy Street.'

'What?'

'Nah. She left by the back way.' He looked around. 'With Trip and Yasmin. So they was the last ones that seen her.'

Whoa. Yasmin told the police Andi had left via the front. Alone.

'They usually all leave together?'

'No.' His eyes narrowed. 'What's it to you anyway?'

'Nothing, mate. Just making conversation.'

'I gotta finish cleaning.'

He sucked on the last of his cigarette, more butt than anything else, and scurried off. I ground mine under my heel. It was freezing and I could feel the hard plastic crate cutting diamond patterns into my arse. Time to go and drag Chloe out of there. I was just getting up when I heard a car coming down the lane and saw headlights moving across the brick walls. I didn't want anyone to spring me out the back so I stayed put, hidden in the shadows, peeping out from behind the bin. Tyres crunched and a white one tonne van pulled up, 'Doyle Food Group' stencilled in cursive script on the side next to a picture of a trout leaping over a cheese wheel, just like the card. A solid looking guy in navy trousers and a matching nylon windcheater got out of the van. He had

56

shoulder length dark hair and a goatee and he slid open the side door and stacked four boxes onto a small trolley.

I heard the unmistakable clomp and rattle of motorcycle boots coming down the hallway and then Trip's voice: 'Hey, Gary.'

'Trip.'

They shook hands and the delivery guy handed Trip an invoice, which he shoved in his back pocket. He wheeled the stock into the restaurant while Gary leaned against the van, having a smoke. A couple of minutes later Trip was back with the trolley.

'All there, mate?' Gary asked.

'Yep. See you tomorrow.' He walked back into the building and Gary started up the van and reversed out.

A restaurant where stock gets delivered in the middle of the night and the chef personally marks it off the invoice? Not in my lifetime. Adrenaline shot into my bloodstream the way it always did when a case picked up momentum, and all sorts of thoughts raced through my brain. Import, export, drugs … Maybe Andi really was onto something big.

I rounded the skip, opened the back door, and ran straight into Trip Sibley.

chapternine

Trip was holding a large white plate loaded with some sort of flan. Cherries oozed from the side, thick cream lolled over the top and the whole thing was sprinkled with icing sugar. He stepped into the yard and I was forced to back up.

'What are you doing out here?' His smile looked like a threat.

'Needed some fresh air.' I realised how stupid it sounded as soon as I'd said it. We were surrounded by rubbish bins.

'Been out here long?'

'Minute or so. Guess I'd better be off home. Grab my friend.' I went to walk around him but he sidestepped and blocked my way.

'Not until you've eaten dessert.' He spooned off a big chunk of pie and cream and advanced, backing me against the wall.

'Trying to stay away from carbs.' I patted my tummy. 'You know, watching my weight.'

'C'mon, live a little. I bet behind those glasses you aren't quite as conservative as you look. Taste it. You know you want to …'

The spoon zoomed closer, laden with sin, smelling as good as it looked. Fantasy food, the kind us hippy kids wished our mothers would bake while we choked down tofu and tahini.

'My clafouti recipe's a secret but I can tell you I fly the cherries in from California, use vanilla bean, clotted King Island cream …' He pressed the cold metal against my lips and when I opened my mouth to protest he pushed it a little way in. Heaven hit the tip of my tongue. Buttery crust, cherries sweet and tart, silken cream. An involuntary moan started low in my throat and I shut my eyes and sucked off the lot.

He dug out another chunk, hovered it near and when I opened up he jerked the spoon back a bit. Bastard. I grabbed his wrist and pulled it towards me, got the pie in my mouth and held it on my tongue to prolong the sensation. God. I hadn't even finished this morsel and already I was wondering how long it would take to get my next fix. Normally I was a savoury girl, mad for cheese in all its forms. It was the first time I'd met a dessert worth selling your arse down Grey Street for.

I chewed slowly, swallowing just a little at a time. Just as well my eyes were still closed 'cause I had a feeling they were rolling back in my head.

Trip chuckled and I thought that he must really get off on being able to do this to people.

'And you want to know the most important ingredient of all?' he said. 'Kirsch.'

My eyes snapped open and I choked on pie. He smirked, eyes black and glinting in the low light.

'Patsy finally figured it out when your friend asked him to work for her. Chloe. The stripper off the tele who got kidnapped and was rescued by her friend, fellow stripper and sometime PI Simone Kirsch.'

He set the plate and spoon on top of a wheelie bin and reached for my face. I ducked but not fast enough. He plucked off the fake glasses, tossed them over his shoulder, then reached around and yanked off my clip so my hair fell around my shoulders.

'Now you look like those pictures in the paper. Still got that sparkly red bikini?'

'Fuck you.'

He just laughed. 'After Patsy worked it out Yasmin remembered a call she'd had from a female private investigator. So the infamous Simone Kirsch is spying on me. It's an honour.'

'You can stop taking the piss, Mr Sibley. I'm looking into Andi Fowler's disappearance and it's pretty damn weird that no one here seems concerned or will talk to me about it.'

'People come and go all the time in this biz.'

'Why won't you answer questions then?'

'That was just Yasmin. I'll answer anything you like.'

'When did you last see Andi?'

'Staff party,' he said without hesitation. 'She left about two. Toddled off down Fitzroy Street to catch a cab.'

Liar. But I didn't let on. For the first time I noticed a scratch on his cheek, opposite side from the scar.

'How'd you get that scratch?'

'You wouldn't believe it but I was bending over in the cool room to get some stock, and a fucking pineapple attacked me. I've got nothing to hide, darlin'. You want to check the rest of my body for suspicious marks? Maybe take a DNA sample?' He moved his hands toward his belt, laughing at his own joke.

'That won't be necessary. I'm going now.'

He didn't try to stop me. Just stood there and ate the rest of the dessert.

If I'd thought things were a disaster before, they were more so by the time I got back into the bar. Everyone was hammered and Chloe was making Patsy audition by giving her a lap dance.

'That's right, baby,' she said. 'Who's your momma?'

Yasmin was leaning against the bar, mouth pursed into a cat's bum. She grabbed my arm as I walked past.

'I told you not to bother us,' she spat. 'Now take your slut friend and get out of here.'

I shook out of her grasp. 'We were just leaving.'

I marched over to Chloe. 'Come on, babe, we gotta go.'

'Just a sec.'

Patsy, still sitting on her lap, said, 'I have to ask, darling, are those fucking gazoongas real?'

'Why don't you have a feel and find out?'

He put a breast in each hand and weighed them up. 'They are too!'

'I don't believe it,' said Dillon. Chloe tipped Patsy off and marched over to Dillon, grabbed his hands and put them on her tits.

Patsy suddenly gasped and clapped his hands to his mouth. 'Oh my god, Dillon, you are sooo busted.'

I followed Patsy's gaze to the front door. A dark haired woman in her early thirties started pounding on the glass, a baby in a front pack and a pissed off expression on her face. Dillon's hands recoiled but it was too late. Gordon, the fat sous chef, leapt up sneering and let her in.

The woman stomped over to Dillon. 'Just staying back for a couple of staffies, huh?'

I grabbed Chloe and her handbag and dragged her toward the entrance. Gordon turned the lock as we approached and reached out his hands. 'But I didn't get to see if they were real.'

Chloe giggled and I stood in front of her. 'Party time's over, mate, let us out.'

I went for the lock and the prick made a swipe at my boobs so I grabbed his chubby hand and dug my fingernails into the palm until his eyes started to water. 'Try it and I'll slap a sexual harassment suit on you so fast your head will spin.'

He looked me up and down, stood to the side and waited till I'd passed before he muttered, 'Bitch.'

Chloe stepped out the door and fell on her arse on the footpath. I put my arms around her waist and hauled her up. 'Come on, babe.'

She struggled against my grasp. 'I'm going back in. I was having fun.'

'No you're not. I'm driving you to my place.'

'Don't wanna. Let go.' She made herself floppy, like a kid chucking a tantrum at the shops, and slithered to the ground where she sat, legs stretched out, laughing.

I'd really had enough. 'Damn you, Chloe, you've fucked up my undercover operation, made a dick of yourself and pissed off somebody's wife. Not to mention humiliated your own boy-friend. I'm not Curtis's number one fan but that was awful. What the fuck's wrong with you tonight? You'd better get your shit together because you're fucking embarrassing.'

Soon as I uttered the last word I regretted it.

She picked herself up and stood in front of me swaying, one eye squinted. 'You're ashamed of me?'

'I'm not—'

'You fucking hypocrite. It's okay for you to be a stripper because you have to do it to save for your business. But me, who does it 'cause I like it, that makes me a dumb slut, right?'

'I didn't say—'

'I'm so fucking sick of you, Simone. Ever since you started being a PI you take yourself sooo seriously. Ooh, I'm too good for jelly wrestling. Ooh, I can't share an office with my tarty friend. Well I don't fucking want you anyway. Fuck off. Just don't forget where you came from.'

'Screw you, Chloe. I don't need this shit. You're the worst sidekick a girl ever had.'

She staggered towards me, pointing. 'Ever thought that maybe you're just my sidekick? Ever thought of that?'

'In your dreams.'

She slapped me. I raised my hand to slap her back.

'Come on.' She put up her dukes.

I glanced inside the restaurant. Dillon was arguing with his wife. Patsy was passed out on a banquette. Trip and the other chefs were watching our bitch fight through the window, laughing and putting bets on who would win. I turned and walked away.

chapter**ten**

First thing I did when I got back to my one bedroom flat was open the fridge and reach for the wine. I wanted to obliterate the whole evening and thought a litre ought to do it. I grabbed the handle on the four litre box then paused. I'd gone all night without a drink, why start now? I could go to bed sober. It's not like I was totally addicted to booze.

I let go of the cask. I'd wake up early and have a run and be all fresh and sparkly and put the debacle at Jouissance behind me. The fight with Chloe was completely mortifying but I supposed the night hadn't been a complete waste of time. I'd found out Andi left with Trip and Yasmin, and they'd lied about it. Now I just had to decide how to follow up on that information.

I grabbed a couple of cheese singles, sat down at my computer with a cup of camomile tea and googled the Doyle Food Group. It was a Sydney based company that owned a boutique hotel there called the Villa, a food importing business, a restaurant in Kings Cross and half of Jouissance. The CEO was a guy named Sam Doyle and I searched his name and discovered he was fond of yachts and horseracing. He was generally described as 'colourful' but I couldn't find out why.

It was two in the morning and my head was starting to pound again so I brushed my teeth, filled up a hot water bottle and tucked myself into bed. I knew the best way to achieve instant unconsciousness was by sorting myself out so I stuck my hand down my pyjama bottoms and tried to rustle up a romantic fantasy of Sean and me making mad, passionate love on a palm fringed beach.

It didn't work. As hard as I tried to concentrate on Sean, Trip Sibley kept popping up, leering and brandishing desserts. Damned if I was going to mentally cheat on Sean with a bloody celebrity chef. I gave up on the idea and kept my hands to myself. Simone Kirsch, sober, chaste, on the right side of the law. Alcoholic nympho my arse.

Next morning I woke at nine thirty, drank two cups of coffee (no need to mainline the entire plunger when you weren't hungover) and called the number on the card I'd found in Andi's bin.

'Doyle Food Group, Rochelle speaking.'

'I'd like to speak to Sam Doyle, please.'

'I'm afraid Mr Doyle is not available. What's it regarding?'

'An employee of his has gone missing from the Jouissance Restaurant in Melbourne. I'm a private detective retained by the family. Could you get him to give me a call when he has the chance?'

'Certainly. If you'll leave your name and number.'

'Simone Kirsch.'

'Excuse me?'

'Kirsch. K–I–R–S–C–H. It's German for cherry.' Most people had a little chuckle at that but she didn't laugh. I'd had about enough of bitchy broads but stayed polite and left my mobile number.

I went through Andi's address book, dialling every number. Some were disconnected, others, including her best friend Daisy, I left messages for, and the few who answered didn't have a clue where she was. I got onto her ex boyfriend, Liam, who also had no idea, but I asked if we could meet up anyway. He was a student at RMIT, doing the same course as Andi, and told me he could meet me there at one thirty. It was a date.

Since I had a few hours to kill I pulled on my winter exercise outfit of black tights, faded Mickey Mouse t-shirt and grey hooded top, laced up my runners and jogged down the canal toward the beach. On the way I decided that I was absolutely not ringing Chloe to apologise after our first ever fight, she could call me, and I was going to spend the day finding out everything I could about a certain arrogant chef. I powered up the Elwood hill, calves aching, and checked out the bay as I leaned against the old wooden lookout, foot to butt, stretching out my quads. The water was choppy and steely blue and when I turned my head to look at the city skyline, I saw that the tops of the buildings were obscured by dark wispy clouds.

I decided to stop for supplies on the way home, and by the time I ducked into the Ormond Road IGA, pellets of freezing rain were attacking my head.

Bypassing the stuff I really wanted—crusty ciabatta bread, unsalted butter and frozen lasagne—I bought a cauliflower, homebrand tuna and a tub of cottage cheese. It was too cold for salad and I'd recently figured out I could mash the three ingredients together for a cheap, low fat, no carb dish that was just like tuna mornay. But not.

I lived on Broadway, a wide, tree lined street with renovated bungalows on one side and a mixture of units, townhouses and thirties flats on the other. Rain pocked the surface of the canal as I crossed the bridge and a fishy smell rose from the water. There was no shelter under the bare branches and by the time I retrieved a couple of soggy bills from my letterbox, I was soaked and shivering. I'd just turned to walk up the path to the security entrance when I heard a voice behind me.

'Simone.'

I turned. Detective Senior Constable Alex Christakos stood on the footpath, rain pattering the fabric of his large, dark blue umbrella.

Alex always looked good and that day was no exception. Thick dark hair swept back from his forehead, his eyes were their usual dark chocolate and his wide mouth was just plump enough to bite. A slight five o'clock shadow darkened his jaw even though he must have shaved only a few hours before. He wore a long charcoal wool coat, a well cut suit and navy tie with a subtle pattern of little squares.

My hair was plastered to my scalp and water ran down my face.

'Alex. Shit. Haven't seen you for months.'

'Been a while,' he agreed.

'You here about the court case?' Alex and I were going to be prosecution witnesses in a major trial later in the year.

'No.'

'What then?'

'I can't make a social call?'

'Ha. Suzy wouldn't let you.' I blinked through the rivulets of rainwater running into my eyes. 'You are still engaged, aren't you?'

'Wedding's in November. Why don't we go inside. You look like a soggy chihuahua.'

Thanks. 'I warn you. Place is a mess.'

'I'm sure it's not that bad.'

'This place is a shitfight!' Alex hung his coat on the back of the door and surveyed the room with his mouth turned down.

'It's not that bad.'

I switched on the gas heater, dumped my shopping bags on the kitchen counter and ran back in to the combined lounge/dining room to gather up newspapers, copies of *Australasian Investigator* magazine, and bowls encrusted with cauliflower mash. Alex was about to sit in the overstuffed armchair I'd found in the street on hard rubbish day, looked behind him and plucked something from the cushion. A pair of my oldest, daggiest knickers dangled from his index finger. Faded black, elastic peeping through holes in the fabric, not entirely clean. I snatched them off him so fast I nearly dropped the bowls.

'It's cold. I get dressed in front of the heater.'

'I can see that.' With one shiny black lace-up he nudged the flannelette PJs lying in a heap on the floor. He always wore nice shoes.

'Sit,' I said. 'Stay. I'll be five minutes.'

I dumped the newspapers in the cardboard box I used as a recycle bin, chucked the bowls in the sink and ran to the bathroom, ripped off my soaking outfit, had a quick shower and dressed in jeans, an oversized man's shirt and thick socks. I ran a comb through my wet hair and put on a little powder, mascara and lip gloss. Not that I was trying to impress him or anything.

When I returned I found Alex had disobeyed my instructions and was rummaging around my kitchen, opening cupboards and drawers. It had last been renovated in the late eighties so the surfaces were all grey laminate with pink trim.

'Got anything to drink?'

I opened the fridge to display the cask and his top lip curled back.

'I was thinking more like Jameson's.'

'Sorry.'

'Coffee?'

'Is a bear Catholic? Does the Pope shit in the woods?'

I stuck on my white plastic kettle, rinsed out the plunger and pulled the coffee tin from the freezer. As I scooped grounds Alex went through my shopping bag.

'Do you mind?'

He held up the no name tuna. 'You're eating cat food now? Must really be doing it tough.'

I snatched the tin. 'Not cat food. People food. Check the can. Nowhere does it say unfit for human consumption.'

'I tried to feed my cat this shit once, he wouldn't touch it.'

'You have a cat?'

'Uh-huh.'

I leaned back on the bench and studied him.

'What?' he said.

'Nothing. I just thought you'd be a dog person.'

'Why?'

'Need a pet that obeys.'

'Shows how much you know. I like how cats are independent and don't take any shit. Plus, you don't have to walk them.'

I stuck my cauliflower on to steam and we took our coffees into the lounge. Alex checked out my CD collection, picked one of the few jazz disks in a wall of alt country, and put it on. Miles Davis.

'Make yourself at home,' I said as he sat back down.

'Really into that country shit, huh?'

'You'd better believe it.'

I flashed back to the night I'd forced him to see Doug Mansfield and the Dust Devils at the Greyhound. We'd ended up in a laneway with his hand up my dress. He must have remembered too because he suddenly became very interested in his coffee cup, as though an image of Jesus had just appeared in the crema.

Alex and I had gotten into a lot of passionate clinches without ever going 'all the way'. I guessed we never would now that he was marrying fellow officer Suzy McCullers and I was going out with Sean, his best friend. It was just as well. I'd first met Alex at a strip club and I'm not convinced a relationship can ever work if the guy sees you naked within ten minutes of meeting you.

'How're the wedding plans going? Bet you're excited. Been practising the bridal waltz?'

He groaned and ran his fingers through his hair. 'You know I've been married before, when I was twenty-one? Big Greek wedding? Didn't want to go through all that shit again so I thought we'd just do the registry office thing, then out to dinner with a few friends and immediate family. But she's got her mother involved. Eight bridesmaids, as many groomsmen, flower girls, page boys. I ever tell you little kids in suits freak me out? Guest list's blown out to over two hundred and, get this, she wants a carriage, with horses, and for us to dress up in poncy medieval gear.' He leaned forward, elbows on knees. 'This fucking outfit she's picked for me, it's got, like, gold brocade. It's got puffy sleeves.'

I choked down a laugh. I knew it wasn't nice, but Alex bitching about Suzy's bad taste made me feel really good. She had punched me unconscious once so I felt entitled to a little gloating. I rearranged my face to look serious.

'C'mon, Alex, let her have her princess fantasy. It's every little girl's dream.'

'Not yours.'

'No. In the unlikely event I ever get hitched it'd take place in Vegas with Elvis impersonators, strippers and a shitload of Bolivian marching powder.'

Alex shook his head at the mention of drugs. He was so straight I was willing to bet he'd never even smoked a J. Unlike his best mate.

'I could see Sean being in that. Heard from him lately?'

''Bout a week ago.'

'Miss him?' The question, coming from Alex, made me uncomfortable.

'Of course.'

Enough pussyfooting around. I tucked my legs under me, sipped my drink and rested the cup on the coffee table. 'So spill, Senior Constable. Why are you really here?'

He slid an envelope out of his inside jacket pocket, handed it over and I pulled out a stack of photos. The shots were grainy and it took me a moment to realise what I was seeing. Holy shit. It was me and Trip out the back of Jouissance.

'Where did you get these?' I asked, flipping through them.

'Get these? I took the fucking things.'

'What?'

'From a unit block behind the restaurant.'

'I don't understand. You're looking for Andi Fowler too?'

'The missing waitress? Hardly. I'm fraud. We've been investigating Trip Sibley.'

'What's the fraud?'

'Can't talk about an official police case. What's going on with the waitress?'

'Sorry.' I said. 'Client confidentiality.'

71

We stared at each other over the coffee table, a Mexican standoff. I tried to look inscrutable while my mind raced at a million miles. I was dying to know what Trip was being investigated for. It had to have something to do with Andi going missing. I couldn't help myself and broke first.

'It's to do with the suss deliveries after midnight, isn't it?' I blurted. 'The ones courtesy of "colourful" Sydney businessman Sam Doyle.'

Alex shrugged and put on a blank cop face that infuriated me so much I briefly considered slapping some expression into it. Instead I grabbed the empty coffee cups, marched into the kitchen, clattered them into the sink and turned off the stove. Alex followed and leaned against the slatted door of the pantry, wrinkling his nose at the farty, sulphurous smell.

'I'm not stupid, Alex.' I tonged the cauliflower into a bowl, picked up a fork and mashed it into a lumpy paste. 'You're obviously here to pick my brains, but you know how it works. I won't give up shit unless you share information with me.' I opened the tuna and realised he was right, it did look a lot like pet food.

'I'm not here for information,' he said.

I snorted, mixed in the fish and opened the fridge to retrieve the cottage cheese. 'Yeah, right.'

'I'm here because I'm not the only one who recognised you in the photos. Our case is at a critical juncture and my boss ordered me to tell you to stay the hell away from Trip Sibley.'

I was halfway through peeling the foil back on the plastic tub and froze, every muscle tense. 'Why?'

He laughed. 'C'mon, Simone, you've said it yourself. You're trouble with a capital T.'

I swung around and when he saw my face he held out his palms. 'Hey, I'm not saying you're a bad investigator but you have to admit, things have a habit of going pear shaped when you get involved and we can't risk tipping the suspects off. Look, it'll only be for a week or so, just until we've wrapped things up. If I find out anything about the waitress along the way, I'll let you know.'

He thought I was a fuck-up. The whole goddamn police force did. I was about to tell him just where to shove his orders when I had a better idea. It was risky, I might not be able to pull it off, but if I did I could possibly help Andi and prove Alex wrong all at the same time.

'Okay, sure. I'll back off.' I turned and scooped about half the cottage cheese into the bowl, added salt, pepper and Tabasco sauce, and stirred.

'Really?' He sounded like he didn't believe me.

I leaned back against the bench, bowl in hand, and tried to look sincere. 'Yeah. I don't want to piss off you guys and risk losing my licence again. And realistically, I blew my cover last night. There's no way I'd get away with waltzing back into Jouissance. I was already thinking I'd concentrate my inquiry on other avenues, like the boyfriend and stuff. You promise you'll let me know if you find anything on Andi?' I forked the cauliflower mixture into my mouth. It really was a taste sensation.

'Absolutely.' He smiled, relieved, then screwed up his face when he saw what I was eating. 'That smells like an old folks' home and looks like something my cat sicked up. What the hell is it?'

'Kind of like tuna mornay?' I said through a mouth full of slop. 'But not.'

chapter**eleven**

The Royal Melbourne Institute of Technology was sprawled across a couple of city blocks on the northern edge of the CBD and comprised maybe twenty different buildings, from gothic bluestone to modern structures of concrete and steel. I drove to the city and parked under a new shopping complex that took up a whole block between Lonsdale Street and Latrobe, then followed Liam's instructions to Bowen Street. It was more of a lane really, blocked off to traffic, skinny trees and wooden benches lining either side. Students in coats and bulky jackets, weighed down with backpacks, hurried into buildings, out of the cold and rain. Wherever Andi was, I hoped it was somewhere warm.

The cafeteria where I'd arranged to meet Liam was a couple of hundred metres down the lane and the entrance looked like something out of *Playschool*, a wall of glass squares coloured blue, yellow and red. I looked around. The only person I could see was a gangly guy leaning against a tiled pillar, smoking a cigarette and sheltering from the rain.

'Liam?'

He was all in black, from his jeans to his gel-spiked hair. He had a long neck with a prominent Adam's apple and the face on top was slightly beaky. He was no more than nineteen, with remnants of teenage acne that looked raw and inflamed where he'd shaved. Guys that young did nothing for me, but I noted he had a kind of intense poutiness that might turn into something in five years time.

'Simone Kirsch?' His voice was a little strangled.

'That's me.' I held out my hand and the wooden beads around his wrist rattled as he gave it a limp shake.

'I've read all about you. Big fan of Curtis Malone. You look different than I imagined.'

'I'd normally show up in a g-string and pasties, drawing a gun from my garter belt, but it's too fucking cold.'

He laughed and stubbed out the ciggie under one of his Doc Marten boots. 'You're not wrong, let's go inside.'

The cafeteria was set up like a food court with a linoleum floor and counters selling coffee, sandwiches, burgers and noodles. The air was muggy and the smell reminded me of school in winter: wet wool and tomato sauce. I bought us both a coffee, Liam grabbed a bucket of hot chips and we sat at a metal table beside another glass wall, this one clear glass, posters advertising dance parties and student rallies fixed to the squares.

'Thanks for agreeing to speak to me.'

'No problem.' He blew on a chip and the sharp scent of vinegar hit my nostrils. 'Just tell me to shut up if I talk too much. Got up early and popped six Sudafed so I could finish off an assignment. Works like speed, turns me into a motor mouth.'

'Motor mouth is good. Tell me everything. Talk all you like.'

'Sure, but like I said on the phone, I don't know where she is or what happened to her. I mean, we were still friends but we broke up a couple of months ago.'

'How long were you guys going out for?'

'God, not more than three months. I met Andi when we started at the beginning of the year. We were in a lot of the same classes and I liked her on sight but I never thought anything would happen. She was one of the mature age students and I'm just out of school. I still live with my parents. You know, majorly uncool. But we worked together on this project for Introduction to Journalism and just clicked. After we'd handed it in Andi took me out to the Stork Hotel and we drank about fifty million beers and played pool and, shit, she totally whipped my ass, drank me under the table then took me back to her place and … you can guess the rest. We were pretty much inseparable for the next three months. God we had a good time. Saw heaps of bands, drank probably half the beer in the state and the sex … my last girlfriend was sixteen, she just used to lie there. So being with an experienced woman … wow. My friends were so jealous. They thought she was ace. She's the only girl I ever met who actually liked playing video games, she could burp the alphabet at will and she'd fart on people, as a sign of affection.'

'Really?'

'She was way cool.'

He shoved four chips in his mouth at once and licked the salt off his fingers and I resisted the urge to peck at his carton like a seagull. If there was anything that tasted better than somebody else's hot chips, I'd never heard of it.

'Sounds like you really dig her, but you don't seem upset you've broken up.'

'Man, I knew it wouldn't last from the start. She didn't want anything serious and I'm too young to anyway, so I decided just to have fun and go along for the ride. Isn't that what going to uni's all about? Andi took me to see some awesome music, taught me how to brew beer and then there was the other stuff she showed me, in the bedroom, if you know what I mean.' He wiggled his eyebrows and one side of his mouth tugged up in a lopsided grin. 'Plus there was the added bonus that my parents hated her. They're really straight. I took her around once and she called my mum mate, and she argued with my dad about politics, and then when we went to bed she was so fucking loud. Holy shit. I mean, I'm allowed to have girls home but they didn't expect that.'

'Sounds like a real wild child.'

'That's what my folks thought. But what they didn't realise was that she was a really dedicated student. She'd work three nights a week, party with me, and get top marks on her assignments. I worked hard on my VCE to get into journalism, but I'd never seen someone so determined.'

'Why do you think that was?'

'She wanted to get the fuck out of the hospitality industry. She'd never liked it but kind of fell into it, you know? Andi told me that when she first finished school she was accepted into law at Sydney uni, but decided to defer and go backpacking for a year. She waitressed to get the money and when she came back she did it again to pay off her debts. By this stage she wasn't interested in law anymore and spent the next six years in restaurants, trying to figure out what she wanted to do with her life. Now that she has, she doesn't want to waste a second.'

Liam shoved in another handful of chips and his motor mouth was temporarily silenced. Chairs scraped the lino. Noodles sizzled. Chatter, laughter and mobile ring tones filled the air. Students passed by in duffle coats and scarves, arms loaded with folders and books and I thought back to my two years at uni. I wondered how I'd got any assignments in at all considering I'd pretty much majored in sex, drugs and rock'n'roll.

'Why'd you break up?' I asked.

'It happened after she started at Jouissance in July. We were fine when she worked at Bistro Verve but within a week of changing jobs she was different.'

'How?'

'Distant, unavailable, there but not there. I knew it was over.'

'Why'd she change jobs anyway?'

'No idea.' He shrugged. 'She visited her mum in Sydney in the June holidays, came back and a week later she'd quit and started at Jouissance. I know why she was acting weird though.'

'Why?'

'She'd met someone.'

'At Jouissance?'

'Maybe.'

'How did you know?'

'She never said anything, but I could tell from the way she behaved. Like, when I first started seeing her, I was still going out with my sixteen year old girlfriend, right? I wanted to break up with her but I didn't want to be the bad guy, so I did the same detached act that Andi ended up doing to me. Serves me right, I guess. Anyway, I pulled the plug, Andi seemed relieved and we stayed friends. End of story.' He swirled the last scraps of chip around in the carton, tipped them into his mouth, and drank them down with the vinegar.

I thanked Liam for his time and finished my coffee. 'If I wanted to speak to one of her lecturers, who would you suggest?'

'Derek Canning knew her best. I've got his class in an hour so he'd probably be in his office. Building six, second floor, turn right at the glass. Hey, you got time for a beer, game of pool?' He wiggled his eyebrows again. Cheeky bugger.

I patted his hand. 'It's a lovely offer but I'm sure there are a heap of girls on campus in need of your new-found skills a lot more than I am. Go get 'em, tiger.'

chapter**twelve**

The journalism department was located in the School of Applied Communication, six storeys of pale brick with some rather fetching ivy smothering the front and a prison-like stairwell within. I hurried out of the cold, boots echoing on the concrete steps, and turned right at the glass doors. The staff offices were a grey carpeted rabbit warren, and, oddly, every second door was painted peach. I found Canning's room and knocked.

I'd half expected a fusty professor with a white beard and leather elbow patches but Derek Canning was a bit of a spunk. A young looking forty, maybe, with dark brown curly hair, sideburns, grey green eyes and glasses. His jeans were faded, his mauve shirt was rolled up at the sleeves and worn brown Blundstones encased his feet. I wondered if it were possible for me to meet a man, any man, without instantly gauging his rootability. Wasn't it a bit sexist? Wasn't it something a nymphomaniac might do?

'Simone Kirsch.' I flashed my licence. 'I'm looking into the whereabouts of Andi Fowler. Can you spare a couple of minutes?'

'Absolutely. Simone Kirsch, huh? We had a friend of yours in here a few weeks ago.'

An image popped into my head. Chloe in her cowboy hat and leather chaps riding a naked Canning through the hallway, whipping him with a crop.

'Really?'

'Uh-huh. Curtis Malone was guest lecturer and the students hung on to his every word. I don't know which stories they liked better, him covering the strip shows for *Picture* or the time he got shot in the hip hanging out with you.'

'Arse.'

'Excuse me?'

'He was shot in the butt.' Trust Curtis to make himself sound cooler than he was.

Canning ushered me into a tiny rectangular office dominated by a large desk covered in newspapers. Crowded bookshelves reached the low ceiling and posters for the Art Gallery, an industrial relations rally and Triple R community radio filled the remaining space. A small window looked onto the back of a brick building where rusted pipes leaked steam. Derek took the high backed leather swivel chair and pointed to a padded vinyl number that sighed when I sat down.

'I've actually spoken to the police on the phone,' he said, 'but there wasn't much I could tell them. She hasn't shown up for class this week, totally out of character, and nobody knows where she is or where she might be.'

The coffee percolator on the filing cabinet hissed as the last drops trickled through the filter. I must have been ogling it because he offered me a cup, which I accepted, then poured one for himself. Nolan and his crony hadn't said anything about me being a dirty, low-down caffeine whore.

'That's what everyone says, so in the absence of any concrete information I'm trying to get a sense of her. What was she like?'

'As a student or a person?'

'Both.' I sipped my coffee. It burnt the tip of my tongue and I placed it on the corner of the desk, on top of the *Age* business section.

'Great student. The mature age ones are often a lot more diligent than the school leavers. Perfect attendance, very good writer, always got her work in on time. You wouldn't believe how many of them ask for extensions. You want to be a journalist? It's all about deadlines. I despair sometimes.'

'And as a person?'

'Well, things have been a lot quieter around here since she's been missing. Very forthright, curious about the world around her, highly intelligent, down to earth. She's first year so I haven't known her very long, but that's what I've picked up from the tutorials. I think she'll do very well. We're constantly drumming into the students that it's not enough to be able to write well, to report, but you've also got to be able to find the news. Andi certainly wasn't shy. I think if anyone could ferret something out, it'd be her.'

'Find the news, huh? It's interesting you should say that because I found a lot of library books at Andi's on investigative journalism and a book called *All That Glitters*, about corruption in Kings Cross, was missing. Is that related to something she's working on here at uni?'

'I seriously doubt it. We don't get into investigative journalism until third year. Right now it's basic reporting and news writing, the ethics of journalism, that sort of thing. She could be interested in it for the future. As for the book on Kings Cross, that was written by a Sydney journalist, Chris Ferguson. He did a guest lecture for us here just before the holidays in June. Anyway, I've got to get ready for this tutorial. Sorry I couldn't have been more help.'

'No, you've been great,' I said. 'Do you have a contact for Ferguson?'

Derek checked his computer and scribbled an email address on the back of a card. My brain was buzzing. And not just from the coffee.

By five that afternoon the rain had cleared and a half assed sun hung low in the cold blue sky. I was standing outside Jouissance peering through the slatted wooden blinds into the restaurant. Silver cutlery and Riedel glasses glinted in the lemon yellow light and Gordon and the apprentices buzzed about the kitchen, stirring pots, chopping vegetables and joking around.

I walked up the road a couple of paces. The sign on the glass door read 'Closed', but Dillon and Yasmin were at the bar chatting, him polishing glasses, her cutlery. I knocked loudly and windmilled my arms and she turned, set down a knife and chamois and swished over. Adrenaline bubbled and every instinct told me to piss-bolt down the street. She'd kicked me out sixteen hours earlier. Would she recognise me now?

She unlocked the door and propped it open with one shiny court shoe. Her black shirt was immaculate, her long apron crisp and her blonde hair was twisted into a neat chignon.

'Yes?'

'I called ya about the dishie job, aye? You Jasmine?' I'd lifted the accent from the rednecks who'd tormented me at my country high school, and was determined to end each sentence in a question.

'It's Yasmeen.' She looked down her perfect little nose at me with undisguised revulsion.

I can't say I entirely blamed her. I'd spent the afternoon trawling secondhand shops and buying up big at a place in Richmond that stocked theatrical makeup supplies, then gone home and really done a number on myself. I'd tucked a Garfield the Cat sweatshirt into high waisted, multi-pocketed, acid wash jeans and slipped on a pair of green army boots a couple of sizes too big. A mullety brown wig hid my real hair, and a bright yellow trucker's cap disguised the fact that it was a wig. Special contact lenses made my eyes bulgy, like I had a thyroid problem, and the fake teeth weren't too far removed from the kind you get at a joke shop. Still, when I'd checked myself out in the mirror I realised something wasn't quite right. It was the eyebrows. I was really proud of my brows. They were dark, not too thick or too thin, had a nice, forties style arch and just wouldn't do. There was no way in hell I was shaving them so I brushed over the hairs with flesh coloured concealer. That did it. I was unrecognisable. Actually, I was worse than unrecognisable. I was a no-eyebrowed freak.

'Follow me,' said Yasmin.

So far so good. She led me past the bar and through the archway to the kitchen, and as I passed Dillon he gave me the same revolted once-over she had, shuddered and looked away. I almost said, 'Don't hate me because I'm beautiful,' but stopped just in time.

Yasmin snaked between the tables and I shuffled along behind her until she halted in front of the kitchen like she'd come to the end of the Armani runway, jutted her hip and pouted. The kitchen ignored her.

'Gordon,' she addressed the fat, red faced chef, 'someone here for the dishwashing position.'

'Kerry,' I piped up. 'Me mates call me Kezza?'

Gordon was chopping onion so fast his arm blurred. He didn't look up. 'What do you want me to do about it? I'm flat out finishing tonight's prep and bloody Trip isn't in yet. You know he'll freak if I put someone on trial without his say-so.' He dipped his head and raised his shoulder to wipe sweat from his temple.

'Right, well.' Yasmin bit her lip and knitted her pretty brows. I imagined she was figuring a way to make me wait out by the bins without violating some equal opportunity statute. 'I suppose you'd better take a seat then.' She led me back to the bar.

'Dillon, make, uh, Kezza, a coffee, would you.' She gestured for me to sit on one of the padded stools and he gave me a look like I might leave skid marks on the lily white leather. And to think he'd been so charming the night before.

I clambered up enthusiastically and sat swinging my legs, looking around. Yasmin collected her cutlery and cloth and took them into the restaurant so she wouldn't have to sit next to me. Above my head Dillon mouthed, 'Help,' and she stifled a giggle. I pretended not to notice.

He flipped his tea towel up over his shoulder, crossed his arms and screwed up his cute Leo DiCaprio features. 'Let me guess,' he sneered, 'macchiato? Ristretto?'

I could have gone a short black but knew Kezza would loathe it.

'Cup of chino thanks, mate. Extra froth.'

Dillon made the cappuccino, watched me spoon in five sugars, shook his head and turned his back to start juicing limes. I decided to punish him for all his smirky looks.

'So, mate, good place to work?'

He sighed. 'It *is* one of Melbourne's best restaurants.'

'Been here long?' I sipped the coffee and nearly gagged. Froth got up my nose.

'Six months.'

'Good job, aye, bein' a waiter?'

He stopped juicing and his shoulders tightened. 'I'm not a waiter, I'm bar manager. And when I'm not here I'm an actor, and an auteur.'

'Like a writer?'

'Like a film maker.'

'Struth, an actor, aye? You been on TV?'

He turned, leaned back on the bench and tossed his head, flipping hair out of his eyes. 'Pepsi ad, Hungry Jack's, Kahlua, small parts in *Secret Life of Us* and *Blue Heelers*.'

'*Blue Heelers*? That was a top show. Which one were you?'

'Drunken B&S ball guy number three.'

'You're famous. Whatcha doin' workin' here?'

Dillon sighed, displaying infinite patience and vast annoyance both at the same time. Maybe he *was* talented. 'Do you know how hard it is for good actors to forge a career in this country? The state of the industry's abysmal. Reality TV has absolutely decimated Australian drama. If you want to get anywhere you have to move to the US, which I plan to do, but in the meantime I'm making a short film, being proactive, showcasing my talents. I'm going to enter it in Tropfest.'

'Whatfest?'

He stared at me then turned back to his limes.

'You should go on *Big Brother*.'

His arm flinched. I hadn't had so much fun in weeks.

The back door banged and I heard the jangle of motorcycle boots coming down the hallway. I swivelled on my stool. The apprentices stopped laughing and hunched over their benches, heads down. Gordon's face flushed redder. The door to the corridor swung open, slammed against the wall and everyone's shoulders jumped.

Trip stood there in his usual ripped black jeans, speed metal shirt and a motorcycle jacket, holding a waxed vegetable box in front of him. With his long hair and earring he looked like a cross between Michael Hutchence and a pirate on the cover of a romance novel. A pissed off pirate.

'Trip, sweetie.' Yasmin dropped the ice queen routine, ran up to him on tiptoes and tilted her head for a kiss. I hadn't realised they were on together. Interesting.

Trip ignored her, strode into the kitchen and slammed the box down on the bench next to Gordon. Small round leaves scattered everywhere. 'This fucking tatsoi is shit,' he growled, English accent coming through.

'Mate,' Gordon shrugged, palms up, 'I have tried every supplier from Gippsland to Queensland. It's the rain. It's the best we can get. Over there—' he nodded in my direction, eager to change the subject—'applying for the dishpig job.'

Trip looked at me. It was make or break time and my legs felt weak and pins and needles buzzed my palms.

'You. Come here.'

Slinking from the stool I shlepped over, playing with a belt loop on my jeans.

He grabbed a handful of leaves and waved them under the brim of my cap. 'What do you reckon, pig?'

A couple had tiny brown speckles you'd never notice if you weren't looking for them.

'S'alright. I'd eat it.'

'"I'd eat it",' Trip mimicked. 'You'd probably eat plastic cheese too, huh?' He turned his back on me and rooted through the contents of the box, hurling most of the leaves over his shoulder onto the floor.

I'd failed the test and was obviously being dismissed. Great. I'd screwed up my undercover job before it'd even begun. Maybe Alex was right.

I'd started creeping out of the kitchen when I realised Trip was speaking. To me.

'Eight bucks an hour. Cash. It's a good deal. You can still collect the dole, or sickness benefits, or whatever the hell you're on. Two days a week and on call when our regular dishie doesn't show. I hope you scrub pots better than you select produce.'

When I didn't reply he whirled around, eyes black and glinting. 'Comprende? You fucking hear me?'

I nodded.

'You're on trial, starting now. Bad Boy'll show you the ropes.'

Bad Boy?

Trip pointed to the corner of the kitchen hidden from diners. There, by the bins and sinks, half concealed behind a commercial dishwasher, lurked the dishie I'd talked to the night before. He gave me a shy smile. He didn't have many teeth.

One of the apprentices, a sallow youth with Tweetie Bird boxers sticking out of his low slung chef's pants, sniggered. 'Look, Bad Boy's got a girlfriend.'

There was a slight pause, then Trip's mood flipped one eighty degrees. Laughter exploded from his mouth and he doubled over, helpless. The other chefs glanced at each other then joined in. It was great how I could amuse so many people, all in the one day.

Trip straightened up, clapped the apprentice on the shoulder and the kid beamed. The tension was broken.

'Fuck me,' said Trip, wiping his eyes and pointing at me. 'I didn't even realise that was a chick!'

chapter**thirteen**

Bad Boy handed me a stained white apron and an old tea towel and I was immediately elbow deep in a filthy brown soup. I'd forgotten how awful dishpiggin' was. It sucked alright. It sucked the big one and the huge dishwasher didn't make it any easier 'cause you still had to scrub everything before you put it in the machine. I'd seen relatively mild mannered chefs pick up a plate and go ballistic upon finding a hardened speck of cheese, so Trip's reaction would probably make the Arab–Israeli conflict look like a hippy love-in.

I spent the first few hours scouring burnt food off pots and pans, then plates, cutlery and glasses entered the mix as the restaurant started to fill. After the first ten minutes I was soaked with perspiration. The sweat never managed to dry, becoming a breeding ground for bacteria, and after an hour the smell that wafted up from my Garfield sweater was a heady mix of football locker room and teenage sports shoe. It mingled with Bad Boy's personal odour, a kind of bum/old man funk with hints of jail tobacco and top notes of rancid tin cans.

Since I had to smell him he could at least have been helpful, but Bad Boy had taken it upon himself to be a kind of executive dishpig, in much the same way that Trip was executive chef. He leaned against the wall, telling me I was stacking the dishwasher wrong, and kindly pointing out spots of food I'd missed, before disappearing out the back for a smoke. Whenever a plate landed on the sink with a significant amount of food still on it, Bad Boy would scrape the remains into a plastic takeaway container he kept hidden on a shelf.

In between washing dishes I snuck looks at Trip. It was hard not to. Just as some movie actors light up the screen, he certainly drew the eye. I'd always thought the whole idea of 'auras' was so much new age bullshit but you could practically feel the energy waves pulsing off him, and if I'd had to describe the colour I would have said scarlet.

He stalked the kitchen like a jungle cat, pulling from a vodka and Red Bull, praising the staff when they did well, berating them loudly and obscenely when they messed up. He particularly had it in for Gordon, his second in command. At one stage Trip stuck his finger in one of Gordon's sauces, tasted it and threw the whole lot in the sink. The apprentices flinched but kept their heads down.

'What the fuck do you think this is, an RSL bistro?'

Ouch. Gordon didn't react but his face reddened and his pale blue eyes glazed over like reflective glass.

As the night wore on the washing-up turned to lipstick smudged coffee cups and dishes smeared with cherries and cream. I remembered the sharp, lush sweetness when Trip had forced the spoon into my mouth and almost licked one of the plates before the thought of hepatitis and cold sores stopped me.

The apprentices cleaned their work spaces, Trip ripped off his black chef's jacket so we could all admire his bi's and tri's, Yasmin and Patsy set the tables and everyone but the dishpigs repaired to the bar for knock off bevvies. Ah, hospitality. It was where I'd learned to drink like a particularly thirsty Oliver Reed.

Bad Boy grabbed his takeaway container, the entire menu slopping around in its plastic confines, pointed to a laminated sheet next to the dishwasher that explained what was required at the end of the night and muttered something about having to leave for a while to 'see a man about a dog'. The instructions were pretty much what you'd find anywhere. Sweep, mop, empty bins, drain dishwasher, except at the bottom of the page bright red letters warned NO ONE EXCEPT CHEFS TO ENTER COOL ROOM AT ANY TIME NO EXCEPTIONS THIS MEANS YOU!!!

I knew a lot of restaurants had problems with theft. At a joint I worked in Sydney a kitchen hand once got busted with a whole lobster down his pants. And personally, I wouldn't have trusted a dodgy mother like Bad Boy as far as I could kick him … but it still seemed a bit extreme.

I swept, getting right under the stove and benches, and was just filling a rolling bucket with hot water and detergent when I saw Trip leave the bar and stride out towards the back. Maybe he was just going to hang a leak but I knew it was delivery time. My heart picked up the pace and started thudding.

Yasmin left the bar and crossed the restaurant floor just as Trip came back carrying four boxes. He plonked his cargo on one of the padded chairs, grabbed her around the waist, pulled her to him and ground his pelvis into hers. Subtle. He whispered in her ear.

'Trip!' She giggled and shook her head.

He took her hand and placed it on his groin.

'You have to unpack the deliveries,' she protested.

'After. I'll be quick.'

Not the sort of line that ever worked with me, I have to say, but Yasmin seemed amenable.

'I'll just pop to the ladies then I'll see you in the office.'

'Nah, stay in the dunny, I'll meet you there.' He licked her neck.

He picked up the boxes, headed to the cool room in the far corner of the kitchen, opened the door and placed them inside on the floor. I kept my head down and pushed sudsy water around with the mop and he hardly seemed to notice I was there. Soon as he left for his rendezvous I scuttled to the cool room and pulled on the door. There was a bit of suction, like with a giant fridge, so I yanked harder and the seals popped and it opened. All in the wrist. I slipped inside.

The room was dimly lit and the size of a small garden shed. Jars and plastic containers, cheeses and meats and every conceivable gourmet foodstuff jammed the metal shelves lining the walls. The sharp scent of basil and coriander mixed with parmesan, raw meat, salty oysters and olive brine. Cold air chilled my damp clothes and after a few seconds the hairs on my arms stood on end.

The cardboard boxes sat stacked on the floor in front of me, sealed with clear packing tape. Damn. How to peek inside without leaving any evidence? With the door seals and the hum of the cooling fan I realised I wouldn't be able to hear anyone approach. Trip had told Yasmin he'd be quick. What did that mean? Ten minutes? Or one premature grunt and a mess on her skirt?

I looked at the boxes, heartbeat thudding in my ears. I had an idea. I flipped the first one over. Tape wrapped right around, but at the bottom join, where the box folded together, the cardboard depressed when I pushed. I stuck my fingers in the gap and wiggled them around. Crumpled newspaper and cans, by the feel of things. What if there were drugs in the cans? I pushed the cardboard in further and it ripped slightly. Hopefully Trip wouldn't notice. I pulled out a small can labelled broad beans and shoved it in one of my ugly pockets. The bulge was way too obvious so I stuck it down my knickers where it was hidden by the sloppy top. I used the same manoeuvre with the next box and from the squishy coldness I could tell it was duck breasts, as the label suggested. In the third I felt cheese wheels, and perhaps some pate. My heart beat harder. How long had I been in there for?

The fourth and final box was wide and shallow, lighter than the rest. My knuckles scraped the cardboard as I forced my fingers in. Immediately I touched something plastic wrapped and hard, ridged slightly at the edge and a little larger than a pack of playing cards. I scissored my fingers around the object and pulled.

Shit.

It was money. A thick sheaf of vacuum wrapped fifty dollar notes and the box was full of them. I snapped a couple of shots with a small digital camera I'd stashed in my jeans pocket, hoping the door seals would hide the flash and praying that Trip's quickie had turned into a longie. Then I shoved the cash back into the box and had just restacked the final carton when the door whumped open and bright light spilled in.

Trip roared, 'The fuck?'

chapterfourteen

Trip grabbed me by the back of my Garfield sweater, lifted me up and out of the cool room and hurled me into the kitchen. I hit the mop and bucket, tipping them over, skated briefly on the suds then slipped and hit the ground, landing on my arse with a splash. Trip towered over me, face twisted, spitting and screaming. Panic pinballed through my body, bounced around my head and shot down to my toes, forcing them to spasm and curl. I suddenly understood why small dogs shake and wee when confronted with more ferocious beasts.

The rest of the staff raced from the bar, some with drinks in hand, to see what the commotion was. Trip hauled me to my feet by the scruff of my neck and I hoped my wig wouldn't fall off or the can slide down my leg and roll across the floor. So much for being invisible. I kept my head down, hidden by the brim of my cap, and prayed my fabulous eye-brows weren't showing through.

'How many fucking times do I have to tell you thieving little cunts to keep your filthy hands off the fucking deliveries!' Trip ranted, practically foaming at the mouth. 'What were you doing in there? Aye?'

'I—I …'

Yasmin stood with her lips pursed and arms folded, no suspicious white stains on her uniform nor a hair out of place. You'd never have guessed she'd just been rogered in the dunny. 'Yes, Kerry. Please explain.'

'I was, I wanted to, to mop the—'I didn't have to bung on the stammer.

Just then Bad Boy came in from the back and stopped when he saw everyone gathered around. His eyes were blood-shot and he looked tragically stoned. Trip turned to him.

'And you! Where the fuck have you been? I just caught the new dishie in the cool room. Didn't you tell her?'

'It's not my fault, man,' Bad Boy whined. 'I showed her the rules.'

Trip marched over to the laminated sheet, tore it off the wall and shoved it in my face. 'Well, what were you *really* doing in there?' He slapped me around the head with it a couple of times and the rough edge scratched my lip.

Now I was getting angry. I felt like launching myself at him, biting his arm and not letting go. Everyone was watching. Dillon smirked. Gordon actually laughed out loud. Patsy looked horrified, puffed up his already inflated torso and came to my rescue. He snatched the plastic coated rules from Trip, went to put his arm around me, noticed the stench and just patted my shoulder instead.

'Isn't it obvious? You ought to be ashamed of yourselves.'

'What? You're the fucking poofta, mate.'

Patsy gave Trip a stern look and said, sotto voce, 'Kerry can't read.'

It was brilliant. I couldn't work out if he just wanted to get me out of trouble, or if he really believed it.

'Is that true, Kerry?' Yasmin asked in her best 'special school' teacher's voice.

I nodded, hung my head and wiped my nose with the back of my sleeve.

Trip turned to Bad Boy. 'You know about this?'

Bad Boy bounced up and down, shaking his head. 'No, man. She never said nuthin' to me.'

Trip's anger spiralled around him, nowhere to go, and the others stayed silent lest he direct it at them. With visible effort he clamped down the rage, breathed hard out of his nostrils and said, 'Well, fuck it. Yasmin, give her fifty bucks and send her home.'

I decided to push it. 'But I—'

Trip held up his palm and looked away. 'Yeah yeah, it's a fucking tragedy you're illiterate and all that but it's really not gonna work out. Okay? Try Sizzler or something.' From him that was probably an apology.

I trundled out to the bins and when I'd made sure no one had followed me, waved at the window where Alex was conducting surveillance, gave him the finger with both hands and performed a twisting, prancing, piggy little dance of joy.

I drove home on a total high, fanging for a drink and a cigarette. There were no ciggies but I slammed down a well-earned glass of cask then poured another. A good result in undercover gave you the same kind of high as a great strip show. The buzz beat any drug, and I knew 'cause I'd tried them.

My phone was ringing but I ignored it. Probably Alex. I'd talk to him eventually, but first I had to get out of the wig and the rest of the crap and wash off every last disgusting trace of Kezza. I'd just stepped out of the shower, wrapped myself in a towel and was combing out my wet hair when the intercom squawked. I picked up the plastic handset and answered.

'It's Alex. Let me up.' He didn't sound happy.

After the previous night's abstinence and no dinner, the wine had gone straight to my head and I was feeling a little cheeky. 'Jeez, I dunno. It's pretty late.'

'Open the goddamn door.' His voice had lowered an octave and I imagined the tone was the same one he used to apprehend fraudulent scoundrels. I couldn't wait to let him know how clever I'd been so I buzzed him in, quickly swiped on some lip gloss and refilled my wine glass. When I opened the door I noticed his eyes wander over the towel, a quick up and down, then focus back on my face. Men.

'To what do I owe this unexpected pleasure?' I smirked.

'I told you to stay away.'

'I'm sure I don't know what you're talking about.'

He pushed past to the bathroom and came out holding the wig and the Garfield shirt at arm's length. The wig looked like a dead fox terrier.

I smiled. Revenge was so fucking sweet. 'Alright, you got me, babe. Drink?'

'Are you deliberately trying to get me in trouble?' He threw the top and wig back onto the bathroom floor.

'Oh relax, Detective, I was brilliant, the pig of glory, a master of disguise. No one knew it was me and I bet you your colleagues didn't recognise me either. And the shit I found out … but you wouldn't want to see the photos, would you? Maybe you should leave now before things go … how did you put it? Pear shaped?'

'Photos?' he asked.

'Uh-huh.'

I sashayed over to the coffee table, booted up my laptop and plugged my digital camera into the USB port, preparing to download. As I bent over the towel almost fell off, as they do, and Alex fixed his eyes on a *Beyond the Valley of the Dolls* poster over my right shoulder.

'Put some clothes on.'

'In a sec.' I sat on the couch in front of the computer and patted the cushion next to me.

He paused, then finally walked over and sat down. The faintest trace of faded aftershave reached my nostrils and his trouser leg brushed my thigh. I busied myself transferring photos and lifting my glass for a couple of comprehensive swigs. I clicked open the first image.

'Check it out,' I said. 'A whole box of plastic wrapped cash. Money laundering, has to be. And I got that.' I pointed to the can. 'Probably just broad beans but it could be full of drugs. Sam Doyle's doing, you reckon?'

'I really can't say.'

'Maybe I'll have to find out on my own then.'

'This isn't funny.' He sighed. 'What do I have to say to get you to leave this angle alone?'

I glanced at him, trying to think of a witty riposte, but the wine had kind of floored me and my mind went liquid and blank. I got caught up checking out his straight black brows and the coffee-coloured eyes fringed by surprisingly long lashes. Then my gaze dropped to his large hands, veins on the back of them, and a smattering of dark hair. I remembered a time not so long ago when he'd kissed me at the entrance to my flat and those same hands had snaked under my top and I'd felt his erection pressing against me. God.

He looked up from the computer. 'What?'

I leaned over, put one hand on his upper thigh and moved my lips to his. He abruptly turned his head and my mouth brushed his ear. I sat back. He removed my hand from his leg and stood up.

'Simone, I'm getting married. You're dating my best friend.'

Before I could say anything he turned and walked out the door. As his shoes echoed down the concrete stairwell mortification hit me like a punch in the stomach and my skin prickled with a full body blush. I must have seemed like a desperate freak. I jumped up from the couch, threw off the towel and grabbed my jammies from in front of the heater, dancing and hopping as I pulled them on. I raced down the stairs, out the security door and down the concrete path, twigs and gumnuts digging into the bare soles of my feet. I had to catch him and explain that I hadn't really meant it, it was the wine on an empty stomach.

But I was too late. I heard the low growl of his Commodore starting up and by the time I popped out of the gate his tail lights were disappearing down Broadway, halfway to Glenhuntly Road. I groaned and slapped my forehead. Idiot. Idiot! I turned and walked up the footpath to my block, pausing to stick my hand in the letterbox as I'd forgotten to check it on my way in.

What I felt in there made me scream out loud.

chapter**fifteen**

It was a possum. Not a whole one.

I grabbed a plastic wrapped community newspaper and swept the severed head out of my letterbox. It fell onto the concrete path and rolled a small way and I crouched down to examine it in the yellow glow of the night lights lining the walkway. What I'd plunged my hand into was the meat and bone of the neck, chopped clean through with an axe or a cleaver. I nudged it face up with the rolled newspaper. The lips were drawn back, exposing sharp teeth in speckled grey gums. Worse than that were the bloody sockets. Someone had plucked out its eyes.

Upstairs I scrubbed the hand covered with dark specks of possum viscera and shuddered, a convulsion like you get slugging cheap scotch. I badly needed a cigarette and reached into the cupboard above the fridge where Chloe stashed one of her many travel bongs. I pulled down her mull bowl and found a Winfield Blue nestled in a cone's worth of debris, half the tobacco rubbed out and the cigarette paper twisted up. I lit it. Dry, stale, but better than nothing.

After finding the head I'd checked the street to see if anyone was watching but all I saw were leafless oaks, parked cars and dark, silent houses. I'd briefly debated calling Alex but decided he'd see it as some bid for attention, since my lunge on the couch hadn't worked. I could call the cops but honestly, what would they do? Pull out the blue and white tape, get the medical examiner and cart the evidence off to the morgue? Yeah, right. They already thought I was flaky. Eventually I'd picked up the head using two rolled-up community newspapers like giant chopsticks, carried it around to the back of the flats and dumped it in someone else's wheelie bin.

I stubbed the cigarette out and tried to rationalise the possum head as the cops would have done. A prank. Kids. The work of some random freak. And I might have believed it if it wasn't for the eyes. That was a message meant for me.

After the late night I woke at ten and when I wandered out onto the balcony in my jammies, steaming cup of coffee in hand, I discovered there was a heatwave going on. Seriously. Blue sky visible between the rooftops and bare branches, no freezing wind and had to be at least sixteen degrees. In the warmth and light the possum head didn't seem so scary. In fact it struck me as totally lame. In my time I'd been shot at, stabbed, nearly raped. What sort of idiot thought a possum head would scare me off? I wasn't going to waste any more time thinking about it and spent the next half hour jotting notes to myself, trying to figure out what was going on with Andi's case.

I knew she was alive, at least she had been on Tuesday evening, and that certain things had been removed from her place. By her or somebody else, I wasn't sure. I knew she was working on some potentially explosive story likely to ruin reputations at the very least, and I knew that Trip and Yasmin had lied. I'd been attacked, which could have been coincidence, but the possum head was no accident.

I couldn't entirely discount the theory that Andi was a bit unbalanced and had disappeared and made the phone call as a bid for attention, but after all I'd found out, and knowing how ambitious she was, I highly doubted it. They tell you in inquiry agent school that you should keep an open mind and not make assumptions but I couldn't help myself. I knew it in my guts. A story of a celebrity chef involved in some sort of money laundering scam was news alright, and could be just the sort of big break Andi needed to get out of the hospitality industry for good. As Curtis was fond of reminding me, journalism was a hard gig to crack. It had to be about Trip, and Jouissance, and the 'colourful' Sam Doyle.

The next thing I assumed was that someone had found out what she was up to. Trip? Yasmin? Doyle? Had they done something to her? Possibly, but what sort of halfwit would kidnap someone and let them keep their mobile phone? More likely was the possibility that she had been discovered, disappeared before they could get to her and come to grief along the way. Whatever it was, I had to find out what happened that night at Jouissance, and I had to find out more about Sam Doyle. And Alex couldn't stop me.

I could go spend a couple of days trawling through company records and court reports to get more information, or I could do it the easy way and call my old boss, Tony Torcasio. He was an ex cop who knew a lot of Sydney policemen and PIs and he subscribed to databases that I didn't have access to.

Sure, he'd fired me, but in a friendly way, and he'd always said that if I needed any help …

'Hey, Simone.' He seemed pleased to hear from me. 'How's it going? Been getting much work?'

'Matter of fact I'm on a case right now.'

He groaned when I told him it was missing persons, but I filled him in, right up to my triumph the night before. Tony could keep his mouth shut.

'Undercover as Kezza the dishpig. Jesus. Only you.' I was sure he was shaking his head.

'I was just wondering if you or any of your Sydney mates know anything about Sam Doyle?'

'You just said Alex told you to back off from that angle. Stick to the background, family and shit.'

'Yeah but I can't. It's all connected. I reckon Doyle will lead me to Andi.'

'If Alex is already investigating the man then I'm sure he'll keep you posted.'

'Oh, he'll let me know what's going on when it's all over, but that might be too late! She might be dead!'

'Very dramatic.'

'Please, Tony, any scrap you can throw me …'

'No.'

It took me a couple of seconds to register what he'd said. 'What?'

'You heard. I'm not going to say anything except stay away from him. I know you. I give you information and you're straight up there, in his face, following him around, probably fucking up the fraud investigation, and then all hell breaks loose. I don't want to be responsible. So, no.'

He was as bad as those fucking cops at Elsternwick. 'Well thank you very much for your help, Tony, you obviously think very highly of me.'

'Anytime.' Tony hung up.

There was only one thing to do. I called Curtis.

'What's going on with you and Chloe?' he said, instead of hello.

'You're not at hers are you?'

'No, Fitzroy.' Curtis was subletting Sean's place, the downstairs of an old terrace converted into a flat.

'She tell you we had a fight?'

'Uh-huh.'

'Well, I'm waiting for her to apologise.'

Curtis laughed and laughed, then he laughed some more. 'Like that's gonna happen. Just bite the bullet and tell her you're sorry. I did. It's the only way.'

'After what she did the other night? You may be willing to let her walk all over you but I'm not.'

'Hey. She's not walking all over me. I thought it was the best thing to do under the circumstances. Have you noticed she's been acting weird lately?'

'Weird is her middle name.'

'I'm serious. Violent mood swings. Much worse than usual.'

'She smoking more dope?' I asked.

'Not possible—there are only so many hours in the day.'

'Stronger shit, like hydro?'

'It looks and smells like the same old weed to me.' Then he twigged: 'So what are you after? You never call unless you want something.'

'I need to find out about Sam Doyle. Colourful Sydney businessman, runs the Doyle Food Group and co-owns Jouissance with Trip Sibley.'

'What's the big juicy story, babe? C'mon, you don't get nothing for nothing.'

It drove me crazy the way he tried to tough-talk, like a character in a forties film. If Curtis thought he could get away with wearing a hat that had a press card stuck in the band, he'd do it.

'Missing waitress.'

'The one whose poster Chloe's sticking up all over Melbourne?' I heard him yawning on the other end of the line.

'Maybe you could do an article about her,' I suggested. 'Get some publicity.'

'What's the angle? She also a model working part time as a callgirl? Left behind a blood splattered uniform? Having an affair with a high powered government minister?'

I couldn't tell him about the suspected money laundering so I said, 'There isn't one.'

'Then forget it.'

'What about Sam Doyle?'

'Name rings a bell, but that's all.'

'Could you find out?'

'Shit, Simone. If you didn't know, I'm writing a very long, very complex true crime book here and I have a deadline. Do your own research. What are you, lazy?'

'No. It's just that time's running out. If I don't find her soon she might die.'

'And that affects me how?'

I hung up on him, stewed for a while then had an idea. Doyle owned a Kings Cross restaurant and the library book that had disappeared, *All That Glitters*, was about Kings Cross too. I rang all the local bookshops to see if they had a copy and struck paydirt at Chronicles on Fitzroy Street. I drove down there, bought it, and took it to the café next door. I ordered a coffee and flipped straight to the index. Doyle, Sam. There were three entries. Damn I was good.

chaptersixteen

By the time I got home my stomach was baying for food so I set to fixing an omelette, roughly chopping spring onions, red capsicum, zucchini and mushrooms then flipping them around in the nonstick pan, mulling over what I'd read.

Sam Doyle had been a fixture at the Cross in the seventies and early eighties, starting as a bouncer at illegal gambling joints. He was employed by some of the big-time crooks of the day and worked his way up, managing a restaurant, then a strip club, before getting into property development and the hospitality industry and becoming respectable. A black and white photo from seventy-nine showed a lean man out the front of the Love Tunnel wearing an open necked bodyshirt, a gold chain, and a shit eating grin. He had intense eyes, big sideburns, a nose that looked like it had been broken once or twice, and a ton of dark hair boofed up Elvis style. A pretty handsome dude, compared to the rest of the shifty eyed crims in the photos. Of course it had been taken a quarter of a century ago and he was probably a bloated old fat cat these days.

I beat four free range eggs with a little salt and cracked pepper, poured the mixture into the pan and turned the gas right down so the bottom would set. If he was delivering boxes full of cash then maybe he wasn't quite the respectable businessman he appeared to be. I wondered if the author, Ferguson, had any more information on Doyle and slung him an email using the address Canning had given me. I wasn't sure if it'd get to him but it didn't hurt to try.

As I waited for the omelette to cook I wondered how to find out about Andi leaving Jouissance with Trip and Yasmin. I briefly considered contacting Gordon, as he didn't seem to like Trip much, when it hit me. Patsy, the gay waiter. He was the friendliest of the lot, had stood up for poor old Kezza and I knew that Chloe had his phone number. She'd got it while trying to recruit him as a stripper. That meant I had to call Chloe, but it was about time one of us broke the ridiculous standoff anyway. We'd been giving each other the silent treatment for two days now. Time to kiss and make up.

I took the cordless phone into the kitchen so I could keep an eye on my brunch, leaned back on the laminated counter and dialled her number. I was stupidly nervous, like when you call a guy for the first time, and felt relief when her answering machine kicked in. It wasn't quite midday. She was probably still in bed.

'It's Simone,' I spoke into the machine. 'Can you give me a call? I need Patsy's number. The buff waiter from the other night?' I thought about tacking on a quick apology and stopped myself just in time, thank god. I wasn't the one who had behaved like a complete psycho and saying sorry would only condone her behaviour. I finished with a clipped 'thanks' and hung up.

Using an egg flip I scraped the omelette back a little from the pan. The bottom was golden brown and the top was still runny. Every time I tried to turn an omelette it morphed into scrambled eggs so I fired up the grill. I switched on the gas, crouched down, waved a match around and turned my head away, eyes half closed. Flames whoomped out, sucked back in and my heart galloped. I've never gotten used to those things. I scavenged in the fridge for cheddar but all I came up with were singles so I unwrapped four and lay them on top, admiring the way they glistened in the morning light, shining like no cheese had a right to.

My phone rang. It was Chloe.

'Oh three one one two three six three three four.' Her voice was flat.

'Wait, lemme get a pen.' I raced to the lounge room, found a pen and picked up my notepad from the dining table. 'Shoot.'

She repeated the number.

'Thanks. Look, even though I'm searching for Andi I'm still available for shows. What you got this weekend?'

'Nothing.'

'What?'

'I've already got dancers booked.'

'What about a last minute, or if someone calls in sick?'

'Got three girls on standby already. Oh, hang on, there is one spot I haven't filled. You want it?'

'Shit yeah, what is—'

'Jelly wrestling.' Her smug tone infuriated me and I slammed down the phone. What the fuck was her problem? Why was everyone being so mean?

I rang Patsy and he answered straight away.

'Despite the debacle of the other night I'm still investigating Andi's disappearance,' I told him. 'I know Yasmin and Trip don't want to speak to me about her but I was wondering if you would.'

'Of course, darl. I'm so worried. Anything to help.'

My shoulders loosened and my chest expanded. Finally. 'Thank you so much. And you won't mention this to anyone else at Jouissance?'

'I won't if you won't. Yasmin'd fire my arse. I'm just on my way to the gym, but why don't we meet after, say, one?'

'Sure, where?'

'Lobby at the St Kilda Sea Baths Fitness Centre.'

'See you then.'

I became aware of a chemical, burning smell. Shit. The omelette. I pulled the pan out to find the top a blackened mess of blisters, swollen and bursting, like buboes from the plague. I chucked the pan on the side of the sink, let it cool and then dug out a bit with my fingernails. It was probably highly carcinogenic, but the bubonic cheese tasted great.

The Sea Baths were sandwiched between the beach and Jacka Boulevard, opposite the Espy. The big white Esplanade hotel had been built at the turn of the century and if a pub was a person she'd be one of those old women you meet in bars, with the dyed hair and drawn-on face, wearing leopard skin and drinking a martini, once glamorous and beautiful, now ravaged and only just keeping it together. Exactly how I imagined myself at seventy. The Espy held a lot of memories for me. It was where I'd seen Doug Mansfield and the Dust Devils for the first time, picked up one of the best roots of my life, and been kicked out for an impromptu striptease at the tail end of a drinking binge. Not all on the same night. At least I'd have stories to tell when it was my turn for animal print and gin.

The baths, also alabaster and grand, had been built around the same time as the pub. They'd fallen into disrepair and had been done up a few years back. Now the complex had a state of the art gym and a new pool, and restaurants and cafés sprouted round the perimeter like mushrooms at the base of a tree.

I entered the foyer and sat opposite the reception desk, looking around. It was ritzy alright, everything shiny and new, and you had to flash your membership to the door bitch before he'd let you up the stairs to the gym. I picked up a brochure on the table beside the designer couch but it didn't mention the cost. I guess you couldn't afford it if you had to ask. I imagined annual fees would cover ten years' membership at my no frills fitness centre with enough left over for a couple of weeks at a Thai spa. The patrons coming and going were better looking here too. No sagging singlets, no back hair and definitely no guys in those awful nylon running shorts that ballooned so you could see their jocks, if they were wearing any. Just lots of tight, tanned, polished flesh.

Speaking of which, I spotted Patsy trotting down the stairs in immaculate tracksuit bottoms and a tight white t-shirt that hugged his segmented chest and straining biceps. His thick black hair was brushed back off his tanned face, his eyebrows were better than mine and I could just picture him in a tiny red g-string and fireman's helmet, six pack undulating as he bucked a hose suggestively between his legs. He waved, exchanged a few words with the buff dude at the front desk and approached, offering his hand. It was warm and slightly damp from the shower and he smelled sweet and musky. I recognised the upmarket deodorant my brother modelled for. The ads always cracked me up: Jasper draped limply over an expensive couch, his shirt open, pouting and making bedroom eyes.

Patsy suggested one of the cafés downstairs and we ended up under an orange canvas umbrella at a wooden table outside, him ordering a protein shake and me a beetroot, carrot and apple juice. Although it was a week day people were everywhere, eating, drinking, strolling the promenade. First day of warmth and sunshine and Melbourne goes ga-ga.

'Nice gym. Expensive?' I asked.

'Shit yeah. But I train people there in the mornings so I use it for free. My tips are good but not that good!'

'Must keep you busy. Training and Jouissance.' Small talk. Since I had no cop-like powers of persuasion it helped loosen witnesses up.

'Sure does. I have to tell you though, I've had it with waiting tables. All the yes sir, no sir shit. I've been a waiter for, god, too long and I want to get out of it for good. I'm saving to set up a lunch place in the CBD. Kind of like fast food but really healthy—low carb, low fat, low GI, you know? I go into town and you can't get anything that's not on bread. I mean, all I want is a fucking chicken breast!'

I held up my hand. 'You're preaching to the converted. Sounds great. I'd be there in a shot.'

The waiter, a blonde in tight faded denim and an orange t-shirt to match the brolly, set down our drinks. We both watched his arse as he left.

'Anyway,' he said, 'I'm seriously thinking of taking Chloe up on her offer. I need some extra money.'

'You'd make it. Male strippers get paid more than females.'

'Why's that?'

'Maybe 'cause there're fewer around. Supply and demand? Maybe it's danger money. Male audiences are mostly well behaved, they know the rules. Women tend to go a bit mental. Kind of attack the guy, scratching with their nails, grabbing for his bits.'

'Really?' Patsy's eyes went wide and he paled some under his tan. He changed the subject for me. 'So what did you want to know?'

'Anything you can tell me about Andi. Everything you can tell me about the staff party, since that's the last place she was seen. Any gossip you can dredge up. I want it all.'

'Gossip, huh?' Patsy grinned wickedly. The cute waiter was on his way past with a couple of Turkish pizzas for the next table. Patsy flagged him down. 'Oh, fuck it.' He touched my arm. 'I'm having a Corona. Want one?'

'I'll pass.'

'I try to be good ninety percent of the time so I can be naughty the rest,' he said. 'Everything in moderation.'

'I don't know what the word means. I'm an all or nothing kind of girl.'

'Star sign?'

'Scorpio.'

He nodded sagely. 'So's my ex. I know all about you people.'

His beer arrived and he pushed a slice of lemon in the top. Sunlight glinted off the bottle. I really wanted one, but then I'd want another, which would lead to champagne, whiskey, seeing a band, snogging some random guitar player, and then it'd be morning and my brains would feel like they were spilling out of my head as I extricated myself from underneath aforementioned random guitar player's hairy arm, sick with guilt after cheating on Sean. I knew myself too well.

Patsy swigged his beer and wiped his lips with the back of his hand. 'Andi's great. I really miss her. Your friend Chloe reminds me of her, actually.'

My eyes must have been bugging out of my head 'cause he quickly said, 'Not physically or anything. But for all her feminine wiles, Chloe's a tomboy, am I right?'

I nodded. Underneath the big tits and blonde hair I sometimes thought she was just a flannelette wearing, bong smokin',
fifteen year old boy.

'Andi was too. When I first got a look at her I thought she
was so sweet and innocent with those big brown eyes peeping
out from under that short fringe, but boy, was I wrong. She
could come up with some filthy stuff, and believe me, I'm not
easily shocked. I'll never forget the night she explained the
definition of pugwash. Gross!'

I decided not to ask. 'Tell me about the staff party.'

'Oh god.' Patsy slumped back in his wooden chair, cradling
his beer. 'I was slaughtered. I drank so much, you know how
you do when it's all free? It was the shots that did me in. And
someone slipped me an eccy but it didn't straighten me out
much. I was too far gone.'

'Remember anything?'

'Bits and pieces. It was our first night back at work after
the young chef awards had been announced. We closed the
restaurant and hung at the bar, just staff, couple of regular
customers, a few friends of Trip. Lots of booze. Some drugs.
Jesus, there was even karaoke.'

'How twisted.'

'I know! It was a wild night. Andi had a bit of coke. All
of us did. She was talking to Dillon most of the night. You
know when you're on drugs and you get stuck in this really
intense rave with one person, like, for hours?'

'Yep. Were they good friends?'

'Yeah. She was the only one who could stand to listen to
him go on about his fucking short film.' Patsy rolled his eyes.
'Anyway, I danced on some tables—gosh, I would make a
good stripper, wouldn't I? Then Dillon's wife Holly came in,
looked none too happy to see him boozing on and dragged
him out of there.'

'He doesn't seem the type to be married, let alone under the thumb. What's all that about?'

Patsy rubbed his fingers together. 'Her folks have a lot of money. Sam Doyle, the other owner? He's her stepdad.'

I sat up in my chair. I didn't know what the information meant exactly, but was sure it was significant. Patsy was on a roll so he didn't notice my change in posture.

'I think Dillon's hanging around to get his hands on it. Gonna need a motza if he wants to try his luck in the States. He's gorgeous enough to make it though, isn't he?'

Far as I was concerned, Dillon's good looks had disintegrated when I saw how he treated the 'little people'. But I just nodded.

Patsy sighed. 'I was so in love with him when I first met him.'

'But he likes girls.'

'Likes himself more, actually.' Patsy tipped the last of the beer down his throat.

'Meow.' I curled up my fingers and scratched the air.

He laughed and signalled for another Corona. 'You did say you wanted gossip, honey. Where was I? Okay, after Dillon left Andi turned her attentions on Trip. Which was very weird as she was one of the few females I saw that never fell for his charms. We used to take the piss out of Trip, not to his face of course. Andi always said she couldn't stand people who took themselves too seriously. I agreed.'

'So she wouldn't have liked Yasmin then?'

'Oh no. And Yasmin didn't like her. But Yasmin is the type who doesn't like other women, if you know what I mean.'

'What's the story with her and Trip?'

Patsy's second beer arrived and he popped the lemon in the neck and sucked the juice off his fingers. 'He knocked her over about a month after she started. It normally doesn't take him that long but she knew what she was doing—he likes the chase. Then he promoted her to restaurant manager. Talk about sleeping your way to the top! Every night after service they have a knock off shag. Quite the libido, our Trip, and apparently he's mad keen on the old bondage stuff. They used to do it in the office but now they've taken to using the ladies toilets. Thrill of discovery puts a little spice back in, perhaps. Of course they don't live together and Trip still roots anything that moves. She puts up with it, just, 'cause she likes getting in the social pages. Thinks it'll help her modelling career. What career? One tampon ad and some promotional work for the spring racing carnival does not a modelling career make.'

'You are such a bitch,' I said, impressed.

'You love it.' He took another big swig.

'So Andi started flirting with Trip?'

'I could hardly believe it myself. Of course she was on a bit of the Bolivian and we all know how frisky that gets a person. And despite being an arsehole Trip is a very attractive guy, especially next to that awful piggy Gordon and all those pimply apprentices, right?'

'How'd Yasmin take Andi's flirting?'

'If looks could kill! Of course that didn't work so she just sort of adhered herself to Trip like a limpet on a rock. It was so funny. Andi on one side, Yasmin on the other. Then Andi upped the ante by sitting on his lap! If Yasmin had been a cartoon there would have been steam bursting out her ears and a squiggly little black cloud above her head. I think I passed out not long after that.'

'Can you keep a secret?'

'Probably doesn't sound like it, does it?'

'Trip and Yasmin said Andi left by the front door and went off towards home that night. But I have a witness who saw her leave the back way, with the two of them. I'm just wondering where they were going and why they'd lie about it?'

Patsy sat back and looked into the middle distance, pondering, a blank look on his face. Then his eyes widened, his mouth fell open and he slapped his forehead. You could practically see the light bulb flick on above his head.

'Oh my god, I just had a flashback. From the party. Seriously. I can't believe I forgot. It's too fabulous.'

'What?'

'It must have been just before I passed out. Andi was on Trip's lap, right, then she slid off to stagger to the loos. Yasmin followed and in my fucked-up brain I thought they were going off to have more coke and I wanted some, even though I was so far gone it wouldn't have done me any good. I opened the first door, but not the second, so I could hear them and they couldn't see me. You would not believe what they were talking about.'

'What?' I was leaning forward now.

'It was hilarious. Yasmin was negotiating with Andi. Said something like she knew Trip was after a threesome, and she'd do it, but it was strictly a one-off and she wasn't eating any pussy. Then she said that Andi had better not go falling in love with him, and that if she ever told anyone she'd fire her arse.' Patsy shook his head. 'I can't believe I forgot that. I must have been really fried. I remember giggling silently at the door, thinking, this is just too funny, and I was gonna run back in and tell everyone, but the next thing I knew it was four am and someone was hustling me into a cab.'

'Andi went back to Trip's for a three-way?'

'I think so.'

Like hell she did. She was looking for something and needed an excuse to get into his place. It sounded like just the sort of crazy plan I would have come up with, when I was drinking to excess.

'Is there anything … suspect, going on at Jouissance?'

Patsy laughed. 'It's a restaurant. Of course there's dodgy shit happening. The scams I've seen in my time …'

'Anything in particular?'

'In my long and illustrious career I've made it my business to turn a blind eye. If I have to be a waiter I wanna work in a three hat place with big tips, not Luigi's spaghetti emporium with a whole bunch of backpackers.'

I tried to think of where to go next. I knew Yasmin would never talk to me so I said, 'If I wanted to run into Trip, you know, by accident, where would be a good place to do it?'

'He goes to this heavy metal bar in the city a lot. Chrome Lounge. But you'll have to wait a few days. He's just gone to Sydney to film an episode of *Chef of Steel* at Food Expo tomorrow night.'

'Think Dillon would talk to me?'

'If his wife didn't catch him. I can give you his number and address, but don't tell him you got it from me.'

'Thanks. What about the sous chef, Gordon?'

'What do you want to talk to that prick for? Andi never had anything to do with him.'

I shrugged. I thought Gordon might know about Trip's scam, but I didn't tell Patsy that. 'Just trying to be thorough.'

'You can catch him at Greasy Joe's on Acland Street most days before work. Goes a burger and fries with the lot. The calories … I shudder to think.'

On the way out I paid for the drinks. Well, Joy did.

chapter**seventeen**

As I drove along Beaconsfield Parade I thought about what Patsy had told me. Did his information square with my theory that Andi got busted snooping into Trip's dodgy deals? From the conversation in the toilet it sure didn't sound like Yasmin was onto her, but maybe Yasmin wasn't savvy to the cash deliveries anyway. Hang on, she was the manager. How could she not be? And what about Trip? Was he pushing for a three-some so he could satisfy his depraved lust before disposing of Andi? If so, how come she still had her phone? None of it made sense and my brain felt like it was about to leak out of my ears.

Dillon lived in Bridport Street, Albert Park. I could have just called him like I'd done with Patsy, but I had the feeling he wouldn't be quite so eager to speak to me and I'd be better off fronting up. Harder for people to weasel out of talking when you're face to face.

Dillon's house was a double fronted Victorian bungalow of immaculate cream brick trimmed in tasteful slate blue from its front door to its neat picket fence. Rose bushes sprouted from a tidy strip of grass in the narrow front yard and lined up in an orderly fashion, off-white blooms matching the brickwork. I was no property expert but I'd seen the inserts fall out of the local paper and figured, what with the location, you'd be talking at least six hundred thou, enough to make a bayside real estate agent squirt saliva. Not bad for an out of work actor and a stay at home mum. I rang the doorbell.

'Dillon? Simone Kirsch.' I stuck out my hand and he took it, but his perfect forehead crinkled and two hollows appeared under his already razor sharp cheekbones. I quickly weighed up how to play it. After posing as Kezza I knew more about him than he did about me and I reckoned a bit of non-threatening ditz would go down well, especially as he must already have thought I was an incompetent idiot after the display Chloe and I put on. I immediately giggled and tilted my head to the side.

'Remember me? I was at Jouissance the other night looking for Andi? God, what a disaster that turned out to be! Anyway, her mum hired me so I'm just going around and, like, talking to everyone who knew her. Do you think you could spare a couple of minutes?' I looked over his shoulder. No sign of the wife.

The frown relaxed a smidge. 'I'm pretty busy …'

I decided to throw a bit of ego massage into the mix. 'Sure, no worries, I can come back later if you like, but can I ask you something before I go? This might sound crazy, but are you an actor?'

He stood up a little straighter, flipped his hair out of his eyes and the corners of his mouth twitched. 'Yeah.'

I did a little bounce. 'Oh man, I knew it! Me and Chloe were arguing about it the other night. I said you were on *Secret Life of Us* and she insisted it was *Blue Heelers*.'

'Both.'

'Ohmigod that's so cool. What you working on now?'

'A short film I wrote, directed and starred in. I'm actually editing it at the moment.' He pointed his thumb over his shoulder, toward the back of the house.

'I love short films! You gonna enter it in Tropfest?'

'Uh-huh.'

'Fantastic.' I gave him a starry eyed gaze, then made a show of snapping out of it and looking at my notebook. 'Is there a time I could come back tomorrow?'

Dillon glanced from his watch to me. 'I could talk to you now, I guess, if you don't mind sitting in while I edit. I'm on a tight schedule, want to lay down the soundtrack before work.'

'No, that'd be awesome. I'd love to have a peek!'

Dillon opened the door wide and put his finger to his lips, inclining his head toward one of the bedrooms, and I tiptoed inside and looked through the half open door into a nursery containing a large white cot, padded change table and a mobile of bunny rabbits hanging from the ceiling. Stuffed bears, lambs and tufty-tailed tigers stared beady eyed from their lair atop a chest of drawers, and the room smelled of wet wipes, powder and the not entirely unpleasant aroma of regurgitated milk. I spotted the kid mercifully asleep under a lemon yellow crocheted blanket, mouth open, one fat fist flung above its head.

'Gorgeous,' I cooed, recognising it was cute, much like Dillon was handsome, and that they both left me cold. 'Girl or boy? How old?'

'Boy. Eddie. He's, um, eight months?'

He took off down a wide hall and I followed, treading lightly on floorboards of polished Baltic pine. When we entered the lounge I revised my initial estimate and added a couple of hundred thousand to the value of the house. The massive living room opened into a designer kitchen, and was furnished with expensive looking items—wide grey couches, a matching rug, and some brown cylindrical vase things with twigs and spiky grass poking out. There was no mess or clutter and the only personal touches were a large painting hovering on the wall above the plasma TV and framed photographs on a mantelpiece.

'Eddie's a cool name.' I wandered over to take a closer look at the photos while Dillon walked into the kitchen.

'It's short for Edwin. After Holly's real dad.'

'He must be flattered.'

'He's dead.'

'Oh, sorry.'

Dillon shrugged. 'I never met him, died when Holly was a kid. I'm having a coffee, want one?'

'Sure.'

He retrieved a tin from an enormous silver fridge and fiddled around with a stainless steel coffee maker that gleamed under the downlights.

Most of the photos were cheesy eight by ten studio shots of Dillon and the rest were of the baby and the three of them as a family. No one else. I checked Holly out closely as I hadn't got much of a look at her when she'd stormed into Jouissance. She was shorter than Dillon, a little wide in the hips and had dark brown hair that curled forward under her ears in a mumsy bob. A thin patina of freckles floated just under the surface of the skin on her pale, round face. She was attractive, sure, but nowhere near Dillon's league, and I wondered if that's why she was so possessive. Perhaps she had to contend with hot chicks throwing themselves at him all the time, actresses and drunk girls like Chloe hanging around his bar. Although I had to admit Dillon hadn't struck me as that much of a slut. I picked up a curiously asexual vibe from him and his flirting with Chloe had seemed more of an act, as though he were channelling Tom Cruise in *Cocktail*, than a serious attempt at cracking on.

I turned my attention to the painting and a laugh bubbled out of my lungs so fast I had to fake a coughing fit.

He looked over from the kitchen where he was depressing a lever on the espresso machine. 'What do you think?'

Thick oil paint swirled across the canvas in lumpen swabs of dark green, burgundy and brown, and it had taken me a couple of seconds to register the subject matter: Dillon, done up as a modern day Hamlet. He wore ripped jeans and a t-shirt and stared at a skull, his eyes intense black whorls. Two theatre masks hung in the air, one smiling, the other frowning, and crawling out of some mist behind him were other Hamlets—Laurence Olivier, Kenneth Branagh and, shit, was that Mel Gibson?

I wanted to throw myself onto the polished floor and roll around convulsing, but instead I took a deep breath and placed a hand on my chin. 'It's very … powerful …'

'Mmm, I think so too. He really captured my eyes. Holly had it commissioned for my birthday.' He held up a coffee cup and I strolled over to the kitchen to take it, refusing milk and sugar and glancing out the French doors to the timber decking, wall-mounted water feature and padded outdoor setting that made up the back yard.

'Great house. Do you own or rent?'

'Own.' Dillon leaned back on the bench and sipped his coffee. 'It actually belonged to Holly's dad. He came out from England in the seventies when some rich rellie died, and inherited a couple of places in Melbourne, a country property and a hotel in Sydney. You might have heard of it—the Villa?'

'I think I have. Has a really good restaurant?'

'Yeah. It's where Holly and I met. I was working as a waiter, you know, in between acting jobs, and Holly was managing the restaurant. She managed Jouissance, too, before she had Eddie. Of course by rights, the whole bloody hotel should be hers. I mean it belonged to her dad, but her stepmother Rochelle inherited the lot and acted like we should be grateful to get this place and a bit of land in a one-horse town called Kangaroo something-or-other.'

I saw his jaw work and I must have raised my eyebrows because he shook his head suddenly. 'Sorry. My stepmother-in-law's a bitch on wheels. I get angry every time I think of her.'

'Holly has two step-parents?' I asked. 'What happened to her real mother?'

'Died when Holly was a baby. Then Edwin brought Holly to Australia from England, married Rochelle and after he passed away Rochelle got hitched to Sam Doyle, they adopted her, and basically cheated her out of her inheritance. *Days of Our Lives* shit. I won't bore you with it. Come to the edit suite and you can ask me about Andi.'

He led me to a small study dominated by a large, matt black desk with an outsized, flat screen computer monitor on top and a Macintosh computer humming underneath. The room was dark and smelled like electricity and warmed-up plastic and the whole set-up looked new, right down to the instruction manuals stacked next to the keyboard. Dillon sat in a high backed leather chair, I took a swivelling stool, and when he swished the mouse the screen crackled to life and I saw a black and white close-up of his pretty, pouty face. A window at the bottom of the screen operated as a control panel and contained film frames and squiggly soundwaves.

'Final Cut Pro,' he said proudly, and I guessed he was talking about his software. 'It's an amazing program. I had to fire my editor because he just didn't get my vision for the film, but with this baby, I don't need him. Most people don't realise editing is a huge part of the creative process.'

'Fascinating.' I stifled a yawn. 'So, do you have any idea what might have happened to Andi?'

'Beats me. She seemed fine at the party and we all thought she was off to Sydney to visit her sick grandma. I left before it finished, so that was the last time I saw her. I told all this to the cops …'

'She wasn't behaving unusually the week before? It's just that she withdrew five grand, all her savings, before she disappeared.' I waited while he clicked and dragged a sound file and punched a button on the keyboard. He sat back in his chair and pointed at the screen. First a title flashed up, 'In My Father's House', and then Dillon himself appeared wearing a flannelette shirt and sitting on a broken armchair in a shabby flat. He stared into space, pale and haunted, and the lighting made his cheekbones jut like rocky outcrops on a cliff face. The music he'd added was a single mournful, wavering note that sounded like someone had pressed a minor key on an electric piano and held it there. A voiceover kicked in, Dillon's voice. 'In my father's house, there were no clocks.'

He seemed pleased with the way the sound and image had hooked up, paused the film and looked at me, a vague expression on his face. 'Sorry?'

'Unusual behaviour?'

'No. Same old Andi.'

'You get on well?'

'Yeah, really well, but she got on with everyone. Nice girl.' He fiddled with the computer as he talked.

'You have much to do with her outside of work?'

'Nah. I don't really socialise that much, now we've got Eddie. Stay back for a couple of staffies most nights, and once Holly and I got a babysitter and went out to dinner at the Flower Drum with Patsy, Andi, Trip and Yas. But that's the only time we hung out apart from work.'

'Did Andi get on with everyone?'

'Yeah, even Yasmin, who can be a handful.'

'Did she ever talk about the stuff she was working on in her journalism course?'

'Journalism?'

'Uh-huh.'

'She wasn't doing journalism. She was doing arts. I re-member she was talking about it at the Flower Drum. Majoring in … shit … linguistics? Anthropology? Something like that. To be honest I sort of tuned out.'

Andi must have been lying to them. I was about to say something when he nodded at the monitor.

'Check this out, let me know what you think.'

The film started playing again and for the next five minutes I simulated fascination while attempting to work out what the hell it was about. Dillon, looking tortured and gorgeous, ran through empty city laneways to a soundtrack of heavy breathing, a heartbeat and an overwrought cello. He ended up in a cemetery chasing a girl in a white dress who kept dis-appearing behind gravestones. The film cut to the exterior of the flat, which I recognised as one of the Housing Commission towers in Collingwood, and the girl leaned out of a window and dropped a flower, which spiralled to the ground in slow motion. He ran up some stairs back to the flat, but the girl was gone and he sank to his knees on the carpet, hands over his face. Again, the voiceover. 'In my father's house there were no clocks,' before the image faded out to the sound of the heartbeat. The film finished and he looked at me.

'Wow,' I said.

He nodded as though he understood that the powerful emotional impact of his crap film had left me lost for words. 'It's my best yet.'

'You must have been to film school?' I laid it on thick.

'I applied but those fuckers wouldn't know talent if they fell over it. For a start they're biased against actors and they just didn't get what I was about. No wonder the Australian film industry is shit—all these idiots making stupid comedies about ocker dickheads. I come more from the European school of film making. It's a bit of a homage, really. I'm trying to combine the alienation of Bergman with the … the … stylised realism of Godard. I wanted to make something gritty, something that pulled no punches.'

Stylised realism? I smiled, impressed. 'So is it, like, based on your own life? Did you used to live in a Housing Commission place?'

'Not my actual life, no. I grew up in Canberra. My parents work for the government. But the inner life, the existential … stuff … you know what I'm saying?'

'Absolutely.'

He looked at his watch. 'Shit, I've got to start getting ready for work and Holly will be home soon. Sorry I couldn't be more help. I told you it'd be a waste of time.'

'It wasn't a complete waste,' I said, thinking it wouldn't hurt to butter him up in case I needed more info. 'At least I got to see your movie.'

He nodded seriously, but seemed lit with an inner glow as he led me back up the hallway.

'Did Andi ever ask you about Sam Doyle, your father-in-law?' I enquired as he opened the front door.

'Why would she do that?' His eyes narrowed slightly.

'He has a colourful past.'

'We talked about lots of stuff. You do when you work together, anything to while away the time.'

He looked over my shoulder and I saw his jaw start working again. I turned around. A burgundy four wheel drive pulled up in front of the house, a black and yellow diamond shaped baby-on-board sticker on the back window. I'd never understood those things. Were they supposed to make drunk drivers think twice before slamming into you?

Holly exited the car and pushed through the gate, dressed in a pleated skirt and fluorescent bib and carrying a long, zip-up sports bag with a hockey stick poking out of it. As she approached I stuck out my hand, hoping to ward off a possible jealous scene. I'd had enough of that with Alex's fiancée Suzy, months before. She shook it.

'Simone Kirsch, inquiry agent.'

'She's looking for Andi,' Dillon said quickly.

'And I'd just like to apologise for my friend the other night,' I told her. 'She was drunk and totally out of line.' Simone Kirsch, liar and total suck. I should have run for parliament. 'Did you know Andi very well? Dillon mentioned you all went out to dinner one time.'

'No.' Holly sidled up to Dillon and put her hand in the back pocket of his jeans, but she didn't go mad and I could tell he was relieved. So was I. 'She started at Jouissance after I left and I'd run into her from time to time but I didn't really know her. She seemed lovely though. Everyone's worried about her. Have you found out anything?'

'Afraid not. Okay, well, I won't take up any more of your time. Thanks for speaking with me.'

'No problem,' Dillon said.

Holly smiled. She seemed pleasant enough on the surface, but something in her eyes told me she was glad I was leaving. I tried to imagine the eternal vigilance her relationship must have required and felt exhausted just thinking about it. I'd always subscribed to the 'if you love something, set it free' school of thought. Not that it had done me any good.

I checked the clock on my mobile phone. I was just in time to catch Gordon at Greasy Joe's.

chapter**eighteen**

Greasy Joe's Bar and Grill was one in a row of cafés on the intersection of Acland Street, Carlisle and the Esplanade, where fat palm trees sprouted from the concrete and the St Kilda and Caulfield tram lines converged. The outside dining area was circled by a waist high brick wall and ubiquitous café umbrellas, red this time, shaded square wooden tables where people hunched over giant burgers, sipped lattes or got stuck into beers.

I spotted Gordon sitting by himself wearing a grey zip-up jacket over his chef's outfit, a light breeze ruffling his receding orange hair and bringing with it the smell of spun sugar and Dagwood Dogs from nearby Luna Park. His plate was empty except for a smear of tomato sauce and his head was down as he concentrated on a hand held video game. I heard the rickety rollercoaster tick along the tracks, took a deep breath, strode over and sat opposite him. Whenever faced with an unpleasant task I found it best to jump straight in.

He looked up, surprised, but covered it quickly by fixing his thin lips into a supercilious smirk and continuing to play his game. With his doughy face and small eyes he looked like an evil gingerbread man.

'Hi, Gordon.'

He grunted. He probably didn't like me after I'd dug my nails into his palm and threatened a sexual harassment suit two nights ago at Jouissance, but hey, you couldn't please all the people all the time. The only trump card I had was his obvious hatred of Trip, so I played it.

'Tell me about the scam your boss has going on.'

He lifted one corner of his small pink mouth and kept his eyes on the Game Boy. 'I'm sure I don't know what you mean. Trip Sibley's a model citizen. He's Nelson Mandela, Mother Theresa and Gandhi rolled into one, an inspiration to us all.'

'Yeah, right. I know Trip's up to something and I think Andi Fowler did too. She was a journalism student writing an exposé of his dodgy deals. I reckon he took exception to it and that's why she disappeared. If you know anything you should tell me.'

'Why?' His chubby thumbs blurred as he hit the controls.

'Most people like to fulfil their civic duty, get a nice warm fuzzy feeling. I guess you might want to do it because the sooner Trip gets in trouble the sooner you can take over his job.'

Gordon furiously punched buttons, then swore as the game trilled a sad little refrain. He looked up at me, eyes like currants. 'I know a lot of things about Jouissance.'

I waited but he remained impassive. Over his shoulder the lights on the Club X store sign blinked red and yellow.

'Like what?' I prompted.

He shrugged. 'What's in it for me?'

'Besides saving someone's life and getting your dream job? Jeez, I dunno. Nothing. What do you want? Sexual favours?'

'Grow some tits and I might be interested,' he sneered. 'I'm talking money. There a reward?'

'Her mum's poor. She's a school teacher.'

He shrugged again and picked up his game.

'Let me get this straight. You know something but you're not going to tell me unless I cough up the cash. How much we talking?'

'Won't open my mouth for less than fifty thou.' He started up with the thumbs and the game beeped and buzzed. I wanted to shove the thing down his throat. I stood up instead.

'What's your problem? Not breastfed enough? Got picked on at school? What?'

'There's nothing wrong with me. It's bitches like you have problems. You all think you can wiggle your arses and guys'll bend over backwards. I don't fall for that shit.'

And I wasn't falling for his. He didn't know anything but was obviously making out he did just to have something over me. I had a flash of what his life must be like, copping abuse from Trip then home to an empty flat, playing computer games and, judging by his prolific use of the word 'bitches', probably listening to gangsta rap.

'You're pathetic.' I turned and walked away, crossing the road and heading up Acland. My car was parked somewhere behind the Esplanade hotel. I hadn't got very far when I heard a shout.

'Hey, Stripperella!'

I turned. Gordon was standing on the opposite footpath, hands in the pockets of his grey jacket, bobbing up and down on the balls of his feet. 'I can tell you one thing,' he yelled.

Somewhere down Carlisle a car revved and tyres squealed. Bloody hoons.

'What's that?'

'You're completely on the wrong track. You're so on the wrong track it's fucking funny to watch. You don't know what the hell you're doing, do you?' He shook his head, and started walking toward Fitzroy Street.

I got so angry a pale red wash seemed to cloud the air. I'd had enough and I wanted to wrap my hands around his throat and throttle him, or at least kick the bastard in the shins. I stepped off the kerb and was about to run across the road when I spotted the dark blue sedan and jumped back. It had turned off Carlisle and was speeding up Acland, doing at least eighty in the fifty zone. The car passed me, swerved, mounted the kerb opposite and ran straight into the back of Gordon's legs.

chapternineteen

Time seemed to slow down and shuttle forward, frame by frame. The car scooped Gordon up and somersaulted him backwards onto the bonnet, smashing his head into the windscreen. He didn't stop there, the momentum propelling him upward, flipping the chubby little chef like an aerial skier, until he'd cleared the car and torpedoed head first into the middle of the street. The crack when his skull hit the asphalt was the most nauseating sound I'd ever heard. The car tore off. At the cafés down the road women screamed and a couple of guys came running, calling for help on their mobile phones.

I got to Gordon's body before them, desperately trying to remember my first aid training. Check breathing. Roll to the side. Find a pulse. Was that the right order? Shit. He was lying flat on his face in a pool of sticky blood and I turned him over.

His features were pulped, flesh scraped off and nose mashed, white shards of bone poking through. One eye was swollen closed and the other half open, staring over my shoulder, pupil big and black. Even worse was the fissure cleaving his head from eyebrow to crown. Loops of pink tissue speckled with burst blood vessels bulged through the fleshy crack. My stomach heaved. I looked away from his head and put my fingers on his wrist. I thought I felt a pulse, weak but …

More shouting. I looked up. The guys who'd been hurrying over to help were now running in the opposite direction as the blue car raced back down Acland. I lurched to my feet and jogged towards the cafés, looking back to keep an eye on the vehicle. It went straight for Gordon's body and one of the tyres bounced over him, splitting the skull wider, forcing more blood and brain to gush onto the road. I stumbled into the gutter and fell, hitting my hip.

The car reversed back over his devastated head then turned and pointed towards me. I made out a guy in the front seat, square jawed, sunglasses, cap, but I wasn't sticking around to get a full description. I sprang up from the pavement and bolted for Greasy Joe's, probably moving faster than I ever had in my entire life, dimly aware of bystanders screaming at me to run. The engine revved as it picked up speed and became louder as the car caught up with me. Any second I expected to feel the bumper biting the back of my legs but I didn't look back, just ran towards the outdoor dining area and, as soon as I was close enough, dived over the wall, onto a table of four, eyes squeezed shut, forearm shielding my face.

Half a second later the car hit the bricks in an explosion of crunching metal and splintering plastic. At the same time I slid off the table, taking crockery, food, tumblers and beer bottles with me. I hit the ground covered in broken glass, kicked off a chair that had fallen on me, struggled to my feet and ran straight through the restaurant, pushing gawkers out of my path. No way did I want to find out what sedan guy had in mind for plan B. Dashing past a couple of startled chefs I punched out the screen door into a back lane, veered up a side street and wound my way around, finally closing in on the Espy and my car. I got in, fired her up, turned left onto the Esplanade and headed for my place, filthy, cut, bleeding, hands and elbows scraped raw.

I felt no pain, but my heart was racing at a thousand miles an hour and my breath came out in panicky little gasps. Shit. I couldn't go to my place, what if they knew where I lived? God, they probably knew my car. I had to go to the cops. But who'd believe a hysterical woman ranting about hit and runs, crazed chefs, three-ways and money laundering, all the while stinking of burgers and booze?

I needed to talk to Alex. He could vouch for me. He'd know who I should talk to and would come with me, hopefully. I pulled over on Ormond Esplanade, opposite the boats bobbing around the marina in the afternoon sun, and called his mobile. Thankfully he answered.

'Someone just tried to kill me,' I blurted. 'I want to go to the cops but I need to talk to you first. You at St Kilda Road?'

'No, I'm home, Mentone.'

'Gimme the address.'

'That's not such a—'

'They tried to run me over. They got Gordon from Jouissance. His brains are splattered all over Acland Street.'

'Shit, Gordon Lamb?'

'I don't know what the fuck his surname is. Was. Please. I need your help.'

He gave me the address.

Alex's apartment was in a new block fronted with slatted wood and grey-blue concrete, one street back from the beach.

I parked and approached a corrugated iron gate, pushed through and crunched up a neat gravel path lined with spiky plants in square ceramic pots. I climbed the metal stairs to the landing and knocked on the back door. When Alex opened it he was wearing suit pants, a white shirt with the sleeves rolled up and a worried expression.

'Holy shit. You're bleeding.'

'A bit. Most of it's tomato sauce.'

He moved back and opened the door wide. The first thing that hit me was the view. A wall of tinted glass overlooked a wooden deck complete with a barbecue and outdoor setting. Across the road a strip of green parkland gave way to the sand and then the bay where the sun was rapidly moving towards the horizon, reddening and swelling. I stepped into the room. The living area was open plan, granite and stainless steel kitchen by the front door, suede covered lounge suite and entertainment unit with a flat screen TV over by the picture window, glossy black baby grand to the right of the couch. All the furniture matched, and didn't look like it had come from IKEA—or, in my case, the side of the road on hard rubbish day. The apartment smelled of clean washing and tumble-dried towels.

'So what happened?' he asked.

I leaned forward on the polished granite benchtop and told him everything.

'Why didn't you go straight to the police?'

'I need you to come with me. You can explain about the fraud case so they know I'm telling the truth. Think Trip and Sam Doyle organised the hit on Gordon? He told me he knew a lot of stuff about Jouissance, but he wouldn't give me any details. Why would they knock him though?'

Alex didn't answer but there was something in his eyes.

'The way you said his surname when I told you he was dead …' I tilted my head. 'You know something. What is it?'

'I'm really not supposed to—'

'They tried to murder me too.'

Alex sighed and leaned back on the counter. 'Gordon's the one that dobbed Trip in to the Fraud Squad.'

'Shit.'

'Shit is right. You're not safe. After we see the police we need to find somewhere for you to stay.'

'Sure, whatever.' I checked my watch. 'You wanna get going?'

'I'll call Homicide first and while I'm doing that you should have a shower. I can see a slice of pickle in your hair.'

'Can I borrow a clean top?'

'Sure.'

Alex's bathroom was ensuite to his bedroom and I got a brief glimpse of a queen ensemble neatly made with a dark grey doona and matching pillow cases. Seeing Alex's bed caused certain images to pop into my head but I banished them immediately. I knew thoughts of sex were a natural reaction to death but it was a bit goddamn sick getting the horn when you'd just seen someone's head split open like a watermelon.

I soaped up with his nice shower gel, washed my hair with his shampoo, dried off with a big fluffy towel, decided it would be best for everyone if I didn't spritz on a bit of his aftershave and dressed in my jeans, boots and an old grey Melbourne University sweater he'd dug out of the closet. When I emerged into the lounge room he was off the phone, standing at the kitchen bench, unscrewing the cap on a bottle of Jameson's.

'Want one?' He tilted the bottle.

'What do you reckon?'

He poured a generous slug over a couple of ice cubes and held out the glass. I'd thought I was doing alright but when I took hold of it my hand shook so violently that the cubes rattled and whiskey slopped over the rim.

'You okay?' His dark brows knitted together and he put his palm on the back of my hand. Sympathy was bad, guaranteed to make me lose it.

'Sure.' I pulled my hand away, bottom lip trembling despite myself.

He studied my face. 'You could be in shock. Maybe I should take you to the hospital first.'

I forced a laugh, aiming for lilting and carefree but getting cackling and hysterical instead. 'I don't get shock, or post traumatic stress, or anything. Seriously. We'll finish these drinks, go to St Kilda Road and get this over with.'

I turned and walked to a modular shelf unit made of big metal squares and started checking out books and photos, mainly so he wouldn't see my watering eyes. Inclining my head I read the spines. Mailer, Hemingway, Proust. 'Jeez, literature with a capital L.'

'What did you think I'd read?'

'You always struck me as a Wilbur Smith sort of man.'

'Thanks.'

It was working. The joking around was drying my eyes. I sipped my drink and examined the framed photos: Alex and Sean in full dress uniform with their arms around each other, graduating from the police academy; Alex and Suzy at their engagement party, him wearing a suit and her a pink dress and a beatific smile. I supposed she was pretty in a bland, girl next door sort of way. Another frame held a photograph of Alex and his family standing beside a whitewashed building in front of a bright blue sea.

'Who's who?' I held it out and he strolled over from the kitchen and pointed. 'Mum, Dad, my brothers Con and Theo, and my sister Athena. We were on Mykonos, couple of years back.'

'Sister looks young.'

'Just turned eighteen and she's already at uni, studying law. After three boys and fifteen years her arrival was a bit of a surprise. Shocked the hell out of me—didn't think my parents still had sex.'

'What do your brothers do?'

'Theo works for the CSIRO in Canberra. I've never been able to figure out what he does exactly. Con went into the family business. My dad's an electrician. I had an apprenticeship with him after I left school but it wasn't for me.'

I moved to the couch to watch the sunset while I finished my whiskey. The sun was an enormous blood orange hovering over the ocean, silhouetting sailboats. Alex sat next to me. The room was awash with peach-coloured light.

'So how did a piano playing ex electrician end up in the police?' I asked.

'I knew it was a bad idea letting you in here to nose around.'

I heard a sound at the front door and jumped, expecting Suzy, but a short haired, glossy brown cat was nosing its way through the flap. It slunk across the room, yawned, stretched and leapt onto the couch, sauntering along the back. I stroked its sleek fur as it passed.

'Meet Graham,' Alex said. Graham dropped into his lap and looked at me haughtily while Alex scratched his chin.

'Graham looks a bit up himself.'

'He's Burmese,' Alex said, as though that explained it. 'So, are you thinking of continuing your search for the missing waitress? I'd strongly advise against—'

'Don't worry.' I held up my hand. 'I'm so off this case you have no idea. Joy's money's almost run out and after what happened today Homicide are gonna pull out all the stops to find Andi. I'll give them my case notes and that's it for me. I'm a private detective, not a freaking superhero. I don't have a death wish. That could've been me with my face scraped off and my brains spilling out onto … Jesus …' The hand holding the glass started trembling again and I tried to set it down on the moulded perspex coffee table but missed the edge and it fell to the floor, whiskey and ice soaking into the immaculate carpet.

I burst into tears. Not cute, dainty ones but gulping, shuddering sobs. Alex wrapped his arms around me and drew me to him but that made me cry harder. For a moment there I thought he might have been going to make a move, but he just held me close and squeezed my shoulder and patted my hair. Things usually got pretty steamy when we touched but not this time. I felt secure and comforted and kind of like a little kid, what with the oversized sweater coming down over my hands. I stopped blubbering after a minute or so, and realised that Graham had become sort of squished between the two of us, half on Alex's lap, half on mine, and didn't seem to mind. His eyes were closed and he was purring.

'Check it out,' I sniffed and rubbed the cat's head.

'I'll get you some tissues.'

He put his hands under Graham but before he could shift the cat onto my lap I said, 'About the other night, on the couch, I'm really sorry. I must have come across like some kind of freak. It was the wine on an empty stomach. I didn't mean anything by it and I swear, it won't happen again.'

He put his hand on my shoulder and said, 'Simone,' just as the front door opened and his fiancée walked into the room.

chaptertwenty

Alex pulled his hand back. A dumb move because it made him look guilty when we weren't even up to anything. For once. Suzy was wearing a skirt suit, her dark blonde hair tied in a ponytail and her arms full of packages. Her eyes flicked over us, noting the whiskey glasses, Alex's sweater and how close we were sitting, before she quickly plastered a bright smile onto her face.

'Simone, what a surprise.'

'Hey.'

Alex jumped up and hurried over, kissed her cheek and grabbed her bags, placing them on the benchtop. 'We're just on our way to St Kilda Road. Simone witnessed a hit and run, then the driver tried to take her out, too. It's tied up with that restaurant case I'm working on.'

Suzy widened her eyes. 'How awful, are you alright?'

'Fine. Just a few cuts and bruises.'

'I know we're supposed to meet the florist in half an hour …' Alex said.

'Don't worry about it. This is much more important. I'll be fine on my own.'

Alex disappeared into the bedroom to get changed and it was just me and Suzy. I had to admit she looked better since she'd quit drinking. Clear eyes. Glowing skin. Or maybe it was true what they said about blushing brides.

'How are the wedding plans going?' I tried to nudge Graham from my lap but he flexed his claws and they pricked into my thigh.

'Good. Lots to do but we're getting there.'

'Set a date?' I stood up. Graham hung on. His hind legs were skipping about on the couch and his front paws were hitched to my jeans. It must have looked like we were dancing.

'November seven. I'm glad you're here, actually.'

I found that hard to believe. I dislodged Graham by un-hooking each individual claw, then scratched him behind the ears to show there were no hard feelings.

Suzy rummaged in one of her boxes and pulled out a white card with embossed lettering. She wrote on it and handed it to me.

'You're inviting me to the wedding?'

'That's not all. I was wondering if you'd be a bridesmaid.'

Was she completely tripping? Alex walked out of the bed-room wearing a suit jacket and doing up his tie. By the way he stared at her I could tell he thought so.

'Jeez, Suzy. I'm flattered, I really am, but we hardly know each other. Isn't there a friend, a relative …?'

'One of my girlfriends just found out she's going to be overseas, so I thought that since Sean's a groomsman and you guys are going out, it would be nice if you were both in the bridal party.'

'Won't he still be in Vietnam?'

'Gets back the morning of the wedding,' Alex said. 'Misses the buck's though.'

They were both looking at me. 'Um. Well. Sure. Be delighted.'

I'd never been a bridesmaid before and wondered what sort of flouncy pastel monstrosity I'd be forced to squeeze into. At least there would be free food and booze and the opportunity to observe Victoria's finest pissed to the eyeballs and dancing to 'Nutbush City Limits'. I wondered what you got a couple of cops for a wedding present. Fluffy handcuffs? Matching flak jackets? A toaster?

'Great. There's a dress fitting in a couple of weeks so I'll get your number off Alex.'

Graham sprang onto the granite benchtop and Suzy smacked his nose and pushed him straight back down. 'Bad cat! You shouldn't let him up there, Alex. It's unhygienic.'

The cat flattened his ears, got down on his belly and shimmied under the couch.

Alex grabbed his keys and his phone. He was kissing Suzy goodbye when my mobile rang. I turned away to answer.

'Simone Kirsch.'

It was Joy. 'There's been a development,' she said. 'Andi's credit card's been used—in Kings Cross.'

The interview with the Homicide Squad took a couple of hours. I told them everything I could remember about the hit and run and all I'd uncovered regarding Andi's disappearance. The shit was gonna hit the fan at Jouissance, but it wasn't my problem anymore.

Alex had driven us to the police complex in his Commodore, and I'd had a long chat to Joy during the ride, telling her what had gone down. She'd agreed it was best I back away from the case and I assured her that after Gordon's murder the cops would go all out to find Andi, including following up the Sydney lead.

By eight o'clock I was waiting for Alex in the lobby, watching cars and trams flash by on St Kilda Road and plain clothes and uniformed officers come and go through the automatic doors. Before becoming a PI I'd applied to join the Victoria Police and had been rejected, probably because of my 'showbiz' past and the fact that I'd spent my formative years with a whole bunch of dope growing hippies.

I'd always thought the urge to enlist stemmed from a childhood incident in which a female copper saved my mum from a violent boyfriend, but there was probably a bit of rebellion involved as well—what better way to flout an alternative upbringing than join up with the filth? I also had a sneaking suspicion that prancing around doing policewoman shows had made me hot for the uniform, cuffs and gun. It was probably just as well I'd never gotten in. Kowtowing to authority wasn't exactly my strong point and everybody on the force except Alex and Sean seemed to hate me. The Homicide detective sergeant who interviewed me about Gordon actually said he'd find something to charge me with if I showed up again, which was so unfair. It had been at least three months since I'd visited the squad.

My mobile chirruped. I was expecting my mum, knowing Joy would have talked to her as soon as I'd hung up, but it was Curtis.

'What's the deal?' He didn't bother with the usual pleasantries like hello.

'What deal?'

'The missing waitress, the murdered chef and Trip Sibley. Word on the street is you were almost roadkill.'

'Don't know what you're talking about.'

'C'mon, I heard you've given a statement.'

Word sure travelled fast out there on the street.

'No comment. How's Chloe?'

'Fuck. Even more psycho than usual. You know those posters she stuck up? Put her own phone number on them and in between strip shows she's running around interviewing every basket case who calls. Hey, you're not giving someone else an exclusive, are you? John Silvester? That bloody Andrew Rule?'

They were the big guns of Melbourne crime writing and Curtis couldn't stand it. I suspected he had an inferiority complex after years of writing for a titty magazine.

I decided to wind him up. 'So what if I talked to them?'

Curtis sputtered down the other end of the phone. 'But, but what about our friendship? And all the times I helped you out with information? Look, I need this story. I've been working on the book full time and my byline hasn't been seen for months. This is my career we're talking about.'

'And that affects me how?'

I hung up and was just thinking I ought to write a book of my own—How to Lose Friends and Alienate People— when the phone rang again. This time it was my mum.

'Joy told me what happened. Were you actually going to call or was I supposed to find the story on page three of the *Sydney Morning Herald*, like last time?'

I explained that I'd had to turn my phone off during the interview and she settled down some. When she asked who tried to kill me I told her I didn't know, despite my suspicions.

'Are you alright?' she asked.

'I'm fine.'

'Have the police caught them?'

'Nope.'

'What are you going to do?'

'Well, I can't go home. The cops agreed that whoever tried to run me down probably knows where I live so I'm looking for somewhere else to—'

'Stay here.'

'What?'

'It's perfect. You'll be miles away, safe, and you can go home when the police make an arrest. I'll buy you a ticket on the internet. Can you make it to the airport before nine?'

I thought about it. Surely things would be resolved by the end of the weekend and in the meantime I could stay at Mum's, eat her gourmet food, drink her pricey wine, enjoy the warm Sydney weather and loaf around. Sure, I'd have to put up with her hassling me to finish my degree, and the occasional dig about stripping, but it'd be better than staying at some crap motel on my own. I had clothes and stuff stored there and it would end up being a cheap weekend, which I desperately needed since my erstwhile best friend had cut off my only source of income.

'Sure. I can make it by then.'

She rang off and called back a couple of minutes later. The flight left at nine fifteen. As I hung up Alex emerged from the lift.

'How'd you go?' I asked.

He loosened his tie. 'Reprimanded for failing to warn you off and my commanding officer told me to stay the hell away from you, said you were a jinx.'

'You believe that?' I was starting to think it wasn't too far off the mark.

'I'm not superstitious.'

'Give me a ride to the airport then? I have to fly to Sydney.'

He narrowed his eyes. 'I thought you were off the case. You're not—'

'My mum wants me to stay with her till the trouble blows over.'

He looked like he didn't quite believe me. 'Promise you won't start chasing Sam Doyle around?'

'Cross my heart.'

chapter**twenty-one**

I opened my eyes, blinked and looked around. I was in the spare room, lying on a single bed beneath a quilt embroidered with the astrological wheel. A large mahogany wardrobe loomed directly opposite, and my old student desk was to my left, petrified chewing gum stuck to the underside. Sun streamed in the window, passing through a translucent parrot sticker, and when a grevillea rasped against the pane the colours danced on the wooden wall. For a moment I imagined I was ten years old, in my loft bed in our house in the bush. Mum's Sydney Queenslander was a lot like our old place, only bigger and plonked down in inner city Annandale. It was painted forest green, surrounded by native plants, and Tibetan prayer flags hung from the rafters of the bullnose veranda.

The springs squeaked as I got out of bed wearing a pair of

men's paisley pyjamas I'd picked up from Newtown St Vinnies ten years before. I opened the door to the lounge and padded through a dark room crowded with bookcases and over-stuffed thirties furniture, passed through the kitchen, with its scarred oak table and garlands of chillies and garlic hanging from the curtain rail above the sink, and headed for the bathroom at the back of the house. The mirror was all steamed up and the clear shower curtain hanging over the old claw foot bath was new and patterned with multicoloured fish. I peed then wandered back to the kitchen and opened the freezer, rooting around for the coffee tin like a rat in a rubbish bin.

'Hey, honey, sleep well?'

Mum walked in clipping small silver hoops into her earlobes. She was shorter and thinner than me, with close cropped brown hair, high cheekbones and blue-green eyes. In her grey hipster pants, thin red belt and fitted white shirt she looked hot, especially considering she was pushing half a century. The only signs of age were the fine lines around her mouth and eyes and a sprinkling of silver hairs that glimmered in the light. They did say fifty was the new forty. So what did that make twenty-eight? The new eighteen?

I let her hug me for a few seconds before I pulled away. 'Can't find coffee,' I croaked, opening and closing cupboard doors.

'There isn't any.'

'You're kidding.'

She always had the good stuff, a special blend from Jamaica, hand harvested by Rastafarians, apparently.

'It's no joke. Steve and I have been detoxing. Organic food, no dairy, wheat, coffee, alcohol. We've been making our own tofu, too, fermenting soybeans in the laundry.' She picked up her rectangular, black framed glasses and slid them on her face. They were her trademark, along with the burgundy lipstick she was never without. 'We feel great.'

'Absolutely fantastic.' Steve appeared in the doorway. He was in his late fifties, wiry, and always wore his white hair back in a ponytail. He walked over and shook my hand. He'd been on with my mum for ten years, but we still hadn't got to the hugging stage. Give it time.

'How've you been?' he asked.

'Great,' I said, which was a complete lie considering I'd almost been killed and there was no coffee in the house.

Steve checked his watch. He was usually a massage sandals and drawstring pants sort of guy but was dressed in jeans, a black t-shirt, corduroy jacket and desert boots. I guessed he was off to TAFE where he taught environmentally sustainable building techniques. Mudbricks and shit.

'We should get going,' he said.

'Yep.' My mum gathered a couple of takeaway containers from the fridge that held either vomit or baby shit, it was an each-way bet.

'Chickpea curry,' she explained. 'There's more in the fridge if you want some for lunch. As for dinner I'm thinking of organising a barbecue.'

'Won't all the little bean sprouts fall through the grate?' Not my best effort, but my bloodstream was completely devoid of caffeine.

'We're allowed seafood. You should try to detox while you're here, cut out the booze and coffee, lose the stress. Your whole lifestyle is no good for you.'

I smiled through gritted teeth. I didn't just crave coffee now, I also wanted whiskey and a cigarette. Hell, I could have gone some crack.

She hugged me again, kissed my cheek and rested her hands on my shoulders. 'It was good of you to help Joy, even though you didn't find Andi.'

'I just hope the cops can.'

'Don't we all. I'm so glad you're here and you're safe. I worry about you, do you know that? When Joy told me someone had tried to run you down, my god. I had heart palpitations, I could hardly breathe. Do you have any idea what that's like?' She'd started shaking me a bit.

'Jeez, Mum, settle down. I'm fine.'

She let go my shoulders and took a deep breath. 'We'll be back at six. Oh yeah, before I forget.' She dug around in her voluminous shoulder bag, pulled out a glossy brochure and threw it onto the table next to the carved wooden fruit bowl. Sydney University. Bachelor of Arts. 'Thought you might want to take a look.'

A couple of hours later I'd been to the shops and back, got my coffee fix, eaten some eggs, an organic tomato and a piece of soy cheese that tasted like a pencil eraser. I'd showered and dressed in an old pair of ripped black jeans, a Breeders tee, a red flannelette shirt and a pair of chunky Rossi boots I hadn't worn for years. I slapped on a bit of my mum's dark lipstick and bam, it was the nineties and I was on my way to uni. Or, more accurately, the uni bar.

I wandered around the house scratching myself, perused a bunch of books whose titles were enough to put me to sleep and watched a half hour of daytime TV before switching it off and lying back on the couch. The lounge room smelled faintly of charred wood from the open fireplace, and the sandalwood/vanilla scent of burned out Nag Champa incense. Above my head there was a square hatch with dirty fingermarks on the edges that led to the attic, and a round, rice-paper shade hanging from a light bulb. Probably the same one we'd had in seventy-nine. Mum was a hoarder, never threw anything out. I stared at it, trying to breathe in the white light and expel the negative energy, as she would have wanted, but I couldn't stop thinking about the case.

After the hit and run I was convinced the attack by the wheelie bin was no random mugging, but what was the point of it? Who had been hiding there, all dressed in black, and why? I had a feeling it wasn't the dude in the blue sedan. Anyone who was capable of running over a guy, twice, wouldn't have settled for a love tap in a laneway. My mind was going around in circles. Trip Sibley. Sam Doyle. Yasmin. Andi. What had she been working on and where was she now? I knew there was nothing I could do and that the police would be going gangbusters, but it didn't stop me feeling guilty, like I'd abandoned her. After all, she'd called me for help.

I rubbed my eyes, struggled off the couch and wandered to the fridge where I rested one hand against the open door and leaned forward to stare at the shelves, just in case some brie and pate had miraculously appeared. They hadn't, so I mooched back into the lounge, moved some books and journals from the piano seat and sat at the upright bashing out 'Chopsticks', willing the harsh jangling to clear my mind. I noticed a bunch of old photo albums stacked on the bottom shelf of the nearest bookcase and after I finished the only tune I knew how to play, I flopped down to the floor and lay on my belly on the faded oriental rug, hoping the proverbial trip down memory lane might distract me.

The album was bound in orange vinyl with a spiral spine, and the first few pages contained pictures of my mum and dad before I was born. Her: a hippy goddess with a waterfall of waist length, centre parted hair and the widest flares I'd ever seen. Him: a kind of bohemian surfie with a shoulder length blonde mane, straggly goatee, and perpetually toting a guitar. He'd moved to America over a decade ago and apparently worked with computers, was remarried and had a couple more kids, but I hadn't spoken to him in years.

Leafing through, I came to my baby pictures. I'd like to say I was a gorgeous infant but the truth was I had a widow's peak and an intense stare which combined to produce an interesting 'spawn of Dracula' effect. My brother was a different story. The next sequence of photos had all been taken in New Zealand and after a couple of pages of my heavily pregnant mother backdropped by rolling green hills and snow-capped mountain peaks, Jasper appeared with his angelic smile, big round eyes and shock of dark hair. His father was part Maori, hence his exotic good looks, and damned if the kid hadn't known how to work the camera even then. On the next page there was a photo of me holding him, and none too happy about it by the way I was staring into the lens like Damien from *The Omen*. For half siblings we didn't look at all alike—in fact with their shared ancestry he could have passed for Andi's brother much more readily than my own.

Andi. The photos of us at Potts Point should have been in between my baby shots and the ones of New Zealand, but they weren't. When I thought about it I couldn't recall ever having seen any, but they'd definitely been taken. I remembered my mum urging me to stop crying and smile for the camera during the Tonka Truck Christmas. I checked the rest of the album, wondering if receiving a prime mover as a four year old was the reason I was so fucked up in the present day, then flicked through the others but couldn't find the pics and resolved to ask my mum about it.

The absence of photographs reminded me of Andi's missing pictures and then I was back to obsessing about her, wondering if the credit card being used meant she was in Sydney, or if someone was laying a false trail. An image of Trip Sibley flashed into my head. He'd been here since this morning. I got a wobbly feeling in my guts and my pulse started to race. Maybe I could just have a look around … No. I'd promised everyone I'd stay here, let the cops work it out and wait for everything to blow over. Hey, maybe it already had.

I scrambled off the floor and jogged up the hallway to the room Mum and Steve used as an office. It was crammed with shelves and filing cabinets and two huge desks covered in books and papers were wedged adjacent to each other. Mum's overlooked the veranda and a paperbark tree in the narrow front yard and I sat, booted up her iMac and checked the *Age* and *Herald Sun* websites. The vehicle used in the hit and run had been found burned out in semi rural Hallam. It had been stolen from a supermarket car park earlier that day. I also learned the police were questioning all the employees at Jouissance, and that the restaurant was closed for a few days. I wondered if they'd talked to Trip yet. I checked my email next, hoping for something from Sean, but it wasn't to be. There was, however, a message from Chris Ferguson, the journo who'd written *All That Glitters*. I opened it.

'Sorry for lateness of reply, been away. Re: your question. Yes, Andi Fowler did contact me. We met up in June. Give me a call.' Then his number.

I hesitated. I'd told the police about the missing library book, but didn't know if they'd follow up on it. And even if they did, it might be days before someone got around to interviewing Ferguson. If I spoke to him, then passed on any relevant information, it wasn't like I was actively investigating the case. It was just, like, being a concerned citizen, right? I picked up the phone.

chapter**twenty-two**

At ten minutes to midday I emerged from the Kings Cross underground station and walked up Victoria Street, past majestic plane trees and three storey terraces, some immaculately renovated, others with sagging roofs and crumbling brickwork. It was a gorgeous spring day, a deep sapphire sky peeking through branches dotted with budding green leaves. At eighteen degrees it would have been a heatwave in Melbourne but a fair few Sydneysiders considered it cold enough for a scarf and beanie. Puhlease.

I was too hot in my flannie so shrugged out of it and knotted the sleeves around my waist. Bad move. I instantly felt like the world's biggest bogan and untied the thing, bunched it up and carried it in my hand. Did I really used to dress like this? And more to the point, had I ever dressed like this and picked up guys? I seemed to remember that I had. The world was indeed a strange and amazing place.

I'd wanted to meet Chris Ferguson in person as visual cues are the only way to tell if someone's being straight with you, and also because I'd been desperate to get out of the house. After giving him a brief rundown over the phone he'd suggested the Goldfish Bowl, a bar attached to the Crest Hotel and so named because of the plate glass windows that made it a cinch to see in and out. Not the best place to hang if someone wanted you killed, but then no one knew I was in Sydney.

I was a couple of minutes early and the bartender, a chunky blonde guy with fat sideburns, was just upending barstools and laying down beer mats. I ordered a Virgin Mary that came in a tall glass with a giant stick of celery poking out, took it to a high round table and watched the passing parade on Darlinghurst Road. Not that there was much to see. Even Sydney's most notorious vice district was pretty quiet before noon on a Friday. Apart from a couple of dodgy guys in thongs and jail tatts, all I saw were tourists: an endless parade of khaki shorts, polo shirts, chunky sandals and bumbags. Suddenly I didn't feel so daggy in my nineties jeans and band t-shirt.

A skinny older guy pushed through the glass door and glanced over at me. Chris Ferguson had told me I'd recognise him by his facial hair and he wasn't fucking kidding. He had a beard a bushranger would have been proud of. He would have looked like he'd sailed in on the First Fleet if it hadn't been for his faded red t-shirt, Dunlop volleys and jeans with a yellow form guide sticking out the back pocket. I waved, he nodded, and after ordering a schooner of beer, he ambled over and sat opposite.

I shook his bony hand. 'Thanks for meeting with me.'

'No worries. How long's she been missing?' His voice was sandpaper.

'Five days, give or take.'

He nodded. His cheeks were hollow, deep lines bisected his forehead and his thinning hair was the same grey-brown as his beard. He dug around in his front pocket and produced a pack of unfiltered Camels. 'You mind?'

My throat hurt just looking at them. 'Go for your life.'

Ferguson sparked up, shook out the match and gazed at me from behind the billowing cloud of smoke. 'What do you want to know?' he asked.

'When exactly you talked to Andi, and what about, if that's okay?'

He sipped his beer and foam clung to his moustache. 'Let's see, Andi called me in mid June. Said she was in Sydney and wanted to meet up to talk about the Cross, in connection to some story she wanted to write. I'd met her once before after my lecture at RMIT and we'd had a smoke and a bit of a natter. She'd lived around here till she was fourteen and it turned out I knew her mum, vaguely.' He drew back hard on his ciggie, as if it were a joint.

'Really? You might have met mine. Peta Kirsch ring a bell?'

'Can't say it does. I've met a lot of people over the years and this doesn't help.' He lifted his beer and took another mouthful. 'Anyway, I arranged to meet her, mainly to turn her off the idea.'

'Why?'

'She's a good kid, and Canning told me she was talented, but it's all been written about before. Corrupt cops and politicians, dodgy developers, Juanita Nielsen going missing, Sallie-Anne Huckstepp murdered. And by people who actually lived through it, not some journalism student who was in nappies at the time. I was gonna suggest she devote her time and skills to something more original, more relevant to her experience and what's happening today.'

I was listening to him, pulling little stems off the top of the celery and gnawing on them. I nodded so he'd go on.

'Anyway, turned out the story hadn't been covered after all.'

'What was it?' I stopped chewing, sat up straight and stared at him. Finally, I was getting somewhere.

'Article about a missing person.'

'The one she wrote for uni in May?'

'Nah, new one.'

'She writes about missing people and she becomes one. That's too weird.'

'It does have a certain irony.' Ferguson sucked on his smoke and the ash grew long but didn't fall.

'Who's it about?'

'Melita Kracowski.'

'Who?'

'Her working name was Melody and she disappeared from around here in nineteen eighty. Andi came across her on the national missing persons website while researching her earlier piece. Wanted to know if I knew her.'

'Did you?'

'Not personally. Knew of her.'

'Pro?'

'Dancer. Well, she did work at the Love Tunnel so who knows what she was doing out the back. They're not all strictly strip clubs around here.' He nodded at me knowingly, and I realised he knew exactly who I was. Christ, the whole world did these days.

'The Love Tunnel,' I said. 'I read in your book that Sam Doyle used to run it. I'm starting to see how this all came about …'

'How what came about?'

'Andi started working at a restaurant Doyle co-owns after she got back from Sydney in June. She befriended his son-in-law and … it was all to investigate her article …' Things were becoming clearer, but not clear enough. Did the money laundering have anything to do with the story or was that just coincidence?

'You write about Melody in your book?' I asked.

'No. There were rumours, but I'd have got my scrawny arse sued if I printed them. The fucking libel and defamation laws in this country.'

'What rumours?'

'Well, Sam Doyle was a suspect for a while. He was her boss and he'd been shagging her.'

'Really?'

'Yeah, but he was rooting most of the girls at the Fuck Hole—sorry, Love Tunnel. It's what everybody used to call it way back when. Not very subtle.'

'Forcing himself on them?' It was a sore point with me.

Ferguson laughed, dragged on his ciggie to the butt then crumpled it in the glass ashtray. 'From what I heard it was the other way around. They didn't call him Hollywood Sam for nothing. Bastard was good looking, especially compared to most of the other weasels on the scene. And charming, so I've heard. Everyone liked him, it's how he worked his way up from being a shitkicker at the illegal casinos.'

'And he was investigated in Melody's disappearance?'

'Yeah, but never charged. No evidence. You won't believe his alibi for the night she went missing—he was swanning around at a bloody police retirement do.'

'A gangster who ran a strip club?'

'It was the eighties. Maybe you'd better read the rest of my book.'

'Why would he have killed her?'

'They say all murders come down to sex and money, or variations thereof, so take your pick. Not long after Melody disappeared Sam came into a whole lot of dosh. A girl he used to go out with at the club got hitched to some rich druggo, Edwin someone, and inherited the lot when he OD'd on smack. Then Sam married her and they were both on easy street after that. Got out of the strip biz and into property, a hotel, restaurants, gourmet food importing. Both well off and living the straight life ever since. Well, so they reckon.'

So Holly's dad had been a junkie and Dillon's despised stepmother-in-law, Rochelle, a dancer at the Love Tunnel. Dillon hadn't been kidding when he referred to the whole situation as *Days of Our Lives*.

I absentmindedly broke the celery stick in half, took a bite and pointed it at him. 'Andi was so sure Doyle was involved that she went to work at his restaurant. Why, when no one else had any evidence?'

'No idea. I can tell you she had a photo of Melody though.'

'What, from the missing persons website?'

'No, this was an original.'

'Where'd she get it?'

'Wouldn't tell me, cagey little thing. Even after three more schooners I couldn't pry it out of her. We played a bit of pool, put a couple of bets on and all she'd tell me was that the story had fallen into her lap. Saw it as a gift, and reckoned it was a ticket out of her McJob. She also said she was becoming completely obsessed with the case and I told her that was a good thing. Can't be an investigative journalist without it. How else you gonna see the whole thing through to the bitter end? In hindsight, maybe that was the wrong fucking thing to say.'

If Andi was anything like me, I thought, it wouldn't have mattered what he'd said.

Ferguson glanced at the clock above the bar, slid his form guide from his back pocket and tapped it on the table. 'Gotta get a bet in on the second at Rosehill. Anything else you want to know?'

'Sam Doyle. People reckon he's a real badass. Ever met him?'

Ferguson scratched his beard and the hair rasped against his fingers. 'I've only heard stuff secondhand and I don't know how much is real and how much is folklore. He used to work for Don Davison, heard of him?'

'The name rings a bell …'

'He was a Mr Big who used to own half the Cross, moved to the Gold Coast and became a property developer before all the royal commissions went down. Anyway, I know Sam used to crack some heads for him back then, he was an ex boxer, but he'd have to be pretty straight now, living in his Balmain mansion, running with the yacht club crowd. You still see him around the Cross sometimes, checking out the old haunts. This place has that effect on you, addictive, I reckon. I tried to move down the south coast once, couldn't handle it. The silence was deafening.' He checked the clock again and smoothed down the newspaper in front of him.

'Think he'd kill someone, or have them killed?' I asked.

He looked at me, green eyes like marbles. 'I wouldn't put anything past anyone.'

Ferguson went off to the sports bar down the road to put a bet on and I sat there finishing my Virgin Mary and crunching on celery, briefly wondering if it was true you burned more calories eating the stuff than you received in-gesting it. It was a relief to finally know what Andi had been working on, even though it didn't help me find her. I was pretty confused about where Trip fitted in though, and why Andi had gone back to his place when she was investigating Doyle. Hell, maybe I'd been reading too much into it, maybe she was just drug-fucked and horny. Bit of a coincidence though, that Trip had been the last one to see her …

I rang the detective sergeant who'd interviewed me at Homicide, Duval, and left a message on his phone telling him that although I was no longer investigating the case I'd come up with some new information. I gave him a rundown and Ferguson's phone number, then sat there tapping my fingernails on the stainless steel table top considering my options. I could go back to my mum's and spend a fun filled day staring at the lampshade trying not to worry about Andi, or I could continue on with my 'concerned citizen' shtick and possibly come up with some more useful information for the police.

It wasn't a difficult choice. I drained my drink, slipped on my sunnies and stepped out the door onto Darlinghurst Road, heading into the heart of the Cross.

chapter twenty-three

Sun glimmered off the freshly hosed footpath and the windows of passing cars. Playbirds International and Porky's were closed, the neon hushed and unblinking, but McDonald's was open and a shop assistant was rolling up the shutters of an adult bookstore. I hadn't been to the Cross in years. The last time it was three in the morning and I'd been off my face on a cocktail of speed, ecstasy and booze. I hadn't realised there were so many trees. Solid old oaks and smaller, more delicate plants with fluttering yellow-green leaves grew from the pavement and clustered in the square near the famous fountain that looked like a dandelion bursting into seed.

Another thing I'd never noticed was the architecture. Above their sleazy, street level facades the buildings were old and ornate. Flats down winding alleyways sported leadlight windows and wrought iron balconies, and ivy climbed up the walls. The place reminded me a bit of St Kilda: the back streets corralled by the Esplanade, Fitzroy and Barkly. I started humming a Paul Kelly song: 'From St Kilda to Kings Cross'.

I saw an internet café and ducked inside to look up the national missing persons website. Andi wasn't listed—maybe it took a while—but I found Melita's name and clicked on it.

'Have you seen this person?' The question was typed in bold at the top of the page and a head and shoulders shot sat underneath. Melita was pretty, with a heart shaped face, thin eyebrows and a bleached blonde, slightly poodle-esque perm. Her boobs looked too big for her slight frame, and too round and upstanding to be real. Did they have tit jobs back in the olden days? Must have done. Her vital statistics told me she was one hundred and sixty centimetres tall, had brown eyes and was twenty-four when she disappeared. It shocked me to realise she'd be my mum's age, if she happened to still be alive.

At the bottom of the page a paragraph explained the circumstances surrounding her disappearance, but didn't tell me much at all: 'Melita aka Melody was last seen leaving work at Kings Cross in the early morning of 28 May 1980. She did not return home and her bank account has not been accessed since. There are grave fears for her welfare.' The Missing Persons Unit urged anyone with any information, no matter how trivial, to call their hotline. It made me think of Chloe putting her own phone number on Andi's posters and I shook my head and almost chuckled fondly until I remembered I didn't like her anymore.

I printed out the page, folded it and stuck it in my notebook and sat for a bit, wondering how exactly this story had fallen into Andi's lap. I reckoned it had to have happened in the June holidays when she was staying in Sydney, and I wondered if Joy knew anything about it. I rang and left a message on her mobile asking her to call me. Who else had Andi seen in Sydney who might know something? Maybe Daisy, her old school friend. I still had Andi's address book so called her, got another darned answering machine and left another message.

I walked out of the internet café and strolled down Darlinghurst Road, looking for the Hot Rock Karaoke Bar where Andi's credit card had been used, and found it wedged between a kebab shop and a bureau de change. The place was closed but I peered through the glass door and saw a set of stairs leading up to a black curtain. Was it just a karaoke joint or a front for something more sinister? And what the hell had Andi been doing there, if she'd been there at all?

I straightened up and that's when I noticed something reflected in the glass. A figure across the road was facing me, holding an object that glinted in the sun. I whirled around, pulse suddenly racing, but it was only a tourist, a guy in khaki shorts and a shirt with big red flowers, taking pictures of the strip. I told myself to get a grip. No one knew I was in town, I was just another anonymous chick who hadn't updated her wardrobe in ten years.

I watched the starburst fountain across the road, waiting for my heart to slow down. The Kings Cross police station was in the same paved square and I decided I might as well flash my licence, tell them I was working for the family and ask if Andi had been spotted. Surely the Melbourne police would have faxed through a picture after her credit card had been used?

The station was a sixties building trimmed in yellow and blue with the chequered police symbol above the automatic doors. I climbed a set of stairs, passing a straggly palm tree, approached the desk and showed the young uniform my licence, explaining why I was there. I took a seat while he picked up the phone, and a couple of minutes later an older male detective came out and looked me up and down. Hopefully he was a Breeders fan.

'Working for the family, are you?'

'That's right. We've had word her credit card was used in the area. I was wondering if she'd been sighted at all?'

'No. I've canvassed the Hot Rock and businesses in the local area but no one recognised the photo. Just this morning someone was picked up using the card in a local bottle shop when the signatures didn't add up. Renee McPherson. She's known to police.'

'Have you got her here?'

'No, she's been taken to the police centre in Surry Hills for charging.'

'Did she say where she got the card?'

'Refused to talk to us.'

'If I fronted up at the centre would they let me speak with her?'

He laughed. 'Not unless you wanted to bail her out.'

I left the police station and sat at the side of the fountain, smelling chlorine and feeling a fine spray of water trickle down my cheek. It was stupid, it was dumb, and I wouldn't be able to pretend I was just a concerned citizen anymore, but I couldn't help myself. I walked to Darlinghurst Road and hailed a cab.

chapter**twenty-four**

A bleached blonde with two inches of black roots staggered into the reception area of the police centre. 'Who the fuck are you?'

I took in her pasty complexion and overplucked brows and figured she could have been anything from a ravaged twenty-five to a drug-preserved late forties. Her off the shoulder broderie anglaise blouse showed the rose tattoo on her right breast and a slice of white belly wobbled out over the waistband of her denim mini.

'My name's Simone Kirsch.' I stuck out my hand but she ignored it. 'I'm a private investigator and I'd like to talk to you.'

'I don't fuckin' think so.'

'I need to know how you … found the credit card.'

'See ya.' She reeled out the door and the desk guy laughed and shook his head.

I ran after her, overtaking her on the steps and blocking her way. 'Come on, Renee, I just bailed you out.'

'So?'

I tried another tactic. Begging. 'Please. I'm looking for a missing girl and her mum's really worried. I just want to know where you came across it.'

'An alley.' She sidestepped me and staggered off on white, spike heeled ankle boots, her pantyhose sagging so I could see the cotton gusset drooping out below her tiny skirt.

'Which alley?'

'I don't fucking know the name of it,' she muttered over her shoulder, then tried to hail a taxi coming down Goulburn Street. It didn't even slow down.

'Can you take me there? Please, Renee, stop.'

She slowly turned around, swaying slightly. Pink blusher striped her face in the general direction of her cheekbones and arcs of blue shadow decorated her lids. She narrowed her eyes and licked her bottom lip. 'How much is it worth to ya?'

'What?'

'Look, I gotta fix before I get sick. So if you don't have any money—' she shrugged—'I hafta go make some.'

'How much?'

'Hundred.'

I crossed my arms. 'I wasn't born yesterday. You can easily fix for a fifty.'

She shrugged and held out her hand. I shook my head.

'No way. I'm coming with you.'

'Dwayne doesn't like strangers.'

'Then we'll tell him a stranger's just a friend he hasn't met.' I pulled out my wallet, showed her the fifty then slipped it back in.

'Whatever.' She thrust her arm up, a taxi actually stopped and I jumped in after her.

Ten minutes later we pulled up in front of a block of ugly brick flats in Rushcutters Bay and I paid the driver. Renee talked into an intercom at the security door and we were buzzed inside. We climbed two flights of carpeted stairs, smelling cabbage and bacon, walked down a corridor and knocked on a door. A man with dark curly hair peered through the crack, unhooked the chain, looked up and down the passageway and let us in.

Dwayne wore a silky tracksuit and his hair was long at the back and short on top. His furniture was upholstered in squeaky black vinyl, his coffee table made from pine and the air was opaque with cigarette smoke. I handed Renee a fifty and she paid him and immediately started fixing up with a spoon, lighter and syringe he had thoughtfully provided. I wasn't freaked out, I'd seen it all before. As far as I was concerned, junkies were far more frightening when they hadn't shot up. She found a vein, plunged in the spike, loosened the belt, slid out the needle, pressed the puncture with her finger and sank back on the couch.

Dwayne was offering me a deal, a small square envelope made from the page of a glossy magazine.

I shook my head. 'No thanks, mate. Trying to cut down.'

'How long you and Renee been friends?' He leaned forward and the gold chain around his neck swayed.

'Not long.'

'You work?' He didn't mean nine to five.

'Nah, up from Melbourne. Holiday.'

'You should go to Darling Harbour. They've got an aquarium there. Or get a ferry to the zoo. Or Manly. Manly's nice. How about a bridge climb? Did you know you can climb right to the top of the Harbour Bridge? Pretty expensive, but.'

I smiled politely. Renee had nodded off on the couch holding a lit cigarette in her hand and the ash was getting really long.

'Renee,' I nudged her. 'We gotta go.'

'What?' She raised her thin brows but her lids remained half closed.

Smack. Such an unattractive look. I couldn't believe it had been trendy back in the nineties.

'We're going to find that alleyway.'

'Oh.'

Dwayne stuck his hand out. 'Nice to meet you. Remember, Darling Harbour. It's ace.'

We walked back up to the Cross, stopping every now and then for Renee to light a cigarette. It was three o'clock now and more shops were opening up. I was so starving that even the chickpea curry would have looked good, but I wanted to get this business over and done with before I ate. We hit Darlinghurst Road and I pointed across the street to the karaoke bar.

'You use the card at the Hot Rock?' I asked.

'Fuck no. I'm good at a lot of things, but singing ain't one of them. Haven't been in that joint since it was the Love Tunnel.'

'The what?' I stopped short outside an ice cream parlour.

'The Love Tunnel. Used to be a strip joint but, you know, with extras going on out the back.'

Now it was making sense.

'Can I have an ice cream?' she whined, pointing to the waffle cones.

I bought her a double scoop boysenberry ripple with chocolate sprinkles on top and we continued on our way, passing the McDonald's where a group of bikies leaned against their Harley Davidsons.

A fat one with bits of Chicken McNugget in his beard grabbed at me as I passed. 'How much, sweetheart?'

I looked him up and down and wondered briefly if he was the one who'd chased me and Andi down Parramatta Road all those years ago. They all looked the same to me. 'I don't go with guys who need their mates to hold their dicks,' I said, shaking him off.

They catcalled as we walked on and Renee looked at me, eyes wide and pupils pinned. Impressed or horrified I couldn't tell.

'You should be careful, darl. You shouldn't talk to them like that.'

'The shit I've been through I'm not scared of guys who have to hang out in groups of ten and dress alike. Talk about insecure.'

She abruptly hung a left down a side street, then a right, and we were in an alley full of bins and one giant rubbish skip. The air smelled of rotting food and the ground was littered with syringes and used condoms. A cockroach scuttled by, big as my mobile phone.

She pointed to the back door of a restaurant. 'The bag was there, on the step. Black backpack thing. I took the cards out and left it.'

It wasn't there anymore.

'When did you find it?'

'This morning. Early. Anyway, I'm getting back to work. Thanks for bailing me out and the ice cream and the smack.' She threw the last pointed scrap of cone over her shoulder. 'You know, I might have chucked the bag in that skip there.'

I tied my flannie around my waist, hitched up my baby backpack, climbed onto an upturned milk crate and peered over the edge of the giant bin. Oh goody. Rancid food, more condoms and syringes, and shit, was that a dead cat? Below me, underneath a mouldering cabbage leaf, I thought I saw a leather strap. I pulled a pen from my bag and hoisted myself up so my hips rested on the lip of the dumpster, then I bent at the waist, trying desperately not to overbalance and holding my breath against the stench. I extended my arm and strained my fingers until I'd looped the strap over the pen, hooked it and then swung back up in gymnastic fashion, like I was taking a turn on the uneven bars. I lowered myself down to the crate. Nice work, if I did say so myself.

A low whistle from the corner of the alley made me turn. Two of the bikies stood with arms crossed, watching me. The one who'd asked 'how much?' was more than fat. He was a land whale. The other was wiry with straggly blonde hair and a ferret-like quality. I knew they'd expect me to shriek and run so I climbed down from the crate real casual and dropped the bag behind me. My hands had gone trembly and I stuck them in the back pockets of my jeans so it wouldn't show.

'Hey, guys. What's up?'

The skinny guy said, 'Macca didn't like what you said to him.'

Macca shook his head. Under the beard I could see some chins wobble.

'Can't he take a joke?' I asked.

'He's not exactly renowned for his sense of humour.'

'Well, sorry if I offended you, man.'

They moved forward. I stood my ground and sighed like this was all just too boring.

'What do you want? My wallet?'

'We're not after money.'

'Well, you wouldn't want to do anything stupid. I'm a cop.' I flashed my PI licence. I'd had it in my pocket since the police station.

'That's not a police badge.'

'PI. Same diff.'

'Bullshit. You don't even carry a gun.'

They took a couple more steps forward. My heartbeat cranked up like a lawnmower. I could run down the alleyway behind me but it turned a corner and I didn't know what I'd find there. Maybe it doubled back to Darlinghurst Road, and maybe it was an isolated dead end where nobody could hear me scream. Why had I never learned karate? Or kickboxing? Or fighting with a sword?

'I wouldn't come any closer.' I pointed to a security camera mounted above the restaurant's back door. 'They'll get you on CCTV.'

Macca took a length of chain from inside his vest, wrapped it around his fist and swung it at the camera, which shattered and fell off the mounting. Ferret man grinned. So much for that.

I said, 'Well, if you wanna rape me, fine, whatever, but I should warn you I have herpes.'

'Who doesn't?' Macca finally spoke, and I wished he hadn't.

I glanced at the alley behind. Did it lead to freedom or would I be trapped like a rat? Maybe the rest of the bikies were down there, waiting for me. I'd seen those sixties bikie films with Peter Fonda and Bruce Dern. I didn't want to be anyone's momma.

I thought of one more tactic before bolting into the un-known. It was a long shot but anything was worth a try.

'Listen, guys, I know you bikies get a bad rap about the drug dealing and the gang banging and bombing each other's clubhouses, but it's all a media beat-up, isn't it? Just one more example of how people who are a little different from the rest of society are constantly marginalised, right? Marginalised … and criminalised … and … and … even demonised, don't you reckon? Well, I say we shouldn't take it anymore. Let's dispel the myth, reject the stereotypes and, like, together we can work toward a better future, not just for us, but for our kids …' I was really babbling by the end. So much so that it took me a while to notice they were staring at me strangely, and actually backing away.

'You're right,' nodded ferret man, walking backwards, palms out in front.

'Sorry to bother you,' Macca mumbled, eyes downcast.

I couldn't believe it had worked. Maybe Dr Phil was right. No matter who they were, people just wanted to be accepted. Communication, that was the name of the game.

'Give peace a chance,' I yelled after them, and let out a long breath. Damn. Close one. I turned to pick up the handbag and came face to face with the barrel of a gun.

chapter**twenty-five**

I yelped like a seal pup and hopped backwards before I realised the hand holding the weapon belonged to Alex Christakos. He smiled at me, slipped the piece back into his shoulder holster and returned his police ID to his coat pocket.

'What the fuck are you doing here?' I asked when I'd regained enough composure to speak. I'd gone all sweaty and my t-shirt was stuck to my back.

'Saving your arse.'

'I didn't need saving. I was fine.'

'I have herpes? Give peace a chance? Yeah, that was really working for you.'

I glared at him.

'I was right,' he said, smug look on his face. 'I knew you'd go after Doyle.'

'I am not going after Doyle,' I said, and Alex raised his eyebrows. 'I'm just hanging out in a skanky alley. Nothing wrong with that.'

'Out the back of one of his restaurants?' Alex pointed to the doorway with the smashed security camera.

'You serious?'

'Uh-huh. La Petite Courgette.'

'Fuck,' I said. Then, 'Seriously. What are you doing here? Don't tell me you came all this way to save me.'

'Don't flatter yourself, babe, I'm up here for the fraud case, liaising with the Sydney guys.'

'The same time I'm here? What a coincidence.'

'Isn't it? I was just leaving the police station when I saw you cruising up Darlinghurst with that tragic hooker. I knew nothing good could come of it.'

'Oh yeah? Well I got Andi's bag.' I dangled it in his face and he recoiled at the smell.

'Sure it's hers?'

That was a point. I crouched down and went through it. The wallet was empty of cash, her credit and key cards and her driver's licence, but her Medicare and student cards were still there. I flashed them triumphantly, then frowned. 'Her bag is dumped out the back of one of Doyle's restaurants, her credit card was used at the Hot Rock Karaoke Club, which used to be the Love Tunnel, and I just found out the article she was writing was about a girl who went missing from the club in the eighties. Doyle was a suspect. Are you thinking what I'm thinking?'

He nodded. 'Let's take the bag to the police station and I'll call Detective Duval and let him know what's going on. It'll be enough for him to send someone or come up here himself.'

'Won't you get in trouble for hanging out with me?' I smiled sweetly.

'Probably, but I'd say he'll be more pissed off with you.' Alex looked me up and down then pressed his lips together like he was trying not to smile. 'And don't take this the wrong way, but I think grunge officially died with Kurt Cobain.'

After handing over the bag and giving a statement we left the police station and walked out into the square, which I had discovered was called Fitzroy Gardens.

'You busy right now?' I asked Alex.

'Nothing till tomorrow.'

'Hungry?' I was starving. It was almost four and I hadn't eaten since the rubbery soy cheese.

'Sure.'

There was a café adjacent to the police station, but I was a bit over the Cross.

'I know somewhere,' I said.

The Sydney Oyster Bar was at the east end of Circular Quay, not far from the Opera House and opposite the historic Rocks area and the Museum of Contemporary Art. From our outside table we could see the Harbour Bridge stretch across the water to North Sydney and the towering hotels and skyscrapers that made up the city skyline. The late afternoon sun had turned the clouds apricot and the harbour was lavender, reflecting the sky. Huge ferries navigated in and out of the quay sloshing water against the old stone parapet and a warm breeze ruffled my hair so it tickled my shoulders. I fancied I could smell summer in the air: salt water, coconut oil and tropical flowers.

Alex took off his suit jacket, rolled up his sleeves and leaned back in his chair to admire the view. 'Wow.' He sipped his schooner.

I had to smile. It was pretty damned impressive. I'd come here every now and then when I lived in Sydney and feel like a millionaire for an hour before scurrying back to my inner city hovel.

'Not bad, huh?' I had a glass of champagne in front of me that cost the same as an entire four litre cask and had ordered a platter of oysters. So much for my cheap and cheerful Sydney weekend.

It was strange to see Alex drinking a beer by Sydney Harbour. He was so far out of his natural habitat it was like running into a wallaby on the arctic tundra.

'How long you here for?' I asked.

'Couple of days.'

'Where you staying?'

'The Villa.'

'Sam Doyle's hotel? For your investigation?'

He nodded.

'Lucky bastard,' I said.

'What's wrong with your mum's?'

'Where do I start? They're on a detox and there's no mini bar, bathrobes or little shampoos. Plenty of chickpeas and guilt trips though.'

The oysters arrived and I ordered another champagne from a waiter whose eyes flicked from my flannie and boots to Alex's suit and tie. I hadn't been able to decide on natural oysters, those topped with caviar, neufchâtel and dill, or the ones with wakame seaweed and soy, so had ordered a combination of all three. Alex and I had gone to dinner once and I knew he liked them. I hoed straight in, sucking the little morsels straight from the shells, practically having food orgasms and squirming in my seat.

He was a little more reserved, but did let out a low moan when he tasted the first one. 'I forgot how good they are. It's been too long.'

'How come?'

'Suzy can't even stand the look of them. I made her try one once and she spat it straight out.'

An incredibly crass remark about oral sex entered my mind and I stuffed another oyster in my mouth before it could escape. Talking about head jobs could be construed as making a move and I'd promised I wouldn't. Easier said than done. To stop myself flirting after two glasses of champagne was so against the natural order of things I would have had more luck commanding the sun to rise in the west.

I lowered my gaze from his eyes to his shirt. This was not such a good move as he'd opened the top button when he'd loosened his tie and I made out a small v of chest hair. I gulped some champagne and turned to stare at an old sailing ship, moored across the cove in front of the Park Hyatt.

'So how come you're back on the case?' Alex asked. I'd expected him to scold me but he just sounded resigned.

'I tried to drop it, honestly, but I just couldn't get it out of my head. I'm no good with unfinished business. You don't have to worry though, no one knows I'm in Sydney and I'm not doing anything dangerous, just following up a few leads, you know, to pass on to the cops. Haven't told Joy or my mother yet.' All the oysters were gone and I picked up a lone sliver of seaweed and popped it in my mouth.

'You wanna order more?'

'Nah, Mum's having a barbecue. I should go soon.'

I didn't want to though. I wanted to stay there with Alex and drink champagne and eat oysters and pretend I was on holiday. I suddenly realised how crap my existence was: working all the time, squirrelling away money, going home alone to a cold, empty flat. Some people had fun lives and did shit like this all the time. What the hell was wrong with me? I took a tiny sip of champagne knowing that as soon as the glass was finished I'd have to leave.

'So that was weird, Suzy asking me to be a bridesmaid,' I said.

'She likes you. I told you she's fine when she lays off the booze.'

'You sure about that? I thought it might have been one of those keep your friends close and your enemies closer sort of things.'

Alex shook his head and sipped his beer. 'You've got her wrong.'

Had I? How could someone go from pathologically jealous to sweet as pie? Sure, she wasn't drinking, but I'd always thought that what you did when pissed was exactly what you wanted to do while sober, only you didn't have the guts. In vino veritas and all that.

I reluctantly drained my glass and was just about to get up when something glinted, reflecting the setting sun and flashing orange light into my eyes. I kept my head straight but moved my eyes to glance over Alex's shoulder. At the entrance to the Dendy cinema, a tourist was leaning against a pillar, photo-graphing the harbour with a really long lens. A tourist in khaki shorts and a short sleeved white shirt patterned with big red flowers.

'Don't turn around,' I said, 'but there's a guy behind you taking pictures of us.'

'Sure it's us and not the bridge?'

'Yep. He was snapping shots of me in the Cross earlier today.'

Alex stiffened. 'I thought nobody knew you were here.'

'So did I.'

'Don't move,' he ordered. 'I'll go inside like I'm paying the bill.'

He scraped his chair back and walked towards a small brick building that housed the kitchen, bar and toilets. I stayed put. The guy still had the camera on me. Out of the corner of my eye I saw Alex slip through the building, and stroll up the walkway towards the Opera House so he could double back and approach the guy from behind. It was all going well until the photographer got antsy and turned his camera onto the building where Alex had disappeared, then swept the lens along the side of the harbour and zoomed in.

Alex, to his credit, kept strolling nonchalantly but the man stuffed his camera into a padded bag, turned and started to race-walk towards the ferry wharves. He glanced over his shoulder and when he saw Alex catching up he bolted. Alex started running too, but was about a hundred metres behind. As the guy ran past the Oyster Bar I leapt out of my seat and took off after him, ignoring the shout of the waiter who must have thought I was doing a runner.

Camera guy was short and rotund and although his chunky legs were really pumping it didn't take me long to close in. He ducked and weaved through the crowd, and almost fell after he leapt over a busker playing a didgeridoo. He staggered, caught himself, whirled around to see Alex and me gaining ground and took off again. I was in front of Alex, only a couple of metres away from camera guy and so close I could hear his panting and smell his acrid sweat.

I was just about to lunge when the guy veered towards one of those sketch artists who draw everyone's faces exactly the same. Grabbed the guy's easel and chucked it at me. I put my arms up to deflect it, almost tripped over my boots and he gained a few metres. Alex caught up and ran past me, tie flying over his shoulder.

'Go back,' he shouted.

Not likely. Zigzagging between tourists and crowds of commuters I chased both of them into the station behind the ferry wharves. The train lines ran above the Quay and to reach them you had to take the escalators or stairs up to the platforms. Two rows of ticket barriers stood opposite each other and Alex covered one while I blocked the other. We had him cornered and the guy whipped his head around, sizing up his chances. He obviously decided I was the best bet, rushed me and darted away at the last second, scrabbling over the far turnstile.

I lunged and had just grabbed the tail of his shirt when I felt a crushing weight on my back and went down hard, hit the concrete with my palms then crumpled and rolled on my side, someone on top of me. I screamed and kicked and the weight lifted. Alex had the waiter from the Oyster Bar by the back of his shirt.

'Go after him,' I yelled, pointing towards camera guy, who had made it inside and was running up the escalator. Alex took off and the waiter pounced, pushing my face into the ground, wrenching my wrists behind my back and shouting to the gathering crowd that I'd done a runner and he was making a citizen's arrest. Children pointed and old people tut-tutted and I wanted to explain but couldn't open my lips lest I copped a mouthful of filthy concrete. Alex eventually returned, puffing, flashed his badge and the waiter finally let me go.

'He slipped into a train,' Alex said. 'He's gone.'

chapter**twenty-six**

After we'd cleared things up with the overzealous waiter, paid the bill and collected Alex's jacket, he insisted on driving me back to Annandale, which was fine with me. On the drive we threw around ideas about who the guy had been, and who'd want me under surveillance. I put forward a theory that whoever had attacked me at Andi's, left the possum head, organised the hit and run and now the surveillance were not necessarily connected. The methods were too diverse. Unless of course some evil genius was just trying to do my head in, in which case they were succeeding.

I'd braced myself for Alex to lecture me about dropping the case and getting the hell out of Dodge but he didn't, and I was glad. I thought my information was really going to help the cops find Andi and from the way photo guy had taken off through Circular Quay it was obvious he wasn't any sort of threat. After an eternity stuck in rush hour traffic on Parramatta Road, we pulled up in front of my mum's.

'Thanks,' I yawned. I was tired and dirty and just wanted a shower and another drink. 'Guess I'll see you back in Melbourne. Call me if you find out anything about Andi during your travels.'

'Can I come in for a sec?'

'Best if you don't.' I didn't particularly want Alex meeting my mum and there was a good chance Steve was still growing a hydroponic dope crop out in the back shed.

'Come on, I'm busting for a piss after that beer.' He slipped out of the car before I could protest. Damn.

Opening the front door I heard muffled music and conversation wafting through the house. I crept down the hallway, Alex following close behind, and was relieved to find the lounge room and kitchen empty. Peeping out the windows above the sink I made out approximately fifteen people, some sitting at a table on the back deck, the others milling around the yard.

I shoved him into the bathroom. 'Hurry up. Soon as you're done you're out of here.'

'Can't I meet your mum?'

'No. She won't like you. Nothing personal, but she loathes cops. Just pee and get out, okay?'

If Alex had been a wallaby on the tundra earlier, seeing him in my mum's house was like watching the Reverend Fred Nile go-go dance in an Oxford Street gay bar. I stood outside the bathroom, bobbing up and down on the balls of my feet and keeping watch through the open back door. The yard was paved and ringed by native plants, except for the lemon tree dragging its branches in the far corner. Mum and Joy were sitting on an old church pew next to it, deep in conversation.

Steve had the barbie set up on the other side of the yard, in front of his mudbrick shed, and the orange glow of bamboo torches cut through the twilight.

I heard the toilet flush, seat flip down—good man—and tap begin to gush.

'Come on, come on,' I muttered under my breath. Just as Alex emerged from the bathroom my mum looked up and saw us. I grabbed his elbow, pulled him through the kitchen into the lounge and was just about to race him down the hallway when I heard her right behind us. I hadn't known she could move so fast.

'Simone! Who's this?'

Alex turned and beamed at her.

'He was just leaving.'

'Don't be rude,' Mum said. 'Introduce us.'

I sighed. 'Mum, meet Detective Senior Constable Alex Christakos, Victoria Police. Alex, meet my mum, Peta Kirsch.'

Alex stepped forward and shook her hand. 'Ms Kirsch. It's terrific to finally meet you. Simone talks about you all the time.'

No I didn't. What a bullshit artist.

'Are you Simone's …?' She tilted her head.

'No, Mum.' I said quickly. 'That's Sean. This is Sean's best friend.'

'So how did you two …?' She pointed from him to me.

'Alex is in Sydney following up a fraud investigation and we just happened to run into each other.'

'Where?'

I gave him a look that said *lie, damn you*, but he chose to ignore it.

'Kings Cross,' he offered.

My mum frowned.

'I was doing a little sightseeing,' I said. 'Anyway, Alex was nice enough to give me a lift home and now he's going back to his hotel.' I grabbed his arm and tried to hustle him up the hallway but he stood his ground and smiled at her.

'Before I leave I want to tell you I really enjoyed your dissertation. What was it called? "Politics and Power"? "Formations of Identity in Gendered Hierarchical Cultures"?'

I did an actual double take. Say what?

'You read it?' Mum's hand fluttered up to her chest. 'Christ, I wrote that for my PhD.'

'I actually cited you in my Master's.'

'What did you study?'

'Criminology. My thesis examined redressing the masculinist nature of policing and I particularly liked what you said about proactive equality strategies. I thought your ideas were spot on.'

I stared at him, mouth dropping open. He'd never let on that he knew anything about my mother, let alone studied her.

Alex pointed at the piano. 'You play?'

'I've just started lessons again. Got grade five exams coming up.'

'They're tough. What piece are you performing?'

'I haven't decided yet.' She looked him up and down. 'Would you like to stay for a drink?'

'Love one.'

'Come out and meet Steve. I have to warn you we've been smoking a joint. You're not one of those overzealous "war on drugs" cops, are you?'

'Not at all. Whatever consenting adults want to do in the privacy of their own home is fine with me.'

'Did you want a toke?'

'The drink will be fine.'

I crossed my arms and turned to my mum. 'I thought you were detoxing.'

'It's organic, darling.'

She stepped around me and hooked her arm through Alex's. As she led him out he glanced over his shoulder and winked at me. I stood there wondering if there'd been a tear in the space–time continuum and I'd inadvertently blundered into a parallel universe. Sure felt like it.

I jumped in the shower and scrubbed off the day, dabbed tea-tree cream on my scrapes and dressed all in black: a pair of stretch pants left over from my waitressing days, the boots I'd worn down from Melbourne, and a long sleeved, scooped neck top of my mother's. I brushed my hair, whacked on a bit of makeup and checked the fridge. My mum may have been detoxing but her guests certainly weren't. I grabbed the biggest wine glass I could find, filled it with someone's sauvignon blanc and considered my chances of scabbing a cigarette. Probably not good. Perhaps I'd have to stand over the barbecue and inhale.

The back veranda had been extended into a wooden deck and a bunch of people in their forties and fifties sat at a stained pine table eating olives and drinking red wine from outsized glasses. Lights shaped like chilli peppers wound round the railing, glowing red, and Joni Mitchell emanated from the stereo speakers. A few of the people looked familiar so I waved in their general direction, muttered a quick, 'Hi, everyone,' and descended the porch steps. Others hung around the sizzling barbecue where Steve, back in his drawstring pants and sandals, was rotating vege skewers and laying down marinated fish fillets and Balmain bugs. The seafood smells mingled with the scent of frangipani and smoke, a plane roared overhead and in the distance cars beeped their horns and trucks growled, air brakes spitting as they stopped and started on nearby Parramatta Road. The evening was getting darker but there was a preter-natural orange glow in the sky.

Alex was sitting on the pew by the lemon tree, drinking a Coopers Red, Mum on his left and Joy to his right. As Joy wasn't yelling at him and calling him a pig it seemed he had charmed her also. Jesus. No one was that good.

Mum, who appeared to be stoned and in quite good spirits, waved me over. 'I was just telling everyone about when you were a kid, how you got lost in the bush and we found you wedged down a rabbit burrow. Should have known you'd end up a PI.'

'Alice in Wonderland?' Alex looked up, amused.

'*Watership Down*. I thought Hazel and Pipkin might be down there. I lived in the bush. I didn't have any friends.'

I grabbed a canvas deckchair and sat close to Joy. Alex turned his attention back to my mum and said something in her ear, causing her to lift her chin and laugh. Good god, was he flirting with her? Steve glanced over before turning his attention back to the barbecue.

'How you holding up?' I asked Joy.

'Not so good. It's the not knowing that's the worst.'

I leaned in close, elbows on my knees, and lowered my voice. 'I tried to call you today but your phone was switched off.'

'I was at the hospital with Mum.'

'Of course. Look, I was just wondering, when Andi was in Sydney in June, did she ever mention anything about a woman named Melita Kracowski? Melody? She disappeared in nineteen eighty, used to work at the Love Tunnel for Sam Doyle.'

Joy went pale all of a sudden and her pupils expanded. Her hand started shaking and her wine glass slipped from her grasp, bounced off her lap and shattered on the ground. Her t-shirt was soaked with red.

'Are you okay?'

She didn't reply, just shot a look at my mum and disappeared into the house. My mother stood and followed her. Steve grabbed a dustpan and brush from underneath the barbecue and Alex and I helped pick up the large pieces of glass. I was just about to go after them when I got cornered by some guy with a beard and elbow patches who asked if I thought real life PIs were influenced at all by their fictional counterparts, since he'd just written a paper about the effect of TV cop shows on police recruiting campaigns.

Steve and Alex started bringing the barbecued food to the table and arranging more chairs. Joy and Mum had been gone about ten minutes so I told beard guy I had to pee, went inside the house to look for them and ran into them in the kitchen. Joy had changed shirts. I'd thought she might have been having another one of her freak-outs but she was dry eyed. Mum, who looked more distressed than she did, went straight to the fridge, poured herself the rest of the sav blanc then drank about half of it in one go. She was holding two sheets of paper and her hand was trembling slightly.

'I'm sending you back to Melbourne,' she said.

'Excuse me?'

'It's safer.'

'Mum, I'm not unsafe.'

Alex walked in from the deck and looked around. 'Bottle opener?' he asked. Mum reached to the bench behind her, picked it up and held it out.

I glared at him. 'You told her about today.'

'No I didn't.'

'Bullshit.'

'I swear. I didn't tell her about the bikies who almost molested you, or the guy following you with the camera, the attack in Melbourne by the wheelie bin, the severed possum head, and, let's see … the hit and run she already knows about …'

Bastard. No wonder he hadn't said anything in the car. This was his grand plan to get me off the case. Mum looked me over. I tried to hide my grazed palms but just drew more attention to them.

She crossed her arms. 'I was right. It's far too dangerous. I've already bought your plane ticket over the internet. You leave tonight.' She handed over a piece of paper: a printed itinerary.

I stood there with my mouth open, hardly able to believe what I was hearing. 'You're the one that asked me to stay.'

'And now I'm telling you to go back to Melbourne.'

'But my flat isn't safe.'

She thrust out the second sheet. 'I've booked you into a motel near the airport. It's out of the way, and in Steve's name. You can stay there until this is all over. It's for the best, considering the circumstances.'

'Sam Doyle circumstances?'

They just stared at me. Mum gulped more wine.

'Soon as I mentioned his name the two of you scurried off. Will you just tell me what's going on instead of treating me like I'm ten? You know him from the Cross, don't you, and you're scared of him. Why? What happened?'

Silence.

'Couple of great fucking feminists you are. The chick PI can't do it 'cause she might get hurt. Leave it to the big strong men with guns. Leave it to Alex.'

He appeared at my shoulder. 'You should listen to your mother, Simone. Joy's taken you off the case and Homicide are onto it. Just let it go.'

'Homicide are only onto it because of my information. Andi's in danger and just as I'm getting close to finding her everyone tells me to drop it. And you're all lying to me. Even you, Alex. I don't know where the Sydney Fraud Squad's located but I doubt it's in the Kings Cross police station. What the fuck is going on?'

'No need to get paranoid,' he said.

The other guests were craning their necks and peering through the kitchen window, trying to see what all the commotion was about.

Mum drained her wine and turned to the fridge to refill her glass. 'Nothing's going on, Simone. It's just that I've heard some bad things about Sam Doyle, and I don't want you getting involved with him.' She turned back and tried to smile, but it came out wobbly. 'Now let's calm down and have something to eat. The plane doesn't leave till eight forty-five.'

'I don't think so. Since I'm not welcome here I may as well fuck off now.' I picked up the wall phone and started dialling a cab.

Mum looked at Alex.

'I'll take you,' he said.

I was going to tell him to piss off but I had an idea. 'Fine,' I said.

Alex and I didn't speak at all on the drive, and when he dropped me off I checked in, passed through the metal detector and went straight to the departure lounge. I waited half an hour, in case he was loitering outside, then strolled through the exit, out of the terminal and into a cab.

'Darling Harbour,' I said.

chapter**twenty-seven**

Sydney's annual Food Expo was being held in the exhibition centre at Darling Harbour, the precinct on the western edge of the CBD home to the casino, aquarium, Maritime Museum and lots of large, loud restaurants and four star hotels. I paid twenty bucks and hurried through the enormous aircraft hangar of a space past a village of little booths displaying samples of everything from gourmet vinegar to instant mashed potatoes.

They'd given me a map with my ticket and the 'Chef of Steel—Live' stage was at the far end of the building. It had been scheduled to start over an hour earlier and I was hopeful they'd still be filming, but when I got there my heart sank. The rows of seats were empty and a lanky janitor with a scraggly ponytail was vacuuming the stage. Great. Trip was gone and I had no way of finding him. I sank down into a chair at the front and the janitor looked up.

'You're a bit late, babe, missed a good show. The young chef was really giving some shit to the older guy. They almost got into a fight.'

'Suppose the young chef's long gone, huh?'

'Nah, he stuck around to chat up these two promo chicks, hey? Last I saw he was over by Lickety Split Gelato.'

The guy pointed and I was out of my seat like a shot, heading for a booth with a giant ice cream cone sticking out the top. Rounding the corner of the stand I saw the two promo chicks behind a counter, one blonde, one brunette, both wearing hotpants and tight t-shirts with a picture of a tongue and the slogan *Lick It* screenprinted over the breast area. It was like Sexpo, but for the digestive rather than the reproductive system.

'Oh my god,' the blonde was stage-whispering to the brunette. 'He's crazy. I think he's on something. He tried to get me to go into the toilets and when I wouldn't he bent down and licked my shirt.'

'No way,' said the brunette.

'Way.' She held out the fabric. 'You can see the wet spot.'

'That would be sooo gross if he wasn't famous and hot.'

I cleared my throat and they looked over and plastered big smiles on their faces. 'Cup or cone?' asked the brunette.

'Neither. Trip Sibley. The shirt licker. He still around?'

They looked at each other and raised their eyebrows.

'He left, like, two seconds ago,' said the blonde. 'See that door? It goes to the car park.'

I turned and bolted out of a glass exit door, flew down a set of concrete stairs and into a low ceilinged car park. I heard a motorbike start up but couldn't tell where the sound was coming from so ran to the exit and planted myself in front of the boom gate, breathing hard. Seconds later the Ducati came roaring toward me and stopped with a yelping skid. Trip hadn't bothered with a helmet.

'Simone fucking Kirsch. What are you doing here?'

'Gee, let's see. Someone tried to run me over right after they killed your sous chef. I was wondering if you knew anything about that?'

'I heard it on the news. Shame, hey? Never liked the guy but no one deserves that.'

'And I think Andi's being held in Sydney. You're in Sydney. Your mate Sam Doyle's in Sydney. I found her bag behind his restaurant. Give it up, Trip. I know you've been lying to me. It won't be nearly as bad for you if I get her out of here alive.'

He started laughing and shaking his head. 'Man, I do not know what the fuck you're talking about.'

'Oh, I think you do. Remember the possum head?'

He laughed so hard he doubled over the handlebars. After a minute he swiped the tears from his eyes. 'Remember the— am I just out of it or was that a really trippy thing to say?'

'Have the police interviewed you about Gordon and Andi yet?'

'This dude rang from Homicide. Duval or something. I haven't called him back yet.'

''Cause you're guilty?'

''Cause I'm on acid. Think I wanna hang out in a cop shop and ruin my trip? No thanks, darlin'. I'll talk to them tomorrow when I've straightened out.'

'This is serious. Andi's in big trouble. If you know anything at all …'

A car drove up behind him and revved its engine.

He glanced back. 'I may know something.'

'What?'

'Look, I'm late to meet someone. Jump on the back, I'll tell you when we get there.'

'Tell me now.'

The car behind beeped.

'Sorry, babe, I gotta go. Jump on.'

'With a suspected murderer?'

He sighed and pointed to the security camera mounted above the boom gate. 'If I was a murderer do you think I'd abduct you on candid camera? Christ, give me some credit.'

Getting on a bike with an LSD fuelled criminal was definitely a risk, but my only other option was to go straight to the airport, hide out in a crap motel on my own for a week and probably never ever find out what was going on.

'What are you waiting for?' Trip said.

The driver was leaning on the horn now, and another car had pulled up behind him.

'Helmet? I don't have a death wish.'

He pulled one out of his side saddle, thrust it at me and I jammed it on and hopped on.

'You're gonna fucking dig this, darlin',' he shouted, cranking the throttle and going straight for the wooden bar.

Was he insane? I squeezed my eyes shut and at the last minute he dipped his weight and we slipped past, so close I felt it rush by my shoulder and then we were cresting the ramp and speeding through Darling Harbour, coloured lights reflecting off the water, the tang of food and barnacles in the air.

Ten minutes later Trip parked the bike on Darlinghurst Road. Neon pulsed, music throbbed and the footpaths teemed with clubbers, junkies and wide eyed couples out to dinner. Touts in black suits shouted from strip club doorways, trying to coax roaming buck's parties and embarrassed tourists inside. I dismounted, slipped off the helmet and shook my hair out, heart fluttering and legs so shaky I could barely stand.

Trip grabbed the helmet, tore off his chef's jacket and stuffed both into the bike bag. Underneath he wore a sleeveless Metallica shirt, and his triceps looked cut, as usual.

'Tell me that didn't get you hot,' he growled, 'speeding through the night with nine hundred and ninety-six cc's of premium Italian engineering throbbing between your legs.'

He was right. Tearing through the city on the big red bike with my arms wrapped around Trip's muscular mid-section had given me a serious thrill, but he didn't have to know that.

I put my hands on my hips and attempted a school marm expression. 'Riding without a helmet, exceeding the speed limit and disobeying the rules of the road is not exciting or clever. It's just plain immature.'

Trip blew me a raspberry, turned and headed for a door-way. I followed and suddenly realised we were entering the Hot Rock Karaoke Club, and I hadn't even mentioned Andi's card being used there. I clutched the back of his black t-shirt and pointed to the sign.

'Is this some kind of joke?'

'Darlin', we must have a breakdown in communication 'cause I don't get half of what you say.'

Upstairs tiny red and orange bulbs twinkled in sequence around archways, the bar and the edge of the stage. The catwalk was covered in multicoloured squares, just like the dance floor in *Saturday Night Fever*, and round tables filled with a mix of Asian and Caucasian clientele dotted the room.

I followed Trip to the bar as a man in his early sixties climbed the stage, grabbed a mike and sauntered out into the red spotlight, trailing the lead behind him. He had thick dark hair and sideburns, was dressed all in black and started belting out 'In My Hour of Darkness' with a deep gravelly baritone that sounded a lot like Johnny Cash.

Trip ordered a beer and two tequila shots for himself and a glass of champagne for me and we took the drinks to an empty table at the back of the room. I didn't know what the hell we were doing there, so decided to play it casual and act like I spent every other night hanging out in karaoke bars with possibly murderous, drug crazed chefs. Inside I was hyped up and as vigilant as the meerkat who stands guard while the others do their digging. At least we were in a public place, with heaps of other people around.

'Gram Parsons.' I sipped my drink and nodded toward the stage. 'Good song.'

'If your taste is in your arse.' Trip knocked back a shot of tequila, yowled like a dingo and slammed the glass down.

'So what are we doing here?'

'I thought you wanted my help.' He slugged another and this time clucked like a chicken, tucked his arms in and flapped.

'I want the truth. Why the Hot Rock? Is Andi here somewhere?'

'You've heard of sex slaves? Well, that's sooo early noughties. Latest thing is karaoke slaves. We've got her chained out the back with a bunch of chicks from Thailand and Eastern Europe and we force them to sing "Hotel California". It's depraved.'

The guy onstage wrapped up to loud applause and a tiny Asian woman got up and belted out 'Respect', sounding just like Aretha Franklin. I'd always thought karaoke would be the same as the first round of *Australian Idol*, but these people were good.

'Stop fucking around, Trip. Tell me what you know.'

'In a sec. I want to introduce you to someone.'

He was looking over my shoulder, grinning, and I turned my head to see the guy from the stage standing behind me. He was handsome for an older bloke, a little thick around the middle, but by no means fat. His slightly weathered features made him look like an ageing Hollywood star playing a grifter in a noir film.

'Meet Sam Doyle,' Trip said.

chapter**twenty-eight**

I started, bumped my champagne and caught the glass just before it fell. Doyle sat down and when he offered his hand I reached across the table and shook it. The palm was warm and dry and he had an effortlessly strong grip. I'd momentarily forgotten to breathe and my voice came out all strangled.

'Simone Kirsch.'

'Kirsch, hey?' His voice was low and raspy and he drew out my surname, savouring it like the liqueur. 'So you're the young lady set the Homicide Squad onto me.'

'What?'

He took a pack of Lucky Strikes from the breast pocket of his black shirt and lit one with a book of matches. 'Detective Duval paid me a visit this evening, asking questions about a dead sous chef and a missing waitress. Seems Andi Fowler wanted to write an article about me, and he thought I might've taken offence.'

My stomach flip-flopped but I tried to appear nonchalant. 'Duval said it was me?'

'No, but young Trip here told me about you a few days ago. It wasn't too much of a stretch.' He turned to Trip. 'You talked to the Melbourne coppers yet?'

'No.'

'Well you're doing it tomorrow, before the party. I'll have my QC mate sit in. Now get me a tequila.'

'Yes, Dad.' Trip held his hand to his head in a mock salute and sauntered off to the bar.

'Dad?' I asked.

'He's taking the piss.' Sam draped his arm over the back of the chair. His sleeves were rolled up and I saw a faded tattoo on the inside of his forearm. Looked like a horse, maybe a mustang. 'We're just friends and business partners. He's a mad fucking bastard, as I'm sure you know, but that's what I like about him. Everyone's so well behaved and sanitised these days, and I'm too old to raise any hell. Someone needs to grab the baton.' He took a deep drag and ashed his cigarette.

Sam hadn't tried to kill me yet, or even do anything remotely nefarious, so I relaxed a little but didn't entirely drop my guard.

'What exactly did Trip tell you about me?' I asked.

'That you were sniffing around Jouissance, looking for Andrea Fowler. I did the rest of my research on the internet. From what I saw you'd be almost as crazy as he is.'

'Don't believe everything you read,' I said, and sipped my champagne. A candle flickered inside a bobbled red vase in the middle of the table.

'Trip also said you thought he had something to do with it. Why's that?'

'Because he lied.'

Trip returned to the table and handed Doyle a shot glass. Sam sniffed it, then took a small taste.

I glared at Trip. 'He said he last saw Andi leave a staff party and catch a cab on Fitzroy Street, but I have witnesses who saw her going home with him and Yasmin.'

Sam frowned.

Trip shrugged. 'Okay, I lied. Yeah, she did come back to mine for some fun and games but I didn't say anything 'cause I was being discreet, for once. Didn't want to screw and tell.'

'So what happened?' I asked.

'You want details, baby? I knew you weren't as straight as you made out.'

'Just tell her,' Sam sighed.

'Okay. Nothing.'

'I find that hard to believe,' I said.

'You're telling me. We hung out for an hour or so, more drugs, more drink, then just as I suggested the girls should kiss, you know, get the ball rolling, Andi's got a text message and she reckoned she had to leave. Ripped off!'

'Who was it?'

'How should I know?'

Sam signalled to a passing waitress for another round of drinks. 'Why do you think Trip would harm her?' he asked me.

I didn't want to mention the fraud stuff, so I said, 'Hell, I dunno. Thought it might have been a B&D session gone wrong. I just got suspicious when he lied. Why did you lie?'

'Yasmin didn't want anyone to know, thought it would undermine her authority or some shit. And it was kind of fun messing with your head.'

Jesus, what a dick. I couldn't believe I'd actually been turned on before.

'You came to Sydney to question Trip and me?' Sam crushed out his cigarette.

'No. I came to Sydney because someone tried to kill me, right after they killed Gordon.' I looked into Sam's eyes. Even in the dim light I could see they were a bright, intense blue, but completely unreadable. I imagined he'd be damn good at poker.

'Tragic, although I can't say I liked the guy myself. And they're sure it was no accident?'

'I was there. Some thug driving a stolen car ran him over. Twice.'

Sam sipped his tequila. 'And you're wondering if I had anything to do with it. The waitress too. You're barking up the wrong tree. I was here in Sydney, a dozen people can vouch for me, and like I said to the cops, why would I go knocking off my own employees?'

I couldn't mention the money laundering so said, 'Gordon, I don't know. Andi because of the article. It was about the Melita Kracowski case in nineteen eighty. You know, Melody?'

Sam didn't react, just lit another Lucky and studied my face.

'And there's the fact that Andi's credit card was used in this bar, and her handbag was found on the back step of La Petite Courgette this morning.'

'Duval mentioned that. I showed him security footage from the restaurant. We saw you, right before the camera was broken, but there was no sign of Andi Fowler in the alleyway. No footage of anyone dumping the bag.'

'But how?'

'The camera has a blind spot. If someone stayed flush to the wall they could have placed it on the step without being filmed.'

'So someone planted it?'

'I can't imagine why else they'd be sneaking around.'

'You think someone's trying to frame you?'

'It wouldn't be the first time.'

'Why?'

'I'm an easy target. Shitkicking Balmain boy made good. Australia, people just love cutting down tall poppies.'

'Who?'

He shook his head and laughed. 'Take your pick.'

Trip had been sitting silent, apparently fascinated by the mirror ball patterns sliding across the wall. Now he piped up. 'Have you thought that Andi might have faked her own disappearance? Maybe she's a vanilla bean short of a crème caramel.'

I almost mentioned Andi's desperate phone message but stopped myself just in time. They didn't need to know she'd had her mobile, even though I was now convinced Trip had nothing to do with her disappearance. He wasn't a good enough liar. And Sam? The man was a little gruff, but basically affable and answering every question I threw at him. Hard to get my head around when I'd been expecting the Lord of Darkness himself. I liked to think I had good instincts about people and my gut feeling was telling me he wasn't a threat. Of course he could have been some kind of evil genius with a talent for lulling unsuspecting PIs into a false sense of security, seducing them with his so-called 'Hollywood' charm. I'd seen it in Mafia movies, the wiseguys all laughing and drinking, slapping each other's backs and then bam, one was garrotting the other with a length of piano wire. Sam had even managed to tame a wildcard like Trip. He was sitting there as docile as a pony in a petting zoo. That took talent.

The drinks arrived and I had a big gulp of champagne and asked the question that had been playing on my mind all night. 'Do the names Joy Fowler and Peta Kirsch mean anything to you?'

He kept the poker face but I could've sworn something

flickered in his eyes. 'Never heard of them.' He didn't pause to think or even remark on the surnames. It was suss.

'They used to live around here,' I said. 'Joy's Andi's mum, Peta's mine.'

'Sorry.' He shook his head. If it had been me I would have asked what they had to do with anything. Doyle didn't.

Trip had started to shift in his seat. 'I'm bored with this. I'm gonna do a song. Anyone else wanna do a song?'

Sam and I shook our heads and Trip bounded off to put his name down. Sam stubbed out his smoke, drank some beer and checked his watch.

I asked him for a cigarette.

'You don't want one,' he said.

'Yes I do.'

He opened the first three buttons of his shirt and showed me his chest. A pink scar, raised and ropy, slashed straight down his sternum. 'Triple bypass. Never thought life'd catch up with me, but it did. Don't do it.'

'Good advice, but it might have more impact if you weren't downing tequila and sucking the guts out of those Luckys.' I reached across the table and grabbed the pack. Sam laughed. He seemed amused that I'd given him shit.

'I have a proposition for you,' he said.

I really hoped he wasn't trying to crack onto me. He didn't seem sleazy, but I remembered what Chris Ferguson had said about him rooting all the dancers at the Love Tunnel. I lit the cigarette and drew back, waiting for him to go on.

'Since someone's doing away with my staff and trying to frame me, I ought to hire you myself.'

I tried to imagine what my mum would do if I swanned back into her place and announced I was working for Sam Doyle. Probably drop dead of a heart attack. A perverse part of me considered it … briefly.

'I can't I'm afraid. Conflict of interest.'

He raised an eyebrow that had a scar running vertically through it. Lines cut deep channels from his nose to his mouth. 'I always pay above the going rate and if you're investigating anyway, which you seem to be … how long you in Sydney for?'

'Not sure.'

'Where are you staying?'

'Nowhere at the moment. I have to find a hotel.'

'Stay at my joint. Villa.'

'A little out of my price range.'

'It's on me. Trip's staying there.'

Alex was too. It would be just like school camp.

'I couldn't.'

'Why?'

I considered telling him it would be foolish to let him know exactly where to drop off the horse head, but said, 'I'd just rather not.'

'Suit yourself. I know you don't believe me, but we're on the same side here. Listen, think over the job offer, sleep on it, then call me in the morning.' He took out a card, scribbled his mobile number and address on the back and handed it to me. I stared at him and he shook his head and laughed. 'Look at you. You still think I'm a bad guy.'

'I don't know what to think. Someone's had me under surveillance while I've been in Sydney. Following me, taking pictures.'

'Believe me,' he said, 'it's not one of mine.'

'And here you are being all friendly and offering me a job and a hotel room. I don't mean to seem ungrateful but it's a little odd. The people I investigate usually try to beat me up, or at the very least threaten legal action. Why are you doing this?'

Sam leaned his elbows on the table and looked me in the eye. 'I'll tell you what I'm about, Simone. I'm a big fan of people who show a bit of get up and go, even though life wasn't handed to them on a silver platter. Especially if life wasn't handed to them on a silver platter. I'm keen to help them out, especially if they interest me. Christ, you wouldn't believe how many boring fucking stuffed shirts I've had to deal with in the property business. It's why I got into restaurants even though they're shit from an investment point of view. It was a buzz and I met some real characters, same with the Cross. Of course round here's nothing like it was twenty years ago. I blame your generation, so bloody straight. Forget live sex shows and cheap blowjobs, you all want lattes and wilted spinach.'

I laughed and Sam smiled at me. 'You shouldn't be scared of me.'

'I never was.' The champagne had boosted my confidence.

'Is that why you nearly knocked over your drink when you heard my name?'

Damn, I thought he hadn't noticed. 'You have to admit, you've got a fucking terrible reputation.'

He gave me a wry grin, pushed back his chair and stood up. 'Don't believe everything you read.'

'I liked that song you did, by the way.'

He smiled and his eyes crinkled at the corners. He looked genuinely pleased. 'You like country?'

'Seriously dig it.'

'Call me.' He pointed to the card in my hand, then strolled away.

I glanced at the stage as I finished my drink and cigarette. Trip was singing a Sex Pistols number, 'Pretty Vacant', thrashing around and swinging from a pole that must have been left over from the bar's strip club days. The other patrons were looking faintly alarmed. I left him to it and walked down the stairs.

chaptertwenty-nine

I knew I had to find a motel, get something to eat and buy supplies, but having a surprise encounter with Sam Doyle had left me a little hyped up and I needed another drink to level out. I bypassed the nightclubs with their swirling disco lights and chest thumping bass and ducked into the Goldfish Bowl. On the video jukebox Billy Idol sneered and sang 'Forgot to Be a Lover' and the bar was crowded with backpackers, dodgy looking dudes, working girls and trannies. My kind of place.

I bought a champagne and took the only vacant seat, a stool by a bench facing a window that looked out onto Victoria Street. I was still reeling from the fact that Doyle wanted to hire me. There had to be more to it than his fondness for interesting people with a bit of 'get up and go', but I wasn't sure what. I also didn't know what the hell his connection to my mother and Joy was and it was driving me crazy. The only thing I could think of was they'd been radical feminists and he'd managed a strip club. Maybe there'd been some sort of run-in.

I hoped it wasn't too late to find a motel and I pulled my phone out of my bag to check the time. It was ten o'clock and I had one message. It was Andi's friend Daisy telling me we could meet up the following afternoon at the Coopers Arms in Newtown, before her band played. She was a singer, apparently.

My heart sank. Newtown was my old stomping ground and the one place I'd wanted to avoid while in town. I considered calling and asking her to meet me somewhere else then decided I was just being paranoid. It had been five years since I'd moved away and it was doubtful any of the old crowd still lived around there. Hadn't property prices gone through the roof? And even if they did, surely they'd gotten over the whole thing by now? I ought to have, too. It was a long time ago, water under the bridge.

I texted Daisy back, told her I'd see her at the pub at five, then realised my buzz was wearing off and drunkenness was setting in. I asked the bartender if he could recommend a cheap hotel and he said there was a whole bunch down Macleay Street. I left the pub and stopped by a 7-Eleven and bought a pack of cheese singles for dinner and a toothbrush and tube of paste. Deciding that my knickers wouldn't dry by morning if I rinsed them out, I popped into a sex shop and bought the only pair of undies I could find that actually had a crotch: a black cotton g-string with 'come and get it' written on the front in red.

As I wandered down Macleay humming 'In My Hour of Darkness' and admiring the trees and the architecture I passed a side street whose name I recognised. Wasn't Doyle's joint down there? It wouldn't hurt to have a squiz. I wandered along for a bit and came upon a mansion with columns, turrets and sweeping verandas. A glowing sign out front read The Villa, Boutique Hotel, Restaurant and Bar. If Andi had indeed been in Sydney then she may have checked it out. I still had her photo in my handbag, so figured I'd flash it then retire to the hotel bar for a nightcap. A double Jameson's would surely provide the knock out blow I needed to sleep the night through in whichever scuzzy motel I decided on.

Entering the open gate I found myself in a modern take on a formal garden. There were hedges galore but they'd all been clipped to resemble rolling waves. Gravel paths snaked between the plants and terminated in alcoves where curved sandstone benches sat in pools of dim yellow light. Instead of a cupid peeing water, the fountain in front of the entrance consisted of three large metal balls stacked on top of each other, water sheeting down the silver surface. A three scoop ice cream? The Michelin man? Abstract art wasn't exactly my forte.

I entered the marble reception area and approached the desk, black and s-shaped like the benches. The willowy young man standing behind it wore a crisp black suit with a mandarin collar and shook his head when I showed him the photograph, but told me I could find the bar to the right of the lobby.

Gold curtains draped the walls, spherical light fittings hung low and the chairs were curved and upholstered in gold and black and red. Apart from the structure itself, the whole hotel had no straight lines and I was starting to feel kind of seasick. A few business types were scattered around and a white jacketed guy whose nametag read Jose was tending bar. I ordered a double Jameson's that cost a whopping twenty bucks and showed him Andi's photo. He studied it for a long time, which got my hopes up, then dashed them when he told me he'd never seen her before.

I took my whiskey to a red couch, and when I swallowed the liquor it burned a satisfying path down my gullet. I leaned my head back. Theories spun around in my brain but I was too exhausted and tipsy for them to make any sense. It had been a hell of a day. I closed my eyes and enjoyed the heavy feeling in my limbs. I'd finish this drink, toddle off down the road, check into the first place I came to, and collapse on a saggy single bed which would have either a chenille spread or an ugly flower printed duvet. I was feeling so relaxed I almost fell asleep until I sensed a presence. My eyes snapped open and I groaned. It was Trip.

He sat next to me, made a hand signal to the barman and stuck his arm along the back of the couch. I hauled myself forward so his hand wouldn't brush my neck.

'You take up Sam's offer of a room?'

'Nope.'

'Then you must be waiting for me.'

Did the guy ever give up?

'Thanks for finally telling me what happened that night, and introducing me to Doyle, but I'd really appreciate it if you'd just fuck off.'

I'd hoped he'd get offended and storm out but he just grinned and raised those devilish eyebrows. 'Hard to get, huh?'

'For you? Impossible.'

'Mr Sibley?' Jose set down a brass tray bearing a bottle of expensive looking tequila, sliced lemon and a salt shaker. Trip completed the lick, sip, suck ritual then placed his hand on my knee.

I pushed it away. 'Trip, piss off. I'm tired.'

'I've got a king sized bed in my room …'

Wanting to get out of there fast I finished my drink in a giant swig that burned my throat and brought tears to my eyes. Crunching through the last shards of whiskey flavoured ice I said, 'This might be hard for you to accept, being in *People* magazine's sexiest and all, but I just don't fancy you.'

'Why not?'

'Let's see. You're arrogant, up yourself, violent. Do you want me to go on?'

'Simone, that's all an act. I'm different deep down. Why don't you give it a chance, get to know the real me?'

I snorted. That was almost as bad as this cop who'd once told me he knew how to make me feel like a woman. What did he think I felt like? A rhinoceros? A single celled amoeba? A bloke?

'Call an escort if you've got the horn,' I told him. 'We're in Kings Cross, shouldn't be too hard to find a fuck.'

Trip reached out his index finger and, before I could stop him, slid it down my cheek and neck and along my collarbone, a surprisingly delicate move for someone who had, half an hour earlier, careened around a pole like a frenzied chimpanzee. I shivered. A reflex action, but he saw.

'Ha!' he said.

'Doesn't mean anything.'

'You sure? Kiss me.'

'What?'

'I'll tell you about Andi ...'

'You already did. She was at your place and nothing happened 'cause her phone rang.' I wondered if the cops had traced that call. Probably. Would they tell me who it was from? No way.

'There was something else too ...'

'What?'

He pointed to his mouth. 'One little peck.'

'You're full of shit.'

'No I'm not. I worked with her four nights a week. I think I have a fair idea what might have happened to her.'

'And you'll only tell me if I kiss you? That's somewhere between sexual harassment and bribery.'

'I wouldn't go that far. Unethical, possibly. Certainly sleazy. But I'm a chef, not a Catholic priest, so who gives a shit?'

I finished my Jameson's, reached over and sprinkled salt on the back of my hand, threw back a shot of tequila and sucked hard on the lemon. A shudder ricocheted down my spine. I looked at Trip. It's not like he was hideous or anything. In fact, as much as I hated to admit it, *People* had been on the money. And it was just a peck. What was a peck if it led to the one clue I needed to find Andi?

'So help me,' I said, 'if you're lying …'

He opened his eyes wide, attempting to look innocent.

I repeated the process with the tequila, spat the lemon onto the tray, squeezed my eyes shut and said, 'Okay, do your worst. But no ton—'

Too late. He'd tilted my chin up, brushed the hair back from my face, and licked my bottom lip. The shiver returned. Not that I was keeping tally or anything but it had been four months, one week and five days since I'd kissed someone, and the aborted attempt with Alex didn't count. I tried very hard not to feel anything, but my lips had started to tingle, not to mention everywhere else. Trip tasted like tequila and he smelled like sweat, but good sweat, the nutmeg and cinnamon aroma you got walking past a bakery.

I started sinking back into the couch but he wrapped his arm around my waist and pulled me up. I touched his arm and felt a ridge of tricep. Gosh, he sure was buff. Probably strong enough to be able to actually lift me up and carry me around the room while he … I tried to block out the image. He pushed his tongue in, just a little way, not at all the arrogant thrust I'd imagined, and, well, I couldn't just leave my tongue lying there like a dead slug. What if word got around that I was a lame kisser? So I kissed back, thought of Sean, briefly, but reasoned that kissing wasn't cheating, not if the former president of the United States of America thought a blowjob didn't count. And anyway, I wasn't doing it for fun. This was for Andi, the greater good … and stuff …

Trip slipped one hand up my back, tracing my spine, and rested it on my neck, fingers playing with my hair. I got even more tingly until I couldn't help it and pressed myself up against him, hard, and then he pulled me onto his lap and crushed me into his chest and I was just thinking that being a chef, he probably wasn't averse to getting his tongue around all manner of exotic fare, when I heard a sound from across the room, the sort of pissed off 'harrumph' that old farts make when they can't handle people making out in public. The disapproving grunt flashed me back to Elsternwick, and the fat cop's words. *Alcoholic nympho … gets all her information rooting people.* Holy shit. I'd been so indignant when he'd said it, but wasn't that exactly what I was doing now?

I wrenched my lips from Trip's, turned my head away before he could lunge in for another pash and saw Alex standing under the archway between the bar and the lobby, glaring at us.

chapter**thirty**

'Let me in!' I hammered on the door and pressed my ear against the wood. All I could hear was the sports channel, turned up loud. 'Alex!'

He'd turned on his heel after I'd spotted him, marched through the lobby and jogged up the sweeping staircase. I'd shaken Trip off and bolted after him but when he'd reached his second floor room he'd slammed the door and nothing I could say would make him open it. My stomach sank and tears pricked my eyes. What had I done? Would he tell Sean? If only I could explain that it wasn't what it looked like. Christ, who was I trying to kid? It was exactly what it looked like, probably worse since I was still feeling all breathless and trembly and more than a little damp in the knickers. I couldn't decide if the sick feeling was real guilt, or just the shame of being caught.

'Alex!'

My banging must have woken the other guests, or perhaps Alex himself had summoned the security guard who was jogging toward me down the hall.

'Open the door!'

'Ma'am.' The guard was an older guy in a beige uniform, keys jangling from his belt. 'I'm going to have to ask you to leave the hotel, immediately.'

I ignored him and thumped the door with my fist. The guard grabbed my upper arms and started dragging me backwards. I dug my feet in and took a deep breath in preparation for yelling louder. I really wanted Alex to hear what I had to say before the guard hauled me off.

'You of all people have no right to disapprove of me! No fucking right!'

The door opened inward and he stood there in his shirtsleeves. 'Let her go.'

The guard wasn't sure. 'You know her?'

Alex nodded.

'Sir, we can't have this sort of carry on. If it happens again I'm going to have to call the police.'

Alex nodded. 'It won't happen again.'

'It had better not.'

Alex stood back and let me into a room with high, ornate ceilings, long gold curtains and a Juliet balcony. All the furniture was modern, moulded and curved like the seats in the bar, and multicoloured. A chaise longue was bright red, the kidney shaped writing desk purple. A feature wall behind the king sized bed had been painted aquamarine. I sat on the bed and stared at the enormous flat screen TV on the wall opposite. An AFL game by the looks of things, but it was hard to see through my watery eyes. I sniffed, determined not to cry in front of him again.

'I decided not to go back to Melbourne. I went to Food Expo and saw Trip Sibley instead and then we ended up at the—'

'Hot Rock. I didn't think you'd leave that easily. I knew you'd come back to the Cross so I hung around. I saw you leave the bar thirty seconds after Sam Doyle. I followed you.'

'Why?'

He stared at the wall for a while and sighed. 'I can't tell you exactly what I'm working on, but it's big and there are some very fucking dangerous people involved. You should take your mother's advice. Go back to Melbourne, stay in that motel. What did you talk to Doyle about?'

I flopped on my back on the billowy doona and stared at the ceiling. My eyes were starting to dry. 'Andi. My mum. I think he was lying about some stuff but I just can't believe he's evil incarnate like everyone's telling me. He's dodgy, sure, but I don't think I'm in danger from him and I don't think he did anything to Andi. Whether he had anything to do with Gordon's murder, who knows? As for Trip, well, he said he'd trade information for a peck on the cheek and things just got a little out of hand. You won't tell Sean?'

Alex shook his head. 'Telling him wouldn't serve any purpose and you weren't joking when you said I had no right to disapprove. When I think of what you and I almost got up to while I was still dating Suzy, before I asked her to … but you know what really pisses me off about tonight? You're a good investigator. You don't need to flirt with Trip Sibley to gather evidence. It cheapens you.'

Cheapens me? I had a flash of anger. He'd done a bit more than flirt with me for information once and I bet that didn't make him 'cheap'. Being a guy it probably meant he was a stud. I breathed deeply in and out of my nose but let it slide 'cause I really didn't want him to tell Sean. 'I haven't been flirting with Trip,' I explained. 'I've been a total bitch.'

Alex crossed his arms. 'Sometimes not flirting can be flirting.'

The fuck? 'Well shit,' I laughed, 'damned if I do and damned if I don't. Got anything to drink?'

'You don't need another drink. Eaten anything apart from the oysters?'

I shook my head.

'Where are you staying?'

'Nowhere.' I rolled on my side and looked at him. I really didn't want to get off that mattress, it was like floating on a cloud. Alex leaned back on the desk, arms still crossed.

'Right,' he sighed. 'You can sleep here. I'll order some room service and one of those rollout cots.'

'No, it's fine.' I struggled to sit up, but the bed was so big and soft and fluffy.

'Your mum would kill me if she knew I'd turfed you out onto the streets of Kings Cross. So would Sean. No argument.'

I yawned. 'Can I have a shower?'

He went to the cupboard, extracted a bathrobe and held it out to me. 'All you ever do is shower.'

'I'm always dirty.' I shrugged.

He opened his mouth to say something, but stopped himself just in time.

chapter**thirty-one**

The next morning I woke to find myself sprawled diagonally across the king sized bed, still wearing the bathrobe. I'd fallen asleep watching a cheery little show about plane crashes on the Discovery Channel and by the looks of things had forced Alex onto the rollout. Oops.

Squinting at the clock I saw it was eleven thirty and a note on the bedside table told me he'd gone out and would be back around four. I yawned, stretched, rolled out of my feather down bower and staggered over to the mini bar to pillage a tiny, outrageously expensive packet of real coffee I'd spied there the night before. I shook the precious grounds into a small plunger and snooped through Alex's things while I waited for the trendy stainless steel kettle to boil. I was hoping to find something pertaining to his fraud case, but all

I came across was a black leather toiletry kit, a copy of *Time* magazine and a pair of balled-up socks.

Alex's room was at the back of the hotel and when I took the plunger out onto the small semicircle of a balcony I expected it would overlook another garden of shiny sculptures and undulating shrubs. Instead I was confronted by an ugly eighties apartment building blocking out the sky.

I sat back in my wrought iron chair, propped my feet up on the rail and sipped the steaming black coffee, wondering what to do. If the interview with Andi's friend Daisy didn't yield any clues I'd have to accept I'd hit a dead end … unless I could find out who'd texted Andi before she left Trip's. If he'd gone to his interview and told the police what he'd told me then surely they'd have checked the phone records by now. They'd never tell me who the message was from, but they'd probably let Joy know. I wondered if she'd even answer my calls after that shit with her and my mum at the barbecue. Probably not, but I'd try later on, regardless.

I finished the coffee and, not really knowing what to do with myself when I wasn't taking my clothes off for a living or skanking around wheelie bins, decided to have a spa. The bathroom was massive, decked out with gold plated taps, rose coloured marble, mirrors and glass. I ran water in the giant tub, whacked in some bubble bath that had been laced with essential oils and labelled 'Romance Blend', ponytailed my hair on top of my head and fired up the jets. In no time a cappuccino-like froth was threatening to spill over the sides and I slipped into the warm, sweet smelling water. Bliss. I frolicked for a little while, pretending to be a seal, then piled suds on top of myself, blew them off and flicked them across the room. No matter how old I got, bath foam and bubble wrap never lost their charms.

Finally I settled down and rested my head back on the rim, feeling my flesh wobble pleasantly in the simmering water and sticking my feet in front of a jet so the air tickled my soles. I fiddled with a dial on the rim of the bath and there was a low volcanic rumble as the pressure increased, not only on my feet but coming up between my legs. I shifted slightly and—goddamn—that was the spot. I twirled the control a little further. Whoa. Unfortunately the bubble bath company seemed to have mixed up its 'Romance Blend' with its 'Filthy Slut' line of aromatic oils because instead of an awfully chaste fantasy of skipping through a field of daisies with my boyfriend, I was imagining myself bent over Trip's Ducati while he slapped my butt and pulled my knickers to the side. I was seconds away from coming when I heard the door to the room slam shut then a sharp rap on the bathroom door and a high pitched voice calling out.

'Housekeeping!'

I reacted faster than when that car had tried to run me down. I sat up, half fell over the side of the spa, struggled into my robe, looked around wildly for the belt and had to settle for holding it together at the chest. 'One moment!' I called. I swallowed, tried to steady my breathing and opened the door.

Trip was leaning against the frame, holding a stack of folded towels. Little packages of soap and shampoo balanced on top. 'How did you—?'

'The maids love me.' He flipped an electronic key between his fingers like he was doing a card trick. 'Your boyfriend about?' He peered over my shoulder into the bathroom.

'He's not my boyfriend.'

'Riiiiiight. That's why he was looking at me like he wanted to kill me.'

'Get the fuck out of my room.' I pushed the door shut. He stuck out his motorcycle boot and kicked it back in. Dramatic.

'Your cheeks are flushed.' He checked out my face, then the spa and the bubbles all over the floor. The motor was still on high and water spumed out. 'What have you been up to?'

A flashback from my sexual fantasy inserted itself into my mind and I felt my face get hotter. 'I was just getting dressed,' I replied through gritted teeth.

He bent forward and dumped the towels on the marble sink, then leaned against the doorframe. 'There's no use lying, babe, we're the same, you and me. Kindred spirits, lust for life and all that.'

'What are you doing here, Trip?'

'Asking you out on a date. The Doyles are having a garden party.'

'Did Sam put you up to this? So he could have another crack at hiring me?'

'No!' Trip came over all wide eyed and innocent. It really didn't suit him.

I hadn't fallen for Doyle's 'I just like interesting people' shtick either. He wanted me onside because he thought I was close to finding something out. Pity I didn't have a clue what that was. I didn't say anything and Trip was forced to go on.

'I'd really like you to be there. And, you know … it'll be fun. French champagne, great food and who knows, maybe you can get Sam drunk and interrogate him some more. I know you think he's got something to do with Andi.'

'Actually, I don't anymore.'

Trip raised his eyebrows in a reverse v. 'I'll tell you my information.'

'You were supposed to tell me last night.'

'And I would have if you'd stuck around. Not that I blame you for running away, darlin'. That much sexual heat can be hard to cope with, 'specially if you're not used to it.'

'You are such a wanker,' I said, and he beamed like I'd paid him a compliment.'Just give me the goddamn information.'

He checked his watch. 'I'm running late 'cause of my interview with the coppers. Why don't I tell you there?'

I crossed my arms and glared. He shrugged, turned and slouched out of the room. Good. I wasn't at his beck and call. I wasn't going to be summonsed to Doyle's party, go hang out with a whole bunch of rich people, possibly get Sam to admit why my mum was so scared of him …

'Wait!' I called.

I hated to admit it but I was growing fond of the big red Ducati. I dug the speed, the way you had to move your body with the bike. And Trip had been right, the damn vibrations coming up from the engine weren't bad at all. We flew through the CBD then across the Anzac Bridge: a sweep of concrete connecting Pyrmont to Glebe and Balmain. Stay cables fanned from two giant towers giving the bridge a futuristic look, and in between them I glimpsed the fish markets and Blackwattle Bay. The western view of the city skyline rose up on the right and below the bridge container ships docked next to a port where rows of identical white sedans glinted in the sun. The sky was pale blue but for a faint smudge of smog clinging to the horizon, and along with exhaust fumes I could smell the jacket Trip had given me to wear, cracked leather over a quilted lining infused with sweat.

Leaving the bridge we tore up Victoria Street and hung a right, twisting our way onto Darling Street and heading further down the peninsula. Balmain had once been a mostly working class enclave of rundown cottages and cramped terraces with a grotty pub on every corner, but like most suburbs close to the city it had undergone a revival during the previous twenty years. The houses had been immaculately renovated and the shops lining Darling Street now sold posh furniture, designer clothes and gourmet food. Real estate was expensive anywhere in Sydney, but in Balmain a half decent two bedder wouldn't leave you much change from a million.

Trip turned left and we wound down sloping side streets till we reached a narrow road one back from the harbour. He slotted the bike in between a BMW and a Mercedes that were both parked half on the footpath, and we approached a high wall with concrete lions guarding the entry. Trip talked into the intercom, the gate clicked open and a two storey glass and sandstone villa came into view. The building followed the contours of the slope and was surrounded by a rockery jumbled with ferns, staghorns and palms.

I trailed Trip down worn steps, through an open front door and into a marble entrance hall that led to a formal living room filled with pristine white furniture. French doors opened onto an enormous terracotta tiled entertaining area where fifty or so guests milled around a blue tiled swimming pool and a quartet played jazz standards inside a pergola. 'Toto, we're not in Elwood anymore,' I whispered as Trip and I crossed through the living room to the patio, our boots clicking on the polished parquetry floor.

The pool rested on the edge of the property so that the water appeared to merge into the harbour beyond. A half sized tennis court was wedged to its left, a grassy area led to a white wooden boathouse on the right, and small olive trees and Grecian urns bordered the yard. The band started performing an instrumental version of 'Bewitched, Bothered and Bewildered', the song that had been playing when Sean and I first kissed, and I felt a pang in my stomach when I realised I hadn't thought of him all day.

Waiters sashayed to and from a trestle table shaded by a sail and laden with canapés and top shelf booze. Trip swiped a champagne and a beer from one of their trays, handed me the glass and as I sipped I noted the palate was completely devoid of cat piss, unlike the shit I usually drank. Seeing all the beautiful people in their pricey duds made me glance down at my own outfit. As well as being not entirely clean, the stretch pants were faded and Mum's black top was pilling and covered in little white specks like a tissue had got loose in the wash. The waiters were better outfitted than me.

'I'm so not dressed for this,' I muttered.

Trip, as usual, wore ripped jeans and a sleeveless heavy metal t-shirt. 'Don't worry, neither am I.'

'Yeah, but you're Trip Sibley.'

'True.' He swivelled his head, surveying the crowd, 'My agent says I've got to project a consistent image if I want to establish myself as a brand. Speaking of which, that's him over there, talking to a chick who was on the cover of last month's *FHM* magazine.' He pointed his beer bottle at a balding guy in an open necked white shirt and khaki pants, deep in conversation with a pneumatic redhead. Double sided tape had to be the only thing stopping her tits popping out of her plunging, emerald green minidress.

'Check you later, Simone.' He started over and I grabbed his bicep with one hand.

'I thought I was your date.'

'No need to get jealous, babe,' he winked. 'I've got plenty to go around.'

'Information first or I tell that buxom wench you've just given me a bad case of the clap.'

'You would, wouldn't you?'

'Better believe it, chef boy.'

'Fine. Okay.' He sighed. 'My theory is that Dillon killed Andi.'

chapter**thirty-two**

Yachts bobbed around a nearby marina and a ferry headed for Birchgrove, which shimmered in the distance.

'You're full of shit,' I said.

'Am I? They were always hanging out, and the way she used to look at him is exactly how all those middle aged society broads are staring at me ...' Trip squared his shoulders and flexed his biceps and I couldn't tell if the pose was an unconscious reflex or completely contrived.

A lot of the women *were* gazing at him, some subtly from behind their wine glasses, others giving him a bold up and down. I supposed I couldn't blame them. After a couple of decades with a squishy, golf playing investment banker I'd be gagging for a bit of well-built rough trade.

'Why would Dillon kill Andi?'

'It stands to reason.'

'How?'

He sighed, like I was a little dense. 'Well, it's always the husband or boyfriend, isn't it? Statistically speaking.'

'Statistics?' I skolled my champagne, royally pissed off. I'd been busted kissing Trip for that? Jesus.

'Don't knock 'em. Right now they're telling me there's a ninety-two percent chance me and the redhead'll end up in one of the spare bedrooms within the hour.'

'Dillon wasn't Andi's boyfriend,' I hissed, 'she was just playing him, trying to find out about Sam for her article. What better way than through his stepdaughter and her husband?'

'You sure about that? I saw them together, outside of work.'

'Where?'

'Mink. You know, the bar under the Prince of Wales? They were sitting real close in one of those dark, curtained booths.'

'So?'

'Why would you be there unless you wanted privacy? I certainly did. I had a Russian model on each arm and Yasmin would have—'

'Did they see you? Andi and Dillon?'

'Nah.'

'When was it?'

'I dunno, maybe a week before she disappeared.'

'You tell the cops?'

'Nah. Doesn't prove anything and I need all the fucking staff I can get. Anyway—' he nodded towards the redhead— 'I've got business to attend to. You wanna join in it's the first on the right at the top of the stairs. Expect us at about, oh, twenty past?'

'You just don't stop, do you?'

Trip necked the last of his beer and his Adam's apple bobbed up and down. 'You're a long time dead …'

He stalked off in pursuit of his quarry and I stood alone in my shabby clothes feeling out of place and nervous. The only other person I knew was Sam Doyle and he hadn't even noticed I was there. He was standing by the pool with his back to me, smoking cigars and drinking spirits with a couple of older guys. All of a sudden my plan to grill him about knowing my mother seemed stupid. If he hadn't wanted to enlighten me the night before, why would he do it now? It had been a mistake to come and I'd hightail it back to the hotel just as soon as I'd stuffed a few of those gourmet snacks into my mouth. I was starving. It was one o'clock and I hadn't even eaten breakfast.

I wandered over to the trestle table, put my empty glass down and hoed in, starting with little stacks of eggplant, goat's cheese and red capsicum, dolloped with pesto. Divine. Tiny wontons nestled in Chinese soup spoons, floating on puddles of sesame scented broth, and I tipped a couple between my lips, bit into the slippery suckers and tasted prawn, ginger and coriander. After living on cauliflower, home brand tuna and individually wrapped cheese singles for so long it wasn't just a party in my mouth, it was a goddamn revolution.

Behind me Trip's agent was reassuring him that the network was thinking of expanding the proposed cooking show into an 'extreme' lifestyle program, but I tuned out as I hoovered up a mini pancake loaded with crisp Peking duck, sweet hoisin sauce and crunchy spring onions, visualising the flavours exploding like incendiary devices, causing all my little taste buds to dance and hug, sing in Spanish, throw off their bandanas and fire automatic weapons into the air.

Across the table I spied cone shaped nori rolls dangling from red laquered holders, crammed with salmon, rice and wasabi. Peaks of Japanese mayo crowned their tops, and tiny, translucent pearls of orange salmon roe glistened in the sun.

I reached over and plucked one out, sucked off the top and pressed the fish eggs between my tongue and palate till they burst and their salty juice mingled with the creamy mayonnaise. It tasted so good I did a Chloe-style butt wiggle as I bit through the rest and barely heard the cough behind me. I only registered a presence after a high, nasal female voice said, 'Excuse me!'

I turned around. The woman glaring at me was tanned to within an inch of her life and wore a tight white miniskirt with a matching jacket and camisole top. The teased and curled blonde locks cascading over her shoulders were the texture of fairy floss and a marvel of modern hairspray, and her clinking jewellery was the same yellow-gold as the chardonnay in her oversized glass. Judging by her smooth forehead, plump lips and slightly starey eyes, she'd had a bit of work done and it was hard to tell how old she was. From the wrinkling on the back of her hands I guessed she was somewhere around my mother's age. That and the skin on her surgically enhanced chest, which was as brown and speckled as a free range egg.

'Mmm …?' I hadn't managed to bite all the way through and the roll was hanging together by a slender but stubborn thread of salmon. If I kept gnawing the thing was likely to disintegrate all over my top, so I shoved the lot in and felt my cheeks bulge like a chipmunk's. I tried to chew but there was so much food in my mouth my teeth couldn't get any purchase. If anything, the roll was expanding and the rice transforming into a swollen, glutinous glob.

The woman crossed her arms, one high, strappy sandal tapping and her whole body quivering with suppressed rage. 'Standing idle, eating my food and drinking my champagne while my guests go without. This is not what I'm paying you for. It's a disgrace. Get your apron back on or I'll call the agency immediately.'

'Buuuh …' I tried to talk and white paste oozed out my lips and trickled down my front. I clamped my mouth shut and swallowed painfully as the roll went down sideways and ended up somewhere behind my clavicle, perhaps lodged in a lung. The wasabi kicked in like a nest of fire ants had scurried up my nose and tears sprang from my eyes. Trying to explain my situation through mime, I pointed to where Trip had been standing but he, and the redhead, had disappeared. Damn that man was a slut.

Luckily Sam Doyle saw what was happening and hurried to my rescue. He was wearing a black outfit very similar to the one he'd had on the night before, his hair was quiffed back, and dark sunglasses hid his bright blue eyes.

'Rochelle, she's not a waitress, she's the private detective I was telling you about, Simone Kirsch.' He pulled a bottle of Veuve Clicquot from an ice bucket, filled a glass and handed it to me. I gulped half in one go and the liquid dislodged the sticky mass from my throat. I gulped for air.

'Oh.' She looked me up and down, laughed nervously and then said, 'Goodness. I'm so sorry.'

I coughed and took a deep breath. 'That's okay. It's not your fault. It's Trip's actually. He insisted I come along and I really didn't have anything to wear. It was a mistake. I should leave.'

'Nonsense.' Sam refilled my glass and a froth of bubbles foamed over the side. 'Stay.'

'I'm really underdressed …' I gestured toward my outfit.

Rochelle smiled, teeth white and even as piano keys, and grabbed my free hand with hers. 'I can lend you something. It's the least I can do after mistaking you for one of the serving staff. Honestly, how embarrassing.'

'No, it's—'

'Please,' she said. 'Sam told me about how you're trying to find our waitress, and that you were with Gordon when he … I'm very interested to talk to you.'

Very interested? Most people blocked me and I was forced to lie, misrepresent myself and break and enter to get information. Here they were offering me clothes and champagne and inviting me in with open arms. I was desperate to know why.

'Well …'

'Great.' Sam smiled and patted my shoulder. 'Rochelle will sort you out. God knows she's got enough bloody clothes in that closet of hers.'

Rochelle rolled her eyes and clucked her tongue as if to say 'Men!' She led me back through the immaculate living room and up a set of plush, gold carpeted stairs. I tried to tread lightly knowing there was probably dirt on the soles of my boots.

At the top of the stairs we passed a closed door and I could have sworn I heard the faint rhythmic thumping of a bedhead whacking into a wall, although Rochelle didn't appear to notice. A pornographic image manifested itself and I shook my head to dislodge the thing. Trip Sibley had half the female population fantasising about him, and probably a fair proportion of the males. One more might cause his already inflated head to explode.

At the end of a carpeted hallway we reached a series of interconnected rooms. The first was an office, the last was the master bedroom and a walk-in wardrobe separated the two. Each of the rooms was fitted out in the same plush, minimalist white and gold scheme as the rest of the house, and all opened out onto a veranda that wrapped around the first floor and overlooked the harbour. Rochelle ushered me into the walk-in and pressed a button that made a mirrored wall slide open, revealing row upon row of designer clothes, most in plastic drycleaner bags. Coathangers clicked as she riffled through the outfits.

'You have a lovely home,' I said. I knew this was how you talked to rich folks. I'd seen it on TV.

'I'm going through a bit of a white and gold phase, can you tell?'

'Wasn't going to say anything.'

'It's just so crisp, classic. Timeless, don't you think?'

'Absolutely.' God I could be a suck.

'Dress?' she asked. 'Suit? Skirt and blouse?'

'Maybe just a top to go over my pants so I don't get mistaken for a waiter again.'

'Sure. How about this? It's from my hot-pink period.' She selected a hanger and lifted the plastic, revealing a sleeveless top with scalloped lace around the edges and a little bow on the front. Not exactly my style but cute nonetheless. I just hoped I could fill out the boob area.

Rochelle pulled at the fabric as though reading my mind. 'It stretches. Try it on, I'll be back in a second.'

She disappeared into the bedroom and I removed my black top and dumped it on the dressing table that ran the length of the wall. Picking up the pink number I got a squiz at the label. Chanel. Holy fuck. I couldn't. Okay, I could, but no red wine, rolling in the dirt or inhaling finger food like a pig at a trough. I slipped the blouse over my head, careful not to swipe lipstick or mascara on the neckline, and checked myself out in the mirror. The garment sucked my gut in and spilled me out above, creating the illusion of a small waist and abundant bust. Wow. The tops I bought from the five dollar rack had no such supernatural powers. A knock on the door and Rochelle pushed her head in.

'Looks great on you.'

'Thanks. I'll try my best not to spill anything on it.'

She laughed, thinking I was joking. I turned to head back downstairs. She held her hand up.

'Not so fast, miss. You can't wear Chanel without hair and makeup.'

I was already wearing makeup, but obviously not enough. 'It doesn't bother me … if you have to get back to your guests …'

She nudged me onto the bench seat and flicked a switch so the bulbs around the mirror lit up. 'I'm very fast. I have a knack for this sort of thing.' Rolling over on a padded stool, she set down her wine and rummaged around in the drawers underneath the table, pulling out Velcro rollers, hairspray, and a big silver cosmetics box. Her French manicured fingernails clicked against everything she touched and I decided that if she'd sworn a bit more and had a pack of Winfield Blue stashed between her tits, she'd have been a dead ringer for a fifty-something Chloe. I missed my ex best friend for a second, until I remembered the fight on Fitzroy Street and how she'd only give me work if I stooped to jelly wrestling. With friends like that …

Rochelle began winding my hair onto fat pink and yellow rollers and up close her perfume had a strong, almost powdery scent. She sniffed, pinched her nose as though trying to stop herself sneezing, tipped her head back and apologised. 'Sorry. Terrible hayfever. So how did you get involved in the search for our missing waitress?'

'My mum and Andi's mum Joy used to share a house. Joy hired me.'

'Sam's talked to the police about it. They told him she was writing an article about the girl who went missing all those years ago.'

'That's right.'

I wondered where she was going with the conversation as she brandished the largest can of hairspray I'd ever seen and aimed it at me. I must have looked alarmed. 'Don't worry,' she said, 'this stuff is fantastic. It has polymers. Close your eyes.'

I squeezed them shut and held my breath as a toxic cloud enveloped my head. When I finally opened my eyes I had to snap them shut again because she was coming at me with an eye shadow applicator.

'You know I met Andrea on a couple of occasions when we were down in Melbourne,' said Rochelle. The brush tickled my lids and it was like being nuzzled by a baby rabbit. 'She seemed so nice. It was a bit of a shock to find out she was dredging up that horrible business. It was hard enough the first time around.'

The stroking stopped and I opened my eyes. She was looking at me, green irises flecked with amber, eyebrows perfectly arched and coloured fawn, her nose too thin for her face. Probably the result of an overenthusiastic eighties rhino-plasty and it gave her a pinched look. She sipped chardonnay and I took the opportunity to toss down some champagne.

'The police exonerated Sam.' Her tone was almost pleading. 'There was absolutely no evidence. The only thing they had against him was the fact that he used to go out with her. You'd think that would be the end of it but mud sticks and we've spent the last twenty-five years trying to distance ourselves from the past. We've built up a successful business, contributed to the community, Sam's donated a lot of money to the church lately but no, he'll always be the "colourful" Sydney identity and I'll always be his slutty wife.' She took a large mouthful of wine and put the glass down next to the makeup case.

'Because you used to work at the Love Tunnel?'

'Mmm-hmm.' She swished a larger brush through a compact containing bronzer, tapped the excess into a tissue and swept it onto my cheeks in downward circles. 'Of course stripping was a lot different then to what it is now. More of a cabaret, I suppose, feathers and sequins and artistic routines. We didn't even go nude and honestly, people wear less at the beach these days. If I'd known it would follow me around for the rest of my life though, I don't think I'd … not that I had much choice. I was only nineteen when I started, from a broken home in the western suburbs, no prospects, no education. Sam was in the same boat. He grew up very poor, big family all squeezed into a two room cottage. I think that's why we got on so well, we both aspired to something more. In America they consider that admirable but here in Australia no one lets you forget where you came from. Trip mentioned you were a dancer too?'

'Yeah. I'm saving up to open my own detective agency.'

'That's great, but remember what happened to Sam and me.'

'I don't really care what people think of me,' I said, wondering whether that was actually true.

'Well, good for you, honey. I wish I could say the same.' She picked up a lip brush and dabbed it in a pot of gloss. 'Now open your mouth, just slightly.'

After she'd painted my lips she began to unravel my hair.

'Did you know Melody, the girl who disappeared?' I asked.

Rochelle pursed her fleshy lips and snorted air through her nose. 'Horrible little thing. A junkie. Lying, thieving. Rip you off as soon as look at you.' As she talked about her she tugged harder on the rollers, pulling my hair. I didn't squeal, just made like a kung fu master and took the pain.

'Half of Kings Cross probably wanted her dead. I don't like to speak ill of … but you're in the industry so you'd know what I mean. Some girls are bad news, looking for trouble.' She took a break to sip her wine and my scalp was grateful.

'God, listen to me, I must be boring you to death going on about myself like this. Tell me about you. Are you married? Kids?'

I laughed so hard I almost choked. 'Hell, no.'

'What about your parents?'

'Divorced. Dad's in computers, lives in the States, new wife, young family. Mum lectures in gender studies. She's here in Sydney.'

'Has she married again?'

'No, but she lives with a guy. Actually, I wanted to ask if you knew her. Peta Kirsch. Or maybe Joy Fowler, Andi's mother?'

'No.' She frowned. 'Should I?'

'It's just that I mentioned Sam's name to them and they freaked. It's like they were scared or something, and that doesn't seem to square with the man I met last night. Sure, he might have been a hell-raiser in his younger days, but your husband doesn't strike me as particularly evil.'

'Did they tell you why they were so frightened?'

'Nope. Wouldn't reveal a thing.'

'Sorry, but the names don't mean anything to me.'

'Sure? They both lived in Potts Point, were involved in the women's movement, radical feminists …'

'Feminists?' Rochelle sat straight up. 'I think I know how they know Sam.'

chapterthirty-three

'Tip your head forward, shake it out and flip it back.'

I did as Rochelle asked, endured another squirt of noxious mist and looked in the mirror. Bloody hell. I was her twin, only dark haired and twenty years younger.

'Thanks,' I said, not adding 'I think'.

'Now let's go talk to Sam. He can tell you what happened.'

As we passed the bedroom I noticed the thumping was still going on. The same session or were they onto round two or three? Not that I gave a shit, I reminded myself, gritting my teeth and walking on by.

Downstairs the party had gotten louder and the band was bashing out an instrumental version of 'The Lady Is a Tramp'. I sang along under my breath, substituting 'lady' with 'chef'. Sam was talking to a group of urban professionals and when

Rochelle trotted over and whispered in his ear he turned to me and held up his finger as if to say 'just a moment'. On her way back Rochelle dragged a pink-shirted man over to meet me.

'Simone, this is Perry, a good friend of mine.'

Perry had straight, light brown hair, a square jaw and was handsome in a bland, forgettable sort of way. I shook his hand. His grip was strong and his teeth were almost as white as Rochelle's.

'Nice to meet you.'

'Same,' I said, glancing over at Sam, eager to find out what he had to say.

'What do you do?' Perry asked.

'Private detective. You?'

'Kickboxing instructor, consultant.'

'Great,' I drawled, trying to be polite.

'Perry won silver in the last WSA Championships at Surfers,' gushed Rochelle. 'He is sooo strong.' She squeezed his bicep and looked from me to Perry and back again. It was an odd, almost expectant look and I couldn't quite work out what was going on. Was she matchmaking, trying to set us up? She'd been terribly nice and forthcoming and although she didn't seem to be quite the 'bitch on wheels' Dillon had described, I'd never been able to do the whole 'instant best friend' thing. I was starting to feel a little hemmed in and decided that as soon as I'd talked to Sam I was out of there.

Sam excused himself from the group he was talking to and walked over. He'd rolled up his sleeves against the heat and un-buttoned the top of his shirt and I noticed the ropy scar and a small crucifix nestling in his chest hair, dangling from a chain. I hadn't picked him for a god-botherer, especially after his comment about blowjobs and wilted spinach, but with a surname like Doyle and a cross around his neck—Irish Catholic for sure.

'I think I do know your mother,' he said. 'Come to the boathouse and talk?'

'Sure.'

We dodged a couple of Grecian urns, rounded the swimming pool and crossed the manicured lawn. Sam looked me up and down.

'When you and Rochelle came down the stairs it was like some mad scientist was cloning a master race of big haired ex strippers.'

'Tell me about it.' I patted my 'do'. 'I get back on the Ducati there'll be no need for a helmet.'

We reached the bright, white boathouse via a worn set of steps, sandstone like the house. The abundance of yellow rock gave Sydney a sunny, colonial air and made Melbourne's buildings seem dark and brooding by comparison. Of course, dark and brooding had grown on me in the past few years.

Water sloshed around the wooden piles, the jetty creaked and a strong salt and barnacle smell rose from the harbour. Sam held the side door open and I saw the sparse, rectangular space had been converted into a very basic studio apartment. The bare floorboards were unpolished, a small bathroom with a sliding door slotted into one corner and in the middle of the room a kitchen of sorts hugged the wall. Sink, bar fridge and a bench with one of those two-plate gas burners you get from camping stores. There was no TV, but a stereo unit sat on a wooden packing crate opposite the kitchen. A row of mostly black shirts and pants hung from a pine clothes rack, next to a neatly made futon on the floor. At the end of the room, where double doors opened out onto the water, two red vinyl arm-chairs were angled to take in the view. I thought back to the master bedroom. There had been no sign of Sam, none of his clothes hanging in the closet, no blokey stuff that I could see.

'You live out here.' It wasn't a question.

'Yeah.'

He didn't elaborate and I thought it best not to pry into the state of his marriage before he'd spilled the beans on my mum.

'No boat?' I asked.

'Sold it.'

'Nice boat?'

'Yacht. Want a drink?'

I nodded. I didn't want to get pissed but I had a feeling the unholy glob of rice was soaking up all the booze.

'I hope you like tequila, 'cause it's all I got.'

'It's okay,' I shrugged. 'Bad hangovers though. I remember this one night drinking El Toro with a bunch of backpackers and—'

Sam shuddered and I thought he might spit on the floor. 'Calling that shit tequila's like comparing Passion Pop with Krug.' He pointed to a row of bottles on the shelf above the sink. They were squat and rounded and looked like something you'd dredge up from a sunken pirate galleon. 'Blanco, Reposado or Añejo?'

I had no idea what he was talking about. 'You choose.'

He pulled down a bottle and a couple of shot glasses and told me to put some music on the stereo. I walked over to a black box with a record player on top that would have been state-of-the-art fifteen years earlier, crouched down to switch on the power then stood up to check out the records and CDs crammed on the shelf above. Lots of country, a bit of soul, some sixties and seventies, Mozart requiems. Nothing from the eighties onward but I could hardly imagine Doyle bopping around to 'Girls Just Wanna Have Fun' or donning a flannie and playing air guitar to Nirvana. A bunch of dog-eared novels by the likes of Hemingway and Faulkner were lined up on the shelf, and I'd already spotted a bible with a faded leather cover on the floor by the bed.

The man was freaking me out. I much preferred your classic bad guys with evil laughs, fast cars and noses full of cocaine. Crooks like the murderous lawyer I'd tangled with a few months before. My relationship with him had been quite simple: he'd wanted to kill me and I'd refused to die. Not so great at the time, but at least I'd known where I stood. Not anymore. Doyle was being friendly, as though he wanted me to like him. Was he really a nice guy, despite what everyone said, or a criminal mastermind and me the biggest dupe of all time?

I considered putting on a Gram Parsons record but having grown up in an era of tapes and compact disks I was scared I'd scratch it, so I picked out a Johnny Cash CD, *Unchained*, and stuck it in the player instead. Sam took the shot glasses over to the armchairs and clinked them down on a scratched little side table in between. The first song on the disk was 'Rowboat', appropriate considering the location, and Sam smiled.

'Why'd you pick this?'

'Are you kidding? I've loved Johnny Cash since I was a kid, which is totally fucking bizarre.'

'How come?'

''Cause I grew up listening to a bunch of hippy shit … bongos, whales mating, protest songs. If I never hear another pan pipe in my life it'll still be too soon. I remember hearing "Ring of Fire" when I was little but I'm not sure where. My mum hates country. Reckons it's redneck music and refuses to let me play it in her house.' I lifted my glass to slam it down and Sam held out his hand to stop me.

'You don't shoot it. This is Gran Reposado, one hundred percent blue agave, aged for two years. It's meant to be savoured.'

'Oh.' I took a tentative sip and a mellow, smoky liquid seeped across my tongue. I hadn't known tequila could be so smooth and I wished I'd never found out. I didn't exactly need a new drink to become obsessed with. 'Wow. That's amazing.'

He nodded.

As my brown-nosing had gone down so well with Rochelle I decided it wouldn't hurt to try it on Sam. 'You know, you've got a bit of a Johnny Cash thing going on yourself,' I said. 'The black outfits, gravelly voice. You even sounded like him at that karaoke bar last night.'

'That's very flattering but it's not true. There's only one Man in Black.' His voice was stern but I saw a corner of his mouth lift, and could tell he was pleased. I was almost as accomplished at sucking up as I was snuffling around rubbish bins.

'So how do you know Mum?'

He was silent for a second and I followed his gaze out over the water. Clouds were banking up, coming in from the west. Huge clumps piling on top of each other, purple-black like a bruise.

'She ever told you about the Cross in the late seventies?'

'No. Can't get a thing out of her. Weird, because on most topics she won't shut up.'

Sam ran his hand over his chin. I couldn't actually see any stubble but heard it rasp against his palm. He put down his shot glass, rested both hands on the arms of the chair and leaned back, like someone about to take off in a plane.

'There was a protest, outside the Love Tunnel.'

'I knew it. When?'

'Jesus. I don't know. Seventy-nine, eighty?'

'What about?'

'Exploitation? Promoting violence against women? Take your pick.'

'Mum and Joy would have definitely been in that. What happened?'

'A group of about twenty of them were marching around on the footpath in front of the Tunnel, carrying placards, yelling slogans and generally intimidating anyone who tried to enter the club. First I asked them to leave nicely and when that didn't work I shouted, demanding they piss off.'

'I'm guessing that wasn't successful either.'

'No. By that stage Don, the owner, had got wind and rang to call me a soft cock for not doing anything about it. We had two bouncers who were itching to have a go, but I told them to back off, hoping the protesters would get bored and pack it in. Don ordered me to ring some of his friends from the Darlinghurst and Kings Cross police.'

Sam finished his drink, got up with a sigh that made him seem every one of his sixty something years and crossed to the kitchen, retrieving one of the tequila bottles and bringing it back to the small table. Up close I could see the brand was Patron. The bottle hand blown with little air bubbles lodged in the glass. He refilled his drink but I put my hand over mine. I still had a little left, and an interview with Daisy in two hours.

'So what happened?'

'Don Davison was never what you'd call a sensitive, new age guy and neither were his cop mates. Violent, corrupt bastards. We used to pay them off every week so we could keep operating. Anyway, it got ugly. Even uglier than I thought it would. I'd hoped the cops would go easy on the protesters, since they were female, but it didn't turn out that way. If anything it was the opposite. The women resisted and the coppers laid into them worse than if they'd been blokes. The guys seemed outraged that a bunch of femos and diesel dykes would challenge them on their turf. It was like …'

'An affront to god, country and scone-baking Australian womanhood?'

'Something like that.'

'You got involved in the stoush?'

'No. Shit no. I used to be a boxer and I'd done a lot of … security work for Don. But I'd never hit a woman.'

'Try and stop it?'

Sam was silent for a bit, staring at the clouds piling up on the horizon as Johnny sang about breaking out of a rusty cage. The music was upbeat, but the lyrics were sad. Sam lit a Lucky Strike and offered the pack to me. My throat was still raw from the one I'd scabbed at the Hot Rock so I refused. Little Miss Goody Two Shoes, paying penance for the night before. He exhaled smoke and a gust of wind sucked it out the double doors and dispersed the plume across the water.

'What could I do? I ran the fucking place, I worked for Don and you didn't say no to him if you wanted a long and fruitful life. Seeing the cops bash the women made me sick to my stomach but I didn't have any say.'

'What happened after they were beaten up?'

'Charged with resisting arrest. Verballed probably.'

'It still doesn't explain why she's so scared of you.'

'It wasn't just the arrests and bashings. The protesters were going to go to the media about it and create a big stink. Don and some of his mates threatened them, their families … their kids. Because I was manager and had a bit of a reputation for standover and so forth, it must have looked like it came from me.'

'But it didn't.'

He looked me in the eye. 'No.'

'Did the protest happen before or after Melody disappeared?'

'Before.'

I sat forward and leaned my elbows on my knees. I was nervous, but I had to ask. 'Did you make her disappear?'

His gaze didn't waver. 'No.'

'Do you know who did?'

'No.' He blinked. Didn't mean he was lying, maybe his eyes were just tired.

I took a tiny sip of smooth tequila and sat back in my chair. 'It kind of makes sense about my mother. Only why would she still be scared now?'

He shrugged.

'And why are you telling me all this when you don't have to?'

'Why wouldn't I? I've got nothing to hide.'

Well that was bullshit. Everybody on earth had something to hide.

'You know, I never even liked running the strip club,' he said, out of the blue.

'Come on,' I laughed, 'it's every guy's dream. Naked chicks, pussy on tap.'

'I started at the illegal casinos, worked my way up from bouncer to floor manager, then Don had me manage one of his restaurants. I liked the restaurants and when he put me in charge of the Fu—' he stopped himself just in time—'the Tunnel, it felt like a step backwards even though he was paying me more. But you didn't argue with the Don. I was there for five years and, sure, I met some good people and we had some times, but it wasn't the life I wanted for myself. The Tunnel wasn't one of your upmarket lap dancing clubs like today. There was plenty of shit going on out the back. Don encouraged the dancers to sleep with his mates and a lot of the girls were addicted to heroin. In fact Don preferred to pay them in smack, if they were that way inclined.'

'Like Melody?' I asked.

Sam shook his head. 'She didn't use. Anyway, it could be depressing. I think I sympathised with the protesters 'cause they weren't too far off the mark.'

I looked at him. Was he playing the SNAG to get me onside? Some guys did that. They'd turn up at a strip club, pay money to ogle your box then come over all reconstructed and say stuff like, 'How awful for you, being exploited.' It always offended me because I knew it was just an underhanded pickup routine. But why was Sam doing it? He definitely wasn't trying to crack onto me, I would have gotten the vibe. Even more interesting was his description of the Love Tunnel and of Melody, totally different to Rochelle's. One of them was lying.

Sam stubbed out his cigarette. 'You going to tell your mother what you know?'

'If she's talking to me. She wanted me to leave Sydney and I didn't. We're kind of having a fight.'

'You should apologise.'

I laughed. 'My god. If she could hear you say that.'

'I'm serious. Cherish your family. In the end they're all you've got.'

I resisted the urge to cross my eyes and poke my tongue in my cheek.

Sam went on. 'I was estranged from mine when they found out what sort of work I was doing, and Rochelle and I never had children …'

'What about your stepdaughter Holly?'

'We never warmed to each other when she was a kid. Not that I blame her, it must have been hard losing both her parents.'

'Do you get on now?'

'We see each other when we have to.'

'And Dillon?' I asked, remembering Trip's theory.

Sam poured himself another drink, slumped in his chair and sighed. 'If I have to hear him go on about another bloody short film … I shouldn't have kept giving him money, but

Holly dotes on him and I guess I've always felt guilty packing her off to boarding school when she was growing up. Must have forked out at least thirty thousand over the last couple of years and nothing to show for it. He never gets selected for any of the festivals because his movies are crap and his head's so far up his arse. In fact, I think Dillon's even more vain than Rochelle, which is a hard ask.' He looked down at his glass then up at me. 'Sorry. Tequila's talking.'

'You don't have to worry about me. I met the guy, thought he was a wanker.'

'Yeah, well, he's up the creek now I've retired and Rochelle's running the business. She keeps a much tighter rein on the purse strings than I did.'

'Rochelle runs the business?'

'Yeah. I retired after the bypass.'

I must have looked amazed because Sam said, 'Don't let that dizzy blonde routine fool you. She's smart and ambitious as hell. Did her HSC by correspondence when she was twenty-eight, commerce at uni then an MBA.'

'It's probably none of my business,' I said, 'but you guys are separated, right?'

'Yeah. We had a good innings, twenty-five years. Just grew apart, had different goals. I wanted to sell the house and business and live more simply and she wanted to get ahead. She's ten years younger so I don't blame her, but I'm over chasing the almighty dollar. It's not what it's cracked up to be.'

The bible quote about the rich man entering heaven and the camel passing through the eye of a needle entered my head, but I didn't say it out loud. The sun dipped behind the clouds, turning the air cold and the water grey. A fishy wind picked up and goose bumps pimpled my bare arms. I finished the tequila and poured another half shot, just for warmth. The title song, 'Unchained', began to play and Sam raised himself out of his chair, turned the volume up then parked himself back down. It was too loud to speak so we sat in silence, him in his takeoff position, me with my legs curled under me, taking little sips of tequila and rubbing the backs of my arms.

I stopped thinking about the case for a moment and let the song wash over me. I'd never really listened to the words before and realised it was a plea for redemption, a lament by someone about to die, perhaps. Cash's voice was low and haunting and the deep bass vibrated in my chest cavity and made the hair on my arms stand even further on end. I decided it was the saddest song I'd ever heard, which was really saying something as I'd spent my adolescence moping around playing The Smiths.

When the song ended I turned to Sam and drew a sharp breath. He'd slumped in his chair, chin on chest, and I thought he was dead until I looked closer and made out the faint rise and fall of his chest. He was sleeping. I grabbed a wispy blanket from the end of the futon, laid it over him and took one last look at the harbour. The clouds were black now, flickering with lightning and spreading silently across the late afternoon sky.

chapter thirty-four

Back at the entertainment area the party had wound up. Waiters cleared glasses, the band packed their instruments in padded black cases and only a few diehard guests remained, guzzling the last of the imported booze, designer clothes slightly askew. Pink shirt guy was standing on his own drinking bottled water and I walked over to him.

'Hey,' he said. 'Having a good time?'

'Yeah, great. You seen Rochelle?'

'She was here a second ago. Must be around somewhere.'

'It's just that I have to get going,' I said.

'Need a lift?'

'No, I'll get a cab, I'm fine.'

'Sure? I don't mind doing it.'

He hadn't even asked where I was going. Creepy. Was he

trying to pick me up? Perhaps Rochelle had told him I was single, or maybe he had a thing for chicks with big eighties hair. Either way, I didn't trust a man who didn't drink.

'Yeah. I have to meet someone. If you see Rochelle can you say bye for me, and thanks for the top? I'll leave it in her dressing room.'

'No worries.'

I headed up the stairs to the master bedroom to change. The door to the first room was open and I glanced inside. No rutting chef, but the king sized bed was all crumpled and empty glasses littered the side table. My mouth pursed. God, I was turning into one of those people I loathed, the types who hated public displays of affection and snidely suggested you get a room. Just because I wasn't getting any didn't mean I should begrudge any one else a root. I should be happy for them. Yeah, right.

I passed through the office into the dressing room, nudged the door half shut with my butt and had just pulled off the pink top when I heard Rochelle talking, coming up the hall. I was about to pop my head out and let her know I was in there when I realised that not only was she talking to Trip, but they were discussing me. I leaned my back against the door and put my ear to the crack.

'… still in the boathouse with Sam,' Trip said.

'Really.' Leather creaked as she sat in her desk chair. 'Do you think he's …?'

'Nah. They both like that fucked-up country music and he's gotta be too old for her. I mean, she wouldn't do me,' he said, incredulous. 'Need a bloody crowbar to get those legs apart. I thought strippers were supposed to be easy!'

'I'm not easy.'

'I'll knock you over one day, babe, soon as you ditch that poofta in the pink shirt.'

'It's the fashion for men on the Gold Coast. And if he hears you call him that he'll whip your arse twelve ways to Tuesday. You know you wouldn't stand a chance.'

'Whatever. So where's this coke? I'm riding back to Melbourne soon.'

'Bedroom.'

The chair squeaked again. Oh shit. They had to come through the dressing room to get to the bedroom. I looked around, mind running a million miles an hour. Closet? Auto-mated. What if it wouldn't close from inside? Snatching up Rochelle's top and my handbag I dashed into the master bedroom, plush carpet muffling my steps, had a split second to decide against the ensuite—coke could be in there, someone might need a pee—and dived straight toward the four poster bed, flattened my body, splayed my limbs and crawled under just like Alex's cat. I lay on my stomach, head turned to the side, lungs bursting, not daring to breathe. A few seconds later Rochelle's strappy heels and Trip's motorcycle boots came into view. Trip sat on the bed and it dipped, pushing springs into my back. Rochelle was rummaging around in the bedside drawer. I couldn't see what she was doing but soon heard the unmistak-able chink and scrape of a platinum credit card on a mirror.

'So what's happening when Jouissance reopens?' Trip bounced and I started to feel exceedingly claustrophobic.

'Nothing. Too much heat.' I heard her snort up a line.

'How about when it blows over?' He leaned over and did one himself.

'With the Fraud Squad sniffing around?' She talked like she had a head cold. 'All business involves risk, but not that fucking much. The deal's over, Trip.'

'C'mon, they won't get anything on us. Yasmin's been great. The books balance and it's impossible to trace all the cash going through a restaurant and bar.'

'You'd be surprised. The police have some pretty sophisti-cated computer programs these days. Look, Don says no.'

Don Davison? But wasn't he ancient history?

'What about the hotel?'

'None of your beeswax.'

'Pity. I was enjoying all the cloak and dagger stuff, as well as the extra money.'

'I don't think money's going to be a problem for you, Trip. Once you're on TV you'll be a bona fide celebrity chef, not just a legend in your own lunchtime. You need extra cash just put out a glossy cookbook before Christmas, or endorse some instant meals.'

'Bitch,' Trip chuckled. 'Rack me up another line.'

She did and they both had another snort. After a minute or so of sniffing Trip said, 'I suppose I should look on the bright side. I won't have to keep lying to Sam.'

'You're hilarious. You'll proposition his wife—'

'Ex, almost.'

'But you don't want to lie to him. Listen, we didn't lie, just omitted certain facts, and we couldn't have told him. Both you and I know he's totally lost it since the heart attack.'

'I wouldn't say that. He's not feeble, or fucked in the head. It's just, shit, having a near death experience, with the tunnel and the white light, that'd freak me out.'

Rochelle scoffed. 'That bullshit is caused by lack of oxygen to the brain, nothing more, and quite frankly I find his whole repentant act pretty hypocritical.'

'Yeah, if I turn all holy roller just shoot me in the head. Guilt's such a useless emotion, don't you reckon?'

'Absolutely.'

'But I have to say, Gordon keeps weighing on my mind.'

'Honey, I told you that was nothing to do with us. I was as shocked as you were. I swear I didn't tell Don that Gordon had spoken to the police. Of course, Don does have connections, but look, it could have been an accident.'

'Not the way Simone tells it.'

'Simone …' She laughed. 'Nice work bringing her, by the way. I found out she's not even interested in us, just wanted to know about her mother and obsessed with finding that fucking waitress. Shit, I'd like to find her myself and slap the silly bitch for disappearing and bringing all this heat. Can you believe she got a job at Jouissance just to go undercover and investigate Sam? Treacherous little cow.'

Trip bounced on the bed another couple of times and sniffed. 'Fuck, this coke's gotten me horny.'

'What a surprise.'

'C'mon, Rochelle.' He patted the bed next to him.

'We've been through this before. I'm old enough to be your mother.'

'And hotter than most chicks half your age.'

'You're very sweet.' I heard her open the drawer and deposit the mirror inside. 'Enough of this gasbagging. You've got to hit the road and I want to check the boatshed. They've been down there too long and I don't trust Sam not to say something he shouldn't.'

'Like what?' Trip said. 'He doesn't know anything.'

'He knows enough.'

I gave them a minute to get down the stairs then dragged myself out from under the bed. As much as I wanted to riffle around in Rochelle's office drawers I knew I had to get out of there as soon as I could. I had a couple of minutes if she made it down to the boathouse, even less if she ran into pink shirt Perry and he told her I'd gone upstairs. I was halfway across the room, heading for the walk-in wardrobe, when I sensed something and froze in the middle of the room in my stretch pants and bra, bag in one hand, Rochelle's top in the other. I slowly turned towards the French doors that led to the balcony.

Perry was on the other side of the glass, standing perfectly still and staring at me.

chapterthirty-five

Perry's mouth stretched into the horribly insincere smile you see on game show hosts and people whose minds have been taken over by aliens, and a creepy feeling rippled across my flesh, like an egg full of spiders had just hatched in my hair and they were scuttling down my spine. He pointed from the bed to me and waggled his finger like I'd been a very naughty girl. Run, I told myself, but my legs refused to move and I was loath to turn my back on him. He reached for the doorhandle, pushed it down and the smile turned to a scowl. The door was locked. The neurons controlling my legs sputtered into life and I spun, dashed across the room, straight through the walk-in wardrobe and into the office.

Perry ran along the balcony at the same time, and burst through the unlocked office door just as I popped out of the dressing room. I stopped so suddenly that my feet skidded out in front of me and I fell on my arse on the carpet. I flipped on my front, struggled to my knees and was about to stand when he grabbed my ankles and yanked them up like I was a wheelbarrow, so my face hit the floor. I clutched at the carpet as he pivoted my body and dragged me back into the dressing room. He threw my feet on the ground, closed both doors then loomed over me with his hands on his hips, the creeped out smile back on his face. I lay there, looking up at him, trying to get my breath back.

'I knew you shouldn't be left alone,' he said. 'Rochelle's going to be pretty pissed off when I tell her you were hiding under the bed.'

'I wasn't hiding, I dropped something and …' I couldn't think of anything and the excuse petered out. Not that he would have believed me anyway. I tried a different tack. 'My police friend, Detective Senior Constable Alex Christakos, knows exactly where I am and he'll—'

'The only note in the hotel was from the cop to you.'

My god, he'd been in the hotel? What was going on? 'I called him.'

'No you didn't.'

'You don't know that.'

'Yeah, I do. If you'd called him you wouldn't have just bull-shitted about a note.'

I suddenly remembered that I *had* texted Alex before I left the hotel, telling him I was going to spend the afternoon at the movies and that I'd be at the Coopers Arms in Newtown at five, figuring the truthful statement would cancel out the lie. Now it was too late.

'Okay … well … I'll scream.'

'Who'll hear you? Trip's taken off. Sam's passed out in the boathouse, the guests have gone and the walls are solid sandstone.'

The bastard had a point.

'So what happens now?' I asked, propping myself up on my elbows and stalling for time. 'You gonna kill me or can we make some sort of deal?' While I spoke I was checking for a weapon out of the corner of my eye. Something, anything, that would give me some advantage against a strong, agile, six foot tall goddamn kickboxing champion.

'It's up to the lady,' he said.

Great. It seemed to me that anybody who had pissed off 'the lady' had come to a bad end. Like Gordon. I thought of the driver of the blue car. I'd only glimpsed him for a split second but he'd seemed tall, square jawed. Put a baseball cap and a pair of dark glasses on freaky pink-shirt Perry …

'You ran over Gordon.'

The grin stayed in place.

'You ran over Gordon … you're too big to be wheelie bin guy … The possum head. You do that too?'

'Possum head? What are you talking about?'

'But I don't think you kidnapped Andi. The way Rochelle was talking, it wasn't you guys …'

'Enough chitchat. I want you to get up, slowly, turn around and put both hands behind you.' He dug about in his pants pocket and pulled out a couple of hard plastic ties, the restraint of choice for riot police and outback serial killers. With those on I'd be even more helpless than I already was.

'And what if I refuse?'

He dropped into a fighting stance and made a couple of fists. 'Then you get a taste of the ancient art of Muay Thai.' He pummelled his fists until they were a blur and kicked one leg into the air for emphasis. Poser. But I was still fucked. And the worst thing was, it was all for nothing. Sam Doyle wasn't involved, and Rochelle? She was caught up in some crooked deal with the Don, probably ordered the hit on Gordon and might have had something to do with Melody's disappearance, but not Andi's. She'd seemed genuinely shocked that Andi had been undercover at Jouissance.

'Stand up,' he ordered.

As I hauled myself to my feet I glanced at the dressing table and spotted the only items I could conceivably use as weapons, but Perry's reflexes were a lot faster than mine and if I lunged he'd stop me before I got hold of them. There was only one thing I could do. No guarantee it'd work, but I had to try.

'Now turn around,' he said.

I started to obey, but at the last second spun back around and launched myself at him, scratching, punching and kicking with all my might. As expected, he retaliated straight away, a sharp jab to the jaw that snapped my head back and clicked my teeth together, then a roundhouse kick in the ribs that sucked the air from my lungs and sent me flying. I crashed against the dressing table, slid along and flopped to the floor, sweeping all Rochelle's makeup and hair products with me. Groaning and gasping for air I curled into a ball, assorted objects digging painfully into my bare torso.

'Get up,' Perry barked.

I just moaned.

He nudged me with his trainer. 'Get the fuck up. That was nothing. I hardly touched you, you stupid bitch.'

I didn't move, just continued to whimper until he was forced to lean over and grab my arm to try and pull me to my feet. As he rolled me around to face him I held out the canister of hairspray I'd been gripping beneath me and squirted it right in his eyes. He bellowed and staggered back and I dropped the spray, seized the metal makeup box by its handle and swung it into his temple. He fell backwards onto his butt and I jumped up and leapt over him, heading for the office door, but he grabbed my ankle and I tumbled to the carpet. I kicked back as hard as I could and struggled free. Knowing he wouldn't be down for long I sprinted through the office, out the door and headed down the hallway for the stairs.

I was on the landing, hands on the banisters, about to propel myself down, when I saw Rochelle on her way up. She looked at me, screeched something unintelligible and I turned and bolted back into the office. Perry was staggering out of the walk-in, swearing and holding his fists against his eyes, and I ran straight out the French doors onto the balcony, looking around wildly. I briefly considered jumping into the pool, but it was so far away I would have splattered on the terracotta tiles before I got there.

A couple of metres beyond the balcony, on the master bedroom side, a palm sprouted, tall as the house. No time to think, I ran toward it, clambered over the railing and launched myself at it, holding out my arms and squeezing my eyes shut. I slammed into the tree face first and slid jerkily down, pants tearing and belly scraping painfully against the rough bark, until I fell in a heap at the bottom. I wobbled into a standing position, didn't stop to look around and took off down the side of the house, ran up the stone steps and tried the gate. Locked.

The sandstone wall was at least eight feet high but I was powering on adrenaline. I took a few steps back, ran and jumped, scrabbling up, fingers searching the crevices, nails breaking, boots scuffing the rough stone. As I rolled over the top I saw Rochelle and Perry run from the house. I wouldn't make it. They'd get me in the lane. I dropped, overbalanced, hit my knee on the uneven footpath and got up. I wanted to scream for help but my lungs were straining so badly I could hardly breathe, and all I managed was a strangled cry.

Looking up the lane I saw a white Tarago twenty metres away, parked half on the footpath, engine idling, rear doors open. One of the guys from the jazz band was loading equipment into the back. I heard Rochelle's heels clicking on the stone steps, knew it was only a matter of moments before they burst through the gate, so I dashed toward the van, pushed past the muso, jumped in and lay flat on my back behind a PA.

'What the—?' The guy scratched his white beard, astonished that a wild haired, half dressed chick had just leapt into the wagon.

'Would you believe I'm a groupie?'

The guy in the rear passenger seat, also sporting a beard but no moustache, put his arm on the back of the seat and turned around. 'We're a middle aged jazz band, we don't have groupies.'

'Okay, I'm a PI and someone's trying to kill me. Drive!'

They looked even more dubious.

'For fuck's sake,' I rasped, tears sprouting into my eyes. 'Look at me. Just get me out of here, please.' The musos exchanged a glance and I heard the gate open down the street and Rochelle's heels click on the asphalt. I hunkered down and closed my eyes reasoning, like an ostrich, that if I couldn't see them, they couldn't see me. Rochelle's voice was calm and bright.

'Hi. Just wanted to thank you again for the show. It was fabulous. Uh, you didn't happen to see anyone come past here, did you?'

The old guy scratched his beard again. 'No, but fuck me if I didn't just see some chick with only a bra on run down to the opposite end of the street.' And he slammed the door and got in the van.

chapterthirty-six

The jazz band wanted to drop me at the Balmain police station but I told them I was meeting a cop in Newtown and they were happy to drive the few extra k's. It wasn't every day a half naked PI jumped into the back of their van and they were so excited they started flapping around like a bunch of chooks. White-hair dude lent me his dress shirt and beard-with-no-moustache gave me a bottle of spring water. The driver wanted to know what had happened. Middle aged was pushing it. He had liver spots on his tufty scalp and was seventy if he was a day.

'Client confidentiality.' I gulped water and wiped my mouth with the back of my hand. 'Can't tell you.'

'Or you'll have to kill us, eh?'

They all laughed and I smiled politely, like I hadn't heard that one before.

We spent the rest of the twenty minute drive listening to Louis Armstrong and I answered general questions about PI work and delighted them with graphic descriptions of peeing into funnels on stakeout. Chatting with the guys helped me calm down but I still shuddered every time I thought about those restraints. The little plastic strips were somehow more threatening than handcuffs and rope combined.

They pulled up on King Street, outside the Coopers Arms, and even from inside the van I could hear a whining guitar and feel the muffled thump of drums reverberate in my chest cavity. I got out and asked the guy how I could return his shirt and he waved me away. 'Keep it. I'll be dining out on this for years.'

I slid the van door until it slammed, waved them off and looked around. The late afternoon sky boiled with puffy grey clouds but there was no rain, only an expectant wind swirling exhaust fumes and food smells. How long since I'd been in Newtown? Four, five years? I'd expected huge changes but King Street was pretty much the same, dirty, narrow and crammed with buses, cars and taxis, all with tail lights flaring crimson in the dusk. Ancient terrace buildings leaned into each other, their ground floors housing Thai restaurants, cafés, bookshops and record stores. Some fancy looking bistros and expensive clothing emporiums had sprung up in a nod to rising real estate prices, but Clem's Fried Chicken still stood on the corner across from the 7-Eleven, crisp mountains of golden wings and drumsticks warming in the display case, filling the air with a moist, salty scent. Good to see the place was still ministering to the desperately hungover, and sending the National Heart Foundation a cheerful 'fuck you'.

I stepped into the pub and was hit by a wall of jangly surf-rock and the yeasty tang of beer. The Coopers Arms had once been the Shakespeare, an early opener full of vinyl-jacketed drug dealers and shuddery old men, and when they'd changed the name they'd done it up, but not much. The walls and wooden tables were uniformly brown, orange pillars held up the ceiling and a flat screen TV fixed high on the wall opposite the entrance broadcast rugby league. The only decoration was a mural of King Street painted on the wall behind the stage, if that's what you called the raised triangle in the corner where a punk chick was thrashing around in front of a drummer and a couple of squished guitar players.

Daisy wore fishnet tights, tartan hot pants and knee high leather boots. Her long black hair was streaked purple, blonde and blue and her net top showed off the bright red bra underneath. She bent over the mike growling a Cramps song, 'Dames, Booze, Chains and Boots', a grungy little refrain that made me want to stomp my feet and bang my head.

I scanned the rest of the crowded room. Locals, students, backpackers and dishevelled dudes I took to be old Sydney rock dinosaurs. Alex sat at the bar, drinking some sort of imported beer and thankfully not wearing his entire cop suit. He'd teamed the black pants with a chocolate top, the sleeves pushed up, but his slicked back hair and shiny shoes still looked too neat for Newtown. Being a suave, piano bar kinda guy the music and grungy surrounds must have pained him, but he seemed to be taking a certain amount of solace in Daisy's skimpy outfit, and the way she was grinding her pelvis against the mike stand. He didn't notice me until I was standing right next to him.

'Hey.'

He pulled his head back, checking out my unfortunate new look.

'Where the fuck have you been? I've been trying to call you for the last hour.'

'I lost my phone, and my bag.' I had to shout over the music.

'What happened to your hair?' he asked. 'And why are you wearing that ridiculous shirt?'

'Long story, let's—' I was just about to suggest we went out back where it was quieter when Daisy finished the song and announced the band was taking a short break. I wasn't sure she'd have any useful information but I had to cover my bases. 'Back in a sec.'

I pushed through the crowd and caught up to her at the other end of the bar just as the barman handed her an icy can of VB.

I tapped one sweaty shoulder. 'Daisy? Sorry I'm late. Simone.'

She swung around in the exaggerated fashion of someone who'd been drinking and doing god knows what other substances for an entire weekend.

'Hey!' She held me to her bosom like we were long lost sisters. 'I didn't think you were gonna show. Whatcha think of the band?'

Really out-of-it people made me feel as prim and sober as a school marm, but I knew that wouldn't score me any points so I summoned up the enthusiasm of a video DJ.

'You guys were going off!' I shouted over the crowd.

'Wooo!' Daisy yelled. She punched one arm into the air and staggered backwards, jostling a guy and spilling some of his beer. He glared at her but she just smiled, a huge grin that engulfed her face. 'I love this chick!' She hugged me again. She was a little taller than me and when my face pressed into her damp chest I smelled beer and cigarettes and some musky essential oil. I pulled away.

'Got time to talk about Andi?' I tried to catch her rather glazed eyes. She was looking over my shoulder.

'Who's that hot guy you were talking to?' She licked her lip stud. 'Boyfriend?'

'No, police officer.'

Cops and punks were natural enemies, in the wild. I'd hoped to turn her off.

'Handcuffs!' She put both wrists out in front of her and thrust her groin a couple of times.

'Not on him.'

She leaned towards me, conspiratorially. 'Big dick?'

'I really couldn't say.'

'Introduce me!'

'He's engaged.'

'And?'

'He's really straight.'

'Ha! So is spaghetti, until it's cooked.' She pushed through the crowd and marched over to him as I trotted along behind, thinking that this had been one more in a long line of really crap ideas.

'Hello, orrificer.' She saluted, swaying slightly. 'Cunt-stable Daisy.'

He looked from her to me, slightly puzzled, until his innate suaveness kicked in. 'Alex. Would you like a seat?' He moved to get up, but before he could vacate the stool she'd slipped sideways onto his lap and sat there, swinging her legs, one arm slung around his neck. I raised my eyebrows. He looked bemused.

'You looking for Andi too?' She put her face so close to his he was forced to pull his head back. She seemed to have completely forgotten about me.

'Yes he is,' I said quickly. 'We'd really like to know what—'

'Man, I thought she would have showed up by now. I love that girl. You know? She's my best friend.' She poked Alex's chest to emphasise each word. 'Just hope she hasn't done anything stupid, like last time.'

'Last time?' I asked. She didn't hear, too busy gazing at Alex and running one black painted fingernail along his jaw. I gave him a look that said 'go along with it'. He nodded.

'What happened last time?' he asked.

She smiled, sighed and leaned back so far he had to grab the bar with one hand and catch her around the shoulders with the other so they wouldn't both topple off the stool.

'Tried to top herself. Year Twelve. Took three packs of Panadol and hid in our shed.'

Joy had told me Andi had run away once before. I hadn't known she'd ended up at Daisy's.

'Doesn't sound hardcore but that shit's toxic. My parents took her to hospital, stomach pumped.'

'Joy didn't—'

'Her mother didn't know. Andi, like, fucking begged my folks not to tell her. Said she wouldn't do it again.'

'Why did she …?'

'That's the stupid part. It was over this cocksucker at school who fucked her, dumped her, broke her heart.'

'She doesn't seem the type.'

'Tell me about it. She's got her shit together in every way except that. Going for the wrong fuckin' guys.'

'Macho arseholes?' I asked, thinking of Trip. 'Good in bed but fuckwits in every other respect?' I'd had more than a few myself.

'Nah. That's my type.' She laughed. 'Rugged, manly, fucks like a jackhammer.'

She pulled on the neck of Alex's top, glanced down at his abundant chest hair and smiled lewdly. It took great effort not to cross my arms and roll my eyes. She was all over him, sexual harassment basically. If the genders had been reversed she'd have been in the local lock-up by now.

'Andi always went for pretty boys, more into themselves than her. Cute faces, smooth chests, probably no fuckin' balls. I always reckoned they looked like girls. Maybe being raised with the lezzies warped her brain. Fuck, I dunno.'

I drew breath. She'd just described someone whose name had been coming up in a damn lot of conversations.

'Daisy!' I had to swish my fingers in front of her face to snatch her attention from Alex's chest. She let go his neckline and it snapped back into place. 'The guy that dumped her in high school. What was his name?'

'Brendan.'

Not Dillon. Of course not. Dillon grew up in Canberra.

'What did he look like?' I asked.

She screwed up her face and looked into the middle distance, trying to think through all that beer. 'Titanic,' she said.

'What?'

'Like the guy in *Titanic*. But before he hit twenty-five and chunked out.'

'Leonardo DiCaprio?'

'That's the one.'

A bad theory came into my head. What if Andi and Dillon were having an affair, as Trip had maintained, and the phone call she received was him breaking it off. She'd been drinking, taking drugs and she freaked, drove into the bush, pills, razor blade, hose to the exhaust pipe ... then left a message on my phone: 'Simone, you've got to come find me. I'm gonna die.' The phone cut out. Bush, bad reception. Jesus. She could've changed her mind at the last minute, too late to save herself ...

Why hadn't I thought of it earlier? I'd been so sure her disappearance was part of some dastardly plot, I hadn't seriously considered suicide. I thought of everything that had made me suspect foul play but was able to rationalise it away. Missing photos? Could be of Dillon. Person who attacked me in alley? Random freak. Possum head? Kids playing a joke that I, paranoid android, took seriously. Andi's laptop and files? They'd find them when they found the body. An image played itself out in my mind, almost like a film, bushwalkers trekking down a lonely dirt track, wondering about the strange smell, finding the Datsun with Andi inside, bloated, unrecognisable, green-purple skin splitting open like overripe fruit.

Hand shaking I reached for the water jug on the bar, poured myself a glass and drank it down in one go. But her bag. How did that end up in Sydney? She couldn't have driven all the way up here, could she?

'You right?' Alex asked. I nodded.

The bass player, skinny lad with shaggy hair, tight black jeans and a studded belt, wandered over. I suddenly felt old. I'd owned a studded belt when they were trendy in the eighties, in primary school.

'Uh, Daisy, we're going back on.'

She slithered off Alex's lap but didn't move too far away. Standing in between his legs, she pushed her arse back into his crotch as she leaned over the bar and waved for a beer. Subtle.

The bartender shook his head. 'You've had enough.'

'But I'm the entertainment! I'm fucking entertaining! Aren't I?'

'Very,' Alex said, and Daisy forgot about the beer, turned around and stood so his knee was in between her legs.

'Come back to my place after the show.'

Christ. She was practically frotting him. Alex glanced my way, a half smirk on his face. If I hadn't known him better I would have said he was actually enjoying himself. Daisy misunderstood the look.

'She can come too. I swing that way. Yeah, the three of us can party, baby.'

She gave an exaggerated wink, rubbed herself against his knee a couple of times then turned and walked to the stage with much exaggerated swinging of hips. Alex watched her go.

'This never happens when I'm single,' he muttered.

'Oh come on—' my eyes were finally free to roll—'she's a total fucking nightmare.'

'Funny,' he said, 'she sort of reminded me of you.'

chapter**thirty-seven**

When I told him Trip had taken me to Doyle's place, Alex's good mood started to dissolve. It had completely evaporated by the time I'd recounted my desperate escape.

'Why didn't you let me know right away?' he said.

'I was about to, but I had to talk to your girlfriend out there first. Sorry.'

He pressed the heels of his hands into his eyes and made a sound halfway between a sigh and a moan. We were sitting at a table in the bistro. It looked just like the front bar except the floor was tiled and chalkboard menus hung on the walls, advertising mezze platters, burgers, chips and dips. I was jamming fries into my mouth, testing a new theory that having a mad bastard try to kill you burned off as many calories as a twenty k run. Alex was still drinking his beer but I was on another glass of water, partly because I was thirsty and partly because I wanted Alex to realise how unlike Daisy I actually was.

'Fuck,' he said. 'This is a fucking disaster.'

'Well, yes and no. I found out Rochelle's laundering money for Don Davison, through the Doyle Group.'

'We already knew that.'

'What?'

'A tri-state fraud and tax office taskforce have been working on this for the last month and simultaneous raids on the restaurants, hotel and Doyle's accountants were scheduled for tomorrow.'

'Why didn't you tell me?'

'I'm not allowed to. It was none of your business and it was my job to keep you out of it. The shit's really gonna hit the fan.'

'You sure?'

'Rochelle knows you were hiding under the bed, listening in. She'll assume you've gone straight to the police. Who knows what she'll do to cover her tracks?' He rubbed his eyes again, like he was trying to sweep them right out of his head. Maybe he was so pissed off he didn't want to look at me.

My 'escape from death' high was gone, replaced with self-reproach. It sat in my stomach like a small, hard stone and made the chips taste like cardboard. I pushed the basket away.

Alex stopped with the eye thing and started rubbing his temples. He had his elbows on the table. 'Right. We're going to the police and then you're going back to Melbourne.'

'I can't go to my place. Where will I stay?'

'A locked box if I've got anything to do with it.'

'I have to go to Mum's first. I need clothes, a shower, money, ID.'

'Shit,' he said.

'What?'

'Chances are that Perry bloke'll be looking for you. They know about your mum?'

'Not much. Just her name and that she lives in Sydney, works at the uni. Phone's in Steve's name.'

'There are other ways.'

'They're not cops and it's Saturday evening. Gonna take them some time.' But he'd got me worried. 'Gimme your phone. I'm calling her.'

I dialled her mobile and she picked up after a couple of rings.

'Where are you?' I asked.

'Out to dinner. Why? Don't tell me you're still in Sydney.'

'Yeah, and we need to talk. Urgently. How soon can you get to your place?'

'The food's just arrived. I don't know, an hour? What's happening? Are you in some kind of trouble?'

'Not really,' I lied. 'Me and Alex are coming around. I'll tell you then. Oh, and look, no dramas, but you might have to move out of your house for a couple of days, just till some shit blows over.'

'No dramas?' She started to go off at me so I made crackling noises, pressed the end button and handed the phone back to Alex.

'Gonna call the taskforce,' he said.

I nodded and took the opportunity to go hang a leak. On the way in I accidentally caught a look at myself in the mirror. Jesus. The heavy makeup had migrated from its intended position, my jaw was swollen and bruised and my boofed-out hair was studded with bark from the palm tree and grit from the van floor. Daisy must have really had her beer-goggles on to invite me to a threesome.

I left the loos and was just passing the back bar, heading for Alex, when a woman with red hair roped into two thick plaits turned around, holding a Bloody Mary. She was about to move aside and let me pass when she glanced up and I caught her eye. My stomach dropped. Her hair was longer, she'd put on a bit of weight, but there was no doubt it was Meg. And I recognised the people she was standing with. Dave, Siobhan, and oh god, there was Ben. Quick exit, my brain screamed, get the fuck out, now! I put my head down and tried to steamroller past but she stepped in front of me, blocking my path.

'Simone?'

I stared at her. I didn't know what to say. Her freckled face got tight, as though someone was pulling the skin from behind, and she smiled like an animal baring its teeth.

'It is you.' She looked me up and down. 'You've got a nerve, coming back here.'

'Don't worry, I was just leaving.' I tried to get around her but she grabbed my shoulder, fingers digging in like claws.

'Somebody told me you were working as a hooker down in Melbourne. Is that true? I always thought it would be a fitting career ...' She'd raised her voice so the whole bar could hear. Alex looked up from his phone call. 'You certainly look like one—tragic makeup, bruise. What happened? Pimp beat you up?' Her eyes turned black and glittering.

I looked past her to the others. Tall, blonde Siobhan had crossed her arms and was staring me out. Dave met my eye, shook his head and glanced away. Ben, who had lost hair and gained a beer gut since I'd seen him last, kept his head down and became very interested in ripping the label off his Coopers Red. If only Matt had been there my humiliation would have been complete, but last I heard he'd gotten married and moved to the North Shore.

'Why'd you do it?' she said.

'Why don't you ask Ben?'

'He's a guy. They're weak. What's your excuse?'

There were a million reasons. There were none.

'What's going on?' Alex stood up.

Meg looked at him and her lip curled. 'Don't trust her, mate, not as far as you can kick her.'

'Bye, Meg,' I said.

'Oh, before you go?' She paused, jerked her hand back and threw her Bloody Mary all over my face.

The whole back bar was watching but I didn't react, just let the thick tomato juice meander down my neck. An ice sliver had lodged in my bra and it burned like a lit cigarette. I kept my back straight, head up high, and strolled out the door as though nothing had happened. The side street was full of cramped terraces, wire fences and bins and once I was out of sight I ran, but only made it half a block before sobs overtook me. I leaned into a wall, pressed my cheek against the scratchy brick and cried. Tears ran into my mouth, mingling with the salt from the chips. I heard footsteps, felt a hand on my back.

'Hey,' Alex said. 'Hey.' He tugged on my shoulder and turned me around to face him. He was clutching a handful of damp serviettes and dabbed at my face and shirt. The harder he tried, the worse it got. The red stain spread and the napkins disintegrated, leaving little spitballs on my skin. I started to laugh and cry at the same time.

Evening had turned into night and the overcast sky reflected the city's orange glow. The air was charged and tasted metallic, like touching a battery with the tip of your tongue. Thunder grunted in the distance and on nearby King Street an ambulance wailed.

Alex finished wiping me down, chucked the sodden mess on top of a bin and put his arms around me, pulling me to his chest. When would he learn that that shit just made me cry harder?

'Let me get this straight.' His voice hummed in my ear. 'You slept with her boyfriend when you lived in Sydney. So fucking what? It was years ago.'

'It's a bit more complicated than that.'

'Tell me.'

'You don't wanna know the whole sorry saga,' I gulped.

'Yes I do. Sit.' He took my hand and pulled me down next to him on a low wall in front of a dirty single storey terrace and handed me a hanky. Who the hell carried hankies, let alone clean ones? I blew my nose and crumpled the hand-kerchief into a ball in my palm.

'I met Meg and the others through my boyfriend. Matt and I lived together in my early twenties when he was a medical student and I was doing arts. We partied, saw bands, had a lot of fun, but it was a serious relationship, we talked about getting married one day. Anyway, Matt finished his degree and started an internship and he couldn't go out much anymore but it didn't stop me. Big weekends, lots of Es and speed.

'I started up this kind of flirtation with Ben. He was a guitar player, funny that, and living together with a chick called Fran. Meg's sister. The flirtation, surprise surprise, turned into an affair and we both knew it was fucked up and bad but that only added to the excitement and when you're on the gear you don't much give a fuck about right and wrong, you're more interested in what feels good. Right here, right now.

'We got addicted. And, of course, one day we got caught. Fran came home from work early and busted me and Ben in their bed. Must have been too dumb, broke or drug-fucked to get a hotel. Can't remember now. Fran ran out, crying, and no one could find her. Not until the next day when the minister discovered a body hanging from an oak branch in St Stephens Cemetery, couple of blocks from here.'

'Fuck,' he said, simply.

'Yeah. So that, in a nutshell, is why everybody hates me and I moved to Melbourne. Can't say I blame them. If I was Meg I'd have punched me out.'

'Hang on, it's not your fault.'

'You sure about that? I knew what I was doing was wrong. I was friends with Fran. I liked her. If she hadn't found me and Ben together she might be alive today. How can I not take responsibility for that?'

'To take her own life she must have had mental problems … a history of depression. You didn't kill her.'

I shrugged.

'And what about the guy, Ben? They're still friends with him.'

'They'd known him for years. I was just the blow-in. And you heard what Meg said. Us women are supposed to be able to control our urges and if we don't we're the evil temptresses that lead the poor, defenceless blokes astray. As you've probably figured, urge control has never been my strong suit. Add drugs to the mix and I have no fucking willpower at all. Meg comforted Ben at the funeral. When she saw me she spat on the ground. No one else would talk to me, or look me in the eye. I couldn't really blame them. I was halfway through my last year at uni, but I just took off. There was no point in staying.'

'And there's no point in continuing to punish yourself. You were what? Early twenties? No one's perfect.'

'You are. Perfect house, perfect life, straight as an arrow. Your only vice was flirting with me and you don't even do that anymore.'

He shook his head and laughed. 'You think you were bad 'cause you took some drugs and fucked someone else's boyfriend? Jesus. When I was in my early twenties I was running around with a gang. Drugs? We were selling the fucking things, doing break and enters, stealing cars.'

'No fucking way.' I sniffed back the last of the snot. 'You're lying.'

'Am I?'

'You can't join the service if you've got a record.'

'Didn't come to that. Got busted knocking off a factory in Brunswick by this cop who was a friend of my parents. He beat the living shit out of me and told me if he ever caught me again there'd be more of the same.'

'You report him?'

'You're missing the point. The bastard actually beat some sense into me. I straightened myself out, took an apprenticeship with my dad, got married … not that that worked out. Think you're debauched for screwing that bloke? I can't count the number of times I cheated on my wife. Shouldn't have rushed into it, like the sparky job. When I was twenty-five I got divorced and joined the police. I'd finally figured out what I wanted.'

I started giggling. It bubbled up and I couldn't stop. Alex frowned. He'd just bared his soul and I was cracking up.

'What? What's so funny?'

'Sorry, it's just such a blokey story. If a cop beat me up I'd be on a vendetta to get even, or at least report the sick son of a bitch. You learned to respect authority and joined the police. It's so …' I caught the look on his face and forced myself to choke down the laugh. I cleared my throat. 'Look, I get what you're trying to say. We've all done stupid shit but it's possible to change, yeah?'

'In a nutshell.'

'But I'm not sure I can change. I mean, I really like Sean, but what if I get carried away again? How do you deal with that?'

'Remember when you tried to kiss me on the couch?'

'Oh god, don't even talk about it.' I groaned. 'I'm still embarrassed.'

'Don't be. I wanted to kiss you back.'

'Really?'

'Yeah, and in the old days I would have. But when I asked Suzy to marry me I made the decision that I was gonna stay faithful.'

'That's all you have to do. Decide?'

'Yeah, if you want something badly enough. I'm almost thirty-six. I want kids and a stable family life and I'm not going to get it if I keep running around after any bit of … It's a choice. You've got to figure out what you want and what you're prepared to sacrifice to get it.'

'I've never been any good at sacrifice.'

'How do you know if you haven't tried?' He stood up and pulled me to my feet. 'We'd better get to your mum's.'

He turned to walk up towards the pub but I grabbed the back of his shirt.

'Alex.'

'Yeah?'

'Thanks. I always thought you were a bit of a prick, but it turns out you're quite a nice guy.' I hugged him and smelled his aftershave and felt his warmth and the span of his hands, one between my shoulderblades and one on the small of my back. I just wanted to bite his neck and throw him to the ground, evil temptress style, but practised self sacrifice, like he'd said. I supposed the moral of the story was, you could think it as long as you didn't do it.

'That'll be a hundred bucks for the therapy session,' he said. 'I take all major cards.' Then his whole body stiffened, but not in a fun way.

'What?'

'Remember our photographer friend from Circular Quay?'

chapter**thirty-eight**

We stood there, clasped in a rigid embrace. I barely dared to breathe.

'White Camry, half a block down from the pub,' Alex whispered in my ear as he looked over my shoulder. 'Same bloke, I'm sure of it. Don't turn around.'

'What do we do?'

'The prick isn't getting away this time. There's a bottle shop next to the bistro …'

'I'm not going back in the pub.'

'You won't have to. Wait outside while I pop in like I'm getting us something to drink. I'll jump the counter, sneak round the back and come up behind him. Just hang by the door and act like I'm in there, yeah?'

'Sure.'

We turned around and linked arms, walking back towards King Street.

'Gimme your phone,' I said.

He handed it over and ducked in the door under the neon bottle shop sign. I leaned on the wall outside and pretended to make a phone call so it wouldn't seem too suss. I even leaned into the doorway at one point, and yelled, 'Not the chardonnay, it's too woody!' The attendant barely glanced up from the street press he was reading. Maybe every night was full of counter jumping cops and crazy ladies ranting at invisible friends.

A few minutes later I heard a car door wrenched open, a muffled curse and scuffling. I whirled around and back down the street to the Camry where Alex was attempting to haul the fat photographer out of the driver's seat. This time the guy was wearing a brown checked shirt and base-ball cap.

'Hey!' he protested. 'Whaddaya think ya—'

'Police, arsehole.' Alex pulled him out and a half eaten kebab and a digital video camera fell from his lap. While Alex shoved the guy over the bonnet and held his hands behind his back I picked up the camera, turned it over and inspected it. Nice. Exactly the same model I wanted to buy for my agency.

'There's been some mistake, mate. I was minding my own business. It's not a crime to sit in a car.'

'Cut the bullshit. Think that cap's a fucking disguise?' He flicked it off, exposing the bald pate and white ring of hair. 'You're the son of a bitch from Circular Quay. Who you working for, huh?' Alex twisted the man's arm behind his back so his face pressed into the duco and his jowls spread out like puddles. Tough cop. Just as well Daisy wasn't around. She might have spontaneously combusted.

'Mate, I dunno what you're talking about. You musta mistaken me for someone else.'

When Tony Torcasio had tutored us in PI school he'd always said if you got made, deny it, then get the fuck out of there.

While Alex patted the guy down I leaned over the bonnet and got in his face.

'We know you're working for Rochelle,' I said. 'We know you cut the head off that possum!'

'The fuck?' He looked at me like I was completely insane.

Some student types sauntered by. 'Police brutality!' They flashed the peace sign.

'Oh fuck off,' Alex told them. 'Simone, check the glove box for a wallet.'

I dived into the car, which smelled very much like a taxi driver's at the end of a twelve hour shift, flipped open the compartment and looked inside. There was a wallet alright, and next to it a small silver pistol.

'Holy shit! He's got a gun!'

Alex slammed the guy's head into the bonnet and the car bounced. 'Minding your own business, huh?'

I pulled out the wallet, held it under the interior light and saw a driver's licence on one side and a laminated ID card on the other.

'There's a New South Wales private investigator's licence,' I yelled, squinting and holding it closer to the light. 'Name of Roderick ... McCullers.'

I poked my head out the car door. Alex and I looked at each other then stared at the man. Alex let go his wrists and stepped back but the guy stayed bent over the car, breathing heavily.

'Who hired you to follow us?' Alex said quietly.

'Wasn't following you ... just parked to eat my kebab ... a misunderstanding.'

'Give it up, mate, you're made, not to mention carrying

concealed.' Alex didn't sound angry anymore, just resigned. 'Who hired you?'

'Suzy McCullers,' Roderick said. 'Your fiancée. My niece.'

We were all sitting in the Camry, Alex in the passenger seat, me in the driver's, Roderick smoking a cigarette in the back. I was watching the video and Alex was scrolling through shots on a digital still camera.

'The McCullers family has three generations of cops,' Alex explained. 'Dear old Uncle Rod here is one of the reasons Suzy joined up. How you finding the private sector?'

'Can't complain. Work part time, bit of extra money. Didn't want to spend my retirement playing golf.'

'And you swear you haven't shown her any of this?' Alex asked.

'Not yet.'

'Suzy saw these she'd go ballistic. Champagne by the harbour, Simone on my balcony in a fucking bathrobe, hugging outside the pub.'

Roderick leaned over from the back seat and pointed a fat finger at the screen. 'Yeah, I really busted youse there. Thought I'd hit the big one.'

'I was comforting her, you prick.'

'Hey, I believe you.' He shrugged and sat back down.

'I love Suzy, that's why I'm marrying her. But she has a slight jealousy problem, understand?'

'Slight?' I was about to laugh when I saw the look he was giving me.

'So here's what we do,' Alex told Rod. 'I delete any photos or video footage that may cause her to draw the wrong conclusion and you report back that there was no evidence of anything going on. When we meet at the wedding, it's for the first time.'

'But—'

'But nothing.' Alex pointed at the glove box. 'That's an unregistered gun.'

'Fair enough,' Rod said. 'Far be it from me to break up a happy home. What do youse want for a wedding present?'

Alex shook his head. I'd swapped the video for the still camera and was going through it. Shots outside my mum's place. Me wandering around Kings Cross. I started looking at people in the background, to see if there was any image of pink-shirt Perry following me. I didn't see him, but I did see something else that was curious. I twisted around.

'Can you enlarge this?' I asked Rod.

'Yeah. Just press menu, then click on zoom.'

'What is it?' Alex asked.

I showed him a photo. 'See this photo of me outside the Hot Rock? Check the figure on the right, sussing me out. Jeans, Nike jacket, baseball cap? The person's small. Reckon it's a woman?'

'I don't know, why?'

'Well, here they are again.' I showed him another photo from the Cross, taken much later in the day. Same person, same outfit, hanging around looking in my direction.

'Probably just a street kid. Take a lot of photos in the same place you'll snap the regulars.'

'Check this out.' I flicked back to one of the first photographs at my mum's house. Walking down the street, back to the camera, was the same person, exact same outfit. In all the shots the person was too far away or at the wrong angle for their features to be clear. But when you zoomed right in you could make out a wisp of dark hair escaping the cap. Maybe I'd been wrong about the suicide. After all, I'd found her bag in Kings Cross.

'Shit,' said Alex.

'Yeah,' I said. 'I'm not a hundred percent sure, but I think it could be Andi.'

chapterthirty-nine

I showed Alex the back way to Annandale and we drove through Camperdown and Stanmore. Streets became wider as we travelled away from the inner city, small front yards appeared and the terrace houses began to expand. Occasional scrubby trees sprouted from footpaths.

We turned onto Parramatta Road at the McDonald's, scooted up Johnston and passed a church with a soaring spire. The whole way I prattled on about the figure in the photos. If it was Andi how come she was in Sydney, why hadn't she told her mum she was okay and what the hell was she doing following me around? Alex didn't say much, just told me not to jump to conclusions when I didn't know for sure it was her. We didn't talk about Suzy or her Uncle Rod, but I could tell he was thinking about it. His mouth was set and he stared hard at the car in front.

By the time we turned into Mum's street it had started to rain, lazy drops exploding sporadically onto the windscreen, crackling like cellophane. The house was dark and Steve's ute wasn't parked out front. Nobody home. Alex cruised around the block, checking for suspicious cars, big-haired ex strippers and pink-shirted kickboxing champs. Finding none, he reverse parked the Commodore into a spot half a block down from the house. Fresh rain on the pavement gave off a faint chemical fragrance that almost made me swoon. It was up there with leaded petrol, new car interiors and that purple ink stuff from primary school. We creaked through the gate.

'Wait here,' he whispered. 'I'm gonna do a circuit of the house.'

'Rochelle and Perry probably think I'm with the police. Or halfway to Melbourne.'

'Better to be safe than sorry.'

All I wanted to do was race inside and jump in the shower but Alex made me wait on the porch while he secured the perimeter. A bunch of potted palms huddled together at one end of the veranda and I felt between them until I found the broad, flat river rock with the smiley face I'd painted when I was eight. The colours had faded long ago and I couldn't believe Mum had carted the damn thing all the way to Sydney from northern New South Wales. I lifted the stone, swept my fingers underneath to retrieve the spare key and waited on the sagging armchair, feeling the coagulated tomato juice itch beneath my breasts and in the creases of my neck. Raindrops pattered onto the grevillea and bottle brush, shicking together spiky leaves as I silently rehearsed the conversation I was going to have with Mum.

'I know about the demo,' I'd say, 'how they threatened you and your family. But it was a long time ago. The danger is past, if it ever existed at all. Is this why you're always so worried about me? Maybe it's turned into phobia?'

And she'd clock the bruise on my face, raise one eyebrow, and say, 'Maybe it's because you keep getting beat up and almost killed.'

Impossible to win an argument with her, even in my own head.

Alex appeared from the opposite side of the house, walked softly onto the veranda and nodded at me as I handed him the key. I watched while he pressed his ear to the door, finally unlocked it and crept up the hallway, crouching into rooms and flicking on lights. His technique was similar to Chloe's, but without so many high kicks. I was just wondering if she was ready to apologise yet when he came down the corridor and gave me the all clear. Under the naked bulb his eyelashes glistened with rain and a fragment of spider web caught in his hair shone silver in the light.

'I'm gonna shower, wash all this crap off me.' I scratched my neck. 'Mum and Steve should be back soon.'

He nodded. 'I'll keep watch from the car.' He turned to leave and I grabbed his sleeve.

'Thanks.'

'What for?'

'Everything.'

The harsh light cast shadows that turned his brown eyes black. He shrugged, half smiled, and closed the front door. He seemed preoccupied, but I could hardly blame him, what with the screwed-up raid and Suzy setting her uncle onto us. I tried to imagine how I'd react if a lover pulled a stunt like that on me. In my case they'd probably be justified, but I wouldn't be fucking happy.

I showered, washed my hair twice with rosemary shampoo, conditioned, brushed my teeth and spat the paste down the plughole. Wrapped in a towel, I painfully combed the knots from my hair then moseyed through to the kitchen and looked in the fridge. Alright! The detox was over. I poured a big glass of pinot grigio, stuffed a hunk of Jarlsberg in my mouth and took the wine to the spare bedroom. Rain thrummed steadily against the tin roof, the most soothing sound of all time, and my earlier sense of anticipation had given way to release.

I kicked the door shut, dropped the towel, opened the big mahogany wardrobe and looked inside. Mum had washed and neatly folded my jeans, flannie and Breeders tee. Bless. I slipped them on, wriggled my feet into a big pair of footy socks and sat on the drooping single bed sipping crisp wine and listening to the rain. I felt like curling up and sleeping for about three days and wished I could be five years old again, tucked up in bed with a cold, Mum bringing me chicken noodle soup and letting me watch cartoons on the black and white TV. The last thing I wanted to do was sit in an austere room, talking to police.

I lay back on the mattress and decided that when the interview was over, wherever they stashed me, I was gonna make the most of it. Lie around, watch *Dr Phil* and *Oprah*, read trashy magazines, recuperate. After everything that had happened I felt bruised, mentally more so than physically, and for the first time since Andi had disappeared I didn't actually give a shit what had happened to her. So she'd killed herself. So she was following me around Sydney. So what? I was that exhausted I just didn't have the strength to care.

I was almost asleep when I heard Steve's ute pull up, its shuddering engine and handbrake's sharp crick audible despite the rain on the roof. Not the most environmentally friendly car, but he needed it to lug around his mudbrick shit. I considered jumping up, meeting them at the door and letting them know I was there, but realised the lights I'd switched on would have alerted them to my presence so I stayed prone for a few more precious seconds. The gate squealed and footsteps thumped as they ran onto the veranda. Mum laughed, the sort of breathless giggle people get when they're caught in the rain, and Steve said something I couldn't decipher in his husky, pot-smoker's rasp. A key rattled the lock, the door creaked on its hinges and I stretched, sat up and swung my legs over the side of the bed. I was just about to stand when the noises went all wrong.

chapter**forty**

I froze.

Scuffling. A muffled scream. A gasp, a whimper, a crack.

The house shook as something hit the floor and my fingers curled involuntarily, clutching the star sign bedspread. I couldn't breathe. After a couple of seconds the initial spike of panic levelled out and I heard footsteps and dragging coming down the hallway, heading for the lounge. I slowly stood, praying the rain would mask the bedspring squeak, padded to the door, knelt and peered through the keyhole, eyeball straining.

Mum entered the room first. I could only see her middle, but recognised her slim hips, grey pants and thin red belt. Someone in a designer trench-coat followed close behind, and when they walked past into the centre of the living room I saw the person had long fake nails and was pressing a dark grey handgun into Mum's back. Rochelle.

Perry came next, backing into the room, dragging Steve by his desert boots. He dropped the feet on the floor and straightened up, pink shirt streaked dark with rain. Rochelle pushed Mum down onto the overstuffed couch and kept the gun pointed at her. Now I could see Mum's face, pale and pinched, tears glittering behind her black framed glasses. Seeing her cry made my eyes prickle and my breath catch somewhere between my throat and my lungs. Keep your shit together, I told myself, no one's dead and Alex is calling in reinforcements right at this moment. The Tactical Response Group, probably, big bastards with boots, tear gas and high powered rifles.

Mum was looking at the floor where Perry had dumped Steve.

'Is he …?' Her voice shook.

'Nah, just tapped him, but he fuckin' went down like a bag of shit.' Perry leaned over him and appeared to be rolling him onto his front. He dug around in his own back pocket and pulled out the nasty little plastic restraints, yanked Steve's hands up and secured them together.

'Are you going to do his ankles?' Rochelle asked.

'Fair go. I've only got four pair and this guy's not going to cause any bother.' He stalked off down the hall and I heard the front door slam.

What the hell was he up to? And where the fuck was Alex? In the meantime, I had to figure out what to do. I couldn't escape from the spare room because the windows were barred, and if I made a break for the lounge Rochelle would probably shoot me on sight. The only place I could hole up was under the single bed or inside the wardrobe. Lame. A toddler playing hide and seek'd spring me in a second. I ran my gaze over the floor, up the wooden walls. There was no escape, I was screwed. In desperation I checked the ceiling and—

There was a square hatch with dirty fingermarks around the edge, just like the one in the living room. It led to the attic. If I climbed from the desk to the wardrobe I could get up there. Would they hear me? Maybe not if I was really slow and careful. After all, the rain was drumming pretty hard, thunder rumbling as the storm closed in. Perhaps I could escape the house through the roof, or somehow slip into Mum's office and use the phone, or make a break for the front door. I had to try. I was just about to clamber onto the desk when I sensed, rather than heard, heavy footsteps trudge onto the veranda. I pressed my eye back to the keyhole. I had to see.

I wished I hadn't.

Perry pushed Alex into the room. Water streamed down both their faces and Alex staggered, dazed. His hands were already fastened behind his back. Mum looked up and let out a clipped yelp. Alex's knees drooped but he remained upright, until Perry planted a high kick between his shoulderblades and he flew forward, smashing his head on the side of the coffee table. Mum gasped. Alex rolled onto his back on the threadbare oriental rug, groaned and lost consciousness. When I glimpsed his face I had to cover my mouth so I wouldn't cry out too. His lip was puffed and split, one eye had swollen shut and there was something wrong with his nose. The shape was different and blood flowed from his nostrils and also from his temple where his head had whacked the table.

I shook with anger and helplessness. Silent tears ran down my cheeks and I pressed my hand so hard against my face my teeth cut into my lip. The SWAT team weren't coming, all the responsible adults were out of action and I was crouching behind the doorway like a scared little kid. Perry reached into the front of his jeans and pulled out Alex's service revolver. Jesus. I wished for a weapon, but I didn't even have any shoes.

'Now search the house,' Rochelle commanded, gesturing towards Perry with her gun.

I backed away from the door but he went straight past, up the hall to Mum and Steve's room. The rain squalled harder, thunder boomed. Someone was on my side. God, Sam Doyle would reckon. Mum would argue Mother Nature but I didn't give a shit who, just knew it was time to get in the goddamn roof. I climbed onto the desk, lay my chest flat on the top of the wardrobe, stretched my arms across, hooked my fingers around the opposite edge and pulled the rest of my body up. The sound of creaking wood seemed deafening. I heard Perry stomp across the hall to the office. It wouldn't take him long to look around.

I kneeled, flattened my palms to the ceiling and pushed the grubby square in, laying it to one side. Holding on to the edges for support I stood so my torso was inside the dark, dusty attic. The wardrobe wobbled under my feet and I quickly hauled myself all the way in, sitting on a splintery wooden beam with my knees drawn up to my chest. I had just picked up the hatch when the door below burst open and Perry marched across the room, upending the mattress on the single bed. Slowly, gently, I replaced the square of ceiling and prayed he wouldn't look up. Then I remembered the wine glass, and my clothes in the wicker hamper in the bathroom. The mirrors were probably still steamed up, and they might twig to the fact all the lights were on. They'd know I was in the house ...

The building vibrated as Perry tromped through the kitchen, laundry and bathroom. I sat on the beam tasting dust, neck and jaw muscles knotted with fear. Beams of light filtered through cracks in the ceiling and as my eyes adjusted I made out a low, sloping roof insulated with foam batts, a couple of rotting cardboard boxes and wooden beams running across the floor. I couldn't see any obvious way out but noticed another hatch like the one I'd come in, directly over the lounge room. Great. The only exit led to the people with guns.

The rain eased off. Good, because I could hear what was happening below. Bad, 'cause if I moved they'd hear me.

'She's not here,' Perry reported back to Rochelle. Luckily for me his kickboxing skills were a damn sight better than his powers of observation.

Mum piped up, sounding defiant although her voice wavered. 'What do you want, Rochelle?'

I started. I'd never mentioned Sam's wife's name to her. Maybe she'd heard it years ago, but the way Mum addressed her sounded strange, almost familiar.

Rochelle laughed. 'What I've always wanted, Cherry Pie. You out of my goddamn life, once and for all.'

chapterforty-one

Cherry Pie? What the hell was she talking about?

'Out of your life?' Mum said. 'Don't you mean Sam's?'

'Sam's not the one you should have worried about, honey.'

'But he—'

'Didn't do shit, actually. Sam wanted the spoils but it turned out he didn't have the stomach for the dirty work needed to achieve them. He promised the world, but in the end it was all left up to me. Don't send a man to do a woman's job, wouldn't you feminists agree? I loved him though, even when he didn't hold up his end of the deal. Loved him and needed his contacts. It was a boys' club in those days. Still is, really. No one would deal with a young ex stripper with an inheritance, except to rip me off. We made a good team for years, Sam and me. Although I have to admit I almost left him when he didn't take care of you.'

'Didn't take care of me?' Mum sounded incredulous. 'He kidnapped—'

'He was supposed to kill you. Instead he just snatched your precious brat and put the fear of god into you so you'd fuck off to parts unknown. Who knew he'd be so sentimental? I had no idea he didn't go through with it until a week later when you hadn't been reported missing. Sam insisted you'd never cause any trouble, and I guess he was right, but he didn't count on your goddamn daughter growing up and sniffing around.'

My mind was reeling. Rochelle had known my mum and wanted to kill her? Sam kidnapped me to scare Mum into leaving town? But why? The demo? It had to be something more serious than that. As serious as murder? As serious as Melody?

The rain was picking up and it was getting hard to hear. Moving in slow motion I spun around and lay down on my belly so my ear was closer to the living room ceiling. Better, but not ideal. I inched along the scratchy beam until I got to the hatch and put my ear to the plasterboard square. I'd thought I was being silent until I heard Rochelle.

'What's that?'

I froze.

'We have a possum problem,' Mum said. 'You want to shoot them, go for it. Nothing else has worked.'

'Where's Simone?' asked Rochelle.

'I don't know.' Mum was lying. She'd seen the lights on, must have known it was me in the roof.

'Don't fucking bullshit me. We've been watching you for hours. Perry followed you to the restaurant, saw you answer your mobile and heard you discuss it with the hippy over there. You left early to meet her. When's she due to arrive?'

'Soon, she should be here soon.'

'Then we'll wait.'

'What are you going to do when she gets here?'

'I haven't quite decided, but the cop's gun is a stroke of luck. Maybe set up some kind of murder–suicide thing? What do you think, Perry?'

Perry grunted his assent.

'You're going to kill us? Why?'

'Because Don likes his people to clean up their own mess, always has. You bring trouble to his door and you don't last too fucking long yourself, know what I'm saying? For a supposed university professor you're not very bright, Cherry.'

'Stop calling me that.'

'I'll call you anything I want, bitch, I've got the gun.'

The rain was heavier now and the only way I'd hear what they were saying was to lift the hatch. I got my fingernails underneath, raised one corner of the square and peeped through. I was directly above Alex, who was out for the count but still breathing, thank god. Perry stood over him, nudging him in the ribs with his running shoe every now and then. Steve was still unconscious, face down on the floor by the sideboard, and Mum was sitting on the couch, Rochelle standing over her with the gun. I saw the top of everybody's head and noticed Perry's hair was thinning, right on the crown.

'Maybe she's decided not to come,' Mum bluffed. 'Gone back to Melbourne.'

I winced. If they thought that was true they'd kill everyone before taking off and looking for me. Luckily Rochelle didn't believe her.

'Oh, I doubt that. After our little chat today she was dying to talk to you. All these deep, dark family secrets she thinks she's uncovered.'

'You talked to Simone?'

'For ages. The stupid little tart was desperate to know why you were scared of Sam so I thought of a fib and got him to go along with it. He told her it was because of the protest. The best lies are based on the truth, don't you agree? She bought it. If only she knew the real story. I might tell her when she gets here. What do you say?'

'I say once a lying junkie slut, always a lying junkie slut,' my mum said, and I clapped my hand over my mouth to stop myself audibly gasping. She never used the S word.

Rochelle slapped her face, grabbed a handful of Mum's short hair and wrenched her head back, digging the gun barrel under her chin.

'Now you're just making me cross. I was going keep you alive in case we needed leverage, but I don't really think it matters. May as well get it over with now.'

Jesus. I had to do something. Make a noise, distract them? But then what? They'd shoot me through the ceiling and we'd all be dead meat.

'Rochelle,' Perry scolded, 'if you're gonna shoot anyone, use the cop's gun.'

He tugged it out of the waistband of his jeans, turned his back on Alex and walked across the rug to hand it to her. Alex's eyes flicked open. Rochelle and Perry were looking in the opposite direction and the rain was coming down hard. In one swift move Alex rolled onto his side, drew his knees up to his chest, slipped his bound hands around his feet so they were in front of him and jumped up. They heard him and had just started to turn when Alex lunged at Perry's back, threw his hands over his head, and yanked on his neck. The two of them fell backwards and the gun flew out of Perry's hand and clattered across the floor, coming to rest by Steve's prone body.

Rochelle pointed her gun at Alex but couldn't take a shot with Perry in the way. A huge thunderclap shook the house and the rain pissed down, booming on the roof, gurgling down overflowing gutters. Alex pulled hard against Perry's throat, the plastic ties digging into his skin, and Perry made a sound like a cat hoicking up its Whiskas and drummed his heels on the floor.

Mum, wrists still tied behind her, leapt up from the couch and ran at Rochelle, butting her like a ram. Rochelle wobbled on her high heels and fell to the floor, and Mum threw herself on her, attempting a head butt. When that didn't work she started biting her neck and face. Rochelle shrieked.

That was my cue and I was about to race back to the spare room, grab whatever blunt object I could find and leap into the fray when Perry elbowed Alex in the guts, struggled free and started stomping him in the head, going crazy. That sort of shit could do serious damage and by the time I hustled through the attic it might be too late.

There was only one thing I could do. I lifted the hatch completely off and threw it to the side. Perry's head was directly underneath me. I squatted over the hole and jumped.

chapterforty-two

I flew through the air, hit Perry's neck with my knees and we crumpled into a heap, his head cracking as it bounced off the floor. We were sprawled half on top of Alex, who was out cold again, and I lay still for a second, stunned and winded, sucking in air. Perry didn't move. Maybe I'd snapped his neck. I hoped so. If I'd broken anything myself I was running on too much adrenaline to feel it. I stretched out towards Steve, reaching for Alex's gun, and my fingers had just touched the butt when I heard Rochelle screech, posh accent completely obliterated.

'Don't fucking think about it! I'll blow her fucking head off!'

I looked over. She'd gotten free of Mum and was picking herself up off the floor, pointing the gun at Mum's head.

Mum lay on her side, hands still tied behind her, glasses askew, dark red lippy smudged.

Rochelle patted her hair-do which had tilted to one side. She was breathing heavily, fake boobs swelling beneath her coat. 'Possums, huh?'

I ignored her. 'You okay?' I looked at Mum.

'I think so.'

'Shut up.' Rochelle kicked Mum onto her back and ground one spike heel into her chest.

'Stop hurting her,' my voice wobbled.

'"Stop hurting her",' Rochelle mimicked, sounding exactly like one of the mean girls at school who flushed heads down toilets and lorded it over the back of the bus. 'Should have thought of that before you spied on me, you stupid bitch. Your mother was actually sensible, believe it or not. Caused no trouble, kept to herself. I didn't even know she was back in Sydney until you rang the Doyle Food Group. Kirsch. German for Cherry. Had a different name when I knew her but when you said that it clicked. Cherry Pie, daughter named Simone. Didn't take me long to find out where she was at and all about you. Of course, I was prepared to leave it until you started sniffing around, hiding under my bed. That was just fucking rude. So whatever happens from now on in is your fault.' She gesticulated with the gun before pointing it back at Mum.

A horrible thought occurred to me. Maybe Rochelle was right. Maybe everything was my fault and I was finally being punished for all the deaths I'd caused in the past. Farquar, Van Annen, Vincent Pirelli, other thugs whose names escaped me, and Meg's sister, Fran. The lyrics from a country song drifted through my head. Something about how nothing was free and everything had to be paid for, in the end.

'How did you know her?' I gasped, still lying on Perry. 'Why do you keep calling her Cherry Pie?'

Rochelle laughed, the same dry cackle that had come from Meg's mouth at the Coopers Arms. Her tongue poked out, flicked at her plump top lip, and her voice turned sickly sweet. 'I call her Cherry Pie 'cause that was her name when she worked at the Fuck Hole.'

'You're full of shit. She demonstrated against that place.'

The corners of Rochelle's mouth curled up. I stared at Mum and she looked back at me steadily, not contradicting her. Even though I was sitting on top of ninety kilos of muscle and bone it felt like there was nothing solid beneath me.

'Yes, but before she cut off her long blonde hair and ditched the miniskirts for boiler suits and sensible shoes she worked at the Love Tunnel under the alias Cherry Pie.'

'But she—'

'She's a fucking hypocrite is what she is! What she always was! I worked there because I had no fucking choice, but she was just a nice middle class girl slumming it. She'd finished high school, could have got any number of jobs but no, working as a bank teller or a secretary wouldn't have fitted into her cool, bohemian lifestyle or given her any street cred.'

'We needed the money.' My mum stared daggers at her. 'We were fucking broke.'

'Oh yes,' Rochelle laughed, 'I remember now. Your father, the musician, couldn't lower himself to work for his rich parents so Cherry just had to get a job at the club. Poor darlings. How else were they going to stay true to their counter-culture values and keep themselves in pot and embroidered flares? You know how I knew she didn't really need the money?' She dug her heel further into Mum's chest and when I moved to get up she tightened her finger around the trigger. I froze.

'Your mother was too good to turn tricks out the back. Oh, all the punters wanted her to. Christ, you should have seen the money they offered. Men, always want what they can't have. Don even encouraged her himself, but no, she refused. It was beneath her, she was the golden girl, untouchable, the prissy little ballerina up on stage. I was forced to do it because I didn't have a boyfriend with rich parents to fall back on.'

Mum raised her head and looked Rochelle straight in the eye. 'Spare me the fucking sob story, Rochelle. The only reason you were forced to turn tricks was to support your raging smack habit.'

Rochelle pulled back her heel and kicked Mum in the ribs. I made to move again and she looked at me, wild eyed, trigger finger twitching.

'What's your problem, Rochelle?' Mum asked, really giving her some sass. I was proud to see her so defiant, but wished she'd shut up. Rochelle had the gun and I didn't think she'd have a problem using it.

'People like you looking down on me.'

'I didn't look down on you. When I became a feminist I thought I could change things from the inside out. That's why I organised meetings, tried to get a union happening and yes, finally demonstrated. I wanted to help you.'

'Save me from myself? You've seen the light so I must too? Oh thanks.'

'No. I was lobbying for minimum wages, decent working hours, women having control over their own bodies—'

'You were stirring up shit. I clawed my way up and learned to make the system work for me—in the traditional way. You catch more bees with honey than with goddamn crew cuts. I'm a strong, successful woman. I'm the real fucking feminist here.'

'Actually, I'd have to disagree with you, Rochelle,' Mum said.

'That so?'

'Yeah. Real feminists don't get their strength holding a big metal dick in their hands.' And she drew back her legs and kicked, her Mary-Janes striking Rochelle's forearms. Rochelle flew back, hit the wall and Mum screamed at me to run. I did, but not in the direction she intended. I bolted forward, my only thought to get in between her and the gun.

I wasn't fast enough. Rochelle straightened her arms, pulled the trigger and shot Mum in the head.

chapterforty-three

I didn't make it to Rochelle. My shin bones dissolved into marrow and I crumpled next to Mum's body like a newborn foal. I knew I should put pressure on the wound but I couldn't tell where the bullet hole was. All I could see was red, gumming up her hair, flowing across the tassled carpet edge, pooling in cracks between the floorboards. I lifted her by the shoulders, put one hand under her neck and rested her head in my lap, then ripped off my flannelette shirt and wrapped it around her skull. So much blood, dripping between my fingers, soaking into my jeans.

I didn't cry, didn't make a sound, but inside my mind was screaming that it wasn't happening, that it couldn't be real. It was. Mum's body was warm and felt light as a bird. Rain roared on the roof. My heart throbbed slow and hard.

I was about to feel for a pulse when I heard a click and looked up. Rochelle stood over me, holding Alex's revolver in both trembling hands, pointing it at my head. Her face was white, except for the red bite marks, and her top lip quivered, as though even she couldn't believe what she'd done. Blood had spattered onto her raincoat and the room smelt of raw meat, burned out incense and the firecracker scent of the freshly fired gun. Sweat rolled down my back although I was shivering, clammy and cold.

Rochelle took a deep breath to steady herself. Her pupils were huge and I saw the tendons flex on the back of her freckled right hand as she began to depress the trigger. My first instinct was to squeeze my eyes shut but I forced them open and stopped trying to deny what had happened. Rochelle had killed my mother and she was going to kill me. I wanted to tear the bitch apart, gouge into her flesh with my fingernails, rip her fucking face off, but I couldn't let go of Mum. I couldn't even speak. A soup of rage, grief and guilt roiled through my veins as the trigger moved and I stared down the barrel's dark round hole and realised it was the last thing I would see.

'Rochelle!'

We both turned our heads. Sam Doyle stood framed in the front door, black shirt and pants soaked and clinging to his solid body. He edged down the hall, arms outstretched, so she could see he wasn't armed.

'How?' Her eyes flicked from him to me and back again.

'The Mercedes has a tracking device. I heard the shot.' He stopped as he entered the lounge and looked around, taking in all the bodies, Mum bleeding from the head. His face went grey and he seemed to age ten years before my eyes. 'Jesus, Rochelle, what have you done?'

She looked at him but kept the gun trained on my face. 'I had to, she tried to kill me. Thank god you're here.'

'She's lying.' My voice choked, like my throat was full of phlegm.

'Give me the gun,' he said. 'This ends now.'

'She's dangerous.' Rochelle nodded in my direction. 'They had a scam going on, blackmail. When I wouldn't pay up they tried to get rid of me, her and Cherry and the cop.'

He shook his head and held out his hand. 'Hand it over.'

'No,' she said.

He took a couple of quick strides and was in front of her, between me and the gun. I still couldn't move. Mum's body had started to twitch. An ambulance. I had to get to the phone.

'Why do you care so much about these fucking bitches?' Rochelle's voice had gone all whiny and ocker, like a strung out junkie looking for a fix. 'I'm the one spent half my life with you, you cunt, played the perfect wife, put up with your affairs.'

Sam grabbed for the gun but Rochelle held on tight. It was pointed at his belly and they started a tug of war. I snapped out of it, flexed my leg muscles.

'And I didn't know you at all,' he said. 'All this time I thought Don killed Melody. It was you, wasn't it?'

I gently lifted Mum's head and placed it on the edge of the rug.

'You never really loved me,' Rochelle screeched. 'Holding a candle for that stuck-up slut.'

'It's over, Rochelle. I called the police when I heard the gunshot. Simone,' he called over his shoulder, 'get out of here. Now.'

I scrambled up but didn't run for the front door. Instead I dashed straight through to the kitchen and picked up the phone, dialled triple 0, screamed for an ambulance and hid behind one side of the arch, out of range.

'What is the exact location of the emergency?' the operator asked.

I'd opened my mouth to speak when I heard the blast, muffled this time. I stuck my head around the doorway. Sam was leaning into Rochelle, and they swayed together, like drunks slow dancing at the end of a wedding. She'd shot him in the guts. His legs buckled and Rochelle pushed him to the ground, aimed the gun at me. I dropped the phone and dashed across the kitchen, heard a sharp crack and the ceramic fruit bowl exploded behind me. I tore through the laundry, launched myself at the back door, lunged for the lock. It didn't turn. Deadbolted. I shook the handle, kicked the wood—nothing. Metal security bars caged the window.

Rochelle's heels clattered through the kitchen and I looked around wildly for a weapon or a way out but all I could see was an energy efficient front loader washer, laundry basin, folded-up ironing board and tubs of fermenting soybeans. I glanced into the bathroom. More barred windows, a flimsy lock and natural products that hadn't been tested on animals. Useless.

In desperation I kicked over one of the tofu tubs, water and white gloop sluicing across the tiled floor. My shoulders strained as I lifted another and when Rochelle skidded around the corner I hauled the bucket back and swung it forward, splattering the contents in her face. Her expensive heels aqua-planed across the tiles and as she fell back I heard another crack, then a metallic clank as a bullet pierced the washing machine. Her arms cartwheeled and I didn't wait for her to hit the ground, just barrelled straight into her, grabbing at the gun. We struck the tiles with a wet slap, Rochelle breaking my fall and letting out a winded 'Oooff.'

I lay on top of her and tried to prise the gun from her hand, but she gripped the weapon so tightly her knuckles almost burst out of her leathery skin. With her free hand she swiped at my hands and face, clawing flesh. One long nail broke off and stuck straight out of my forearm, like a thorn. I got both hands on her wrist and bent it back.

'Stop! You're breaking my arm! I have osteoporosis!'

'Should have eaten your dairy products, bitch.'

A burning pain tore across my cheekbone as one of her nails narrowly missed my eye. I ignored the sting, turned my head and applied more pressure until her wrist cracked like a dried out twig. Her shriek was inhuman, like a demon doused in holy water, so shrill my ears popped. I yanked the gun from her fingers, straddled her inflated chest and stuck the barrel in the socket of her left eye. I'd been so helpless when she'd shot my mother. Now molten energy surged through my veins.

'How's it feel, Rochelle?' I pushed harder, feeling gelatinous tissue tremble beneath the steel.

'Please.' She choked, writhing desperately beneath me. 'Don't kill me. You don't want to do this.'

'Why not? You deserve it and my karma's already shot to hell.'

I was going to pull the trigger and watch her skull explode and brains slop out over the tiles. Blood rushed in my ears, my vision tunnelled and my heart hammered like I'd just OD'd on speed. Sirens wailed in the distance. My trigger finger twitched and a sharp ammonia smell hit my nostrils. Rochelle had pissed herself.

'Bye, babe.'

I tried to press the trigger but I couldn't get my finger to move. At first I thought there was something wrong with the gun but it wasn't that. My body wouldn't obey the instructions from my brain. Pull the trigger, I screamed at myself. Shoot the bitch. Fucking shoot her. My finger wouldn't move. My hand started to shake. My chest spasmed, breath coming out in convulsive gasps. Hot tears streamed down my face, the salt water stinging the scratches.

When Rochelle realised what was happening she let out a mocking, incredulous laugh. 'You've got no balls. You can't do it. You can't fucking do it.'

She was right. I pulled the barrel away from her eye. The lid had turned purple and was almost swollen shut. Then I drew the gun back and smashed it across her temple. That, I could do.

chapterforty-four

Two days later, in the middle of the day, I lay on the couch in striped flannelette pyjamas, a doona wrapped around my body like a cocoon. Hot air blasted from the wall heater's shuttered vents, but I couldn't seem to get warm.

Outside, low lying clouds scraped skeletal branches and every now and then brilliant shafts of sunlight burst through, illuminating dust motes and the general shabbiness of my flat: grimy bookshelves; smudged fingerprints on the doors and light switches; the posters' torn and curling edges. The Russ Meyer chicks didn't seem so cool and cheeky anymore, just tacky, like my whole damn life.

Chloe clattered away in the kitchen cooking up some sort of Polish comfort food and I smelled paprika, onions and frying meat. In front of me the coffee table held a glass of red, a packet of sedatives, cigarettes and an ashtray, and on the television Dr Phil berated a clean cut American couple, telling them to get their shit together and take responsibility for their miserable lives. The TV had been on for the last twenty-four hours, numbing me more effectively than the Xanax. I kept my attention on the screen whenever I was awake, because every time I looked away the memories flooded back, and the pain twisted like a knife in my guts.

Dealing with the police had been a blur. They'd arrived not long after I'd knocked out Rochelle, seen me holding the gun and tackled me to the floor. I'd spent the night in the lock-up, trying to explain what had happened in between bouts of hyperventilating and hysteria, no one able to tell me what had happened to my mum. Apparently Alex's unit and Duval from Homicide had vouched for me, in a fashion, and Sam backed up my story when he awoke from surgery, finally convincing them I wasn't responsible for the bloodbath.

When I was released Joy took me back to her place for a shower and a change of clothes—cords and an oversized burgundy shirt—then we'd driven to RPA hospital in Camperdown, to see if we could find out what was going on. In the car, an old red station wagon, she explained some things about Mum. How she'd worked at the Love Tunnel, quit when she got pregnant with me, then gone back when my dad pissed off. It was around that time she'd answered an ad of Joy's for a flatmate, the two of them sharing babysitting duties and Joy turning my mum on to women's lib.

'But why did Rochelle want to kill her?' I asked. 'Why did Sam kidnap me? It was something to do with Melody, wasn't it?'

Joy nodded. 'After Peta was fired from the club she found a part time job at a shelter for battered women. That's where Melody ended up, after she got bashed.'

'Bashed?'

'Uh-huh. She was walking home from work and some thug dragged her into a lane, started beating her up and said he'd been sent by Sam. Melody reckoned the guy would have killed her if a prostitute and her john hadn't come upon them and scared him off.'

'But why?'

'She had something on Rochelle and Sam. Your mother knew, but she wouldn't give me the details. Said the less I knew the safer I was. I suspected it was information about Edwin's death. Pretty suss how Rochelle married him and less than six months later he was dead. Then bam, Sam's back together with her and they're developing the property with Don Davison. They weren't allowed to knock down the original building, but they got away with putting up that ugly apartment block out the back. Ended up making a lot of money from the deal. If Melody had proof they'd knocked off Edwin, it could have put a major spanner in the works. Your mother told Melody she had to get out of town, disappear, and she did, but while she was getting better she stayed with us for a little while and with other women we knew.'

'Did you know Sam kidnapped me?'

She nodded. 'It was the most hideous moment of my life. I was looking after you and Andi while Peta was at work, left you playing in the back yard and the next time I looked you were gone. The phone rang and a man, Sam, told me to get Peta home, and that if either of us called the police, you were dead. I did as he said. Christ, your mum was beside herself.

'We waited by that fucking phone for what seemed like forever. He didn't call back until three am. Peta spoke to him, left the house and came back with you half an hour later, bundled up, asleep and unharmed, thank god. I said we should go to the police, dob him in, but she said he was in with half the cops in the Cross and she was going to do what he'd told her to. Take you and move away. We decided on New Zealand because I had relatives you could stay with and it was such a long way away. So now you know why we always hated him so much.'

'Yeah, but Rochelle wanted Mum dead. By kidnapping me Sam was saving her life.'

Joy had snorted.

Inside the hospital a young female surgeon with dark liquid eyes and a plait of long black hair took us into her office to break the news and we sat on padded vinyl chairs, Joy gripping one of my hands in both of hers. I hadn't slept, but instead of blurring, everything in the room, from the table edge to the shelf full of medical texts, stood out in sharp relief.

'I have good news and bad news,' she said, and my body tensed, a boxer anticipating a body blow. 'Your mother, Peta, is going to be fine.'

I breathed out and my muscles went limp so suddenly I almost slid out of my chair. Joy let out a victory whoop. The doctor told us the bullet had lodged in Mum's skull, damaging a lot of blood vessels but missing her brain, and they'd managed to remove it without too much trouble. I started laughing and crying at the same time and felt an effervescent fizzing expand through my chest like I'd won the lottery or fallen in love, until she said:

'Stephen Merrick, I believe he's her partner? He didn't make it.'

Joy and I stopped dead.

'What?' I said.

'He suffered a heart attack when he was assaulted. The paramedics revived him at the scene, kept him stable in the ambulance, but when he reached the hospital he flatlined. We tried everything, but …'

'Does Peta know?' Joy voiced the question looming in my head.

'She's only just regained consciousness and is undergoing some tests. I'm planning to tell her soon and I'd like it if you could both be there to provide emotional support.' She shuffled through her notes and told us that everyone else had survived. Rochelle had concussion, Perry was being monitored for a suspected spinal injury, and although Sam had needed a length of bowel removed, he was expected to make a full recovery.

I hardly heard her. Ten years Mum had been with Steve and he'd been good to her, not like some of the losers she'd lived with in the past. My life partner, she'd called him, and I'd always rolled my eyes at the politically correct phrase. Ten years, and I'd never even hugged the bloke. They'd planned to grow old together eating organic tofu, tending their native plants and quietly smoking joints on the back porch. I wanted to throw myself on the linoleum floor and howl like a little kid. Instead I took a deep breath and held it together, just.

'What about Alex?' I asked. 'Can I talk to him?'

She clicked her pen against her teeth and looked at me. 'Were you close to Officer Christakos?'

Why was she asking that? 'You said everyone else was alive.'

'The assault against him was severe and the swelling required us to drill a hole in his skull to relieve the pressure. An MRI scan has indicated he's sustained lesions on the frontal lobe area. At present he's in intensive care in a medically in-duced coma and is requiring a respirator to breathe.'

'But he'll be okay …?'

'Brain injuries are tricky. Even if he does recover there may be extensive damage. It's too early to say.'

My heart clenched and tears ran down my face.

'I'm sorry,' she said. 'Now, do you want to see your mother?'

She took us into a lift and down a maze of green painted corridors to Mum. She was propped up in bed, a drip trailing from her arm, head bandaged like a soldier in a war movie. I rushed over, hugged her gently and tried to hold back the tears.

'Simone,' she smiled. 'You're alright.' Her eyes searched the room. 'Where's Steve?'

My stomach flipped. The doctor came forward and I moved back as she sat on the edge of the bed and spoke to her in low tones. Looking at Mum's face was like watching a cloud pass over the sun. Her lips trembled, her mouth turned down and when she tried to speak no sound came out. She turned her head to stare at the wall. The doctor stood up and I took her place, stroked Mum's forearm.

'It's gonna be okay. I'll stay with you and we'll get through this. Joy's called Jasper and he'll come over and—'

Mum pulled her arm away, tucked it around her waist. 'I think you should go now,' she whispered.

'Sure, okay. Should we come back in a couple of hours?' I glanced at Joy, and back to Mum.

'No. I think you should go back to Melbourne. I don't want to see you right now.'

'But—'

Her voice got louder. 'If you'd gone to Melbourne when I first asked then Steve ... then none of this would have happened.'

'I'm sorry, I—'

'Please. Just leave.' Her voice broke.

I backed out of the room, hit the corridor, ran until I found the toilets and busted through the door. Locking myself in the first cubicle I vomited into the bowl, sat back on my heels, flushed it away. She was right. I could justify it till the cows came home but if I'd done what she'd said then Steve would still be alive and Alex wouldn't be in a coma. It was my fault.

The door squealed as someone entered the bathroom and I remained crouched on the tiles, waiting for them to enter a cubicle so I could make a break for it. It didn't happen and instead I heard a sound like the screw cap of a bottle cracking open. I waited for a bit and when it didn't look like they were going anywhere in a hurry I got up and unlocked the stall door. Too bad if they saw my tear stained face, I had to get out of there, find a pub, have a goddamn drink myself.

The door opened and I stepped out and saw a woman leaning back against a sink, skolling the last finger from a hip flask of Johnny Walker. It was Suzy, Alex's fiancée.

chapter**forty-five**

Suzy looked surprised but quickly recovered and tossed the empty bottle into a wastebasket full of crumpled paper towels. She was dressed in jeans, a chunky knit cardigan belted at the waist, and her blonde hair was tied back in a messy ponytail. Her eyes were red rimmed and puffy, just like mine.

'Simone fucking Kirsch.' She pronounced every syllable separately, slowly. 'You happy now?'

I opened my mouth to apologise but she jumped in before I could get the words out.

'It's not enough that you try to steal him away from me, you have to kill him as well? If you can't have him then no one can?'

She advanced and I backed away until my shoulderblades bumped the air dryer. I smelled scotch on her breath and guessed the hip flask wasn't her first. She bunched my top in one hand and raised her other and I flinched and squinted, waiting for a blow that never came. When I opened my eyes I saw that she hadn't made a fist but was pointing a finger at my face, stabbing it forward, punctuating her words.

'I have tried to like you. God help me, I even asked you to be one of my bridesmaids, but the truth is, I hate your guts. If Alex doesn't wake up, or if he ends up some kind of vegetable, I will fucking kill you, you understand? I don't care if I get sent to jail, it doesn't matter. He's my life. Without him I have nothing. Do you understand me?'

I nodded. 'I'm sorry.'

'That's pathetic.'

'Is there anything I can—'

'Apart from staying the fuck out of our lives?'

'I'm going back to Melbourne, maybe I could feed the cat or—'

'Fuck the fucking cat!'

Chloe placed a steaming bowl of goulash on the coffee table in front of me, garnished with chopped up gherkins, paprika and sour cream. My stomach had a hollow feeling I recognised as hunger, but I couldn't bring myself to eat. She didn't push it, just curled up in the armchair, packed a bong, sucked it down and blew smoke up to the ceiling, then flipped through a copy of *Beat* magazine, checking out the band listings.

When Joy called her from the hospital Chloe had dropped everything and immediately flown to Sydney to escort me home. She'd apologised profusely for our fight and so had I, the whole thing seemed incredibly petty after all that had happened. Since then she'd cooked, cleaned, fielded calls from friends and the media and had refused to leave my side. She'd even conducted a screaming argument with Curtis over my intercom after she refused to let him up to interview me.

'Hey, look.' She pointed at the paper. 'That band you like, Doug Mansfield and the Dust Devils. They're playing at the Standard. We could go for a bit, maybe, get your mind off things …'

I didn't respond, just stared at the TV.

'Or if you don't feel like going out I've got my investigation notes.' She hefted a huge pink shoulder bag onto the table, stuffed with notebooks and loose leaf paper. 'I've got a lot of information here. It doesn't make much sense to me, but if you looked through—'

'There's no point. Andi's dead.'

'Don't say that, you don't—'

'Come on, Chloe, Joy told us in Sydney. Cops finally found Andi's car out in the boondocks, Wattle Glen train station. They traced the call she made to me and one to triple 0, to somewhere in that area. They've done a massive search but shit, it's gonna be one of those deals where a bushwalker stumbles over the body. No one had her, she topped herself.'

'I don't—'

'Just drop it. Even Joy's accepted she's gone.'

'But her handbag, in Sydney.'

'The Datsun was stripped. Someone must have stolen the bag and taken it up there. The computer was gone too, probably ended up in a hock shop in the Cross.'

'The pictures from Suzy's uncle.'

'Joy said they weren't Andi. The clothes, the stance, the shape of the body. Weren't you the one who said a mother always knows?'

Chloe had another bong and changed the subject. 'Want to see some pictures of the place in Balaclava? I'm going to sign the lease soon and the shop downstairs is still—'

'Can't you get it through your head? I'm not interested.'
I was getting fucking sick of her relentless attempts at cheering
me up.

'Is it because of the jelly wrestling? I said I was sorry.'

'It's not that. I'm finished with the PI biz.'

'How come?'

I sighed like she was completely stupid. 'The question isn't
why am I quitting but why did I start? The only motivation
I can think of is the cops wouldn't take me, so I tried to prove
I was better than them. It's pathetic and self centred and has led
to me ruining god knows how many lives.'

'What you gonna do instead?'

I shrugged. All I wanted to do for the rest of my life was
lie around watching TV.

The phone rang and Chloe leapt up to answer it, spoke
briefly and held the receiver to her ample chest. Was it just the
big fluffy jumper or had she put on a winter layer?

'It's Trip Sibley. You wanna talk to him?'

I didn't answer. An ad for washing powder was on the tele.
A happy homemaker hanging out pristine white sheets and
bouncing a rosy cheeked baby. Why hadn't I ever wanted that
shit? If I'd taken that particular path then Steve would still be alive
and Alex would be fine and my mum's life wouldn't be in tatters.

Chloe chatted to Trip for a minute or so, then hung up.

'He's really sorry about what happened and he wants to
come over and—'

'If you want to root him, just root him,' I said. 'You don't
need me as an excuse. He'll fuck anything that moves. Actually,
I don't think motion is even a requirement.'

Chloe tossed her platinum hair over her shoulders and put
her hands on her hips. 'Why are you being such a bitch? I know
you're traumatised but I'm only trying to be a good friend, take
care of you. Do you want me here or not?'

'Can you move a bit to the left?' I said. 'I can't see the TV.'

That did it. Her eyes welled up with tears and she grabbed her smokes, keys and handbag and stormed out, slamming the door. I was alone. Good. It was easier to be by myself than to accept kindness I really didn't deserve. Everything bad that had happened was my fault, had always been my fault. I'd deluded myself into thinking I was trying to help people, but that was a joke, I was only trying to help myself.

Those cops from Elsternwick had been right. I was a fucked-up excuse for a human being. I stared at the cask on the table. Alcoholic? Check. Nympho? Suzy had hit the nail on the head. I did want her man, even though I was supposed to be in love with his best friend. I was selfish and I was a bad person because when you thought about it that's all evil was, complete self centredness. There was a certain satisfaction in finally figuring it out, and I washed down another Xanax with the last of the red, smoked a cigarette and crashed out.

.

chapter forty-six

I struggled awake later that afternoon, legs tangled in the doona, one arm flung above my head. A molten orange sun peeped under the clouds, rays slanting through the bare branches and into the window, and when I closed my eyes against the light all the bad memories returned. I opened them, whipped my head around and gazed at the TV screen. Another ad. A fluffy white dog sat in a restaurant wolfing down what looked like foie gras while a model-type made goo-goo eyes at him across the table. Christ.

I was just about to reach for the sedatives and wine when I remembered Alex's cat, Graham. Maybe Alex's family were feeding him, but what if they weren't? I doubted Suzy would have alerted them and imagined the poor thing hanging around the empty flat starving and wondering what had become of his owner. The thought made me even more depressed but was enough to propel me into a sitting position then lurch off the couch into the shower.

I pulled on jeans and a bulky jumper, slammed down a coffee and drove to the 7-Eleven where I stocked up on tiny packets of fancy cat chow. Graham hadn't exactly struck me as a no frills feline. As I wound the Futura along Beach Road, heading for Mentone, the sun dipped toward the dark denim sea and its rays didn't so much glint off the chrome as become absorbed by the rust. Twenty minutes later I let myself in the corrugated iron gate, clanked up the metal stairs and knocked on the door, just in case, but there was no answer. I sat cross-legged on the landing, cold wood chilling my butt, pushed the cat door in and peeked through. In the sunset glow I made out the granite kitchen and straight lines of the designer sofa.

'Graham? Puss, puss, puss?'

He wriggled out from under the couch, padded towards me and I realised I felt inordinately glad to see him. I held the flap open and he jumped through, did a little skip in order to boof his head against my knee and wound all around me, purring like a two stroke engine. I ran my palm down the lumpy knobs of his spine and he flopped onto his side then rolled onto his back, exposing his belly. I rubbed the silky fur and he clutched my hand with both paws, chewed the spongy pad beneath my thumb and kicked his back legs like a kangaroo. I pulled my hand away and he righted himself and jumped on my lap, put both paws on my chest and kneaded my jumper. He pushed his sharp little chin into my face and his wet nose dabbed my cheek and whiskers tickled the corner of my mouth. I bent to kiss the top of his head and got a whiff of toasty fur and of Alex: aftershave, hair product, tumble dried towels. Graham must have been sleeping on his bed.

My breath caught in my throat as I thought of Alex standing in the hallway at Mum's, just before everything went to hell. He'd looked gorgeous as usual, even though he'd been wet and tired with spider web sticking to his hair. I remembered his melted chocolate eyes and his square hands and the veins that coiled up his forearms, the v of chest hair when he opened the top button of his shirt and the perpetual stubble shadowing his well defined jaw.

Then I pictured how he'd end up if he ever regained consciousness, and an image straight out of a road safety campaign materialised in front of me. Alex strapped in a wheelchair, eyes glazed, mouth slack, one arm curled spastically against his chest. It was too much to bear. Tears spilled down my face and onto Graham's head and guilt shredded my guts, clawing my insides into raw, bloody ribbons. I was responsible for all of it. Alex. Andi. Steve. Mum. Sam Doyle. Even Suzy. I remembered the look on Chloe's face after I'd treated her like dirt and it, too, ate away like acid. I lifted my head and saw the ocean through the balcony railing, blurred and blue. I felt like running across the sand, wading in, swimming out until my sodden clothes dragged me under and freezing water filled my lungs and obliterated my brain.

I sniffed. It wasn't such a bad idea and just thinking about it dulled the pain. I weighed it up and couldn't find any reason not to. Sure, some people might be upset for a little while, but considering my talent for fucking up the lives of everyone around me, they'd be better off in the long run if I wasn't around. The end would totally justify the means.

A perverse excitement buzzed through my veins. Fuck it. Nothing was stopping me. I should do it. I was gonna do it, but not here. I had to go home, leave a note asking Chloe to feed Graham and then I had to get completely fucked up so I wouldn't chicken out. I could go to the Standard, see Doug

Mansfield and the Dust Devils one last time, drink everything in sight, finally kiss that hot bass player then take the rest of the pills and catch a cab to St Kilda Beach and wade on in. Frank Parisi's body had washed up on the same stretch of shore and it was where all my deluded PI shit had begun. You had to admit, it had a certain symmetry.

I heard rustling and looked around. Graham had actually inserted his entire body into the plastic 7–Eleven bag, desperate for food. I shooed him out and peeled back the foil on a packet that claimed to contain smoked salmon mousse with lemon and capers and he hunched over, snuffling, not bothering to chew. I slid a ceramic tray out from underneath a spiky potted palm, opened a bottle of water and filled it for him, not that he seemed interested. He was busy licking the edges of the empty container, scraping it around the balcony. I opened him a package of pork and fennel roulade, apparently studded with juniper berries, and stood up, feeling lighter all of a sudden, better than I had for days.

chapter**forty-seven**

The Standard was in Fitzroy, a two storey pub of white painted brick that sat flush to the pavement in a narrow lane not far off Brunswick Street. I pushed through the door into a room of dark wood panelling, red patterned carpet and a crush of people, warmth, smoke and noise.

Heading directly for the bar I weaved past older guys who looked like they'd been bashing out twelve bar blues since the Jurassic era, and women wearing red lipstick and the sort of cool retro dresses I searched for in op shops but could never find. I wore tight jeans, a black Club X t-shirt and a fluffy white jacket that wouldn't have looked out of place on a New York streetwalker and didn't quite fit in with the crowd but hell, that was the story of my life.

I leaned on the bar and ordered a shot of whiskey and a glass of champagne, realising that for once I didn't have to worry about a hangover. A hard kernel of grief remained lodged in my stomach, but anticipation of what I was about to do tamped it down and gave me a hyperactive buzz. I was gonna make the most of my last goddamn night on earth.

The band was already playing in the next room, and I tapped my foot and swayed my hips as the familiar twang of country honky tonk drifted across the bar. When the drinks arrived I slammed down the shot and a couple of old rock dinosaurs glanced over, nodding approvingly. I picked up the champagne and pushed through the crowd into the band room, a narrow space crammed with tables where families, groups and couples sat eating typical pub fare: steaks, chips, calamari.

The band members were squished onto the tiny stage and dressed mostly in checked shirts and boots. A mural on the wall behind them reminded me of a seventies Marlboro ad, depicting a couple of cowboys on horses silhouetted by the setting sun. The bearded singer, Doug Mansfield, sat on a stool out front wearing a ten gallon hat and nursing a guitar. The bass player I always flirted with, Jack, was wedged to Doug's right. He wore his usual outfit of black shirt and jeans, hair swept back in a vaguely fifties style, and I realised with a start that he was a dead ringer for a young Sam Doyle. Weird. He nodded in my direction and I lifted my glass in return.

As if on cue the band started playing a number I'd pretty much adopted as my own personal theme song, 'Trouble Follows Me', and I mouthed lyrics that seemed more relevant than ever.

I've been round this town too long it's plain for all to see,
there's always something going wrong and happening to me,
no matter what I do or say it's grim reality,
and I don't follow trouble, trouble follows me …

I downed the champagne in record time, ordered another, and when the band launched into a song called 'Standard Time', about the very pub they were playing in, I squeezed through to the front of the stage and thrashed about, even though no one else was dancing. Knowing I wasn't actually going to be alive the next day gave me an incredible feeling of freedom and although people were staring and probably laughing at my overenthusiastic boogie, I really didn't care.

I tossed back another couple of champagnes and whiskeys, hoping they'd play 'She Dances on Tables' so I could do as the song suggested. I'd danced on a table while seeing the Dust Devils at the Greyhound with Alex and he'd become so alarmed he'd literally picked me up and carried me, kicking and screaming, out of the pub. The memory made me smile, then it made me hurt, so I quickly downed another couple of drinks to flush away the pain.

Soon after, Doug announced that the band was taking a break and I decided it was time to make my move. After eight drinks in an hour I should have been falling over but I was raring to go. It was now or never and tomorrow, literally, wasn't going to come. I tracked Jack to the bar and tugged on his shirtsleeve.

'Hey.'

He turned around, a Melbourne Bitter stubby in his hand. He was six foot, give or take, and I had to look up at him.

'Simone. I read about you in the paper. You alright?'

'Right as rain. Can you come outside for a sec? There's something I've got to ask you.'

He looked around, like he really wasn't sure.

'Please?' I said. 'It's important.'

He nodded, finally, and followed me into the covered beer garden, chill despite gas heaters. We leaned against a brick wall

and I smiled, noticing that his hazel eyes were fringed by surprisingly long lashes. He looked a little nervous and I couldn't
work out why, since he'd always been the one asking me out
for a drink.

'I've been following the story,' he said. 'Missing waitress,
shooting in Sydney. What happened?'

I really didn't want to talk about it and gave him the
edited version. 'Apart from trouble following me? Not much.
I pissed off some bad guys but it was all for nothing 'cause it
turns out the waitress topped herself. They found her car out
bush, near Wattle Glen, wherever the fuck that is.'

'Northeast of the city.'

I looked at him and he shrugged. 'Used to go camping in
a national park near there with my parents, years ago. It's an
old goldmining region.'

Whatever. I wasn't interested in conversation, just wanted
to lose myself in his moist, beer flavoured mouth.

'What did you want to talk to me about?' He swigged his
Melbourne.

'The last good kiss.' I tilted my head in what I hoped was
an enticing manner.

'The novel by James Crumley?'

Damn guitar players, always au fait with noir fiction.
I shook my head. 'Not the book. The real thing.'

I stood on tiptoes, parted my lips and kissed him. He
jerked back, just like Alex had in the car.

'What's wrong?' I asked.

He looked at his feet and a faint flush rose to his cheeks.
'Simone, this is very flattering, and if it had happened a few
months ago … but, I'm here with someone.' He glanced over
his shoulder. 'I should get back to the bar … sorry.'

He left and I leaned against the wall. So I'd missed my
chance. Great. It just confirmed that my life was one enormous

fuck-up and I decided there was no point sticking around for the band's second set.

The ladies was decorated with gilded mirrors and dim light emanated from candle shaped wall fittings. Very Melbourne. After hanging a leak I stood by the sink popping downers out of the blister pack and tossing them into my mouth. I cupped my hands beneath the tap, filled them with water and swallowed the pills. Showtime, but as I walked toward the door it burst in and slammed against the tiled wall. I jumped back. A platinum haired pocket rocket stood in front of me with her face twisted up and her lips snagged into a snarl. Chloe.

chapterforty-eight

Chloe rushed into the bathroom, chucked her bulging shoulder bag on the floor, screamed and barrelled into me, pitching me against the sink. I realised I was still holding the Xanax pack and shoved it behind my back. Too late. She reached around, prised it out of my hand and examined it. Tears trembled on the surface of her wide blue eyes.

'What the fuck have you done?' She waved the empty packet in my face before flinging it to the floor.

'Nothing, I …'

She stepped back and I was relieved for a second, until I saw her push up the sleeves of her baby-pink quilted jacket and set her mouth in a grim, determined line. She wouldn't …

Oh yes she would. I turned and bolted for one of the cubicles but she was right behind me, shouldering the door.

It hit my back and I bounced off the opposite wall, then turned and slapped both hands in her direction, fighting like a girl. I didn't stand a chance. I was weak and more than a little tanked and although Chloe was tiny she'd spent her teenage years brawling much tougher bitches than me in the pool halls and sports ovals of suburban Frankston.

She grabbed a fistful of hair—classic scrag fight move— dragged me around and kicked the back of my legs so my shins smacked the tiles and I was kneeling in front of the toilet. She yanked my head back and when I saw her other hand coming toward my mouth I tried to jerk away, but was forced to stop as my hair started tearing out from the roots. Chloe pushed her fingers between my lips, long acrylic nails scratching my palate. I gagged and she thrust them further, into the back of my throat. My oesophagus shuddered and my stomach heaved and she pulled her fingers out just in time for me to fling myself over the toilet bowl and spew out a watery soup of tablets, booze and foaming green bile. No food. Not even a chunk of carrot.

I choked and coughed and finally sat back, eyes watering and sinuses on fire. I heard Chloe wash her hands, then the whine of the air dryer, pulled myself up using the wall for support and stumbled out of the cubicle. After rinsing my mouth and spitting down the sink I leaned back on the wall breathing heavily and feeling sobriety descend like a thick, depressing fog.

'You selfish bitch.' Chloe picked her bag off the floor and slung it over her shoulder. 'How could you do that to me?'

'Nothing to do with you.' I wrenched paper towel from the dispenser and wiped my face.

'No? I found your fucked-up note.' She walked over, clutched the lapels of my fluffy jacket and shook me. 'I've been looking for you, thinking I was gonna find a body. I drove here on the off-chance … fuck, how could you?'

When I didn't answer she shook me harder until my head banged into the wall. Why wouldn't she just leave me alone? I shoved, hard, and she reeled back, bag slipping off her shoulder, notes and papers slithering out across the floor. The bathroom door opened, letting in a waft of plaintive pedal steel and a red lipsticked woman who ignored us, locked herself in a cubicle and pissed loudly. Chloe hugged herself tight, her whole body shaking.

'I'm sorry.' Each time I uttered the phrase it sounded more pathetic than the last. I crouched to gather up the papers and stuff them in her bag. A glossy brochure slipped out of an A4 notebook, advertising a gleaming burgundy four wheel drive. I plucked it off the floor and stared. I'd seen exactly the same vehicle somewhere before.

'Why do you have this?' I held the brochure up.

'What do you care?'

I didn't reply and eventually she said, hiccupping, 'A neighbour of Andi's called up about my poster a couple of days ago. He'd been away for the last week. He's one of those bike freaks that go riding really early in the morning and the day Andi disappeared a car like that was parked in his street and tore out of there so fast it nearly knocked him down. I didn't know if it was a clue or not, but I got hold of that picture and put it with all the rest of my stuff.'

'He get a numberplate?'

She sniffed and shook her head. 'No. But he says that's the exact colour and model. Oh, and it had a baby-on-board sticker on the back.'

I looked up. 'What did you say?'

My hand was trembling. A feeling surged inside me, temporarily washing away thoughts of suicide and diluting some of the guilt. A feeling I hadn't experienced for a long time. Hope.

'It's Dillon's car,' I said. 'I saw it when I interviewed him. My god. Maybe Trip was right. Maybe they were having an affair …'

'But why would he kidnap her …?' Chloe started jigging up and down.

'I don't know why, but there's a chance I know where. You ever heard of a place in the country called Kangaroo something-or-other?'

'No.'

'Got a street directory in the car?'

'Caught a cab.'

The woman came out of the loo, glanced over and veered towards the sink furthest away from us.

'Excuse me—' I tried to keep my tone well modulated because my words were going to sound insane—'do you know of a place in country Victoria called Kangaroo something-or-other? A town? A region?'

She shook her head and hightailed it out of there without bothering to dry her hands.

'Shit, someone's gotta know.'

I headed for the band room, Chloe right behind me, tiptoeing on her spike heeled boots. I scanned the pub. It'd take forever if I asked each punter individually. There had to be a better way. There was.

The band was playing 'She Dances on Tables' but for once it was the furthest thing from my mind. I pushed through the crowd, jostling people and spilling their drinks as I headed for the tiny stage. When I waved my arms at the band they eyed me warily then exchanged glances as they continued to play. Perhaps sobriety hadn't completely descended because as I stepped up onto the stage I tripped over a mike lead, narrowly missed Doug Mansfield and careened into the drum kit, cymbals falling on top of me with a brassy clash.

The music petered out and I crawled to the front of the stage, picked myself up and grabbed Doug's mike from the stand. He didn't say anything, just raised an eyebrow, took a packet of Winfield Red from his shirt pocket and lit up. The pub had gone silent. People crowded in from the front bar and the beer garden to see what was up, staring expectantly. Being Fitzroy natives they probably assumed I was performing some really awful fringe theatre.

'Sorry for the interruption.' Feedback whined as I spoke into the microphone and everybody winced. I saw the barman signal to a bouncer over by the front door and realised I didn't have much time. 'I have a very important question, it may be a matter of life and death.'

'Get off, you crazy bitch,' yelled a guy with a goatee wearing a long leather coat. 'Who do you think you are?'

'I'm a private investigator, now—'

'It's that stripper,' one of the women pointed and squealed.

'Take it off!' called another dude. I ignored him. The bouncer was in the band room now, manoeuvring his bulk through the crowd.

'There's a place in Victoria called Kangaroo something.' I raised my voice. 'Kangaroo Land? Kangaroo Place? Anyone heard of it or know where it is? Anyone?'

People turned to each other and chattered, but no one came up with an answer. Bloody inner city types. Probably thought Preston was the outer limits.

'Have you tried looking up your own arse?' Leather-coat shouted. Goddamn hecklers.

As the bouncer approached the stage Chloe leapt in front of him and started waving her hands around like Elvis during his karate phase. Not surprisingly, it had absolutely no effect, so as he pushed past she launched herself at him, throwing her arms around his neck, dangling like a baby monkey and swinging from side to side as he attempted to dislodge her.

'Please,' I pleaded, 'someone must know where it is.' I felt a tap on my shoulder and whipped my head around. Jack stood there, bass guitar strapped low.

'Kangaroo Ground,' he said. 'It's where we used to go camping. Five minutes from Wattle Glen.'

chapter**forty-nine**

Soon as the bouncer hustled us out into the cold, narrow laneway I borrowed Chloe's phone and called Detective Sergeant Duval. He wasn't there so I left a message telling him what I'd found out, then rang the switch and was put through to another officer whose name I didn't quite catch. I repeated what I'd said on Duval's voicemail and told him they had to search the Kangaroo Ground property as soon as they could. He urged me to come into the station the next morning and I muttered something noncommittal and hung up.

'They gonna look for her?' Chloe's breath came out in misty puffs.

'Shit, I hope so. But I can't see them doing anything till tomorrow.'

'Tomorrow might be too late! Have you heard the radio? It's gonna be the coldest night all year. They reckon it might snow!'

I pulled my jacket tight around my neck. Andi had to be dead. A week in the bush, undoubtedly injured, no food, temperatures close to freezing. But what if she wasn't? The same hope I'd felt when I saw the picture of the four wheel drive bubbled up and my mind flooded with images from every amazing survival story I'd ever heard: a guy lost in the Himalayas with a Mars bar, the plane crash in the Andes where a football team ate each other, dudes trapped under rocks sawing off their legs with pocket knives, people pulled from rubble weeks after earthquakes and terrorist attacks. Andi was a tough chick and if anyone had the will to survive it was her. I imagined how I'd feel if the police found her a few hours too late and I thought of the look on Joy's face if we discovered Andi alive. If there was the smallest chance that one good thing could come out of all the hideousness …

'Let's go get her.'

We had to find the address of the place first. Chloe tried Trip's home and mobile numbers, to no avail, then had directory assistance put her through to Jouissance. I listened in, hopping from one foot to the other, trying to keep warm.

'I'd like to speak to Trip Sibley, please.' Chloe used her best telephone voice. She could be quite polite and well spoken when she wanted to. 'I realise that, but it's urgent. I'm sure he won't mind speaking to—it's none of your business who I am—listen you slack moll, put him on or I'll come around there and stick the frigging phone up your—' She looked up, surprised. 'Bitch hung up on me.'

We caught a cab to St Kilda and by the time we pulled up at the taxi rank outside the Prince of Wales I'd gulped down two cans of Red Bull and was buzzing with caffeine, sugar and rage. Dillon was probably at the restaurant and it was gonna be all I could do to stop myself tearing him a new arsehole. Finding Andi was the priority and I didn't want to waste time getting into a confrontation, but if the bastard hadn't done away with her in the first place, then Steve would still be alive and Alex would be fine and everything wouldn't have turned to shit.

Chloe threw the driver some money and we slammed the doors and hurried down Fitzroy Street. A few people lingered in restaurants and bars but the cold footpath was deserted. Chloe's spike heels echoed off the concrete and the street lamps were haloed by a fine mist of sea spray. We'd just crossed at the lights and were passing the milk bar on the corner when Chloe yelped and grabbed my arm, pulling me to a halt.

'It's the car!' She pointed to the four wheel drive pulling up a few doors down from Jouissance, gasping as though the vehicle itself was evil. Holly emerged from the driver's side, opened the back door, pulled out a baby capsule and headed for the restaurant. Maybe we wouldn't even need to go inside. We ran toward her and she whirled around.

'Simone? Oh my god. I tried to call you when I heard about … I'm so sorry … I knew my stepmother was a bitch but I didn't think she'd ever...I just wish I could have warned you. If there's anything I can do …' Holly was rugged up in a cable knit jumper, beige stirrup pants and a shapeless navy jacket a couple of sizes too big. A long scarf wound around her neck and her dark bob was hidden by a beanie. The freezing night air made her freckles stand out on her round, pale face. I remembered how Patsy the waiter had hinted that Dillon was just after her money and suddenly I hated him even more.

Chloe peered into the baby capsule, easily distracted. 'How cute. The little beanie matches yours. What's his name?'

'Edwin. Eddie. After my father.' Holly jerked the capsule back, glaring at her, and I was shocked by the vicious expression until I remembered that the first time they'd met, Chloe had just placed Dillon's hands on her boobs. Luckily Chloe was too busy cooing at the sleeping child to notice the dirty look.

'Actually, Holly, there is something you can do,' I said. 'Give me the address of the land you and Dillon own out at Kangaroo Ground.'

She started and almost dropped the baby. 'What. Why?'

'Because we're going there to get Andi.'

Her mouth fell open and her hazel eyes went wide. 'I don't understand.'

'I don't understand everything either but it looks like your husband was on with her. I think they had an argument after the staff party and he attacked her and drove to your property to dispose of the body.'

Holly sucked in a breath. 'No, you're wrong. He was home all night.'

She would say that.

'What's the address?'

'I don't remember offhand.'

'But you could get it, right? Must have the title deeds at home?'

'I don't know where exactly. It would take me a while …'

She would say that too. I shook my head. 'Protect him all you like, babe, but I've told the Homicide Squad what I know. Your husband's going down.' I turned and marched off, Chloe following close behind.

Jouissance looked warm inside with its glowing orange lights, flickering candles and dark wood. We reached the door just as Yasmin turned the sign to 'Closed'. She lifted her head, realised who we were and lunged for the lock. Too late. Chloe and I had already pressed our palms to the glass and we pushed with all our might. She tottered back, nearly fell out of her court shoes and righted herself as we barged in. She drew herself up, smoothed her immaculate chignon and pointed.

'That's it, I'm calling the police!'

Chloe rushed into her, head first. The back of Yasmin's knees hit a plush armchair and she fell into the seat. 'Siddown and shut up, you scrawny freak,' Chloe yelled, standing over her. 'I wasn't joking about that fucking phone!'

I glanced around. Trip sat at the bar looking tired and washed out. I'd heard on the news he'd been arrested and charged over the money laundering, but had been released on bail. He raised two fingers in a half hearted wave and didn't seem surprised to see us or remotely bothered by the fact that Chloe was threatening to insert telecommunications equipment into his girlfriend's nether regions. The other chefs, clustered on a banquette, sat and stared. Through the glass panel I saw a couple of diners in the restaurant, lingering over a decanted bottle of red. Patsy had his back to us, setting tables, and Bad Boy was mopping the kitchen. No sign of Dillon.

I rushed over to Trip, no time for pleasantries. 'Where's Dillon?'

'Around here somewhere, why?'

'I need the address of his property at Kangaroo Ground. You were right about him. He did something to Andi and we've got to go find her, there's a chance she's still alive.'

'Shit.' He sat up straight on his padded stool. At that moment Dillon sauntered out of the kitchen, carrying a tray of freshly washed martini glasses and whistling a tune. The jolly little melody enraged me and I couldn't help myself. I ran at the bastard.

chapterfifty

Dillon pulled up short and backed away when he saw the expression on my face.

'Simone. I heard about—'

'Shut the fuck up,' I growled. 'I know all about your affair, and what you did to Andi. We're going there now to find her, dead or alive, and you'd better hope to god the cops arrest you before I get back because I'm holding you personally responsible for ruining my life.'

'You're fucked in the head.' He jerked his chin up, flipping straight brown hair out of his eyes. 'Get out of my way.'

I shoved his chest and he staggered and dropped the tray, the delicate glasses shattering with an almighty crash. Out of the corner of my eye I saw the diners hand Patsy the black folder containing their payment and hightail it down the back corridor. Bad Boy slumped out of the kitchen and he and Patsy inserted themselves in the archway, eager to see what was going on.

Dillon looked at Trip, eyes begging, willing his boss to come to his aid. Trip just shook his head and the other chefs followed his lead and stared at the floor. Chloe had Yasmin pinned in the armchair by the front door. Dillon was on his own.

'I didn't do anything to Andi.' He talked slowly and precisely, his eyes narrowed and his voice simmering with rage.

'Bullshit. You texted her after the staff party, from a public phone, to make sure it couldn't be traced, went round to her place, bashed her probably, bundled her into the Datsun and dumped her body at Kangaroo Ground. Of course you were too fucking dense or panicked to realise she was still alive and in possession of her mobile phone. Then I reckon you left the Datto at the station, caught the first train to the city, another to Ormond, cleaned out her place and drove your four wheel drive out of there so fast you nearly knocked over a cyclist. Home to wifey, back to bed, then the acting role of your life, pretending you were innocent and didn't know what happened to her. Did you cut the head off the possum to freak me out and encourage me to investigate?'

'Possum? I don't know what the hell you're talking about. Why would I kill Andi?'

'I dunno. Maybe she was gonna tell your wife what was going on and there goes your little nest egg. You tell me.'

He scoffed. 'I never touched her. We never had an affair!'

'Come on, mate,' Trip said. 'I saw you two making goo-goo eyes. There was your secret rendezvous in the booth at Mink, the party pash.'

Dillon laughed. 'Sure, I flirted with Andi but not 'cause I wanted to sleep with her.'

'Why then?' Trip seemed puzzled that anyone would be bothered to flirt if they weren't after a root.

'Because …' Dillon flicked his hair again and a pink flush rose to his high cheekbones.' … I wanted her to invest in my film. I knew she had money saved and I thought if I buttered her up she'd give it to me and I could buy the editing equipment. It was a loan,' he said quickly. 'I was going to pay her back when the film started making money.'

A short film making money? He had to be even more stupid than he looked. But if he was that dumb, how had he got away with it for so long?

'How much she lend you?' I asked.

'Five grand. I needed to finish the film. The in-laws wouldn't give me any more money and Rochelle wouldn't let us sell the stupid land. I know I probably shouldn't have led Andi on, but I was desperate. That's what we were doing at Mink. She was handing over the cash.'

It explained the withdrawal from Andi's account but didn't mean he didn't try to knock her.

'Tell me where she is and how to get there,' I snarled. 'I'm running out of time.'

'Can't you get it through your head? It wasn't me and I don't know! I've never even been to Kangaroo fucking Ground. Jesus, I hate the country, it's full of bugs and rednecks. Holly took care of that shit. She went out there when we got the land evaluated, she can vouch for me. She'll tell you I didn't leave the house after the staff party and I slept right through till one in the afternoon, the deepest sleep of my life, god, like I was drugged or something.'

Dillon was expressing a convincing mix of desperation and self righteous indignation and if I hadn't known he was an actor I'd have been taken in. Until I remembered I'd seen him in his short film and he'd been bloody awful. I knew he was under pressure but how could a such crap performer suddenly pull an Academy Award performance out of his arse? Unless it wasn't an act …

'Honestly, Holly'll be here soon to clear up this bullshit. Just ask her.'

I looked at Chloe. I'd thought Holly was right behind us. 'Where's Holly?' I asked.

She ran to the door and looked down the street where the four wheel drive had been parked. 'Car's gone. She's taken off.'

Everything hit me all at once. I'd thought Dillon was an idiot, but it was me who'd been the fool.

'Holly's really jealous, yeah?' I asked him.

'Not really …'

Patsy snorted, leaning against the arch. 'Yeah, right. She's the green eyed monster personified. Wouldn't hire any female staff when she ran this place and I think she was even worried about me! You told me yourself that she attacked a girl when you guys lived in Sydney, a chick who came up and danced with you in a club.'

'That was a long time ago,' Dillon protested. 'She got counselling. She's really mellowed since she had Eddie. She wouldn't. She was home with me all night.'

'You said you slept like you were drugged …' I was almost certain. Everyone else thought Dillon and Andi were having an affair. What if Holly thought so too? What if she'd seen them kiss at the party? I thought through my theory and slotted Holly in, in place of her husband. It all worked out. There was just one more question to ask.

'Did you guys spend all last week together?'

'Except for Thursday and Friday. She had to go up to her old school unexpectedly, to coach some girls in a hockey camp. They couldn't find anyone else and she didn't want to let them down. I stayed home from work and looked after Eddie.'

'Where's her old school?' I asked.

'Just outside Sydney. She flew there on Thursday morning. Why?'

I looked at Chloe. 'She's got a twenty minute head start,' I said. 'We need to find the address and get there, fast.'

I heard a cough and turned around. Trip had slid off his stool and was dangling his keys.

chapter**fifty-one**

Trip took Dillon home to Albert Park and called me as soon as he'd unearthed the address of the Kangaroo Ground property. He also told me that Holly wasn't there, which was no great surprise. By the time he'd returned to Jouissance Chloe and I had printed a map and directions from a computer in Yasmin's office and were arguing in the cobbled laneway out the back.

'We can't fit three on the bike,' I told Chloe.

'Then kick Trip off. I can handle this motherfucker.'

'No way.' He squared his shoulders.

'It's a bike, not your penis.' She put her hands on her hips.

'I've got no problem with either of you riding my dick, but the Ducati's out of the question.'

Jesus.

'Get a cab to your car then catch up to us,' I suggested. We were seriously running out of time.

'No. I'm your freaking sidekick and I'm coming with you!'

He shrugged. 'We can all fit, just. I've had three on the bike before, with the Russian models. It'll slow us down though.'

'What about the police?' I asked.

'Fuck the police!' he yelled and Chloe grinned and high fived him. Friends again.

'Okay, fine,' I said, 'let's just go.'

Trip handed us the two helmets and hopped on, Chloe behind him, me bringing up the rear half sitting on the carry rack. After crawling along the Esplanade he hit Fitzroy and finally we were struggling up Punt Road and onto Hoddle. When we turned onto the Eastern Freeway he tried to gun it but the engine protested against the extra weight.

Then I heard the sirens. I turned my head to see a police car pull parallel, the uniformed officer in the passenger seat waving us down. Trip hit the throttle and the engine groaned. Damn. We couldn't outrun them and the damn cowboys in the cop car were veering over, forcing us onto the verge. Trip stopped the bike before we crashed into the ditch at the side of the road.

He swore. 'It's okay, I'll talk to them.'

He kicked the stand out, left the keys in and slid off the bike. Cars zoomed by, beeping at us, and Chloe and I pushed our visors up and watched as he sauntered over to the cops. I couldn't hear the exact words but within seconds they were arguing and Trip was waving his arms around. One of the officers reached for Trip and he batted him away then both tried to grab him and he whirled and started running down the side of the road. Christ, could it get any worse? Chloe started scooting forward on the seat.

'Kick the stand,' she yelled over her shoulder.

'Chloe.'

'Come on, mate, I can't. My feet don't reach the ground. You wanna find Andi or not?'

Shit. Trip was probably seconds away from getting arrested and she was already revving the engine so I whacked the stand with my heel and we took off down the freeway. I didn't look back to see Trip's reaction.

A little further along Chloe turned off at the Burwood exit. I had to hand it to her, she knew how to ride the thing and was smart enough to follow the speed limit to avoid attention. I just had to remember to put my feet down and balance the bike whenever we stopped at the lights.

We sped through the suburbs and gradually the houses were fewer and the road became lined with ghostly gums, wooden fences and tangled vines. The air was freezing and held the sharp eucalypt scent of the bush. We had to stop a couple of times and pull a torch out of the saddlebags to study the map but eventually we were trundling down a winding dirt road, checking out mailboxes made from chopped off forty-four gallon drums. Finally we found the lot number we were looking for and rode up a gravel driveway, winding around a hillside, traversing steep hills and sharp declines, and although the bike wasn't designed for off road riding and skidded a bit on the pebbly surface, Chloe maintained control. I'd been so wrong that night outside Jouissance—she really was one hell of a sidekick.

We roared up a near vertical hill and rocketed down the slope on the other side, picking up speed. Too late the head-light picked up a metal gate at the bottom, on the far side of a concrete ford. She laid off the accelerator and hit the brake but the bike was too heavy and had built up too much momentum to stop. Just before we slammed into the gate she chucked a hard right and the back wheel spun out. I tried to hold on but couldn't and flew through the air toward the bushes, eyes squeezed tight.

I came to a few seconds later in a clump of bracken, a couple of metres from the Ducati. A rock gouged my shoulder and my ankle throbbed, but my fluffy white jacket must have protected me because I could move my limbs and nothing seemed to be broken. I sat up and ripped the helmet off. In the glow of the headlight I saw Chloe trapped under the fallen bike and I limped over.

'Ow,' she moaned, 'it hurts.'

I don't know where the strength came from but I lifted the Ducati, grunting, and flipped it off her, the bike crunching when it hit the gravel. I found the torch, pointed the light and saw that her leg was twisted underneath her.

'It's broken.'

'Fuck.' I felt in her pockets and found her phone, checked the screen. No signal.

'I'm so sorry,' she cried, 'I've fucked everything up.'

'No you didn't, babe. You got us here. Hold on, okay? I'll get to higher ground, call for help.'

I climbed over the padlocked gate and hobbled up the hill on the other side, the torch beam wobbling over the stony track and illuminating creeping vines and snarled scrub. I constantly checked the phone for the bars that would indicate I had a signal, but there was nothing. The night was freezing, arctic almost, and my ragged breath came out in cloudy puffs as I laboured to the top of the hill and climbed over another gate, the skin of my palms almost adhering to the icy metal.

The full moon behind the cloud cover dispersed an eerie light and ahead I made out a clearing, the hulking shape of an old two storey house and a large shed or barn off to the left. No sign of life, no burgundy four wheel drive. Looked like Holly hadn't come after all. Most likely she'd fled the state— I would've—but I turned the torch off anyway, just in case.

As I crossed the clearing a night bird let out a witchy screech and I stopped dead, my skin prickling with a stupid childhood fear of dead people risen from the grave, zombie creatures lurking and watching from behind the trees. Get a grip, I told myself, get to the second storey of the house, call for help, then look for Andi. You're not a frightened kid, you're a twenty-eight year old, hard-arse PI. I didn't really convince myself but when I heard no more screeching, only the chirrup of a cricket or a frog, I exhaled a shaky breath and took off again toward the house. I'd just put one foot onto the creaky, tilting veranda when I heard a low moan.

At first I thought it might have been a cow but when it happened again I realised it was human and coming from the bush beyond the house. Andi? Had she heard the bike or seen the torch light before I'd switched it off? I didn't want to go into the zombie filled scrub, but I had to, she might be dying, and Chloe would surely be okay for another couple of minutes. I switched the torch back on, stumbled around the side of the house and plunged in, tripping over tree roots, vines and branches slapping my face.

Every few metres I stopped and listened, making sure I was heading in the direction of the noise. I was. The moans were getting louder, more frantic, but just when I was sure I was right on top of her, they stopped. What the hell? I shone the torch all around. The gum trees were bigger here, with peeling bark hanging down in sheets, and right in front of me I saw a pile of huge boulders, speckled with lichen and fuzzy green moss. At the base of the rocks, branches and twigs lay heaped on top of each other, as though someone had stacked them there. Was Andi somewhere under the pile? I shivered and couldn't shake the feeling that I was being watched.

'Andi?' I whispered, picking my way toward the boulders. No response. I tried again, a little louder. 'Andi?'

A twig snapped behind me and all the fear I'd choked down returned, tenfold. I didn't want to see what was back there, anticipating the Blair Witch, or some fucked-up demon from *Evil Dead*, but I whirled around anyhow. I had no other choice.

All my horror film nightmares came true on the spot. It was Holly, a skitzed out look in her eye, holding an axe.

chapterfifty-two

Holly lifted the axe above her head, yelled and charged, and I instinctively blundered back, hit the twigs and plunged straight through. Half a second later I hit hard packed earth, jolting my already sprained ankle and landing hard on my shoulder and ribs. The torch bounced from my hand and the light snuffed out.

I looked up. Holly had switched on a torch of her own and in the ambient light from the beam hovering above I could just make out where I was. The hole I'd stumbled into was narrow, about three metres straight up, and the chamber a couple of metres across. At first I thought I'd fallen into an ancient pit toilet but it was too deep, too far from the house and the floor was hard and rocky—not that I had a clue what hundred year old faeces might feel like. There was a musty smell though, mingling with the dank scent of earth, and as my eyes adjusted I made out a shape across the cave and drew a breath, thinking it was Andi's body. I stretched my leg and nudged it with my foot and to my relief felt something hard and brittle. Probably just twigs fallen down from the pile.

Above me, Holly swore and I heard her throwing sticks aside before the torch light came dancing into the hollow, bobbing along the walls and tracing the floor. I lay still and closed my eyes, thinking playing possum might give me an advantage. The torch light rested on my eyelids, making them glow red inside.

'I know you're not dead.' Her voice echoed slightly as she called down the hole. 'I can see your chest moving and I am not falling for that one again. Could have sworn the other slut was a goner when I took her to meet her little friend, but the bitch must have climbed straight out. With a broken leg, if you can believe that!'

Little friend? Holly sounded like she'd totally lost it. I kept my eyes closed, hoping she'd think I was knocked out.

'Anyway, you're not escaping. I won't make the same mistake twice.'

The light left my face but I stayed still, just in case. I heard her clomp around, then a scraping sound, and even with my eyes shut I could tell the cave had gone pitch black. I opened them. She'd placed something over the entrance to the hole and was throwing stuff on top. It sounded like rocks hitting metal and each clang was more chilling than the last. Then the banging stopped, her footsteps receded and the silence was infinitely more terrifying than the noise had been. It wasn't quite as bad as being buried alive but it wasn't far off and I had to use all the mental strength I had to stop myself collapsing into a quivering heap. Think of Chloe, I told myself. If you don't get your shit together and get out of here Holly will find her and chop off her head with that goddamn axe. The thought was enough to make me sit up and feel for the torch until my fingers curled around the hard plastic handle. Working by touch I tightened the components, jiggled it and the light flickered then steadied. Yes!

I directed the beam upwards. A sheet of rusted corrugated iron lay over the top of the hole. My chances of scrambling up there were virtually nil, even without the metal to contend with, so how the hell had Andi managed, and with a broken leg? I brought the beam down and swept it slowly around the walls of the cave and when I got to what I thought was the pile of twigs, I screamed.

It was a body, slumped against the wall, and the grinning skull stared straight at me, eye sockets hollow and dark. For a split second I thought it was Andi before I realised the corpse was long dead, bone mostly, with only a few shreds of desiccated flesh holding the skeleton together. Clothing remnants hung in rotting ribbons and the cranium was peppered with tufts of curly blonde hair. A plastic bag seemed to be stuck to its chest and another had fallen into its pelvis. I forced my trembling hand to steady the torch and I inched closer. My god, they weren't plastic bags, they were silicon breast implants, perfectly preserved while the rest of the body had decayed. I suddenly realised what Holly had been talking about when she referred to Andi's 'little friend'. It was Melody, had to be, but I didn't have time to wonder how she'd got there, I had to find a way out of the cave.

I swept the light around the rough hewn walls and found another hole behind me, a lot smaller than the one I'd fallen in. What was the place? An old mine? Andi couldn't have climbed up the shaft and must have dragged herself out the back way. I crawled over, shone the torch down the opening and swallowed. Maybe not. The tunnel angled down until it dropped out of sight and, worse than that, it narrowed the further it went along. Could a person actually squeeze through? Surely you'd become trapped and at that steep angle there was no way of inching back up. The thought made my heart trill. No way was I getting stuck down there, I was leaving the same way I came in.

I rested the torch on Melody's brittle femur so the beam angled up, positioned myself under the entrance and for the next ten minutes tried my damnedest to scale the steep walls, hoping to use thin tree roots and minute corrugations to gain purchase. It didn't work. My boots slid off and the roots snapped in my hands. In desperation I attempted to claw my way up but a couple of fingernails ripped off and I crumpled into a heap on the ground, sobbing in pain, frustration and fear.

The only other way out was the tunnel. Just thinking about going in there made my head spin and bile rise to my throat. I couldn't, but if I didn't then Chloe was going to die. Who knew how long the cops would take? It could be morning before they arrived. I was just thinking that things couldn't get any worse when they did. The torch light flickered and died.

I'd never known such total blackness. It was so dark that I started seeing things, shooting stars and colours dancing in front of my eyes. I tightened the torch again and slapped the casing and when that didn't work I carefully removed the back, twiddled the batteries, screwed it together and … nothing. The thing was kaput. Fear rushed back and I started hyper-ventilating, thinking that any second I'd hear a rattle and scrape and feel Melody's gnarled finger bones dig into my shin.

Terror actually overcame me and I curled up on the ground with my knees tucked under my chin, covered my face with my coat and cried. It wasn't just the skeleton, it was the tunnel, because I knew if I was going to have any chance of saving Chloe I'd have to go down there, and if I went down there

I would probably get stuck and die. Sure, I'd wanted to kill myself earlier that night, but drowning was one thing. Being stuck underground, wedged fast and unable to move forward or back … but if Chloe died because of me …

I pulled myself to my knees and crawled through the darkness, sobbing and choking, to where I thought the tunnel should be, felt around the opening with my hands and inserted my head and shoulders. My bulky coat brushed against the narrow walls so I sat back, ripped it off, threw it behind me and forced myself in.

I wasn't sure if my eyes were open or closed, the darkness was so absolute. I managed to move forward by stretching out my arms, wiggling my hips and digging my elbows in when my body caught up to my hands. The further along I went the more terrified I became, and though I tried to control my breathing it was coming out in fast, panicky gasps. After about a minute the tunnel sloped down so sharply that I actually slid for a metre or so and knew there was no way in hell I could inch back. I'd reached the point of no return.

Panic spiralled and it was all I could do to get air into my lungs and keep pushing myself forward. The tunnel narrowed until there was no room to dig my elbows in and I had to squirm forward with my arms out in front of me. I inched along like some blind, burrowing worm until my searching fingers hit wet dirt. There had been some sort of collapse. The passage was blocked.

chapter fifty-three

I wanted to scream but there wasn't enough air and my throat constricted. I heard my heartbeat throbbing in my ears. I thrust my hands into the loamy earth as far as I could but all I could feel was more dirt, going on forever. Thrashing against the compressing walls I suddenly realised that hell wasn't a place of flames and pitchforks, it was dark and claustrophobic and icy cold, and I was there. I knew I was going to die and I'd just started to give up and go limp when a tiny spark fired in my panicked brain. I had to plunge straight into the dirt. There was the smallest chance I'd get to the other side and if I didn't at least I'd die faster in the complete absence of air.

I took a deep, final breath, squeezed my eyes shut tight, moved my hips and plunged face first into the soft moist earth.

I was doomed. The soil compacted as I struggled blindly through, cold dirt cramming into my nostrils, ears and eyes and forcing its way into my clothes. My whole body was encased and my lungs strained as I pulled harder, but it was hopeless, there was no end to the dirt and I had no breath left. My mouth opened involuntarily, my nose and throat filled with grit and as I convulsed, about to pass out, I stretched my arms in front of me as far as they would go and thought I was hallucinating. I felt empty space, cold air on my fingertips, and with my chest and head about to burst I writhed forward one last time, pushed my head out of the tunnel and sucked in dirt and air in one huge wheezing breath. Somehow I pulled my body out and then I was tumbling and rolling down a steep, rocky slope, until I slammed into a tree and came to a sudden stop.

I coughed and spat until I thought I was vomiting up my lungs. Dirt crunched between my teeth, tore at my sinuses and felt like it had been forced into my brain. I didn't care. I was out of the tunnel, alive and in the grip of a near-death adrenaline rush more profound than I'd ever experienced before. Despite the fact that I was freezing in my t-shirt, my whole body shivering with cold, I felt invincible. I was alive. Holding on to the tree I pulled myself to my feet then staggered up the slope, clutching at vines, barely registering my injured ankle and the bladey grass slicing my fingers and palms. I was going to save Chloe and I was going to find Andi. And Holly was going to pay.

I reached the crest of the hill, saw the clearing and slowed, trying not to make too much noise. The shed doors were open and the four wheel drive was parked inside, headlamps spilling light. I pulled the phone from my back pocket and wiped dirt from the screen. Still no signal, but if I could get to the top of the house … It was the highest point around and had to be where Andi had called me from. Maybe she was still there.

As I lurked by the trees Holly stomped out of the shed, carrying her torch and the axe and heading for the house. Change of plan. If I snuck to the car I could drive on out of there, bash through the gates and pick up Chloe on the way. Holly creaked onto the listing veranda and as soon as she disappeared inside I dashed across the clearing to the shed, hopped in the car and felt for the keys, but they were gone. Shit.

I swivelled in the seat and looked around. Jesus, her baby was asleep in the back. I considered grabbing the infant, threatening to harm him for leverage, but what if she realised I wouldn't go through with it and called my bluff? Instead I looked for something I could use as a weapon, spied her hockey sticks and decided they were better than nothing. I reached across the back seat, slid one from its cushioned sheath, left the shed and crept toward the house.

I padded onto the veranda and slipped through the open front door, made out a staircase in front of me and glimpsed flickers of torch light in a room to my left. Holly was in there, muttering, swearing and clicking open ancient cupboard doors. I glanced at the phone. Still nothing, but when I lifted it above my head my heart leapt—one signal bar flashed on the screen. Soon as I brought it down to my mouth, though, the bar disappeared and I knew I had to get up those stairs. I dashed lightly across the floorboards, which were spongy with rot, climbed the first two steps. On the third the stair disintegrated, my foot smashed through and splintered wood bit my calf.

chapter**fifty-four**

Holly popped out of the doorway, torch in one hand, axe in the other, and ran toward me. I pushed on the step above with my free hand and as my leg slid out felt ragged wood tear the flesh from the back of my knee right down to my ankle. Glancing over my shoulder I saw the axe swoop down and I squealed, but she couldn't control it with only one hand and the weapon went wide, missing me by half a centimetre and lodging in the wood. As she struggled to extricate the blade I ripped my foot out and clambered up the stairs, sticking close to the edge and gripping the wobbly banister, praying it wouldn't collapse.

At the top I came to a mezzanine level that looked over the ground floor of the house and turned and headed right, still clutching the railing, afraid of plunging through rotting floorboards. I passed through the door at the end of the corridor, closed it and, finding no lock, scanned the room for something to use as a barrier. In the half light I made out an old bed frame and a chest of drawers. I tipped the drawers over and pushed them in front of the door then backed to the far side of the room where looping reams of insulation material spilled onto the floor from a hole in the wall.

My heel hit the lip of some sort of metal bowl and I almost tripped as it upended, clanging and splashing water on my jeans. I checked the phone, hand shaking. Yes! The bar was back and I pressed triple 0 and held the phone to my ear. Come on, come on, I thought, the whole house shuddering as Holly thundered up the stairs. I became aware of a rotting smell as I waited for the phone to connect, not musty like the cave but sickly sweet and acute, and I remembered the odour from our old house in the bush when marsupial mice got trapped in the walls and died.

Holly bashed on the door and I edged to the window, looking for an escape route. The glass was already broken and I used the hockey stick to smash out the few remaining shards. The window sashes remained intact though, and I was just wondering if I could squeeze through when my call was answered.

'Triple 0. Police, fire or ambulance?'

'All of 'em,' I yelled as the chest of drawers started scraping across the floor.

'You can only pick one.'

'Police.'

'What's your address?'

'Um. Shit. Lot 444, View Glen Road, Kangaroo Ground.'

'Nearest cross street?'

'How the fuck should I know?'

'No need to be rude, putting you through now.'

As I listened to the ringing tone Holly slipped through the gap in the door and I backed up further until I trod on something squishy. I looked down and gasped. In the thin moonlight I saw Andi's body wrapped in the insulation, her head and an arm poking out. I'd stepped on the hand. Her face was drawn, bone white and the smell was terrible. I was too late to save her and if I didn't get out of this then Chloe and I were dead as well.

'Police. What's the nature of your emergency?'

I looked up. Holly had put the torch down on the chest of drawers so she could hold the axe with both hands. She stalked towards me, grinning.

'One dead, one injured and a crazy bitch is coming at me with an axe.'

'Tying up emergency services with hoax calls is a very serious offence if—'

'It's not a hoax! Talk to Duval, Homicide. My name's Simone Kirsch and—shit!' I dropped the phone and clutched the hockey stick like a baseball bat. Holly was getting close.

'Police are coming,' I tried.

'If they can find the fucking place. Nearest cop shop is Eltham. I've got plenty of time. What's that hideous smell?' She wrinkled her nose.

'That smell? It's what happens when you kill someone in cold blood, you crazy murdering bitch!'

'I don't think of it as murder so much as protecting my husband from sluts like you and Andi and your big-titted friend. I was just looking after what's mine. Anyone would have done the same.'

'Protecting Saint Dillon?' I laughed. 'Are you totally fucking deluded? Can't you see he's a vain, self absorbed actor who's only with you for your money?'

'Shut your mouth!' She raised the axe higher. 'He's the father of my child, and a beautiful man, inside and out. He wants to be faithful but your type's always trying to lead him astray. Throwing yourselves at him, flaunting your wares.'

Flaunting my what?

'Babe,' I said, trying to keep her talking so she wasn't chopping at me with the axe, 'I so don't fancy him.'

'Of course you do. I've seen the way you look at him, how every woman looks at him.'

'Just because you like him doesn't mean everyone else does. I can't stand him.'

'You're lying. He's the most wonderful—'

'Like your dad?'

'You don't know anything about my dad.'

I tried for the sympathy vote. 'I know Rochelle killed him. Gave him an overdose, left you an orphan and stole your inheritance. That's harsh. I don't blame you for being pissed off.'

'She ruined my life. Me and Daddy had the best time together until she came along. He didn't need to work, so just painted, and I hardly ever went to school. We'd hang out in our secret garden out the back of the Villa—you know, where they put up that ugly hotel? It was overgrown and had big stone walls and we'd draw pictures and tell stories and sometimes just lie on our backs and stare at the clouds. And we'd have picnics, with custard tarts and vanilla slices and—'

'Junkies do have sweet tooths.' I couldn't help myself, she was making me sick.

'He wasn't a junkie! That was his medicine. He had a bad back and the doctors wouldn't prescribe anything strong enough. Anyway, no one's going to take Dillon away from me. I've made sure of that. Enough talking, I know you're trying to stall me. I'm not dumb.' She raised the axe.

'Wait! Before you kill me I just wanna know one thing. How'd Melody end up down the mine shaft?'

'Rochelle found out she was in Melbourne, promised her a payoff if she didn't say anything about what they'd done to my dad. We met up with her in that park near the St Kilda pier and had a picnic. Rochelle brought me along to put Melody at ease. I mean, who brings along a four year old to murder someone? She drugged her, drove her up here, ran her over and shoved her down the hole. I was actually in the car, pretending to be asleep. It's where I got the idea for getting rid of Andi. Sins of the parents, huh?'

'If you hate Rochelle so much why didn't you just dob her in? Why leave it up to me to get dirt on her?'

'Are you kidding? After she did it she pinched me awake and said if I ever told anyone she'd know and she'd come and kill me. And she would have. Look what happened to your family after you messed with her! But it worked, she's going to jail now and I finally get what's mine.'

'So the possum head?' If I kept her talking maybe I could get her off guard, swing the hockey stick before she was ready for it. 'Taking the handbag to Sydney? Using Andi's card at the karaoke bar?' Suddenly I remembered the figure in the photos I had thought was Andi. 'You were following me!'

'It was so easy to play you,' she gloated. 'All of you. I'd known about Andi's article for ages. You know how I found out? Gordon. He wanted Trip's job and I told him I'd help him get it if he kept an eye on Dillon for me. Yasmin was about to start and I was worried she might go after my man, but Gordon told me it was this little bitch instead.' She pointed to the body.

'I followed her, knew where she lived and even where she hid her spare key. I'd been inside her house before that night, you know, gone through that filthy room of hers and found her notes about Melody and Sam and seen all the photos she had of my husband. There were four in her photo album and a big one, an enlargement, stuck in the middle of her notice-board. Can you believe that?

'Then, when I came to pick up Dillon on the night of the staff party, I saw her kiss him and let me tell you that was the last straw. I took him home, put a couple of sleeping tablets in his nightcap and texted her from a public phone pretending to be him, saying I had to see her at her place, that I wanted her. Like a bitch in heat, she fell for it. I got to her place before she did. I already knew her flatmate was away, and I waited for her in her room. Got the shock of her life when she flicked on the light and saw me waiting there with my hockey stick. Do you know when I confronted her I wasn't planning to kill her, but she actually admitted she was in love with him, and suggested I let him decide who he wanted. Well, you can see where that got her.' She laughed and shook her head and her eyes went hard and crazy again.

'I hit her in the head but it didn't knock her out and she tried to run so I swung my stick and cracked her shin, broke it. That stopped the slut. Then I bashed her on the head again, hard. I thought she was dead. I collected up all the pictures of Dillon, and her computer and all her notes. I had a plan. Shift the blame to Rochelle and Sam and kill two birds with one stone.

'I put her in the boot of the Datsun then drove her up here to dump the body. She started to make noises as I was coming up the driveway so I stopped the car and dragged her out and decided to run over her, like Rochelle did with Melody. She jumped out of the way, though, fell down a goddamned hillside and by the time I dragged her up and dumped her in the hole I was sure she was dead. I even checked for a pulse. It was almost light by the time I drove the Datsun to Wattle Glen and caught the train to Flinders Street, then another to Ormond so I could pick up my car. I got home exhausted but Dillon was still crashed out and so was Eddie. He's such a good baby. Sleeps right through.'

'It was you behind the wheelie bin,' I said, torn between swinging the stick and finding out everything that had happened. My fingers had started to twitch.

'I thought the cops would have been onto Rochelle and Sam from the start, but Andi was so secretive she hadn't told anyone about her article! I put the newspaper clipping and the card in the bin to direct them, but you got there first. Thought you were so clever, didn't you, and that I was just a stupid suburban mum? But you fell for it all—the handbag, the credit card at the karaoke bar. I've always been smarter than you. I wasn't just captain of the hockey team at St Gertrudes, I was dux of my—'

I swiped the hockey stick, hoping to hit the axe handle and bounce it out of her hands. It didn't work. She was too quick, sporting reflexes probably, and when the blade hit the wood one half ricocheted across the room and only a splintered stump remained in my hand. She raised the axe again and I backed into the window, reached behind me and shook the frame, willing it to give way so I could tumble out onto the veranda roof. No dice. Everything else in the house was collapsing but the sashes remained firm.

I glanced to the left, thinking maybe I could dive out of the way, but she saw me looking.

'Just try it,' she said. 'I'm not only smarter than you, I'm quicker, more coordinated.'

I glared at her and didn't think I'd ever hated anybody more, which was really saying something. Everything that had happened was her fault and she had absolutely no remorse. She was actually congratulating herself. I thought of a way to bring her down a peg and get her to finally swing the axe. I couldn't wait anymore. I wanted this over with, either way, and maybe if I made her angry enough her famous reflexes might desert her.

'It's funny that you hate your stepmother so much,' I said sweetly, 'because the two of you are so similar.'

'No we're not!'

'Well, maybe not looks-wise, but your expressions and mannerisms and the way you justify your actions. You're so alike it's uncanny. Nurture over nature, huh?'

'Liar!'

'No, no, I'm serious. You're practically twins!'

She screamed with rage and swung and as the axe reached its zenith I chucked the stump at her. I was just preparing to dive sideways, realising with a sinking feeling that her aim was still accurate, when the insulation paper rustled and Andi's corpse sat bolt upright, grabbed Holly's ankle and said, 'Boo.'

chapter fifty-five

Holly shrieked and automatically whipped her head around and I rushed forward, slamming into her chest. She fell backwards over Andi and the axe slipped from her grip but it was too late, the weapon continued on its downward trajectory and slammed into my back, just inside my left shoulderblade.

The blow made me arch and I felt only pressure, relieved the edge was too blunt to pierce my skin, until a warm wetness gushed down to my waistband and the throbbing and burning kicked in. My legs gave way and I sank to my knees, the axe dislodging from the wound and clattering to the floor. I fell forward onto my stomach, sweating despite the cold, a wave of nausea swamping my guts. Andi had lain back down and I wondered if the whole thing had been some bizarre hallucination.

Holly had crawled halfway across the room to get away from Andi and when she got over the shock she laughed nervously, stood up and brushed herself off.

'Why won't you bitches stay dead? Do I have to chop your fucking heads off?'

The thought must have worked for her because she came toward me, reaching for the bloody axe. I grabbed it first, ignoring the pain and the fact I was probably dying, pulled myself to my knees and swung it at her shins. She yelped and jumped back. Now she wasn't so brave.

I dragged myself to my feet and lurched towards her like something out of *Night of the Living Dead*, the room spinning around me. She turned and bolted out the door onto the landing and half a second later I heard a crack and a scream. I snatched the torch off the chest of drawers and when I got to the corridor saw her trying to yank her leg out of a hole in the floor. I swung the axe, too far away to strike but scaring the living shit out of her.

She wrenched free, scuttled to the top of the stairs and started to propel herself down, but her long scarf tangled in the banister knob at the top. The material tightened and she jerked back and swayed sideways into the railing. It shattered, gave way and she plummeted over the side of the staircase and dangled in the air, legs kicking uselessly.

I sank to my knees on the landing, shone the torch at her and watched as she writhed like a worm on a fishhook. Her face was turning purple and her eyes and tongue bulged like a character from some grotesque cartoon. She was lucky, I thought, practically delirious, the wound in my back pulsing and bleeding. It would all be over for her soon and was a much more pleasant death than being stuck down a dank, dark pit or hacked apart with an axe.

Suddenly incredibly tired, I rested my head against the railing and that's when I heard it, the faint, faraway squawking of her baby, crying in the back seat of the car. A part of me wanted her to die, knew she deserved to, but another part … I put down the torch, lifted the axe, swung it at the banister and sheared through the scarf. The house shuddered as her body slumped to the floor. I didn't know if she was conscious or not, but by that stage I really didn't care.

I crawled all the way back to the room, dragging the axe behind me, and collapsed next to Andi. My shoulder throbbed and my limbs ached and a brown kaleidoscope edged my vision. I needed to sleep, a little nap, just for a few seconds, but before I did I forced myself up on one elbow to look at Andi and at the same time she turned her head to me. In the half light I could just make out a pale, skeletal face.

She tried to laugh, but all that came out was a hacking rasp. 'Scared the shit out of that bitch, huh?'

'Scared the shit out of me,' I croaked. 'You're dead, right?'

'Not quite. Would be if it hadn't rained. I collected water in that old bedpan you knocked over. Roof leaks like a bastard.'

'You smell dead.'

'That's just fucking rude. It's my leg. Gangrene, I reckon.'

'Fuck.'

I rolled onto my back and my eyelids fluttered. So heavy. I forced them open and coughed and rough grit jumped from my lungs to my mouth and crunched between my teeth.

'Thanks for saving me,' she whispered. 'I knew you would.'

I would have laughed except it would have taken too much effort. I was dying, Andi was dying and Chloe too, out on the road. No matter. We'd all meet up in heaven. I had a vision of the afterlife as a tacky, tropical 18–35s resort and the three of us sitting at some thatched cocktail bar drinking margaritas and checking out the barman's butt.

Just before my eyelids sank down for the last time the moon slipped out from behind the clouds and washed the frosty night silver. I looked out the window and saw that it was raining. No, not rain—snow. Soft, sparkling flakes, spiralling in slow motion. Everything went silent, the baby, the night birds, the crickets and the frogs. All was hushed beneath the still, soundless snow.

epilogue

November 1: Six weeks later

It was my twenty-ninth birthday and I was sitting in my new office, a narrow shopfront that had once been a shoe store on Carlisle Street, Balaclava. Music and the smell of frying sausages wafted down from upstairs. It had been Chloe's idea to have a combined birthday party and grand opening for both of our businesses.

I'd painted over the plate glass window for privacy and had partitioned the front of the office into a waiting room furnished with a cheap IKEA couch, rubber plant and a low rectangular table fanned with magazines. The room I sat in, directly behind it, contained the minimum requirements for a fledgling PI: desk, high backed fake leather chair and the two blue armchairs that had come with the couch. A TV and DVD player perched on a unit in the corner, the combined fax, printer and copier sat on the shelf behind me, and a couple of squat filing cabinets were holed up under the shelf. I'd stashed my new cameras, high powered binoculars and listening devices in a safe bolted to the floor and my new computer sat to one side of the L-shaped desk.

Out the back there was a tiny kitchenette with a kettle, microwave and bar fridge and a small, square bathroom containing a toilet, sink and tiny shower. Best of all was the innocuous white secondhand Ford Laser in the parking lot. She had cloth upholstery, airconditioning and power steering, and I was keeping her secret from the Futura. Who knew what sort of expensive repairs the Beast would demand if she found out about my prissy new mistress? The rest of my savings had gone on advertising and a website, and I'd managed to completely max out my credit card. I was four grand in the red and tried not to think about it too much because every time I did I felt like throwing up.

Things had worked out okay in the end, after the showdown with Holly. Well, as good as could be expected. The cavalry had arrived at first light and Holly had been hospitalised then arrested. Chloe had a broken leg and concussion, I'd needed stitches and staples and had ended up with a nasty scar but that was nothing compared to Andi, who'd had her left leg amputated just below the knee. She'd cried nonstop for a week, then suddenly snapped out of it and started making off-colour amputee jokes and bad *Are You Being Served?* style puns about stumps. She was an amazing chick. I'd have been a total basket case if it had happened to me.

Andi told me how she'd got onto the case in the first place. She'd been staying with Joy in the June holidays and one day, bored, she'd started going through boxes of old photos. In amongst pictures of demonstrations and women's lib meetings and even the famous Tonka Truck Christmas, she'd found a photograph of Melody talking to Peta. Andi had studied the national missing persons website for her uni assignment and she recognised Melody straight away, but when she asked Joy, and later Peta, they both said they couldn't remember who Melody was. Andi hadn't believed them and knew she was on to something big.

I did get a major shock at the hospital, though, when I came to and grabbed the nearest nurse's arm.

'My friend Chloe, did she make it?'

She'd smiled down on me and patted my hand. 'Your friend's fine, dear. And so is the baby.'

When I finally figured out she wasn't talking about Holly's kid, I'd almost fallen out of my hospital bed. Turned out Chloe had been more than four months along and hadn't even known. She'd always had irregular periods and thought she could never get knocked up after a number of abortions as a teenager. Curtis had been delighted, until she'd dumped him and said that although she wanted him to be part of the baby's life, she was raising it on her own. On her own was right. Much as I loved her, babysitting wasn't in my repertoire.

Alex had eventually come out of his coma, but he still wasn't a hundred percent and was on indefinite leave while he continued with tests and rehabilitation. I found out from Sean that he had lesions on the frontal lobe, the part of the brain that kept aggression and impulse control in check, and the police service didn't want him back until they were sure he was normal. The injury had also led to problems moving his left arm. He was still getting married to Suzy, with Sean as best man, but not surprisingly the bridesmaid offer had been withdrawn. I'd obeyed Suzy and stayed well away and although Alex had rung me a couple of times, I hadn't returned the calls.

Once … okay, more than once, I'd driven down to his place, parked out of sight and spied on him, telling myself I was just testing my new, high powered binoculars. I'd seen him sitting on his balcony in a bathrobe, patting Graham, and another time I'd watched as he and Suzy walked slowly on the beach. It had looked like he wasn't real steady on his feet and it broke my heart.

And Sean, well, Sean was coming back within the week. I'd actually managed to stay faithful to him, which was a first, and was looking forward to a guilt free reunion. I was excited but nervous as well. Our time together had been so brief and I hadn't seen him for six months. Would we get on? I could barely remember what he looked like apart from the fact that he had reddish hair and looked a little like Ewan McGregor, which was fine by me.

Mum still wasn't speaking to me and I supposed I couldn't blame her. Saving Andi had assuaged the guilt somewhat but Steve's death still ate away at me. I was actually getting counselling for it, but wasn't telling anyone. Didn't want to ruin my image as a tough PI. My brother Jasper was staying with Mum and picking up Sydney based modelling jobs. He'd threatened to come to Melbourne and visit in the not too distant future.

Joy's mum passed on, but Andi saw her one last time before she died and Joy reckoned it was almost like she was hanging on just to see her granddaughter, and after she had she was able to let go.

Jouissance had shut down and another restaurant was about to open up at the same site. Patsy had a job at a three-hat place in the city and was moonlighting for Chloe while he tried to save for his business. Trip, along with Rochelle and a raft of others, had been charged with money laundering, but was free on bail and had started filming his extreme lifestyle show.

Rochelle had also been charged with Melody's murder, but the case wouldn't come to court for a while. Yasmin wasn't working in hospitality anymore, and had actually picked up a lucrative gig as the 'face' of a major brand of panty-liners. With Holly in jail Dillon had been forced to abandon his dreams of making it in LA to become a stay at home dad.

I put my feet up on my desk and leaned back in my leather chair, just like PIs were supposed to, and opened the bottom drawer to grab the bottle of top shelf whiskey that was rolling around in there, courtesy of Sam Doyle. He kept trying to get in contact with me but I didn't think it was right, considering I was still trying to get onside with Mum. Of course, I didn't have a problem drinking his expensive booze.

I heard the front door swing in and glanced up. Bloody Trip Sibley swaggered in, carrying a bunch of flowers in one hand and a six pack of beer under his arm. He'd bounced back pretty quick after losing the restaurant, being arrested and having his precious Ducati destroyed.

He perched on the edge of the desk and put on a forties detective voice. 'A brunette entered the office, eyes like fire and a body for sin …'

'Oh shut up,' I said. He snatched the bottle out of my hand, took a swig then leaned on his elbow, lying sideways across the desk.

'You know, I still can't believe we never got it on,' he mused. 'I think we'd be good together.'

I sighed. 'I'm not gonna fuck you, Trip, we've been through this.'

'Not sex, a relationship.'

The laugh spluttered out of my mouth so fast I think I actually spat on him. He looked hurt, or a facsimile thereof. 'I'm serious. It's time for me to find a good woman and settle down. I mean, I'm going to be twenty-six in April.'

The phone rang and I snatched it up. Saved by the bell. It was Chloe calling from upstairs, wondering why I wasn't at my own party.

I locked the office and Trip and I took the back stairs up to Chloe's concrete deck. It was early evening, warm, still light, and from the top of the stairs you could look out across rooftops and see the trains slink along the raised track, heading south towards Elsternwick.

Curtis manned the smoking barbie and nodded curtly at me, still pissed off I hadn't granted him an exclusive. But it was Andi's story and despite publicity being the kiss of death for PIs, apparently, I'd told her everything. Since I hadn't saved her leg, helping her career was the least I could do. She was going great, though, everyone loved a story of survival against the odds, and her agent had negotiated a deal with a media outlet that guaranteed her a journo job, as well as a lump sum. She couldn't exactly waitress anymore.

The deck was dotted with palms and pots of star jasmine released their sweet perfume into the air. Trip's mouth turned down when he spied the supermarket snags and the bowls of crisps and Chicken-in-a-Biscuit, but he cheered up remarkably when he glanced through the French doors into Chloe's office. The room was full of strippers in various stages of undress, drinking champagne and taking turns on the practice pole she'd had installed. He grinned and entered the fray, thoughts of settling down completely forgotten.

Patsy and Andi wandered out onto the deck and I gave them both a hug and we sat at a green plastic outdoor setting. His pumped up biceps strained the sleeves of his tight white t-shirt. She was on crutches still, and hadn't been fitted for a prosthetic leg.

'How are you?' I asked.

'Legless!' She raised her beer and Patsy and I looked at each other and groaned.

'I know,' she grinned lopsidedly, 'I need some new material.'

'How's work?' I asked Patsy.

'I'm digging the money and the outfits, but I can't believe the women. You were right. They go completely insane, screeching like harpies with this look in their eyes like they want to …' He shuddered. 'I thought you guys were supposed to be the fairer sex.'

Andi and I looked at each other and snorted as Chloe lumbered out of the office, her belly thrust out like the prow of a ship. Despite being nearly six months pregnant she wore gingham pedal pushers, a matching bikini top, a pink cowboy hat and clear Perspex heels. She carried a plate of what looked like chocolate chip cookies and we all stared at her boobs. They were so insanely huge it was impossible not to.

'Watch out,' Andi said, 'you'll take someone's eye out.'

Chloe gave her an affectionate clip over the head and offered the plate. I'd known those two would get along. Andi took two cookies and Patsy declined. Chloe shoved one in her mouth but didn't offer the plate to me.

'Hey,' I said.

Chloe and Andi looked at each other and Andi broke a biscuit open and showed me the inside. Green flecks competed with chocolate chips, primo buds by the look of things.

'Chloe, you're not supposed to!' I pointed to her taut and swollen belly.

'I'm not supposed to smoke. The doctor didn't say anything about eating it!'

Her mobile phone rang and she put the plate down on the table and answered, then held the phone to her chest and looked at me. 'You're not going to believe this, but someone's just called up requesting you for a show right now at a pub in Brighton. Want me to see if they'll take someone else?'

I thought of my credit card and the overdue rent on my one bedroom flat and shook my head. 'If they pay cab fare I'll do it. It's not far, I can be back in an hour.'

'Sure you don't want me to organise a driver?'

'Nah, it's a pub, I'll be fine.'

Chloe shrugged and worked out the details and I slammed down a couple of champagnes to get me in the mood. Turned out they wanted a cop themed show so I dressed in the outfit, put a big coat on over the top and stuffed a CD and the accessories—hat, cuffs and plastic gun—into a zip-up shoulder bag. Chloe covered my scar with makeup just before I left, and I did my face in the back of the cab.

The hotel was a white, two storey building opposite the beach, with function rooms on the ground floor out the back. The one I was looking for had wood panelling, green carpet and an island bar. It was dark inside, thankfully, the windows draped with swathes of black cloth and one of those disco lights swirled coloured dots across the ceiling and walls. The place was crowded with blokes, all pissed and singing along to thumping eighties hits. People often asked if I got scared performing at buck's turns and the answer was no. The guys were loud, but if anything they reminded me of a bunch of overexcited kids hopped up on red cordial.

I ordered champagne off the young barman and asked if he could locate George, the guy who'd organised the shindig. A couple of seconds later he appeared, fat, forties, dark curly hair. He looked me up and down with a knowing smile plastered across his face, as though something about me amused him. Whatever. He handed over the two hundred bucks and I put it in my wallet, slipped out of the coat, put on the police hat and clipped on the belt with the cuffs and the gun. I handed the barman my CD and stashed my bag behind the bar.

'Which one's the buck?'

George pointed vaguely to a crowd of guys in the centre of the room. 'On the chair. Ball and chain.'

The barman hit the play button and 'Bad Boys', the theme song from *Cops*, blasted out of the speakers. You couldn't go past it for a police themed show and to be honest I couldn't bring myself to strip to 'Cherry Pie' anymore. It reminded me of Mum, and all the awful things that had happened. The guys all sang along gleefully and clapped their hands, just like kindergarten kids. I swaggered over in time to the beat, in the mood after a few champagnes and feeling special because it was my birthday. The crowd parted and I found the buck, sitting on a chair in the centre of the room with his back to me. I grinned at the other blokes, unclipped the gun, came up behind my victim, put my hand on his shoulder and pivoted around to straddle his lap, smiling and pointing the gun at him. His jaw dropped. So did mine. It was Alex.

Perhaps I should have been a tad more professional but I squealed, jumped off his lap and ran out of the room. George and the rest of the guys were falling about laughing, obviously all in on the joke. I fled down the corridor, came to a disabled toilet and locked myself in, leaning against the bench around the sink, looking in the mirror and breathing hard. Alex must have been hot on my heels because a few seconds later he was bashing on the door, telling me to let him in. Then I heard another voice. George.

'C'mon, mate, come back to the party. It was a joke! Not much of a show though. Reckon I should ask for my money back?'

'Piss off, George, you're a dickhead. It wasn't fucking funny.'

'No sense of humour, Christakos, that's always been your problem.' His voice became faint as he staggered back down the corridor, muttering about how it had been worth two hundred bucks just to see the look on Alex's face.

Alex kept banging. 'Simone, I'm sorry about my cousin. He's an idiot and he's been shitting me since I was a kid. Open the door, please.'

I sighed and opened it and Alex slipped in and locked it behind him. I leaned back against the bench in my lycra police outfit, tarty makeup, fishnet stockings and thigh high boots. He was checking me out so I crossed my arms and studied him back.

He looked different and the only word to describe it was dishevelled. His usually neat hair was mussed up, his shirt was open, half untucked and one of his pockets had gone inside out. His nose looked different since it had been broken, not so straight and slightly wider across the bridge. He was drunk, granted, but I'd seen him pissed in the past and he'd always kept himself tidy.

Alex fumbled in his back pocket with his right hand, pulled out a hip flask sized bottle of Jameson's and wiggled it at me. That's when I noticed his right arm, hanging sort of limply at his side. He saw me looking.

'It's better than it was.' He screwed up his face in concentration and wiggled a couple of fingers. 'But they still won't let me back on the job. It's not just the arm. I reckon they think I'm too fucked up.'

I grabbed the bottle off him, took a hefty swig, handed it back.

'How come you never answered my calls?' he asked.

'I wanted to, but Suzy told me she'd kill me if I went anywhere near you. After a run-in with one jealous bitch, I believed her. Besides, it's better all round if we stay away from each other. I'm a jinx, remember? I've already ruined your life. Next time I'll probably get you killed. It's not worth it.'

Thinking about what had happened to him made tears come to my eyes and a couple rolled down my cheek. Alex put down the bottle, reached out with his good arm and wiped them away with his thumb. My skin tingled where he touched me and I moved my head away.

'Don't.' I grabbed the bottle and had another drink. The whiskey burned in my stomach.

'Why not?'

'Alex,' I said, 'you're the one who told me it's not too late to change and be a good person. In a few days Sean will be back and you'll be married to Suzy. I know we've always fancied each other but nothing's ever gonna happen. End of story.'

'Sure.' He held up his good hand, stepped back unsteadily and had another drink. But his eyes were travelling down the tight blue lycra like he was trying to mentally undo the zip. I gripped the sides of the bench and silently repeated my new mantra: it's alright to think it, as long as you don't act on it.

'It true that crazy bitch popped you with an axe?' he said, and I was glad he'd changed the subject.

'Uh-huh, forty staples, stitches. I cover it with makeup for shows but it's still a hell of a scar.'

'Can I see?'

'Alex!'

I was starting to think that Sean hadn't been joking about the whole impulse control thing and if that was true then Alex was now on a par with me. The safest thing was to get out of the bathroom, fast. I finished the last of the Jameson's, chucked the bottle in the bin and slid off the bench.

'It's been great to see you, Alex, and good luck with the wedding, but I'm missing my own birthday party.'

I turned the lock and had just started to open the door when Alex came up behind me and slammed it shut again. I whirled around. Up close he still smelled of aftershave but not so much of clean washing, more of spilled booze, cigarette smoke and sweat. I'd never minded that smell and I swallowed, my throat suddenly tight.

'I miss you,' he said.

'I miss you too, but—'

It was all the encouragement he needed. He moved in to kiss me and when I made a half hearted attempt to angle my face away he held my jaw in his good hand and tilted my chin so I would have to look at him. My mantra deserted me. His coffee coloured eyes had such an unguarded look of desire that something melted inside and I couldn't help myself.

When he bent his head and pressed his lips to mine, I kissed him right back.

acknowledgements

Thanks to Anthony Larsen and to my family: Thea Woznitza (who bears no resemblance to Simone's mum in any way, shape or form except for the fact she looks damn hot for her age!), Tony Redhead, Kelly Burke, Bruce Worrall (you're not Steve, okay? Right, sorted), Jesse, Kate, Jasmine and Julian Redhead, Jean and Stella O'Connell.

To the people who took the time to read my manuscript and gave insightful comments: Donna Thompson, who did it with four young kids—yikes; Katherine Howell, crime writer extraordinaire—see you on a panel soon babe; and Michael Lynch—thanks for the constant encouragement, Sicilian olives and everything else.

My friends and people who helped me out and inspired me: Dorothy Mozejko, Juliet Lamont, Donna Butler, Helena

'Hell-Bags' Bond, Scott Wales, Greg Thorsby, Jemina Napier, Andy Carmichael, Amanda Monroe, Rhys Newell, Keith Larsen, Julian Wu, Matt Rasmussen, Carl Donadio, Danielle Johanesen from RMIT and Bob Noreiks from Ducati.

Hospitality veterans: Andy Russell, Bradley Dawson, Kerryn Davies, Siobhan Ryan, Simon from Mecca and Patsy from Mecca—the real Patsy!

All the wonderful Sisters in Crime especially Carmel Shute, Lindy Cameron, Sue Turnbull, Katrina Beard, Vivienne Colmer, Phyllis King, Michelle Cooper, Cathy Martin, Tanya King and Robin Bowles.

Everyone at Allen & Unwin: Annette Barlow, Louise Cornege, Christen Cornell, Clara Finlay, Patrick Gallagher, Andrew Hawkins, Julia Lee, Catherine Milne, Christa Munns, Renee Senogles, Louise Thurtell and anyone else I met at the Christmas party but was too drunk to catch your name.

Jo Jarrah, world's most fabulous editor. With each book she tightens up my writing and I get to teach her a new rude word!

Thanks also to the wild-eyed fisherman at the Tin Can Bay pub, Ray, who bought me a steak and kindly offered me a berth on his boat, which I had to decline.

Everyone I met at UQ: Veny Armanno, Kim Wilkins, Bronwyn Lea, Sue Gough, Megan Jennaway, Alyssa Ryan, Michele Yamada, Geok Ang and a special thanks to Vicky Schinkel for the lend of your house and your cat! Also thanks to all the people from QUT I met along the way, including Nike Bourke and Sally Breen.

Thanks to the management and staff of Café Al Dente who turned me into the dishpig-par-excellence that I am today. Greg and Jo Fowler, Holly Godwin (you did ask me to use your name!), Phil Winters, Jeff and Kristy.

My favourite band, Doug Mansfield and the Dust Devils: Doug Mansfield, Jack Coleman, Bruce Kane, Gerard Rowan,

Nick Del Ray. With a special thanks to Jack for letting Simone flirt with him. The lyrics from 'Trouble Follows Me' are reproduced with permission from Doug Mansfield.

Oh yeah, and to kitty-cats current and departed: Jackie, Leroy, Sally, Harry, Barry and McDuff without whom I could never have created such a deep and multi-layered character as Graham.

peepshow

LEIGH REDHEAD

ISBN 978 1 74114 976 0

chapter**one**

I was lying on my back in the peepshow at the Shaft Cinema, legs in the air, wearing a peekaboo nightie and no knickers.

Two of the six booths were occupied, and every time one of the guys put a coin in I heard a buzz, the glass went from opaque to clear, and a small orange light came on above the window.

It cost them two dollars for forty-five seconds, and I got a dollar of that. The booths were dark and the men's faces shadowy, unless they pressed them right up against the glass. Not a good idea.

They kept putting coins in so I writhed around on the thin mattress, got on all fours, flipped my long dark hair around in faux orgasmic throes and pretended to play with myself. A portable stereo blasted out Madonna and the small room was lit with coloured disco lights. Mirrors on the walls and ceiling reflected each other and there were thousands of me, stretching out into eternity.

The peep's door opened and my best friend, Chloe, pulled across the tatty red curtain.

'Simone!' Her blond hair was in rollers and she popped out of a small pink bikini top.

'You're keen.' I glanced at the clock. It was three forty-five in the afternoon. 'I've still got fifteen minutes.'

'He's dead.' She was clutching the pm edition of the *Herald Sun*. 'That fat bastard's been murdered.'

'What fat bastard?' I lay on one side and lifted my leg up, Jane Fonda style.

'Strip club slaying,' Chloe read from the front page. 'The body of a man discovered floating near St Kilda beach this morning has been identified as strip club boss Francesco (Frank) Parisi, thirty-eight. Police have confirmed Mr Parisi, proprietor of Flinders Street table dancing venue the Red Room, was brutally hacked to death before being dumped in the bay.' Chloe worked at the Shaft during the day and moonlighted at the Red on Friday and Saturday nights.

I bent over in front of the windows and gave everyone a flash. 'Did you knock him off?' I joked.

Chloe wasn't laughing. She hugged the paper tightly to her chest and chewed her bottom lip. 'I think we'd better go for a drink,' she said.

We crossed Swanston Street, dodging trams and Silver-top taxis, and headed to the Black Opal. It was a pokies place with cheap drinks and the men were too busy willing their machines to pay out to bother cracking onto a couple of off-duty strippers. Maxine was covering for us in the peeps. She should have retired back in the mid eighties but that was another story.

I bought bourbon and Coke for Chloe and champagne for myself and we sat at a high table at the back of the bar, the newspaper between us.

I sipped my drink and waited for her to fill me in. She lit a ciggie and looked around the bar with big scared eyes. Drama queen. I slid the paper over and read my horoscope. It worked.

'I never told you what happened on Saturday night,' she blurted out. 'I should've, but I was embarrassed.'

When she paused for effect I flipped through to the employment section. She lasted five seconds.

'It was early in the shift and Frank called me into his office to do a line of coke. You know, kickstart the night.'

I knew, even though I hadn't done any drugs for a year.

'I'd been alone with him before and nothing ever happened. But this time, after we'd done a couple, he gets up and comes over to where I'm sitting and unzips his pants. Gets his cock out and tells me to suck it. Mate, I just fucking laughed at him, thought it was a joke, right? Then he tries to push my head down, like, hard, and somehow I manage to wriggle out of his hands and I bolt back into the club.'

Shit like that made me really mad. If Frank wasn't already dead I would have had to kill him myself. 'Why didn't you tell me?' I asked.

Chloe took another slug of bourbon and rubbed her face with her hands. 'I shouldn't have got myself into that situation. You wouldn't have.'

It was true Chloe flirted and appeared promiscuous and up for anything. But that was no excuse.

'It wasn't your fault,' I said.

She shrugged. 'So there I am at the bar and I'm like, coking off my head but I'm also in shock and a couple of the girls are asking me what's the matter when Frank comes out of his office and tells me to clean out my locker, I'm fired.'

'And I say, well that's OK 'cause I quit anyway and where's the two hundred you owe me from the night before? And he says he's not giving it to me. Fuck, mate, I just went ballistic. I earned that money. I worked fucking hard for every cent of it. I went off at him, called him every name under the sun and told him I was going to report him to the cops, charge him with sexual assault, drugs, you name it.'

I raised my eyebrows. Chloe groaned. 'I know, not the smartest thing to say to a prick like that. So he goes, you don't know who you're dealing with, bitch, you want to wind up dead? And I say, you don't fucking scare me, you better watch your back motherfucker 'cause I know people. And then Flame, she's kind of like his girlfriend, hands me the stuff from my locker and the bouncers drag me out.'

'Do you really know people?' I asked.

'No, that bit was bullshit.'

The card machines sang electronic songs and Chloe lit another Winnie off the butt of the first. I wanted one too but I'd given up a few months before.

'Tell me what I should do,' she said.

I'd finished my investigative services certificate in October and gained an inquiry agent's licence soon after. Since then the girls at work considered me the last word on all matters of law and order. They asked me about custody disputes and apprehended violence orders, taxation and drug busts. No matter that I hadn't found a job and my training covered following people and pissing into a funnel.

'How many people heard you threaten Frank?' I asked.

''Bout fifty.'

'You should go to the cop shop now and tell them about Saturday night. Makes you look innocent.'

'I am innocent!'

I drained my champagne. It had given me a nice buzz and I was tonguing for another.

'Come on, I'll take you.'

We caught the number 16 tram and rattled down Swanston Street. The top end where it intersected Lonsdale was home to the Shaft and a bunch of sex shops and as we moved towards the river we passed takeaway stores, discount clothing outlets and shops with spruikers out front flogging perfume rip-offs and cheap sunglasses. The Flinders Street station end had all the druggies. Junkies in bad tracksuits hung around the fast food joints and the alcoholics congregated on benches outside St Paul's Cathedral. Swanston was the street they never showed you in the tourist brochures. I knew it well.

We passed the Queen Victoria Gardens and the Domain and got off at the St Kilda Road Police Complex. I led Chloe straight up to the reception desk.

'We're here about the Parisi murder,' I told a young cop. 'My friend worked for him and she'd like to speak to someone.'

'I didn't kill him,' Chloe exclaimed.

The uniform grinned. 'That's what they all say.'

Chloe smiled back. She was wearing a low-cut top with 'Pornbabe' written across the chest.

I was good at flirting but Chloe was better. She could flirt for Australia. They stared at each other, smiling, while I picked up the phone and spoke to someone.

'Detective Talbot will be down in a moment,' he said.

I sat in the corner and left them to it. Just as she asked to see his gun a door opened and a female detective with bobbed auburn hair stuck her head out a door. 'Chloe?'

She followed the D and I settled back to wait. Crimestopper's posters adorned the walls and cops went in and out the automatic doors. I watched them and couldn't help wondering what they had that I didn't. I'd tried to join the police force a year before and hadn't got past the application stage. They'd rejected me when I told the truth about my work history. Either I didn't have the moral credentials to be a girl in blue or the Victoria Police had enough scandal without dropping a stripper into the mix.

It was a weird career to aspire to after growing up in a hippy community where the kids were taught to hate the 'pigs' and our parents lived in fear of the choppers that buzzed the hills around harvest time. But aspire to it I did, partly from rebellion and partly because of something that happened when I was thirteen.

My mum had hooked up with a man named Russell, an ex-bikie, straggly but good looking in his own way. He'd come to our town to buy dope to sell in the city, but liked it so much he decided to stay. My younger brother Jasper and I weren't too happy when he first moved in, but he brought us round with jumbo packs of M&Ms and hand-held, battery-operated computer games. He even hooked up a small black and white TV to a car battery so we could watch 'Countdown'.

The trouble was he had a problem with alcohol, and heroin, and when he was really drunk, or couldn't score, he'd lose the plot. Anything would set him off and his arguments with my mum escalated from yelling to pushing, to slapping her in the face.

We wondered why she didn't just leave him. She'd been a women's libber in the seventies and had worked at a battered women's shelter, but Russell seemed to have her under some sort of spell. He could go from frightening to charming, and after one of his outbursts he'd be extra sorry and romantic, and promise never to do it again.

He'd been living with us for three months when Jasper and I were woken by shouting. We peered down from the attic loft where we slept. In the light of the kerosene lamps we saw Russell looming over our mum, hand raised, face twisted with rage. Jasper, who was only eight, started sniffling.

'I've called the police,' she said, but this got him angrier.

'Are you fucked in the head, woman? I've got ten pounds drying in the shed. You have got to be the stupidest fucking unit I have ever met.' He was pacing back and forth on the faded oriental rug, a bottle of bourbon in his hand. All of a sudden he dropped the bottle and punched her in the face. She staggered back, crashing into the unlit potbelly stove and knocking out the flue.

I half climbed, half slid down the ladder and ran at him as he raised his fist again, jumped up and hung off his arm. He swung it back and I flew off onto the floor.

My brother's cry was now a high-pitched wail. Mum was cowering in the corner, Russell advancing on her, when the front door crashed in.

'Police!'

Two uniformed officers stood there, one male and one female. Russell grabbed a poker from beside the stove and wielded it like a baseball bat. 'Come on,' he yelled. 'I'll have ya!'

The woman had her hand on the butt of her gun. The male approached Russell with his hands out, talking in low tones, calling him mate. Russell swung at him and the cop leaned back and grabbed the poker, pulling him off balance, so he fell face first to the floor. It was the coolest move I'd ever seen. The female officer leapt into action, wrenching Russell's hands behind his back and digging her knee in as she cuffed him tight.

They made sure we were all right and took Russell away. It turned out there were a number of warrants out for his arrest, and we never saw him again. And since that day I'd wanted to be a cop. But the cops didn't want me. So I'd done the PI course; it had seemed like the next best thing.

When I'd graduated one of my lecturers said he might have a bit of surveillance work coming up. Tony Torcasio was an ex undercover officer who had his own agency, a good guy, but so far nothing had eventuated. There were ads in the paper for investigators from time to time but if you didn't have experience or weren't an ex-cop you didn't have a hope in hell.

I loved dancing but after three years it was time to quit. I'd turned twenty-eight two days earlier and although I could pass for twenty-three, I felt old. Maxine was a well-preserved forty-five but that didn't stop the younger guys yelling, 'Get grandma off stage.'

'All done.' Chloe stood in front of me, wiggling her hips.

'They're not going to throw your arse in jail?'

'Nuh.' She skipped off to the front counter, whispered something to the constable and handed him one of her cards. I could have sworn I heard 'bring your handcuffs'.

Ten days later, November thirteen, I was sitting on my balcony in Elwood among palms and potted herbs. My first floor unit was in a block of sixteen and although the building was ugly brown brick the one bedroom flats were renovated and the street, Broadway, was full of oak trees. Dean Martin was on the stereo and I had a glass of cask wine and half a pack of individually wrapped cheese singles in front of me. I love plastic cheese. It was Thursday evening, still light because of daylight saving, and I felt the itch to go out. It was a toss-up between seeing a band and getting so pissed I ended up pashing some grungy rocker, or going to the Godard version of *Breathless* at the Astor. Decisions, decisions. The wine flowed through my limbs, relaxing them, and a breeze that smelled of saltwater came in off the bay.

The phone rang. It was my mum.

'You're home, I don't believe it. How's work?'

'Great, fantastic,' I lied.

'I worry about you, you know. Not so much the peepshows but the bucks' parties. What if the guys get out of hand? What if it turns violent?'

'It's really not dangerous. There's always heaps of security. And the bucks are more scared of us than we are of them. Just last weekend—'

'It irks me. It just does.' She actually said irk. I wondered if I'd heard anyone say it in conversation before and decided I hadn't.

'I know.' I started craving a cigarette.

'And apart from your physical safety I worry about your psyche.'

'My psyche?' I would have killed for a cigarette. And something a bit stronger than wine. I leaned back in the canvas director's chair and put my bare feet up on the balcony railing.

'It's got to affect you, pandering to men, reinforcing ridiculous stereotypes about women, buying into the whole madonna/whore thing—'

'I don't buy into—'

'I know *you* don't but by working in that industry you perpetuate the myth. And to think I named you after Simone de Beauvoir.'

My mum was an old school feminist who lectured in women's studies and I couldn't win an argument with her. I turned into a petulant fifteen-year-old every time I tried.

'It's an art form, Mum, like…like Josephine Baker or Gypsy Rose Lee.'

'Did Josephine Baker do "floor work" and show the world what she had for breakfast? I think not.'

I picked at an ingrown hair on my leg and didn't say anything until she changed the subject: 'I heard from Jasper.'

'What's he up to?'

'He's doing really well, said to say hi. He's in New York doing some stuff for *GQ*, then he's off to Canada for fashion week in Montreal.'

My brother had scooped the family gene pool and worked as a model. I considered asking my mother if she didn't think modelling was similar to stripping but restrained myself.

'How's Steve?' I asked instead. Steve was my mother's 'partner'. They met a few years after the Russell episode and had been together ever since, eventually moving to Sydney where my mum became an academic. Steve ran courses in mud-brick housing and solar power at the College of Adult Education.

'He's great, really busy though, organising a rally against the government's stance on greenhouse gas emissions.'

'I've got my inquiry agent's licence,' I said. 'There might be some work coming up.'

'Why don't you finish your degree? You've only got one semester to go and you could finish it in Melbourne. I've looked into it.'

'I'm a bit busy at the moment.'

'You could study part time. A qualification would get you out of the sex industry.'

'I dunno about that, heaps of strippers have arts degrees.'

There was a beep on the line. Call waiting. Hallelujah.

'Mum? I've got another call, I have to go...

'Hello?'

'Simone,' Chloe sounded out of breath, 'you've got to come quick. Someone's trying to kill me.'

NOW READ THE SECOND BOOK IN THE SERIES

RUBDOWN

Simone Kirsch PI has given up stripping and is trying to be straight. But she can never stay straight for long.

Simone is hired by prominent lawyer Emery Wade to follow his wayward daughter Tamara. She's been taking drugs and working in the sex industry and Daddy fears a scandal that will affect not just his reputation, but that of her AFL-hotshot brother and his high-profile fiancée.

Tangling with a drug dealer, a sleazy brothel owner and a bizarre love quadrangle with three coppers, time is running out for Simone to get to the bottom of it all before someone tries to keep her quiet.

rubdown

LEIGH REDHEAD

ISBN 978 1 74114 977 7

chapter**one**

I walked up to the brothel and rang the bell, smoothed my hair and looked around. The South Melbourne industrial area was all converted cottages and boxy factories. A high machinery whine stabbed my ears and my nose twitched with the scent of freshly sawn pine and chemical solvents.

The building was a double fronted, single storey terrace painted livid maroon and a sign in foot high letters told me I was standing outside the Good Times Club. As the mesh door opened I recalled the seventies TV show of the same name and half expected JJ to greet me with a buck toothed 'Dyn-o-mite!'

'Help you?'

The autumn morning was cool and bright and it took a while for my eyes to adjust to the gloom within. The voice had come from a middle aged woman with frizzy red hair and thin eyebrows.

'I was wondering if you had any work available?' I asked.

'Come on in.'

I stepped inside and she locked the screen behind me, crossed to a melamine reception desk and spoke into an intercom.

'Boss won't be long.'

The vinyl couch squeaked as I sat down. Penthouse Black Label magazines fanned out on a side table and the walls and carpet were the same purple-red as the exterior. A large photograph of a blonde draped over a Ferrari hung behind the desk. Classy stuff. I heard the swish of polyester slacks and turned to see a man enter the room. His beer gut forced his red polo shirt to pouch out and his mousy hair stood up in thinning tufts. As he got closer I saw his nose was bulbous and pockmarked, and guessed he was in his fifties. I stood up and shook his hand. The palm was sweaty.

'Neville,' he said. 'I own the joint.'

'Vivien.' It was my old stripping name and I answered to it more readily than Simone.

'What sort of work you after, darl?'

'Dunno, what have you got?'

'Full service or massage. What you done before?'

'Neither.'

Neville and the woman exchanged a glance. He took a pack of Horizons from his pants pocket and shook one out. 'Take her around, Marla, show her the rooms, tell her what's involved.'

I followed Marla down a dim hallway and realised her enormous tracksuit-panted rump was out of proportion to her tiny upper body, then felt bad for noticing. A door with a number three painted on it was ajar and she led me inside.

Marla said, 'Rule number one. If the door's closed, don't open it.'

I could understand the logic behind that.

There was a double bed on one side of the room and a foldout massage table on the other. The bed was covered with a fitted sheet and two pink towels, pleated like napkins at a Chinese restaurant. A bedside table held home brand oil, baby powder, tissues and air freshener. A white shower unit had been moulded into the corner. I smelled damp carpet and that powdery stuff you sprinkle on the floor in the hope the room will smell like a 'Country Garden'. Mirrors were stuck to the walls, along with framed black and white prints of big-boobed eighties gym bunnies in sweat bands and g-string leotards bearing the legends *Sweat* and *Pumped up Down Under*.

Marla was looking at me expectantly so I said, 'Nice.'

She nodded. 'Yes, Neville's recently spent quite a bit doing the place up.' She leaned against the massage table and the joists squeaked in protest. 'How come you're here if you've never worked before?'

'Curious, I s'pose. I've never been inside a place like this.'

'You a student?'

'How did you guess?' I was wearing a miniskirt with black tights, knee high boots and a face full of makeup. So much for thinking I looked like a hooker.

'We get lots of students, need money to study. What course you doing?'

'Um, arts.' I sat on the sagging mattress, careful not to disturb the origami towels. 'So, uh, what do the girls have to do?'

'Massage is full nude, bodyslide and hand relief. Up to you if you let them touch. Most ladies allow the boobs, outside the pussy. It's sixty for the half hour, fifty-fifty split. Full service pays better, naturally.'

'That's sex, right?'

'Uh-huh. Massage, French, then sex. Client pays one-eighty for the hour, a hundred for the half and we have a ten minute special for sixty.'

Thirty bucks a fuck. It wasn't exactly *Pretty Woman*.

Marla went on: 'Fantasies like schoolgirl and light B and D are an extra twenty and Greek's fifty. It's up to you if you do Greek.'

'And Greek is?'

'Anal.'

'Ouch.'

Back at reception Neville was smoking and drinking instant coffee out of a Garfield mug.

'How'd you go?' He forced a smile and crinkled his eyes up.

'I don't know, I've never done anything like—'

'Piece of piss. You've had a fuck before, haven't you?'

'Well, yeah.'

'And I bet you've rooted jerks for nothing. Why not have sex with some nice gentlemen and get paid for what you were giving away for free?'

Gee, now you put it that way…'I'm just not sure I could go through with it.'

Neville slurped his coffee and smacked his lips. 'What about massage then? Money's not quite as good but all you got to do is a bit of a rub, bit of a tug. Hand shandy. Like shaking a Coke can up and down.'

I stared at the blonde on the wall getting jiggy with the sports car and chewed on a fingernail. 'Can I talk to some of the other girls first?'

Neville frowned, sighed. 'Yeah, okay. But don't let them put you off. Like a bit of a whinge.'

Marla led me down a corridor on the other side of the building to the girls' room. Six workers, aged from early twenties to late forties, lounged around on brown velour couches and shabby mismatched chairs. Mugs left wet rings on the smoked glass coffee table and Bert Newton delivered double entendres from an ancient, wooden framed TV.

A blonde girl with a wide mouth and freckled, tip-tilted nose sat cross-legged on the floor in front of an age speckled mirror. She wore a white lace bra and pants set with a pink scarf knotted at the hip, and had her lips open, applying mascara. I casually shifted my handbag so the hidden video camera would get a better shot of her.

Her name was Tamara Wade. I had found my target.